Praise for *Mad Money*
by Linda L. Richards

"Murder, mayhem, humor, romance, and great
characters make this first book in the
Madeline Carter series hard to put down."
—*Booklist*

"A likeable heroine, a strong supporting cast,
knowledgeable insight into the world of stocks without
going overboard, and murder and mayhem in L.A.
add up to a hugely enjoyable read."
—Sarah Weinman, author of
Confessions of an Idiosyncratic Mind

"Readers will enjoy this madcap fiscal adventure
starring a likeable cast, especially the protagonist."
—*Midwest Book Review*

"This novel is filled with enough corruption to keep
the reader turning pages. Anyone who dabbles in the
stock market will be enthralled with the development
of this plot, as well as frightened. Interesting and smart,
and easily worth the price of admission,
this is a recommended read."
—*New Mystery Reader*

"*Mad Money* is no lightweight airplane read; instead, we
have the fiendishly complex tale of corporate swindles,
surreal glimpses into the world of the
stock-trader.... For a debut novel—bravo! If you need
a fast-paced and fun read *Mad Money* is for you, as
it is a light in the noir and far, far from lightweight."
—*Crime Spree Magazine*

"Move over, St
going to g

Also by LINDA L. RICHARDS

MAD MONEY

*Watch for Linda L. Richards's next book
Coming September 2006*

THE NEXT

EX

LINDA L.
RICHARDS

MIRA

ISBN 0-7783-2240-8

THE NEXT EX

Copyright © 2005 by Linda Richards.

www.MIRABooks.com

Printed in U.S.A.

"I've been lucky. I'll be lucky again."
—Bette Davis

Completing a novel provides opportunity for taking stock and reflection. A little like Thanksgiving, or perhaps New Year's. It's a time of accomplishment, because you've done something you set out to do, and it sees a finish to a period of complete emotional and physical immersion.

As I bring my head up to look around after completing *The Next Ex*, I find myself feeling entirely blessed and extremely lucky. I am surrounded—both professionally and personally—by talented, caring people. And these two halves—the personal and the professional—are beautifully entwined. Sometimes I can't tell one from the other. I feel loved and cared about by the people with whom I discuss matters of "work," and I feel creatively nurtured by my friends and family. And vice versa. I wouldn't change a thing.

My editor at MIRA Books, Valerie Gray, is a talented professional for whom there is no "beyond" the call of duty. Valerie does all the things one expects of an editor and then she goes further, imprinting her passion and caring in a real and meaningful way. Thank you, Valerie.

Thank you to my publishing team at MIRA Books— some unseen by me, but never not felt—who have made me the envy of my author pals. Seriously. This team includes Dianne Moggy, Marleah Stout, Sarah Rundle, Sasha Bogin and a whole bunch of others I've not yet met, but who I know are there doing what they do and doing it well.

Thanks to my special friends and cheerleaders, the novelists. M. J. Rose and Alafair Burke. Neither of you will ever know how much your support has meant.

My partner, the artist and photographer David Middleton, contributed to *The Next Ex* in more ways than can be calculated. In addition to making the meanest latté this side of Seattle, David is always my first reader, and he contributes a great deal to the actual plotting of the Madeline Carter novels. In addition, in *The Next Ex* David saved me from what would have been perhaps the worst metaphor in the history of... er...metaphorics. It was so awful that I will not tell you what it was, but— believe me—it was absolutely not worth repeating. David, for all of that and more and more and more, thank you.

My son, the actor Michael Karl Richards, continues to shoot me important advice on living creatively. Michael awes me with his wisdom and his heart. Knowing that I had a hand in the development of this extraordinary person leaves me without words. Thank you, Michael, for your love, your generosity and your presence in my life.

My brother, Peter Huber, has been a constant source of all things good throughout my life. His generous spirit and loving heart inspires everyone he touches, not least of all his youngest sister. Peter, thank you, thank you. Always.

Thanks to my sister-daughter Carrie Wheeler, who always provides a willing ear and an open heart. I'm so happy to have you in my life.

Thank you to Jaymie Matthews, Madeline's rocket scientist on call. Jaymie came through with specifics on how long someone could be expected to breathe in a completely airless place, as well as some delicious details on carbon dioxide poisoning. As Jaymie pointed out, this (ahem) enlivened the proceedings considerably.

Mary Beck, the goddess of compliance, once again had input into Madeline's financial carryings-on. The hours that Mary and her consort, Lang Evans, spent with the manuscript did much to help ensure that the technical portions of *The Next Ex* are accurate. If there are errors in this regard they are mine, but Mary and Lang did everything in their power to guide me to the light. And more.

My trusted earliest readers provided so much more than careful eyes. They are, in some ways, Madeline's soul and probably also her biggest fans: Michèle Denis, Andy Heard, Carolyn Withers-Heard, Laura-Jean Kelly, Jackie Leidl, Patricia McLean, Betty Middleton and Debbie Warmerdam. Your comments were invaluable, your enthusiasm irreplaceable. Thank you.

Thank you to the team at *January Magazine* for your enthusiasm and support. Most especially J. Kingston Pierce, Pamela Patterson, Tony Buchsbaum and David Abrams.

A special thank-you to Linda Murray, Derrick Lloyd and Sara for allowing me to be one of the food people.

In the time since the publication of *Mad Money* I have been humbled on many, many occasions by readers who took the time to write to tell me how much they enjoyed the book and being part of Madeline's world. In many ways, this is the biggest thanks of all. Without you, gentle reader, it really is all beside the point. Thank you.

One

I'll always remember her eyes. They still haunt me in my sleep. Eyes the color of topaz, bright and rare. In that first instant, I thought about a beautiful doll I'd had when I was a child. These eyes were vacant and staring, just like that doll's. And though I didn't want to believe it, I knew in that first moment she was dead.

Though it's sometimes difficult to recall the major thrust of events, horror can make the smallest details jump into your mind with astonishing accuracy. It would, for example, be impossible for me to tell you how long I stood there as what I saw filled my conscious mind, or even to tell you in proper detail what I'd been doing in the moments just before. But the image of her there is imprinted. I've tried to erase it, bury it. I can't.

I could see that she lay where she had fallen, the highly glossed marble that covered the bathroom floor reflecting the curve of her hand, the bend of her leg, the glow of her cinnamon skin.

Her dress was the color of blood and because of it I identified her easily. It was a daringly cut Balanciega gown I'd admired when I'd arrived at the party several hours earlier. Then it had clung to her surgically enhanced curves like a second skin. Now there seemed to be more fabric—it was everywhere!—as though the loss of the essential something that had been her had caused this overabundance of cloth.

When I moved closer I discovered what should have been obvious from the start: the puddle that the gossamer fabric made on the floor was amplified by her own blood. There seemed to be gallons of it; more than I would have thought could fit into her slight frame.

That's when I heard the screaming: a textbook horror-movie sound, the kind that follows nightmares out of the dark. It reverberated, that scream. It echoed through flesh and walls, and rent, almost, the fabric of my reality. It was only later I realized that this world-ending sound had come from me.

I'd met Keesia Livingston a few weeks earlier. It was not a chance encounter. Our lives would never have intersected at a place that would have made that happen.

I'd been renting the guest house in the Malibu home of the director Tyler Beckett and his wife, the actress Tasya Saranova, since I'd moved to Los Angeles from New York. It was a good arrangement for all of us. Tyler was a friend of my old boss, Sal. Sal liked having me at Tyler and Tasya's. It made him feel as though he could keep an eye on me even though I was three thousand miles away and didn't work for him anymore. Distance hasn't stopped Sal from wanting to watch out for me. He'd been my mentor at the brokerage firm where I worked in New York, and he'd stepped into part of the void left when my father died. And old habits can die hard.

Tyler, my landlord, has a teenage daughter from a previous marriage, and he liked having someone— me—around the place to keep an eye on things when he and Tasya were out of town, which was fairly often. I wasn't expected to do anything besides paying my reasonable rent and being there. Since the "there" in question was lovely—an apartment tucked under the deck of a palatial ocean-view home overlooking Los Flores Canyon in Malibu—and the kid, Jennifer, was generally sweet and mostly kept herself out of trouble, the arrangement was never onerous.

So when Tyler knocked on my door one sunny afternoon just as the markets had closed for the day and I was settling in to do a bit of relaxing, I had no reason to be suspicious. It was only later that I'd attribute the grin he wore when I opened the door to sheepishness.

I should, I suppose, have been alerted by his manner. Tyler embodies California casual, right down to his working wardrobe of chinos and golf shirts, but he's a busy guy and gets to the point fairly quickly. Usually. On this day, however, he seemed inordinately interested in…*stuff*.

"The place looks great, Madeline," he enthused. "You've really made it homey."

I looked around the not-many-square-foot apartment, unchanged since the last time Tyler had been there. My desk and computer setup dominated the window wall in the living room. The view over the canyon was spectacular, but I couldn't think of any way it could be accredited to my decorating skills. I had a big, comfy chair that looked as though it was waiting for the imminent arrival of the sofa and coffee table that should have complemented it. I had some art on the walls, but while it was colorful, none of it was noteworthy. I had a little eating area—a small table, a couple of chairs—right outside the tiny kitchen, but they were purely functional. At a glance, it was fairly obvious I wasn't set up to do a lot of entertaining.

"Thanks," I muttered, on gentle alert now. "It's amazing what a computer and desk will do."

At the sound of Tyler's voice, his dog, Tycho, had come padding out of my bedroom, where he'd spent my workday snoring gently on my bed: a fairly usual occurrence. I worked at home and the various Becketts and Saranovas did not. Probably for that reason Tycho adopted me not long after I moved in. Though he scared the bejeebers out of me the first time I met him, the large, hairy beast quickly became a fixture in my life and—when I wasn't using it—on my bed. I kept food and water for him on my little deck, he would run with me in the morning, go for the occasional car ride when I was going somewhere even mildly interesting to a canine and usually watched me while I slept. I guess you could say that Tycho and I had an arrangement, though he was the only one who seemed absolutely certain of the details.

Now Tyler scratched the big dog's head affectionately. "You know, I hardly see this big lump anymore."

I grinned at the big lump description. It seemed so apt. "Well, you always know where he is," I said.

"Yeah. Don't know what I'd do if you moved. Probably have to give him to you and get a new dog."

Though it was a funny thought—and Tyler was clearly trying to be funny—I'd had enough. "Look, Tyler, much as I'm always pleased to see you, I'm pretty sure you didn't drop by today to talk about your dog."

What was my clue? Maybe just that I knew Tyler was one of the most in-demand directors in Hollywood and that he was currently working on at least two important projects. His wife and daughter had been waving to his shadow for the last couple of months, and the most I'd seen of him for a while was his SUV racing up and down the canyon: we'd beep and nod when we passed each other on the road. Tyler didn't have time to breathe right now, never mind stop by to chat with his tenant about decorating and dogs.

Tyler had the grace to look slightly embarrassed, as though he'd been caught at something, which put me further on alert. Then he took a deep breath, shrugged and plunged right in. Once you get him going, he's a pretty forthright guy.

"See, here's the thing. I'm this close—" he held his hands a couple of inches apart "—to getting a green light on the *Race the Dawn* project. I mean, I've really polished the script, Alastair Reynolds's people say he's almost a sure thing for the lead, and Vancouver is looking super good for locations."

"That's good," I mumbled vaguely, wondering why in hell he was telling me any of this. I have no kind of stake in the film industry, though I did know that *Race the Dawn* was Tyler's pet project. He was known as a director, not a screenwriter, yet this was a script he'd written himself and had been trying to get backed for years. He'd put a lot of his own resources into it to get it as far as he had. But he'd known all along that wouldn't be enough.

"And I'm *this* close—" he held up his hands again, this time even less distance apart "—to getting Maxi Livingston to agree to produce."

Maxi Livingston. Even I knew that name. Livingston Studios has had some piece of some aspect of Oscar for almost twenty years. Maxi Livingston was not just one of the most important producers in Hollywood, he was *it:* the cat's ass, the big kahuna. The twinned hyacinths of the Livingston Studios logo were the final seal of approval: even audiences were aware of that and knew what it meant.

Tyler was no schmuck, no slouch: he'd made some wonderful films. But there had been whispers about *Race the Dawn*—to get it made the way Tyler wanted was going to cost a lot of money. The kind of money Maxi Livingston could pony up without even beading the wax on his Bentley. If he produced *Race the Dawn*, Tyler would be able to make it into the kind of film he wanted.

And I found all of this interesting. I really did. I was born and raised in Seattle, the daughter of a golf course manager and an insurance agent. I have a business degree from Harvard and I've spent most of my career as a stockbroker. I've been around a lot of cool stuff. But to me the film industry is separate. Magic. So it still seemed really special to be this close to it. This far inside. I liked hearing about it. I just didn't know why I was hearing about it now.

That's what I said to Tyler. "Why are you telling me this?" I'm not one to beat around any bushes.

Tyler sighed. Ran his fingers through his sparse hair. Sighed again. "You see, Madeline." A beat. A pause. "It's like this." Another sigh. Then a sense that he was just going to rush in and let things fall where they may. "I kinda told Maxi you'd teach his wife about the stock market."

I didn't say anything. I mean, what could I say? I just looked at Tyler. Closely. Tried not to enjoy it too much when he squirmed under my glance. Finally I said firmly, "You did not."

"She doesn't want to be a broker or anything," he said quickly, as though assuring me of something vast. "She just wants to play the market a bit. Like you do." Tyler filled the space quickly with words when he saw my face. "Well not, of course, just like you do. I just meant from home. With a computer. Herself. Without a broker."

"Tyler, I *am* a broker." I hesitated. Went back a few steps. "Well, I was. It's what I did for ten years. It's not like you can just fall out of bed one morning and say, 'Ooh. I think I'll play with stocks.'"

Except, of course, that you can. Ever since the Internet had become so accessible, millions of people had been doing just that. Some of them with incredibly horrible results: buying stuff they hadn't meant to buy, sometimes losing hundreds of thousands of dollars. I told Tyler this now.

"See, that's the beauty, Madeline. Livingston has a pile of money. And his wife wants to do this. Instead, I guess, of opening a dress shop or a gallery. I dunno why, really. Maxi just mentioned it to me and I…"

"…rushed in to be helpful," I said with a little more venom than I'd intended. After all, it was *my* services he was offering here. "And it's not like it's something I can do, Tyler."

"You can't?" he looked genuinely perplexed. The thought obviously hadn't occurred to him.

"Well, I'm not a teacher, for one. I don't know the first thing about instructing someone."

Tyler looked relieved. "Oh, that. Madeline, I've seen

you with Jennifer. You're a terrific teacher. She really listens to you and respects you."

"It's not the same thing."

"No, of course not." Tyler was in heavy placate mode, yet I could see he was determined to get what he'd come for. "Still, I know it's something you'd be great at."

"Tyler, it's just not that simple. I'm not even licensed in California. I can't go around giving financial advice."

Tyler brightened. "See, I knew that, so that's not what I promised. Of course. I just thought you could teach her the mechanical end of things. Online broker-ages and how to—you know—physically buy and sell stocks from her computer. Not *what* to buy," he assured me. "Just how to do it."

"Tyler…"

"And I wouldn't expect you to do it for free, of course."

"Tyler…"

"I'd pay you for your time."

"Tyler don't be an idiot. It's not the money."

He shoved his hands deep into the pockets of his chinos, a sheepish look on his face. Again. "I know that, Madeline. Believe me, I know you well enough for that. It's just that it's so important."

Tyler, usually strong and in charge in every situation, looked so dejected—so *desperate*—I got a sense of how important this really was to him. And I thought about it. It *was* something I was capable of doing. Not so dif-ferent, really, from when I'd shown my mom how to do the same thing when I was last in Seattle. Yet it felt dif-ferent, somehow. More official when it was a stranger.

And I was busy—sure, I was busy. I had a life. But it wasn't the kind of life I'd had in New York. In those days a request like this one would have been unthinkable. Laughable. Working at an investment firm, I'd barely had time to eat and sleep, let alone give one second of thought to babysitting a film mogul's wife. But, I reasoned with myself quickly, wasn't that part of why I'd changed my life? Why I'd left that high-pressure world and ended up day trading in a cliff house in Malibu? Because, among other things, life just gets too short when you see it whizzing past you at the end of a speed dialer. And every day you're trying to cram in more *stuff* and make more money and save more time. And then one day, if you happen to be me, you wake up and realize that the person who dies with the biggest pile of loot is *not* necessarily the winner. And all that time you've saved over the years? It doesn't accumulate in a bank somewhere. It isn't off accruing interest. You've worked and worked to save that time up and for what? It's just as gone as if you'd wasted it, so what, in the end, was the difference?

So, bottom line: I'd changed my life for a lot of big reasons and a lot of small reasons and all of them had to do with Tyler standing in front of me now with a pleading look on his face. If you couldn't make a withdrawal from that time bank to help a friend, what the hell was the point of anything?

"Tyler, I can't take money for this. But maybe the guesthouse could use a teensy addition."

"That's doable," Tyler said quickly.

"You haven't even heard what I want."

He smiled. "I know, but it's still doable. This is *that* important to me." He seemed to think for a second, then added, "And I know you wouldn't ask for anything unreasonable."

"Well, you're right. I'm not thinking anything big. But it seemed to me that if the bathroom incorporated part of the storage space behind it…"

"Or all of it, we don't really use that storage space, anyway. That's a good idea. I should have thought of it myself. We could even give some of the space to your kitchen, while we're at it."

"Wow. Cool. Great. What do I do?"

"Maybe draw up a rough plan. There's a guy in Santa Monica that has done some work for me. I'll give him a call, maybe have him get in touch with you, if that's all right."

"Sure." I was amazed at how quickly all of this was happening.

"Okay, you guys work out the details." He grinned. "And I'll pay. Anything else?"

"What's her name?" I asked, wanting to put a more personal face on the whole thing. "Maxi's wife."

"Keesia. Keesia Livingston."

"I had a friend who had a dog called Keesha once." I had visions of myself teaching the market to a well-behaved poodle.

"Not *Keesha*," he corrected. "Kee-zee-ya," he pronounced carefully.

I rolled my eyes. "Still. Dumb. For a person."

Tyler spread his hands. Clearly he'd had no part in naming Maxi's wife. But he smiled. Despite my rant, he could sense victory. "So, you'll do it?"

"I guess," I sighed. "But I still don't know that I'll make such a great teacher."

"Sure you will," he enthused, obviously relieved. "You'll be great. And you'll like Keesia. I've met her. She's a very sweet girl."

The project took on a slightly warmer tone for me when I found out I'd be doing the instructing at the Livingston's estate in Beverly Hills. Tyler told me it was one of the grandest ever and I love seeing inside other people's houses.

I knew my mom would be excited when she heard. I think she's enjoyed my living in Los Angeles at least as much as I have. She loves hearing about the people I meet because of living in Tyler Beckett's aura, never mind hearing about Tyler and Tasya themselves.

"Oh, but I've heard of Keesia Livingston," my mother enthused on the phone when I called her in Seattle that night. "There was a photo of her and Maxi, beside their pool, in *In-Crowd Magazine* a couple of issues ago. They referred to her as Maxi's 'new wife.' Really. I'm not making this up."

"How new?" I asked.

"They've been married two, maybe three years."

"I wonder what happened to his old wife?"

"*Wives,*" my mother said pointedly.

"Wives? How many?"

"I'm not sure. Three, anyway. Maybe four."

"Wow," I said. That meant a lot of alimony *and* disharmony. Not to mention, potentially, a lot of mouths to feed. "Well, I'll tell you about the house after I've seen it. It's supposed to be gorgeous."

"Oh, it is," my mother said knowledgeably. "It's an estate, really. I saw a photo spread in one of those British magazines when he married this one. Incredible gardens, a huge main house: twenty-six bedrooms…"

"Twenty-six?" I said, startled. I couldn't even imagine. "What do you do with twenty-six bedrooms?

My mother laughed. "Dust them, I guess. And it has

a theater that seats two hundred people. The gardens are supposed to be incredible. It said in the magazine that the whole thing was brought over—plants, garden structures and all—from some important estate someplace in the middle of England. Don't you think it's amazing what enough money will buy? So I'll want to hear all about it! The girls will be thrilled."

"The girls" might either mean my mom's best friends, Clarissa and Ruth, or it might mean my sisters, Miranda and Meagan—which for some reason my family has always insisted on pronouncing as "Miggin"— or it might mean all four. Perhaps even at once. I knew that the bicoastal chapters of my life sometimes made for interesting dinner and coffee conversation at my mother's house in the quiet and pretty Greenwood neighborhood of Seattle.

Tyler made all the arrangements for my visit to the Livingston estate. He knows that, most of the time, my personal work schedule echoes that of the New York trading day. I've always been an early riser. Most people who find themselves truly drawn to the stock market are, or force themselves to be. I get up before the opening bell rings on the exchange floor in New York—that's 6:30 a.m., Pacific Time—and generally spend most of my workday at my desk until the closing bell rings at 1:00 p.m., Pacific Time: that's 4:00 in New York.

The happy part of all this is that it leaves my afternoons free if I want them that way, which is a nice thing when you live in Malibu and the Pacific Ocean calls you from your "office" window while you work.

To be honest, most of the time I don't see it. On one level I might notice the fat cumulus clouds floating over a clear blue sea, or the way the light shifts across the canyon that separates me from the ocean when I sit at my desk. I see the scraggly and picturesque eucalyptus trees that dot—and scent—the sparsely vegetated canyon, and the long stalks of the grasses responding to the play of every breeze. All that stuff is there. Always. And I'm aware of it. But when I'm trading—seriously trading—not much gets between me and my computer screen.

So simultaneously moving to L.A. and deciding to become a day trader suited my mood. And they—L.A. and day trading—suit each other. Because I can spend the day focusing, focusing, focusing. Scanning columns of ever-changing stock prices; reading press releases and news announcements as they hit my in-box; scanning annual reports and detailed company information and—most important and always—buying and selling various securities. But when the day ends—when that distant closing bell at the New York Stock Exchange rings—I'm not only ready to play, I'm in a good physical location to do so.

On the particular Thursday that Tyler had arranged for me to meet Keesia Livingston, playing would not be an option. I spent the forty minutes it took to go from my place in Malibu to the Livingston estate in Beverly Hills regretting my agreement. How had I let myself get talked into this? And while I knew the answer to that— and I felt happy to be able to do something for Tyler: he'd done a lot for me and a bigger bathroom and kitchen *would* be great—the fact that I was now committed to helping a probably ditzy "new wife" learn about the stock market didn't do much to lift my mood. While I have many sterling qualities, patience has never been one of them. I had visions of swallowing my ire when Mrs. Livingston (inevitably, I thought) asked me the difference between a security's trading price and yield for the thirtieth time.

Arriving at the Livingston estate on Benedict Canyon Drive pushed everything else out of my mind. It was in an area that had once housed many of the large multi-acred mansions of the stars—testaments to opulence and poor taste. The visible, earthly trophies of people who had started out with less than nothing and ended up with more than their share.

My mother had told me she'd read that the original Livingston mansion had been built for Lolita Larkin, one of the most golden stars of Hollywood's golden age. The estate encompassed several acres and a fairly famous garden. Even though Ms. Larkin had been dead for more than thirty years, the house and property were still referred to as Larkin House.

Livingston hadn't razed the old mansion like so many others had done with Hollywood landmarks. Rather, over a number of years he'd had the original structure of the house gently augmented and modernized by talented contemporary architects. The resulting property was one of the most celebrated in a town stuffed with celebrated houses. And where a lot of other large estates had been cut up—the big mansions torn down to make way for even bigger mansions on smaller chunks of increasingly valuable real estate—Larkin House survived not only intact, but improved.

As I passed the security gates—probably left open in anticipation of my arrival—and moved my car up the long, curving driveway, the scope of the estate almost took my breath away. Mature formal English gardens thrived in lush splendor, looking not in the least innocuous in an environment more suited to palm trees and desert grass. No doubt some homesick English landscape architect had forced his view of the world on the California earth. And if it wasn't a Brit, it was someone who wished they were: it was in every line of the neatly marching cypress trees, the hard-edged concrete masonry, the formally regular reflecting pools, the regimentally straight flower beds. Generations of gardeners had kept the vision true and the resulting lush oasis was as impressive as the house it framed.

The mansion itself gave a nod to the building's environment: but only a nod. The huge two-level Georgian-style home incorporated a mission-style roof and Spanish arches. And though that sounds incongruous—and it would be on a modern house—it looked quite perfect in its setting: as though it had been standing there for hundreds of years. Another incongruous touch: thick ivy coated two sides of the gargantuan structure, rose vine crept up a third. I'd lived in California just long enough to wonder how many gallons of water it must take to keep that ivy looking crisp and the roses fresh, as though they received daily waterings from an English sky.

I pulled my almost new, nondescript, four-door car only slightly self-consciously into the porte cochere. It was a house that seemed to demand at least a Jag to be parked in front of it, maybe flanked by a Ferrari and a Rolls. Certainly nothing made in the good ol' U.S. of A., as my Chevy was.

When I reached the top of the grand marble staircase that led to the entrance, one of the oversize oak doors opened wide just in advance of my knock.

"Ms. Carter?" the uniformed maid said before I could

announce myself. I nodded mutely, slightly over-whelmed by the deliberate displays of opulence I saw all around me. She answered my nod: "Mrs. Livingston is expecting you."

As I followed her through a labyrinth of hallways, I had a sense of dark wood, old paintings and the smell of beeswax all around me. It was like a well-kept museum.

We emerged into a sunny corridor that followed the contour of one side of the house: a conservatory. South-ern California, with its almost year-round clement weather, hardly needed one. But the original designer must have thought that a proper English country house required a conservatory, and never mind bothering with reality and the fact that it wasn't a proper English house, at all.

The present mistress of Larkin House had comman-deered the conservatory as her own. Light and modern furniture didn't half fill the airy space. Large, indige-nous plants filled much of the area that was left, per-fectly complemented by rustic jade-green tile.

One corner of the conservatory had been given over to a serious-looking office setup. The desk looked as though it was entirely made of huge pieces of glass that converged together at odd angles. The desk's surface was almost covered by a noticeably shiny new com-puter, complete with enough high-tech gear to run a lit-tle corporation. Because of the glass desktop, all of those electronics seemed to float eerily in midair.

Though I'd had a pretty good idea that anyone iden-tified in a national magazine as Maxi's "new wife" would be attractive—it goes with the whole trophy wife mystique—Keesia Livingston was beyond expectation. My first impression was of cinnamon and sunshine:

she was all browns and golds. Red-gold artfully touched the black of her hair. Her eyes rivaled amber, not only in color but in luminescence. She wore a crisp linen blouse open at the throat over chamois-colored khaki pants that looked both tailored and comfortable. She was lithe and slender to the point of delicacy, both of which vouched for the likelihood of the full, round breasts she displayed so carefully being after-market. Her features and complexion were clear and flawless. I'd been told she was twenty-eight, though I would have guessed her age as closer to nineteen and not because of anything I saw in those topaz-colored eyes: her expression was quick and intelligent, her handshake, when she rose to meet me, firm and sure.

"Madeline Carter—" her voice, like her body, was full and lovely "—you are a surprise! I'd expected geek girl—glasses and frumpy. You're beautiful. You're fashionable. Were you ever a model?"

Her words surprised me, as they always have when I hear anything like them directed at me. I'm tall, so the modeling thing is not completely out to lunch: five foot eleven on a slender woman puts that idea into a lot of people's heads. Especially, I've found, in L.A. where everyone is a model, actress or wants to be one. But I can't align the face and the body I see in the mirror with those on television and in magazines. Am I beautiful? Enough people have said so that there are days when I sort of wonder. But it's an abstract wonder, a sort of "what if" wonder. I have enough going on that occasional flashes of beauty—real or imagined—are sufficient in my life.

"No," I said, then decided to answer her frankness with my own. "And why, in L.A., is it acceptable to talk about beauty as though it's an accomplishment?" There was no malice in my voice: I really wanted to know. This woman was, really, nothing to me. But she seemed forthright enough that I had hope of getting an answer.

I was right. She considered a moment, her head tilting ever slightly to one side, giving her the appearance of a lovely and canny fox. Then she laughed, while she waved me over to a conversation area dominated by a brace of comfy-looking jade-green leather sofas and separated by a coffee table that probably cost as much as my car, but managed to look functional, anyway.

"Sit, honey," she said between chortles. "This is gonna take some time." She pushed a button on an intercom I hadn't noticed before and ordered us some tea, taking for granted that I'd want some. I did.

When she was settled across from me, Keesia said comfortably, "When Maxi told me you were going to come and help me with the stock thing, I didn't know how I'd repay you." She was smiling, and it was all said in good humor, but I didn't miss the thread of seriousness that ran beneath what she was saying. "I didn't imagine that it would be an exchange of information," she said with a thousand-watt smile. "Now I know I was wrong." She seemed to consider for a moment, as though thinking of a place to begin. "You're not from around here, are you?"

"You can tell that just by looking at me?" I quipped.

"Actually, I can't," she said quite seriously. "You're beautiful. Poised. Polished." I made to demure, but she held up one perfectly manicured hand to stop me. "See, that's the part that tells me you've not been here that long. You protest, but not too much. It took me a second to see it, but I think it's because you mean it."

She said this last with such earnestness I almost laughed out loud. I guess she could see that on my face, because she rushed on. "No, really. Beauty is a job here." And by "here" I knew she meant the rarified and monied circles in which she traveled. "I have not achieved the things I have by letting my hair go all natural and not taking care of my skin." I ran my hand self-consciously through my own unruly blond mop, but Keesia didn't seem to notice as she continued. "I work out with my personal trainer three times a week. I don't eat carbs. I do yoga. I run at least twice a week. I ride. I swim. I play tennis. And all of that is more for the outside of me than the inside, if you follow what I'm saying."

I did, but I wasn't quite sure I believed my ears. She talked about achievement the same way I would: the same way everyone did. Career advancement, goals attained, financial well-being.

I looked around me. Out the conservatory windows I could see a lovely swimming pool surrounded by those world-class gardens. I could see some employee bent over, scrubbing at the visibly clean concrete around the pool. Another snipped away, doing something unfathomable to roses. Still another clipped at the grass. As we sat, a soft-footed servant—a different one than had answered the door, I noted—brought our "tea," a large, steaming pot of it in bone china, cups and saucers to match, plus carefully prepared fruit, finger sandwiches, cream scones and petit fours so delicate they were almost too pretty to eat: none of which, of course, Keesia touched at all. Except the fruit. But eating wasn't the point. Serving it, showing it, having it, that's what it was about.

So, accomplishment: Keesia had it all, didn't she?

She had accomplished the American dream. More. The big house, the flock of servants, everything she could possibly think to want. She'd not done it with an MBA from Harvard and twenty years of work, but—from her perspective—with the right combination of genes, strategy and trips to the salon. Was her way any less real? I'd have to think about it. In the meantime, I had another question.

"Then why the stocks, Keesia? It doesn't seem to fit into this—" I indicated our sumptuous surroundings "—or your demanding workout schedule."

I'd said it lightly and was relieved when she took it that way and laughed. "Observant girl," she said merrily, but I could see the hint of a shadow in her eye. "You're right. It doesn't, does it? Well, that's the problem—the challenge—of my sort of accomplishment. There's always tomorrow. You've gotta keep lookin' over your shoulder. Besides," she joked, "I'd like to use my computer for something more than keeping my journal."

And with that cryptic remark she seemed to have had enough of talking about her world, and shifted things deftly into mine.

If, before I met her, I had apprehensions about Keesia's ability to grasp the concepts of online trading, she laid them to rest in short order. There was more to Keesia than a flawless complexion and perfect hair. She effortlessly followed the basics as I laid them out for her, interrupting only to ask the occasional intelligent question. The type of question that told me she'd not only been paying attention, but was understanding the things I was teaching her.

When I took her through the application for her online trading account, Keesia unlocked a drawer in a cabinet near her desk to pull out the file that contained the ID she'd need to complete the application. The drawer was between us and, once opened, along with various personal files and other things I could imagine you'd want to keep out of servants' hands, something caught my eye.

At first glance, it appeared to be a rock, roughly the size of my hand, and about the same dimensions: longer than it was wide and perhaps two inches thick. Even from its place in the semidark, I could see that it was roughly carved and carefully shaped.

"It's interesting, isn't it?" Keesia said following my glance. She drew it out of the drawer and offered it to me to examine. I took it eagerly.

When I was a New York stockbroker, I made a lot of money. Stupid amounts of money. But I worked such crazy long hours, I didn't get a lot of time to shop.

Some of my colleagues did. They'd go to Balthazar and drop a couple grand on dinner for two. They'd buy crazy-ass cars that no one in the city would bother driving on a daily basis because it's just way too much hassle to actually try to get around in your own car in New York. A few of them started snorting money up their nose or shooting it into their arms or smoking it in various, creative ways. Those guys called it recreational: said it helped them unwind. And, generally, they didn't last a real long time after they'd started down that path.

None of these ways of spending money appealed to me. I mostly socked it away, invested it, bought a co-op. But I did develop one habit: I started collecting stuff. Not in a big way. In fact, I spent more time thinking about collecting stuff than actually doing it. But I loved nineteenth-century art—mainly impressionist but also some realist—and I especially loved the thought of being able to own it. To me it seemed a vice almost on a par with the coke blowers. To own—actually *own*—something Degas or Renoir or Turner had made with their own hands. To have it and look at it whenever I wanted. This, to me, seemed the ultimate luxury. The ultimate decadence.

The other upside of collecting for me was that I could do it without having it mess up my work schedule. Auctions are often held at night and, if they're not, you can usually participate online. It's almost like being there. I'd buy things and hardly miss a beat out of my trading day.

As a result of my close brushes with the collecting world, I'd gained an appreciation for a fairly wide range of stuff. In Keesia's office, I didn't understand the nature or purpose—if there was one—of the object I was holding, but, on some very basic level, I knew it *was* something to hold.

One side was almost perfectly smooth, save for a series of carvings that I could now see were runes that I judged to be Celtic. The sides had similar, smaller carvings. The other, larger side was quite different. Though it was also mostly smooth, there were no carvings. Instead there were several areas about an inch in diameter where bits of the stone stood out in sharp relief.

"What is it?" I asked as I examined the stone closely.

"I don't really know," Keesia said. "It looks as though it might have a purpose, doesn't it? But I can't imagine what it might be. I found it, right here in the conservatory, when I had the place redone. Imagine—when we pulled up the old flooring, we found it. It looked as though someone had tried to hide it. I've always meant to find out what it was. Just, you know—" she shrugged "—never got around to it."

"It's a wonderful story, though, Keesia. Imagine— hidden in your floor. I love it." I moved a finger through the carvings, "A magical stone, hidden away for who knows how long."

Keesia laughed as she tucked the stone back into its spot in the drawer and we refocused on the business at hand: getting Mrs. Keesia Livingston smoothly into the stock market.

Two

I had a date that night. That may not seem remarkable, but it was to me. Remarkable, that is. It doesn't happen all that often.

If I said it wasn't the worst Southern California date I've been on, you'd get a sense of how wonderful my recent romantic history hasn't been. It wasn't the worst date, but it was pretty much up there.

I'd met him at one of Tyler's parties. It's gotten so that when I start hearing them move the deck furniture around above my head or the sounds of caterers scurrying to and fro, I start thinking about what to wear. I've discovered this is what happens when you live in a guesthouse situated under the deck of a well-known movie director who likes to entertain: you either join in the fun or stay home and grumble at the racket. I am, by nature, not much of a grumbler and the free food is a bonus, plus it's stuff to tell my mother, who thinks my life since moving to Malibu has gone completely glam.

However, for all the perks that go with being Tyler Beckett's tenant, one of them has not been meeting men. Well, I meet them, but most aren't keepers. One of the qualities I admire in a man is that he's more impressed with me than he is with himself. Hollywood parties are *not* a good place to meet that sort.

Clipper Anderson seemed different, despite the stupid name. First of all, Clipper is a behind the camera kind of guy, something that could be deduced from his handle. He's a film editor and Clipper is his nickname. I've no idea what his real name is, and considering how everything turned out, I'm not likely to discover what it is. I'm even less likely to care.

At Tyler's party, Clipper made me laugh: another quality high on my list. We mostly sat on the sidelines, our drinks resting on the deck railing, the Pacific Ocean a velvety drape below us. We'd watch the view for a while, then turn back to the party and make fun of the partygoers from a safe distance.

"Where do you think she got that dress?" he said cattily as one young actress struggled to keep the garment from falling off her when she turned a bit too quickly to snag a passing drink.

"Maybe Ringo Starr's daughter designed it for her?" I offered, a stab at the fact that fellow ex-Beatle Paul McCartney's daughter, Stella, is a fabulously famous designer and movie stars battle for her best designs. And Ringo Starr's daughter is…not. It's even possible that Ringo Starr doesn't have a daughter, I really don't know. But Clipper got my joke. He even thought it was funny.

Okay, making fun of other people was a childish pastime, it's true. But I followed Clipper's lead and we seemed to enjoy each other's company, and so when Clipper proposed we meet for dinner in the near future,

I agreed. More laughs, I thought. And who can have too many of those?

He insisted on picking me up for our date, which is weird for L.A., considering I live two miles up a canyon in Malibu and Clipper lives in Santa Monica. We'd agreed to have dinner in Brentwood, which is a lot closer to his house than to mine. I have a perfectly good car, but I thought: What the hell? Clipper's an old-school gentleman, though he hadn't struck me as the type. I went along with it; though, to be honest, I had a twinge even then.

Things started off fine. The drive down the coast in his brand-new Mustang convertible (another twinge, another hint) with the top down on a perfect Southern California evening was lovely. Textbook. A scene straight off a postcard. I made a mental note to tell Mom about it.

The restaurant was posh and beautiful and tony—the kind of place I generally loathe, except it was also French and I like French food a lot. A gift from my ex-husband, the chef, who taught me a thing or two about cuisine. I don't remember the first gift Braydon—the ex-husband—ever gave me, but I'll never forget the time when we were dating that he made me omelet fourrée à la japonaise followed by squabs en papillotes with pommes de terre farcies à la duxelles and then, for dessert, a financier torte, which he said he thought was appropriate, considering the business I was in.

So, obviously, just being able to *remember* the names of all those things made me something of an expert. I'm not much of a cook. I can manage a bowl of cereal and I actually make a decent sandwich: when I've remembered to get all the ingredients. When I'm sick I can make chicken noodle soup, from a package or a can. But serious cooking? About all I can make is reservations.

Thanks to Braydon, though, I'm good with a menu in almost any language. More: I *like* ordering food. It's practically a hobby. So, when I think about it, it's possible Clipper looked at me archly when I declined his offer to order for both of us but, frankly, I don't remember. I was too busy internally salivating over all the cool stuff I could order if I wanted to. Clipper-schmipper. For a heartbeat, while I drank in all that was on offer, he may as well not have been there.

Fillets of sole à la cancalaise.

Diablotins au fromage.

Côte de veau foyot.

Culotte de boeuf aux poireaux a la bière.

The possibilities had me salivating and I realized I'd been spending too much time thinking about the stock market: getting by on toast with peanut butter and rice cakes with not much of anything while a whole world of food slid by me, unnoticed.

I ordered the foie gras with a tangerine reduction to start, then the diablotins au fromage as my main course and crème brûlée for dessert. I can never resist crème brûlée. Clipper rather predictably ordered the steak frites—i.e., steak and French fries—making me doubly glad I'd declined his oh-so-generous offer of ordering for me.

Did the conversation lag while the foie gras melted on my tongue or the diablotins au fromage sent my eyes rolling heavenward? It's possible. I can't imagine that we *didn't* converse while we ate, but for the life of me, I can't remember whatever it was we talked about. Maybe something about his latest film (it didn't sound like a very good one), his car (he'd only just acquired it) and his trip home to Boston. That is, our conversation centered around Clipper's favorite topic: Clipper. I found my foie gras a lot more interesting.

With dinner done, Clipper ordered a cheese plate, coffee and a bottle of dessert wine for both of us—as though he had to sneak ordering for me in *somewhere*— then excused himself. By the time I'd finished my (really wonderful) coffee, nibbled at the (truly yummy) cheese and fruit on the cheese plate and sipped substantially at my (incredibly sublime) ice wine, I noticed Clipper had been gone a long time. A really long time. A weirdly long time.

By the time Clipper had been gone a full thirty-five minutes I was almost beside myself. Surely there were no manly needs that needed *that* kind of attention on a date. At a restaurant.

I scanned my internal database for instruction. Came up empty. No etiquette lesson I could recall had prepared me for what to do when your dinner companion disappears into the Twilight Zone of the men's room. Obviously, I couldn't sit there all night waiting for Clipper to come back. Something had to be wrong with him. Why else leave me sitting here alone for—I scanned my watch—forty-five minutes now? And counting.

I flagged a waiter.

"Mam'selle?" he queried in his Pasadena-inflected French.

I hemmed a bit. Then I hawed. But I knew I had to say *something*. I couldn't just sit there all night with Clipper in who-knew-what kind of trouble in the men's.

"My…my companion is…perhaps…indisposed. He's been gone a long time. Could you—or maybe someone—could you check? The men's room, that is. I'm getting worried."

"Your companion?"

"Yes, the man I had dinner with. Red hair—" I pointed at Clipper's vacant seat "—he was sitting there."

"Oh, Monsieur Anderson?"

"Yes."

"But he left, *mam'selle*."

"Left." I know I said it stupidly, but the word didn't make any sense. Clipper was in the men's room. Wasn't he? Where else could he be?

"Oui."

"But, the men's room…" The fact that he was gone took a little while to penetrate.

"The check has been paid, *mam'selle*," the waiter assured me, though I hadn't yet gotten around to thinking about that part.

"He left?" I played the possibilities through my mind. Could there have been a family emergency? An *editing* emergency? Either way, it didn't explain why he'd disappeared without saying goodbye. Without saying *anything*.

"Would *mam'selle* like me to call her a cab?"

Here's the thing: if I'd actually *liked* Clipper very much, his actions would have hurt me. As it was, I was just mad. In the first place, Brentwood is a good twenty miles from my place in Malibu. If he'd asked me to meet him at the restaurant like a normal person, I would have had my car there. I would have sipped a little more slowly at the ice wine, sure. But I would have had my wheels. As it was, my wonderful evening with Clipper Anderson cost me thirty bucks in cab fare and slightly more than that in self-esteem.

By the time the cab pulled over to the edge of the cliff

above the house, I'd begun to see humor in the situation. Nothing like this had ever happened to me before, true. But then, the SoCal dating experience was fairly new to me. I kept hearing about how wacky just about everything was out here and Clipper Anderson seemed like a pretty good example. Back in New York you might have to worry about fending off unwanted advances by the end of the evening. Out here, it seemed to be enough just keeping track of your date.

As I made my way carefully down the stairs leading to the house, then cut across the deck to get to the stairs that lead down to the guesthouse where I lived, I felt a couple of chuckles turn into full-throated laughter. I could see I'd either have to keep better track of my dates in future, or maybe just choose them more carefully in the first place.

Tyler, out under the stars with some candles, a glass of wine and a script, intercepted me between decks. "What's so funny?"

"How can you read in the dark?" I asked.

"Candles." He pointed, with an expression that told me he thought he was stating the obvious. "It's a romantic script. And why were you laughing?"

"Do you even want to know?" I chortled.

"Mmm… I'm not sure. Maybe. No, you're right. I don't. How are things going with Mrs. Livingston?"

"Just great, Tyler. You were right. She's super nice. A quick study, too. I'm just surprised she has time for any of this in her busy schedule."

"What do you mean?"

"I dunno." I considered. "Between personal trainers and yoga and all of the attention that needs to be paid to a carb-free diet, her life seems full. Why do you think she's doing this?"

"Retirement fund?" Tyler offered.

I looked at him quizzically. "What do you mean?"

"Well," he said carefully, "Keesia is the fifth Mrs. Maxi Livingston."

"The *fifth?*" It confirmed what my mother had told me, but it was still a pretty big number.

He nodded. "I'd say she's planning for her future. Probably not a bad idea."

It wasn't a bad idea at all. Unfortunately, Keesia didn't know how little future she had left.

Three

Over the next few weeks, Keesia Livingston and I got to be something like friends. When I'd met her, she didn't know how to do much on her computer beyond checking her e-mail and writing her journal. It was more than my mother knew when we'd gone through a similar process after a stock deal went bad on her a while ago. Mom figured she'd better learn a thing or two up close and personal about the market to protect her investments. Mom's zeal cooled a bit when she discovered how much was actually involved.

Mrs. Livingston was a different story. She seemed more open to all of it, perhaps more motivated and, after a couple of sessions and with her application approved, Keesia was ready to activate her online trading account.

She told me she was going to start with $25,000 and invest from there. It seemed like an awful lot of money to be playing with—my mom had started with $5,000. But, like everything, money is relative. Since Keesia probably spent more on makeup in one year than my mom did on clothes in ten, it all sort of made sense.

I showed Keesia how to read the financial section of a newspaper, how to look for stocks that might be interesting, how to read a financial statement and which news and stock Web sites were worthy of attention.

We didn't talk about day trading but about long-term investment. I told her it would make sense for her to start out by looking carefully at parts of the market that she found interesting. No pork bellies or semiconductors for Keesia. I instructed her that, especially while she was learning, she should look for companies with products she actually knew something about and on which she could form an opinion based on her own knowledge of that section of the market. And there are enough publicly traded companies in every sector—cosmetics, hair-care products, magazine and newspaper publishers, clothing designers and retailers, you name it—that she had loads to choose from.

I found I liked making my post-trading day treks up to Beverly Hills three times a week. The estate was so different from the Malibu cliff house where I lived. The ordered grounds at Larkin House were more reminiscent of an East Coast or European estate than one in Southern California, and I found the seemingly endless line of servants fascinating. It was like being on another planet.

The trips to Keesia's even became a relief once the remodeling on my apartment started. The contractor Tyler knew—a long, cool drink of a guy called Gus who looked less like a Gus than anyone I'd ever known—had basically taken over the guesthouse from 8:00 a.m. until 5:00 p.m. every day. While I hated the disturbance that all of this activity created, I consoled myself with the thought of how great it was all going to be once it was done.

When Keesia proposed a trading-day visit—kind of a field trip—to my place, I asked the guys to knock off early. Since mine was only one of several jobs the contractor was working on, he had no trouble rearranging things.

Keesia drove herself up the canyon in her dove-gray Aston Martin Vanquish, a car I'd coveted vocally on several occasions.

I was at the computer when Keesia arrived. I'd left the door open and she let herself in. I motioned for her to position herself behind me while I entered a buy order, then pulled up a chair and showed her through the world of day trading, as viewed from my post above Las Flores Canyon.

I always have about forty or fifty securities that I follow pretty closely—I have them on a "watch" screen on my computer so I can see everything at a single glance. This score or so of stocks are, for me, a microcosm of the market. They are mostly securities that have shown themselves to be recently volatile, or are ones I think will be volatile in the near future. You need that for day trading. But I've pulled them from all sectors. And so, at a glance, I see telecom stocks and electronics firms and gold mines and high-end retailers and glass manufacturers and pharmaceutical companies and so on. What I see on-screen is the name of the company, its trading symbol, what its trading price is at that moment—in green if the price is up, red if it's down and black if there's been no movement. I also see how many buy and sell orders are waiting to be filled—which is important to help predict which way the price will go—as well as volume amounts for each security: how many shares have actually traded hands on that day.

I explained all of this to Keesia and she delighted me by immediately grasping something I thought was quite subtle. "There's a lot of red," she said, indicating the trading prices. "Much, much more than half. Does that mean it's a bad market day?"

I smiled at her, pleased. "Well it does and it doesn't, but it's a great observation. See, there are ebbs and flows. You've probably started noticing that on your own already. The market will start out gangbusters some days. Then—if you're just watching the stock market itself and not listening to the world—it will seem to turn around and everything starts to go down. Almost everything. When it does that—" I looked down, embarrassed "—it feels—" I cleared my throat "—it feels like it's alive."

"The market?" she asked.

I nodded. Smiled gently.

She smiled back. Then a little more broadly. "I *know* what you're telling me. You're saying that, like you told me before, you can't just watch the market. You have to read the newspapers, read the releases and everything. Because the outside world affects the results, right?"

I nodded. That *was* what I meant. Of course. And yet. Watch it some time. Watch any first-rate stock market. Don't read the feeds. Don't listen to the news. Don't actually do any trading while you're doing this; just observe. Watch the ebb and flow. It feels like a creature. Breathing, stretching, growing. I did not say any of this. Some things really are too personal to share. Too esoteric. It wouldn't have helped her education, anyway.

At 1:00 p.m., when the North American stock markets closed, I found Keesia staring around my little apartment.

"Honestly, it's usually a little calmer around here," I told her, indicating the stacks of indigo tiles awaiting installation, and the piles of rubble set aside for the guys to cart away. "Want the tour?" I asked, half in jest.

"Sure," she said, rising.

The tour of Château Madeline took about forty-nine seconds if you stopped to inspect the contents of the refrigerator and I'd been shopping recently. I hadn't, so we didn't. There just wasn't that much to see. Keesia's bathroom in the conservatory would have taken about the same amount of space as my living room, eating area and kitchen. The bedroom was only slightly larger than an international postage stamp, and I have a hunch that Keesia would take more clothing on a weekend trip to the country than what would fit in the fairly small closet. She probably had a larger area just for handbags.

"But the closet has a window," I said lamely. "See? A closet with an ocean view."

"Yeah. Neat," she said politely, but I could see she was less than impressed.

I loved my apartment: my sky cave hanging over a canyon. It was like a dollhouse: everything built in, everything within reach. And the view made up for a lot. Under Keesia's scrutiny, however, the place seemed to shrink by half, even without the mess the guys had been making with my little remodel. And the funky disorder I generally called "home" suddenly seemed an unbearable mess. Of course, I didn't have a fleet of servants to clean up after me. And if I did, where would I have put them?

Keesia broke into my thoughts with her signature frankness. "I dunno, Madeline. I mean, sure it's cute and everything, but listen. You've been sharing your secrets with me. Maybe I should share some of mine with you? With all that hair and those long-ass legs, you could go far."

It was a joke. It *had* to be a joke, right? I laughed as though it was. Afterward, I'd wonder. I mean, you think about things. I've busted my ass my whole life for what? My car is paid for, but it's no Vanquish. I sold the little bit of real estate I owned before I left New York. I have what a lot of people would think of as a whopping amount of cash and equity in my trading account. I could maybe sell my holdings and put a good down payment on a house somewhere in West L.A.—not a great house, but a good one, though not in Malibu. 'Course, then I'd have to look for a job because I use my capital to make the money I live on. But, still, I've been out of college for a long time. You'd think I'd have more to show. I don't usually think of it that way. But I did right then.

Now, here's Keesia: a dozen years ago she was probably the prettiest girl in her high school. She decided she wanted to be a model, but at five foot seven she was too short for high fashion and some boyfriend spotted her the cash to buy boobs so she could do the lingerie thing. Then L.A.: actress (natch) and, before that gets seriously going, she lands what will end up being the biggest role of her career: the wife of Maxi Livingston, a man about as attractive as a jelly doughnut—without the soft center—and a billion (or ten billion?) reasons to find him attractive. Next thing you know (bada bing, bada boom), white wedding, the L.A. version of Tara and she has only to lift her finger and fifty people come running to do her bidding.

On the surface of things, you think: Well, at least I have my integrity. I did it all myself. But that doesn't buy a lot of potatoes. And you scratch and you scrape and you fight the rat race, as I had for a decade in New York, and you end up with what? Well, the ability to look at yourself in the mirror, for one thing. But maybe if, when I looked in the mirror, I saw what Keesia saw, I'd feel differently.

I said none of this. What I did say: "Well, if I could go far, why are you learning to do what I do?"

I saw again that shadow, an almost imperceptible grimace. Then a shrug. "It's complicated."

I went to the refrigerator, inspecting what we'd missed on the tour. No servants bearing crumpets on silver trays here. It was, by now, almost two o'clock in the afternoon and our work for the day was pretty much done. I pulled out a couple of longnecks, handed one to Keesia and said, "So tell me. We've got time."

Almost to my surprise, she took the bottle, cracked it with a single smooth movement and plunked herself down in my big comfy chair. Her elegant legs dangling over the side, she took a pull from the beer and sighed.

I pulled up a piece of the floor opposite the blanket box that passes for a coffee table and likewise cracked my beer. I didn't say anything. I could see she was organizing her thoughts, or perhaps gauging whether or not to take me into her confidence. I was a good bet for that: outside of her circle, yet in a position of trust. There probably weren't a lot of people she could talk about this with.

"Do you know Maxi was married four times before he met me?"

I made a grunting sound. I *did* know, but I wasn't sure it would be polite to tell her it was common knowledge. So common, in fact, that my mother had told me long distance from Seattle.

"Well, he was. I'm wife number five." She said this with such irony I could tell it wasn't a source of pride. "That's what the staff at the house calls me—Five. Not to my face, of course. But I've overheard them. 'What does Five want for lunch?' or 'After Five gets back from shopping, her bath must be drawn.' The staff has been there forever, but wives come and go. It's like they don't even bother to use our names and they know there'll be a new number before long. It makes you think, you know? And I've run the odds on this, Madeline." And when she said it, I knew she had. In the short time I'd known her, I'd seen this unerring instinct for numbers. She would have made a hell of a broker. Or an accountant. Had her life gone a different way. "Maxi replaced all four of his previous wives before they turned thirty. I'm *twenty-eight,* Madeline. It could start happening anytime."

It would not have been possible to look at Keesia Livingston in that moment and not feel completely conflicted about what she was saying. She had this almost unearthly beauty, which I suspected, at twenty-eight, had not yet reached its fullness. But it wasn't just that transient physical beauty. The more I'd seen of Keesia, the more I liked her. She was funny, generous, gentle, strangely wise and furiously intelligent. And yet she was a woman not yet in her prime already looking over her shoulder. I felt a little sad. And, oddly, a little sorry for her.

"But *stocks,* Keesia. It's not exactly a natural progression."

"Here's the thing. Maxi gives me an allowance, you know." I didn't, but I could imagine. There was that Vanquish parked above the house, after all. "I just started thinking about things and decided I'd better…you know…*know* something. And maybe *have* something. Just in case. And it's not just money. I mean, Maxi is generous that way—all of his ex-wives are taken care of. I'd have money. I want there to be something in my life that isn't just about the way I look. Does that make any sense at all?"

Sense? On one level, sense didn't even have a place here. In my world people got married because they fell in love. It didn't always work out, but the level of commitment required to take the step was extreme. There was the expectation—not always fulfilled—that the person you stood next to at the altar was going to be around for a while. That he would see you not only in the smooth magnificence of youth, but beyond the ripe promise of maturity and into the infirmities of old age. You promised, really, to love, honor and change each other's bedpans if that's what it took. *That* was love. *That* made sense to me.

With her words, Keesia opened a window into another world. Her world. It looked like a scary, potentially lonely place. The only commitment was to things that could be counted and stacked. *That* was a love you could depend on. *That* could take care of you in your old age.

It just wasn't the same thing. At all.

So did it make sense? No. But I understood what she was saying. And I told her so. I knew that's what she was asking in any case.

Keesia didn't notice my hesitation. "I know women," she said, "women in my position, who start lining up for surgery and trying to stay young. Fool nature. But…"

I suddenly understood something. "It's not the age, though, is it? It's not about appearances."

Because I'd learned a *little* something about L.A. since I'd been here: forty-five could look like twenty-five with enough money, the right medical introductions and a good enough surgeon. But there were things that surgery couldn't touch.

"No," she said, a little sadly. "At least, I don't think so. It's something about knowing too much. Not about him, necessarily. About the world. It's just, I dunno, experience or something. I think maybe we get too experienced for him. We get too wise." And I wondered if she realized she'd used that "we" as though she were part of some club.

"And the more I see, the more pathetic it seems. These beautiful women, Madeline, looking so desperate. So afraid. I decided I just don't want to be like that." She looked suddenly resolved, as though she'd reinforced something she'd been thinking just by saying it out loud. "I decided I wanted to do something that would give me some control. No matter what."

"So when you said you could teach me…"

"Oh, Madeline. I was kidding. Who wouldn't want to be you?"

I laughed at that. "Well, there are mornings…"

Keesia was suddenly very serious. "You laugh, but it's not a joke. Sure your place is dinky, and you don't have a lot of clothes and you probably even have your own boobs, but there's an air about you. I'm pretty sure you chose this dinky place. Am I right?"

I nodded. Of course. There had been options. There were always options. I'd liked this one.

"You've chosen everything in your life. And you do it so naturally, you don't even know what a gift it is." She sighed again. Took another pull from her beer. "But it's not a gift to you. You *own* that ability. You earned it. I want that, too." She'd said it quietly, as though it were an affirmation. "When the time is right, I'll have it."

Our conversation moved on to more neutral things, but our relationship had altered, deepened. We'd bonded, somehow, over trading and beer, and I found I was glad to have this complex, intelligent woman as my friend.

As she was leaving, she had a thought and brightened right up. "Omigawd! I nearly forgot. I brought you something." She laughed. "My graduation present, I guess."

"Hmm, isn't it me that's supposed to give you the grad present?"

"It doesn't matter, I wanted you to have it. Walk me to my car."

"You're giving me your Aston Martin?" I said as we walked.

"Huh! Nice try. No, it's in the trunk." She pulled a small, deep blue velvet bag with a drawstring neck out of the car and handed it to me.

When I pulled it open, I was surprised to see the hand-size piece of carved rune stone I'd spotted on my first trip to Larkin House.

"You seemed to like it so much, Madeline. And, I thought, a girl whose whole life is about important papers could use something special *and* heavy to hold them all down."

"Keesia, it's beautiful. But I can't take it. Really. It's too wonderful."

She laughed again, the richest laugh I'd heard from her yet. "Well then, it's exactly right."

"Seriously, Keesia, I know a thing or two about collectibles. This looks very valuable to me. I don't think you should give it away without knowing what it is."

Keesia smiled, obviously pleased I appreciated her gift so deeply, but bored, now, of the topic. "Listen, Madeline, it may be an ancient treasure—" she widened her eyes and deepened her voice as she said this "—or it might be just a hunk o' rock. Either way, it's more to you than it is to me. I can see that. And I want you to have it."

"Okay. Thanks. But…"

"But…? After what I just said, there is no but."

"Well, I have to be honest, I'm not completely comfortable with taking it. Just like that. But I know a few people who might have a better idea about this than I do. Would it offend you if I had someone look at it with an eye to appraising it?"

"Offend me?" Keesia said in an amused tone, "No. Not at all. I think it's a little weird. I mean, Madeline, it's just a rock."

I shrugged. "Probably. Actually, I hope so because I like it. But if it's some priceless artifact, you're getting it right back."

"Deal. And if it *is* some priceless artifact and you give it back, I'll give you my Vanquish." She patted the car's gleaming flank, then grinned mischievously. "Maxi can always get me a new one."

She hugged me quickly then slipped behind the wheel of her car. "Thanks for everything, Madeline. It's meant a lot to me." Then she thundered off down the canyon.

I watched her as she drove away, enjoying the cool heft of the carved stone in my hand. Back in my apartment, I put the stone in the window, thinking the direct sunlight would somehow illuminate its purpose. It didn't.

One of the television shows I occasionally enjoy watching is like the original reality program. People bring all of their crusty old crap to appraisers at some central location. Widely varying crap, too. Antique furniture and jewelry and ceramics…you name it. On almost every episode there's a single thing that ends up being worth some ridiculous figure. Invariably it was a gift to the person who brings it in: either a bequest or some loving family member or a friend has passed it along. And when the appraiser names the astronomical figure that the heretofore piece of junk is worth there can be this look of joy and disbelief, which is fun to see. Less fun, however, are the times when the look is tinged with greed and you just *know* that Aunt Bertha is never going to hear a word about what transpired under the appraiser's eye. In fact, you get the feeling that the person with the fledgling greed etched so sharply on their face will go home and make sure that the giver never again gets near PBS.

I've never liked those people. And I determined not to be one of them. If Keesia's rock was worth a bundle, I wanted to know about it now so I could give it back. And she could keep her Vanquish.

As a result of the collecting habit I had when I lived in New York, I still had a few contacts at galleries and auction houses. There was one woman at Bartleby's Fine Auctions in particular. I called her not long after Keesia left.

"Jilly, it's Madeline Carter. How are you?"

I remembered Jilly Rhys-Haywood looking as though she'd been born to be an appraiser. She hails from one of the eastern states and old money fairly drips off her tongue. Vassar, I think. Or Wellesley. She has straight blond hair, blue eyes, very white teeth with only the slightest overbite, and a nose that is straight, long and sharp.

"Maddy, darling! How long has it been? We're much overdue for lunch."

"It'll have to wait, I'm afraid. I'm still in L.A."

"You're in L.A.? Whatever are you doing there?"

"Long story, Jilly. I'll give it to you sometime. Meanwhile, I've come across something that might be of interest." I described the stone—the heft of it, the look of it and the carvings.

"Interesting, Maddy. But not really my field. But, listen, when you're back in the city, bring it by and I'll have Marshall in antiquities give it a peek. It sounds more like his kind of thing."

"Thanks for the offer, Jilly. But I'm living out here now. Is there any way I could send you photos or something?"

"*Living* out there? Oh, Maddy, you're not serious! You're such a New York girl."

I looked down at the gray sweatpants and T-shirt I was wearing. Ran a hand through my unwashed hair. "Huh! You wouldn't think so if you saw me, Jilly. And I'm not planning a trip out there in the near future. But I'd really love this looked at. Any ideas?"

"Well, the photo thing you mentioned might work. If you can get someone to do really sterling photos, that is. All angles, you know, that's what we need. And we need the weight of the item as well, of course. And, for the photos, make sure you include something for scale," she said as an afterthought.

"Scale?"

"You know, like a ruler or a hand or something to compare the size so that the appraiser can tell how big your rock is."

That made sense. "Great. Thanks, Jilly. If everything works on this end, I'll e-mail you photos tomorrow, okay?"

"Super, sweetie. I'll pass them on to Marshall. Make sure you include all your current contact info. I'm quite sure I don't have any L.A. numbers for you."

After I got off the phone, I thought about how far away New York felt right now. Not as though it were on the other side of the country, but on the other side of the moon. Did I miss it? I looked out at the ocean, at the big lump of dog sprawled across my bed. I scratched his tummy and watched him kick at the air ecstatically in response.

So, did I miss it? Not enough.

I was relieved to discover that Tyler's digital camera was not nearly as complicated as it looked. One of the things that de-complicated it—despite all of the mysterious dials and buttons—was the fact that, as he pointed out when he loaned it to me, you couldn't ruin it unless you dropped it and you didn't have to worry about wasting film. So, okay, it took me about one hundred frames before I got the eight photos I was happy enough with to send to Jilly. But an hour later, I sent her a note by e-mail with photos attached, telling her again that I wasn't interested in selling the piece, just finding out what it was and what it might be worth. And then I forgot all about it.

Four

The next day was frenetic for me. I was finding it increasingly difficult to focus on work in the midst of a construction zone. Though I'd started spending some of my working hours at an Internet café in Santa Monica, there's something to be said about being in your own desk chair at your own computer with your own good coffee keeping things buzzing along. Plus, I'd fallen into the home office habit quickly and easily. After what seemed like a lifetime of "getting ready for the office" back in New York, I found it difficult to rip myself out of my little nest and into the real world unless I was supermotivated to do so. On this day I hadn't been. Though, it had been tempting throughout the morning as the noise seemed to escalate and the number of construction guys swarming my place seemed to increase. Perception or reality? It didn't matter. It just seemed like they were *everywhere*.

The phone rang just after the closing bell. Keesia had known that, with the markets just closed, it would be a good time to get me.

"Wanna party?" she said pertly.

"Pardon?" I used to be married to a Canadian. Politeness counts.

"Maxi and I are having a huge shindig on Saturday night. Everyone is coming. And everyone means you, too."

"Sounds like fun."

"And bring someone if you like. Or, if you feel like fishing, there'll be plenty of material—" her voice took on a teasing tone "—I can push you in the right direction. Give you pointers."

"Hah!" I snorted. "Everyone wants to be me, remember? But, you know, I might just take you up on that. My love life has been sucking fiercely of late." I remembered too late that my apartment was crawling with construction guys. When I lifted my head to see if anyone had overheard, six pairs of eyes hastily darted back to their work. Gus, the contractor, didn't bother with this pretense. He was smiling at me innocently, but I knew he'd heard every word. I could feel the color creep into my cheeks as I turned away and directed my attention back to my phone call.

"I take it that's not a good thing?"

"What's that?" I asked, still flummoxed.

"The sucking love life."

I pulled the phone into my bedroom, which was blessedly free of construction guys, since there was no work being done in there. "Oh, Keesia," I said, once I'd closed the door. I plunked myself down on the floor and crossed my legs. "I've even got some good stories. And a very recent one involving French food and dates that need tracking devices. I'll tell you some time."

"Great. If the party is too boring, we'll slip away and have a beer and you can tell me then."

When I got off the phone it became clear to me that I was once again about to float out of my depth, something that had been happening a lot since moving to the West Coast. The rules for parties here seemed different. Or maybe, thanks to Tyler and my friend Emily, who also works in the film industry, it was just that I was traveling in different circles. Hollywood circles. My biggest problem now: what the hell was I going to wear?

Emily, who should perhaps write a book on the social mores of the Left Coast because she knows *every-thing* about it, had a strong opinion. Or six. I called her right after I got off the phone with Keesia.

"Let me get this straight," she said from her condo in Huntingdon Beach. "You're going to a party at Maxi Livingston's house on Saturday night?" Emily had just returned from working on location in Bucharest and had thus missed the Livingston installment of my life to date. She'd need a serious update soon. Emily likes—*demands*—to be kept informed.

"That's right. Larkin House. It's an estate. I've been there a lot lately."

"Oh. My. God. Who do I have to kill to get invited along?"

"Fortunately for both of us—not to mention the world at large—no one, doll. I'm allowed to bring a friend."

"And you're bringing *me?*"

"Against my better judgment, yeah. But seriously, who the hell else would I bring? Don't you think I know that if I went without you and you heard about it, my head would be on a platter?"

She was quiet a moment, as though considering.

"Good point," she conceded at length. "So what are you wearing?"

"Well, that's the other reason I called. I have no idea."

"Hmm. What did the invitation say?"

"I dunno. Keesia just called me."

"Keesia *Livingston?* Cool. So you and Keesia are, what?" Emily said. "Hanging now?"

"Something like that. Look, I'll explain it all when I see you. But right now, I need to know what to wear."

"Okay, without an invitation, it's a little hard to tell. Let me make some phone calls. I'll call you right back."

My phone rang exactly forty-three minutes later. I spent the time straightening my bedroom and generally futzing around. I so did *not* want to go back out to construction land and was putting it off for as long as possible. "Sorry for the wait," Emily said breathlessly when I picked up. "It took me longer than I thought it would to get a fix on this thing."

"Fix?"

"Yeah. Well, it's a huge party. Seems like it's mostly going to be industry." I didn't need her to tell me anymore that when she said "industry" it meant anyone remotely connected with the business of making movies. "And, obviously, it's A-list. Trouble is, my friend David said it's poolside casual."

"I doubt it. Have you seen the place?"

"No," Emily sniffed. "I have not. Yet. Anyway, my friend Jackie says definitely upscale nighttime stuff is in order."

"Like what? Tuxes and stuff?"

"Probably not that upscale, but yeah, close."

"So…what you're saying is we don't know any more than when we started?"

"Well, slightly. I guess. I made five phone calls in all," Emily summarized. She sounded as though she might be checking some notes. "Four of the people I called are going. Three are going as dates—like, with someone—and one got invited directly, but like you did. A phone call, so no invitation."

"Again, this doesn't sound like progress."

"Well, it is because all of *these* people have decided to play it very dressy casual. So that sounds safe."

It sounded nondescriptive to me, but this didn't seem like the time to voice my opinion. Emily would figure it out right. If I followed along, all would be cool. "So... upshot?"

"Upshot—shopping. Thank God we wrapped last week. It means I can give this my full attention. Let's meet at Solly's Deli in Santa Monica at nine tomorrow." I could tell that Emily was, as she said, giving this her full attention. Solly's at nine meant a businesslike breakfast before hitting the mall when it opened: no farting around.

"You mean 9:00 *a.m.*, Emily?"

"Well," Emily said sarcastically, "somehow I did think going shopping while the stores were actually open might be a good idea."

"But I don't think we need to be *that* right on it, Em. The party is three days away."

Emily sighed: long-suffering, but she didn't bother arguing. "Solly's. Nine. See ya." And she was gone. This was going to be the industry party of the year. An entrée had fallen unexpectedly into her lap: she didn't even have to crash! No way was she going to let a networking opportunity like this slip past her or catch her badly or inappropriately dressed. I looked at the dead phone in my hand and sighed. From Emily's perspective, we were going into battle. The only thing I could do was pack my credit cards, run to keep up if I had to and, meanwhile, try to enjoy the ride.

I got off the telephone knowing I couldn't stay in my bedroom forever. I was going to have to face the music. I just had no way of gauging how strident the music might actually be.

When I came out of my bedroom, dragging the phone behind me like a tail, Gus had gone back to work, but a grin still played around his lips. Or the trace of a grin. Or maybe it was just my own paranoia.

I didn't say anything for a while, just busied myself tidying up around my computer: something I never, ever did. I usually looked for things the way you go through an archeological dig: sifting through the strata until you reached the correct time period. But with *people* in my house—especially people who were male and who had overheard me in the middle of a personal *girlfriend* conversation—I felt the need to make myself busy. And right this second I couldn't think of anything else to do. Maybe, I reasoned, if I looked busy enough for long enough, Mr. Construction Dude would get caught up in his own busyness and forget all about me.

A few minutes—and several neatened piles—later, Gus dashed my hopes.

"Sucks, huh?" he said, without looking up from the tiles he was grouting in the kitchen. He'd said the words sympathetically, but I could hear the smile in his voice. "That sounds rough."

I sighed deeply. I'd intended to cast him an arch glance—a *withering* glance—but when I lifted my head, the look caught somehow. There was just this basic niceness in Gus's face, even trapped behind the gentle cragginess of his features. Looking at him looking at me softly from my kitchen, wearing work-lightened jeans and a white T-shirt that had probably had too many washings, I remembered that the first time I'd seen Gus, I'd wondered what he'd look like in a magazine, stripped down to his tool belt and posed next to a pool. I pulled my mind away from that and forced my glance out the window when I answered him.

"Sucks is relative." I shrugged. Cast my eyes at him, then back to the stone Keesia had given me the day before. "It's life, right? Grown-up life." I shifted things to more neutral ground. "It's going to be beautiful, isn't it," I said, indicating my kitchen with a gesture that encompassed the bathroom on the other side of the wall.

I could tell I was going to love the kitchen's new stainless-steel countertops. Stainless steel is very durable, though picky to keep looking really clean. Since I don't cook that much, I didn't anticipate that this was going to be a problem, and it would look smashing against the pale wood of the new cabinets.

Gus seemed aware of the fact that I was changing the subject and, to his credit, went with it. "Yeah, it's going to be pretty nice, all right. And Tyler's gone all out here, you know. The appliances he ordered are top-of-the-line."

"Cool," I said noncommittally. Honestly, to me appliances are appliances are appliances. As long as a refrigerator keeps my beer and my San Pellegrino cold, I'm fine. And almost any stove will do to heat canned soup or fry an egg. Apparently Tyler had other ideas. But there was something more important than appliances on my mind. "When do you figure I'll have my apartment to myself again?"

"Pretty quick now, Madeline." He indicated the indigo-blue tiles I'd chosen for the floor and the backsplash. "Guys got finished with the tile work yesterday. I'll be done with the grout by the end of today. Then we'll give it a couple days to dry before we do the finishing work. Seal it up all nice for you, you know." I didn't, but whatever. I got the drift. "They're finishing the tile work in the bathroom today, the tub guy is coming tomorrow and that's about it for the bathroom."

"So you're saying that you're for sure out of here by the end of the week?" I was excited. I hadn't really thought it would be that fast.

"Yeah. Except for the floors." He grinned long and slow. "I've dragged it on as long as I could, but I can't make it go beyond another couple of weeks."

His grin was infectious. I found myself grinning back. I'm usually not a grinner. "Well, I'll miss you hon'—" I was totally kidding "—but it'll be good to get my place back." I smiled at him again and turned back to my desk. When I looked back at him a few beats later, he was still standing there, looking, I thought, somewhat sheepish.

I grinned at him again, confused. "What?"

"Madeline... I... oh, what the hell." He looked like a man plunging right in. "You want to, maybe, have dinner sometime?"

I looked back at him carefully. Other than the stuff with the pool and the tools, I really hadn't thought of him that way. If I'd thought of it at all, I'd assumed there was probably a Mrs. Gus out there somewhere, not to mention a bunch of little Guses. He just sort of had that look.

In the split second it took for me to decide, I realized

I'd never dated a construction worker before. And while the construction aspect itself didn't put me off, Gus and I had never exchanged any words that didn't include some aspect of talk about my apartment. Would we have anything to discuss over dinner? Would the differences between us prove too much to provide room for commonality? I looked at his softly curling sandy hair and his dark green eyes and realized it didn't matter.

"Sure. Dinner. Sometime." I smiled to take the bite out of the hesitancy of my words.

His grin grew deeper and he looked somewhat bashful at the same time. A funny combination on a man of his height. "Well, great then. How 'bout tonight?"

I considered briefly. That was certainly sooner than the "sometime" I'd imagined. But I didn't have anything else planned and I found that the prospect of an evening of uncomplicated conversation and good food suddenly seemed quite appealing.

"Sure. Okay."

The grin deepened still further. "All right, then. I'll pick you up here at seven."

As seven o'clock approached I found myself increasingly—and inexplicably—nervous about my date with Gus. And was it even a date, I asked myself? Hmm… carefully examined from every angle there was no getting around it: We were going for dinner, without pretext of business. He was picking me up. We were going out. It was a date.

After he'd asked me, and I'd accepted, we'd both been suddenly—perhaps understandably—uneasy with each other. He finished the grouting work quickly and left not long after—ostensibly to check on something that I hadn't paid any attention to. Unfortunately, though, I hadn't asked him where he was planning on taking me.

Part of my uneasiness was due to plain old etiquette. I'd worked at one of the largest brokerage houses in the world for more than a decade, keeping an eye out for improprieties was part of the culture. After a while it was instinctive: a hard habit to break.

Was this, I wondered now, sort of like dating a co-worker? Or, worse, an employee? Was I violating some bit of personal or business etiquette that I hadn't known about before? I thought briefly about calling Emily and checking—never doubting that she'd have an answer—then discarded the idea. Whatever else I needed tonight, Emily's quick tongue and wit were unlikely to be very helpful. I'd ask her tomorrow, when the deed was done. And, anyway, since Emily had summoned me to breakfast, there was little chance I'd be able to escape her company without her sensing I'd had a date and then squeezing every bit of available information out of me. She's that kind of sensitive to subtleties of mood.

Meanwhile, I was back to that age-old dilemma—though this was the first time in recent memory I'd had to worry about it twice in one day. What was I going to wear?

Finally I reasoned that, since Gus was a blue-collar worker, it was likely he'd take me to a place where the waiters sang and they served a lot of red meat. A place that was loud and possibly obnoxious, but fun in the right mood. I gauged my own mood. Was this the right one? I shrugged. Analyzing and reanalyzing might work when deciding on which security to invest, but it wasn't helping me much in preparing for this date.

In the end I put away the black Prada pants and

DKNY sweater I'd been thinking about wearing and opted for Gap jeans and a tailored white blouse. With Manolo boots, a black pashmina to keep off the evening chill and a black Kate Spade Sam bag, I decided there weren't many places in L.A. I couldn't go, especially when I was going to be escorted by a construction worker.

When I opened the door to Gus's knock, I was hard-pressed to keep myself from gaping at him. Like some rugged Cinderella, Gus was utterly transformed. Gone was his daytime uniform of worn jeans, grubby T-shirt and do-rag. His suit was dark, and if it wasn't Armani, it was a good-enough knockoff to wear to the collections. His shoes were black and dangerously polished and his timepiece looked as though I'd be able to swap it for half a year's rent. I felt ridiculously underdressed, like I should at least have added some bling.

"Wow," I breathed. Talk about judging books. "You look great."

He smiled, aware of my surprise. Perhaps he'd even been expecting it, relishing it. "You look pretty great yourself."

"I…I didn't know where we were going. Should I change?"

"You still don't know where we're going, Madeline. But, no. You're perfect just as you are." Though the line was corny, it sounded wonderful coming out of his head.

I was surprised to see a Lexus sports car parked where he usually left his battered bright red work van.

"Yes, it's mine," he said grinning as he opened the door for me.

"Still waters," I said cryptically as he got in beside me. He just grinned again as he took the wheel, and while he steered the car smoothly down the twisty canyon roads toward the Pacific Coast Highway, I digested the fact that we seemed to spend a lot of our time together grinning ridiculously.

At PCH, he surprised me by turning right, instead of left: he was heading away from Santa Monica, Brentwood...the city. If he felt my surprise he didn't comment, just said, "How hungry are you?"

"I could eat, I guess. But I'm not famished or anything."

"Good," he said, his eyes held tightly on the road. I noted Malibu whizzing past and wondered pleasantly what he was up to.

"Why? Where are we going?"

"Oxnard."

"Oxnard!" The community was about an hour's drive up the coast, in Ventura County. "I've never been there."

He smiled, as though pleased at my response. "Excellent. I hoped that might be the case."

The drive passed quickly, mostly in companionable silence. Gus pointed out various sights in the darkening landscape as we thundered over the highway but, mostly, neither of us seemed to feel we had to talk to fill up the empty air between us. Or maybe neither of us knew what to say.

"You seem so different," I said after we'd been driving for a while.

He grinned again. Looked at me speculatively. "Different how? Good different or bad different?"

I considered before I answered. "Not good, not bad, sort of more like someone else. And I like both of you," I assured him quickly. "But it's like the guy I agreed to go out with was a construction worker and you're his older brother, the MBA."

Gus laughed at that. He laughed quite a lot. More, I thought, than the comment had merited, strictly speaking. But he didn't say much. "Clothes make the man," he smirked, but it wasn't an unattractive smirk, more like the way construction Gus would have smirked, so I felt reassured.

Gus had reservations at a seafood house on the water in Oxnard. We could probably have gone just a teensy way either down or up the coast from my house and gotten seafood in Malibu or Pacific Palisades that was just as good or better, but it wouldn't have been in a different county and it wouldn't have been an adventure. And, because it was Ventura and a weeknight, there was hardly anyone in the restaurant. We had a candlelit table with a water view, attentive but not perky service—not one person burst into song—and the feeling that we had a little oasis to ourselves.

Gus ordered an eight-year-old bottle of Napa Valley pinot noir. Though I didn't recognize the name of the winery, Gus said it with authority and the wine, when it came, was smooth and rich and delightful.

He surprised me again when he ordered. I had, it seemed, endless preconceived notions of him. I'd expected him to order a steak or, at the very least, some sort of Oxnard version of surf 'n' turf. To my surprise he ordered a caviar soufflé as an appetizer, for the two of us to share. For his main course, he chose porcini-dusted skate wings with chervil whipped potatoes and truffle oil. By comparison, my grilled tuna with orzo and roasted vegetables sounded mundane.

"What?" he said when our waiter left us alone.

"What?" I repeated.

He smirked again. Construction Gus was back, for the moment. "I think I've surprised you again," he ventured.

"How so?" I asked innocently.

"You were sure I'd order a steak." It wasn't a question.

I shrugged, feeling funny that he'd guessed my thoughts so precisely. "Maybe. To be perfectly honest, I don't know what to make of you at all anymore, Gus."

He laughed, not unpleasantly. "Some days I feel that way about myself. I think that's why I asked you out."

I lifted an eyebrow at him but didn't say anything and he went on. "I had the feeling we're alike that way. Both reinventing ourselves in new places."

"Apparently," I said archly, "you know more about me than I know about you."

"Apparently."

"Old women have nothing on Tyler when it comes to gossip," I said.

This time, when Gus laughed, I could see it ripple through his whole being. "Damn straight." He tipped his glass at me before taking an appreciative sip. "Tyler *can* be a blabberhead. But, in case you get the wrong idea, everything he said, he said with great affection."

I nodded. "Uh-huh. That's what I said—like an old woman. What did he tell you?"

"Not that much. Just that you're from New York and you were a stockbroker, working with a friend of his. That something terrible happened and you came out here. And now you're a day trader." He smiled, then added, "A pretty good one, too, I think. This not from Tyler, just from what I see when I'm hanging around your house."

I laughed at the insider knowledge. Nodded. "I've been having a good month." But it was funny hearing your life encapsulated in such a way. Nothing Tyler had told him was inaccurate. There was just so much more to every bit of it than what he'd said. I let it go.

"So, okay, no fair. You know all about me. And I know nothing about you. No, wait, that's not true. I know you look exceptionally good in both jeans and a great suit." I could feel the flush stain my cheeks almost as soon as the words were out of my mouth, but I couldn't call them back. And I wasn't quite sure I wanted to.

If Gus was offended he didn't show it. "Well, Madeline, I'm flattered. However, I will point out that, if I'd said that exact same thing to you—and I'd mean it, too, by the way—you'd have cause to slap my face and stomp on out of here."

"What? And take a cab home? I've had to do enough of that lately." He looked at me quizzically and I held up my hand, regretting my words already. "Never mind. Forget I said that. I seem to be doing an amazing job of saying the wrong thing tonight. So—like I said—since you seem to know everything about me—" I prompted again "—it's only fair you tell me about you."

Predictably, the only thing not surprising about Gus's story was the fact that everything about him was a surprise. He was from Chicago, he told me. He'd been in L.A. for five years. In Chicago, he'd been a developer: mostly shopping malls, but some housing developments, as well. And I discovered why he'd laughed at my older-brother-MBA crack: he was, in fact—and of course—an MBA. The reason, I gathered, he looked so comfortable in that suit.

"So what happened?" I asked.

"Did you ever hear the song? Something like, 'Is

this my beautiful house? Is that my beautiful wife?'
And so on. It was like I woke up one morning and discovered I had everything I'd ever dreamed of...and I
hated it."

"Beautiful house, beautiful wife?"

"All of that. And more besides."

"Oh, Gus. That *so* explains the Lexus."

"I'm afraid to ask why," he said, but he didn't look
afraid.

"You had a midlife crisis."

Gus grimaced but didn't look offended, which was
a good thing since—upon reflection—a lot of the stuff
I'd been saying tonight seemed somewhat offensive. "I
guess that's one way of looking at it."

"And the beautiful wife...?"

"Still in Chicago. Now someone else's beautiful wife
and the happier for it. We were pretty crappy together."

"But from developer to construction guy. That's a
pretty big leap."

"Not really, Madeline. In the first place, I'm not a
construction guy, as you so sweetly put it. I'm a contractor. With some pretty interesting clients, as you well
know. And, after I got out here, I found what I wanted
to do was get my hands dirty. And get really involved
with my clients on a personal level."

"Like me?" I quipped.

He smiled. "No, Madeline. Not like you. You're not
my client. Tyler is." It was a good point. I was glad he
made it.

The only sour note in the evening happened out of
Gus's presence. Between dinner and dessert he excused
himself to go to the men's room. After he'd been gone
around sixty-seven seconds, I started fidgeting. Two

minutes in I kept checking my watch and berating myself for not coming in my own car. When Gus reappeared, pretty much on schedule after about four minutes, I felt a flood of relief that pushed a smile onto my face.

He smiled back at me as he took his seat and, though I fought it, I could feel a blush creep over my cheeks. "For what it's worth," he said conversationally, "I missed you, too."

The drive back to Malibu was beautiful. Romantic. Perfect. It was one of those moonlit Southern California nights that send songwriters and poets into raptures.

The Lexus buzzed along the highway like a well-muscled cat. Soft jazz spilled out of the speakers and gathered us into well-fed well-being. Outside the car, moonlight reflected off the water. I felt supremely happy in Gus's company that night. As happy as I'd been in a long time. We chatted companionably, our earlier shortness of conversation burned off over dinner.

Gus pointed out that we had a lot in common. We'd both achieved everything we'd wanted in our lives and found, when we'd gotten there, that it wasn't what we'd wanted in the first place. It had all looked different upon arrival. We'd both worn expensive clothes to shiny offices and commanded respect and large salaries. And when the glow had worn off and we'd seen what we'd built, both of us had run to the West Coast and all of the possibilities for reinvention that Los Angeles offered. More: when we'd gotten here, we'd both done that. Separately. In casual clothes.

When I felt Gus's hand caress my leg as we chatted and drove, I shuddered in anticipation. I had a feeling I knew where this would go and I didn't want to fight it. It had been a long time and it felt that comfortable. That right. Inevitable, in a way.

At Zuma Beach, Gus pulled off the highway and parked with the water in front of us. Moonlight, water and sand. We sat in the car while the jazz washed over us. We were suddenly silent, our conversation awkward again. But in a totally nice way.

When he took me in his arms, kissed me, I could feel the rightness all the way through me. I felt like a teenager. Maybe that was the point. Like a teenager, but so much better. There was no fear here. No sense of possible loss or danger. I felt strong, in control and—since there was no back seat—an ever-increasing desire to make like Deborah Kerr and drag that man down onto the sand.

Before I could act out any insane fantasies, however, Gus disentangled himself gently and held me at arm's length. "Gawd, woman. You taste every bit as good as I knew you would. Better." He kissed me again, smiled, then started the car and put it in reverse, all in one smooth motion. I hid my disappointment. "I'm taking you home before I make an ass of myself. You seem to bring out the teenager in me." His words echoed my thoughts so precisely, it startled me.

Outside my house, he kissed me again. Deeply and at length.

"Do you want to come in?" I asked when we came up for air.

He shook his head no, but said, "More than anything. But I'm due here, in your house, with a crew first thing tomorrow. I don't think I should already be here, wearing your bathrobe."

"I meant coffee or something," I laughed, thinking about what he'd look like in my paisley-patterned silk robe.

"I know you did, Madeline. But if I come in with you now, you're going to have trouble getting me to leave." At that moment I didn't see the problem.

Back in my apartment—alone—I sat at my desk for a while, with the computer off, staring at the moonlight over the ocean. Watching the pale outline of clouds in the night sky. I thought about changes in life and coincidences. I thought about sweat-stained T-shirts and a well-made suit. I wondered at the validity of soul mates and how and when you know you've found one. I looked at the calendar, looked at the clock and wondered if I should make a note: this is when I began to fall in love.

Five

I am one of the lucky ones and I know it.

A lot of people spend too much of their lives at work. Think about an eighty-hour work week. That was a low average for me when I lived in New York. I mean, there are only a total of 168 hours in a week. If you take out forty-two hours for sleep—and some would say that six hours a night wasn't enough—and maybe another five to commute, that only leaves forty-one hours for everything else. It's not enough. Forty-one hours a week to brush your teeth, shower, do your makeup, talk to your friends, make love, prepare food and consume it, go through your mail, pay and file your bills, talk to your mom, read a book or do a crossword puzzle, watch a stupid television program or the news or go to the movies, exfoliate, get regular hair and medical and dental treatment, wash dishes, make your bed, do laundry, go to the bathroom. Dust.

When you think about it that way, it's no wonder so many people lose it. It's no wonder that clock towers can hold such attraction. And all of those antidepressants?

Sure: some of them are very necessary. But some people could probably get by with regular naps and the occasional trip to a spa. That is if they could find the time, I guess. Remember: you don't get to make withdrawals from the time bank. Only deposits. It's not such a great deal.

So I'm lucky. And, like I said, I know it. I don't actually work very hard anymore. Or, at least, very hard for very long. Having paid my dues with ten years of lack of a life, I've rearranged things in a way that allows me to trade on my experience in order to make my living. Quite often I don't make fabulous amounts of money. It's mostly pretty modest. But I also don't work very hard. Or rather, I only work hard enough to make what I need. Life can be short and it's often tenuous and I feel lucky on another front: that I discovered all of this early enough to do something about it.

I am the master—mistress? of my destiny. I feel that very sharply now. The captain of my fate. And the way I've arranged things, I have plenty of time for reflections like this one. And for emergency shopping trips and breakfasts with friends and pretty much whatever else I like.

I am one of the lucky ones. And I know it.

On the morning I was to meet Emily for breakfast and a forced shopping march, I let myself sleep in until six o'clock. I reasoned that, since I'd be spending a lot of time in a mall, I'd be getting plenty of exercise and so could forgo my usual workday run.

I showered in fairly leisurely fashion and got myself ready for my day. Not my usual work wardrobe of sweatpants and a T-shirt, but a light knee-length skirt, low-heeled slides and a crisp white blouse. Shoppin' clothes.

By seven I was properly attired for a day in town and brought a cup of coffee to my computer and prepared to do what would pass for my day's work over the course of the next hour. Though the domestic markets had already been open for half an hour, I still had time to check on my current holdings, have a peek at some of the securities I'd been watching, plus read through the news releases that seemed most likely to affect the financial future of my immediate life.

When I'm "on" or when I'm particularly hungry— when I've been having a bad month or for one reason or another just need to make an extra few grand—I get all diligent about my work life. I'll be at my desk at least half an hour before the opening bell at six-thirty Pacific Time, scanning all the news feeds, checking the previous day's biggest winners and losers to see where the action might be heading, even reading the online versions of the financial newspapers to see if I can capture a glimmer of movement or get some idea, usually in the most oblique reference to something entirely unrelated.

On those days, when the market opens, I'm not only in position, I've usually already used the ordering system of my online brokerage to enter a buy or sell order at a price I've predetermined will be the right one for that day. It doesn't always work out the way I've planned, but through the course of the day as I watch things progress, I can always scoot back into the program that connects me with my online brokerage to change my buy or sell orders if necessary.

When the Internet is a component of your stock market experience, as is the case with me, your trading is self-directed. That is, you don't call in your desires to a broker on the phone. A broker who might say, "What are you, *nuts?*" or "Why don't you try this instead?" That is, there is no one with expertise between you and the markets. You're on your own and you interface with your trading account through a Web browser on the Net.

In some ways, for me it's not very different from when I worked at an investment firm. Except, of course, for the lack of the constant hum and buzz of brokers on the phone, the horseplay of the traders, the warning shouts from the managers, the… Okay: it's *very* different. Just me and Tycho and my potted palm. And a gorgeous view of the Pacific Ocean as seen through a Malibu canyon. But, for me, the *trading* part isn't very different. With the horseplay out of the picture, it's just me and my acumen watching the numbers rise and fall.

So on this day, knowing I wouldn't be there until close to watch things, when I approached the market I had my planned absence in mind.

These days, for a safe, solid long-term investment— the type I used to give advice on when I was a broker— I'd give the high-tech sector a pretty wide berth. Too much madness. Too many possibilities for sweeping fluctuations. However, that erratic graph line is the type of environment that lends itself to day trades. A solid little company with a slow but steady upward trend is not what you need to make money on the very short term. For that, you need to take risks. And a little market insanity can actually help with short-term profits.

The week before, I'd bought several hundred shares in an electronics firm on an uptick. It was a company whose books had been under scrutiny over the past few months and whose senior management had been let go during the period of scrutinization. The bloodletting had been a symbolic act. The stock had tanked on news that the company was being investigated on several fronts. On news of the senior staff's "resignation," the stock had plummeted still further, but the name of the new CFO had caught my eye. A former Marine Corps general, his appointment had to be purely for PR. Yet I figured that the PR gambit would work. He'd been a hero when he was in the service. He was generally thought of as the sort of stand-up guy who'd brook no funny business. I saw his name and bought in around the time a lot of other people got the same idea. Hence the uptick: the badly beaten-up security took a little rise. I figured I'd sell my shares before the end of the trading day with a tidy profit.

Within hours, however, the Securities Exchange Commission joined in the feeding frenzy, and when it was announced that the SEC would also be examining the corporation for signs of previous wrongdoing, the market responded predictably with a drop.

It was a game. It's always a game. As in "my investigation trumps your general" and so on. I had no doubt that the huge company with the pull to bring in the general in the first place would rise to the occasion and calculate an answering move that would cause the stock to go up. Meanwhile, however, my day trade wasn't anymore and I had several thousand dollars invested in hoping they got their ducks in a row so I could get out as planned.

With that in mind, I put in a sell order I knew had no hope of getting executed on that day. There was just no way the stock would not only gain back what it had lost after the SEC's announcement, but also add enough to bring me a profit. Not in a single day. But the market is unpredictable. Putting in the sell order at my desired price meant that if some freakishly wonderful thing happened while I was off shopping, my stock would sell and I'd have my profit. With the reverse of the same scenario in mind, I put in a buy order on the same security but at a much lower price. If more high jinks happened while I wasn't looking and the stock plummeted further, I'd buy another few hundred shares. I was confident that the stock would go up, ultimately if not today. However, if it went down first and I bought some more, even the stocks in my initial purchase block would effectively be costing me less. I would be averaging the purchase price down, and when the stock did go up, my profit would be larger.

That was the theory, anyway. It was also a fairly good example of why a whack of experience is as important as having the money in the kind of trading I did. What looks good on paper can lead to a world of hurt if you don't know what you're doing. Even when you *do* know what you're doing, there are no sure things. But I felt pretty good about how all of this was going.

After putting in my orders and checking on a couple of other stocks I was watching, I left my computer a little after eight o'clock so that I'd have ample time to blast down the coast to meet Emily in Santa Monica.

I avoided Tycho's reproachful eyes when I left the house. He hadn't needed to see me heading to my car to know he wouldn't be getting a run again this morning. I was wearing the wrong shoes.

Emily had gotten to Solly's before me. I found her in one of the red leather booths, in the middle of a friendly but heated discussion with our server, who proved to be the son of the proprietor, also named Solly. They were debating the merits and demerits of various things known as "bagels."

Solly Junior, in his mid-twenties and with his alliances in plain sight, was vehement when he said, "And don't even get me started on what the Canadians call bagels. 'Montreal-style bagels,'" he snorted, derisively. "I'd rather eat cardboard."

"Well…" Emily acknowledged my presence with a nod, but didn't allow herself to be diverted from her debate. Her thick, dark hair swung with the passion of her words. "You'd be in no danger of that here, would you? What you call a West Coast-style bagel might as well be an airline roll."

I gasped. It was possible Emily had gone too far this time. To my surprise, Solly chortled, then grinned at me companionably. "Now that you're here, I'll leave you to ponder the menu. But if she orders anything that even resembles a bagel—" he cocked his thumb at Emily "—I'll tell my dad about that airline-roll crack." He wandered off still chuckling.

"What was *that* all about?"

"His company catered a couple of the location shoots I've been on," Emily explained, her fine, dark eyes creased into a smile. "The bagel thing has gotten to be a running gag."

"Weird," I commented.

"You think?" She seemed to consider. "Yeah. Maybe. But it's fun."

Fun is Emily. Emily is fun. This is something I've come to accept about her. People love Emily. All people. All the time. Even when she gently harangues them, as she sometimes does just for sport, people love her. It's one of her gifts, part of her charm. And it makes her very fun to be around.

We did more than order bagels: we ordered lox and

bagels—West Coast bagels, East Coast lox—à deux. The bagels arrived in a basket, still steaming. The cream cheese came in a little pot, ready for us to smear on at will, and the rest—lox, capers, onions and even some tomatoes—arrived together on a plate, awaiting our pleasure. So we had a little feast. The food was simple and satisfying, the coffee blissfully strong, and Emily and I had a little blabfest, our first since she got back from Romania. I hadn't realized how much I'd missed her.

Unsurprisingly, considering her cheerfully obsessive nature and the fact that she never misses an opportunity for career advancement, she tabled almost all talk of her recent trip in favor of discussion about the business at hand. To her, the Livingston party wasn't going to be an evening of entertainment, it was a possible career move and, as such, deserved her full attention.

"So tell me—" she launched in without preamble, the cream cheese still melting over the warmth of the bagels "—Keesia Livingston. How did that happen?"

I told her how it had come about and how, in the end, I'd swapped it for a remodel. I tried not to tell her about Gus—I really did—but she must have felt a thread of it, because she wheedled the rest out of me, just as I'd figured she would.

"So what do you think?" I asked once I'd told her about my date the previous evening. "Is it *completely* tacky to go out with the contractor, or what?"

"Jeez, Mad, you're kidding, right?"

Was I? I had to think about it. "Not really. I don't know. It's just…it's just odd, is all."

Emily's laugh, when it came, had a warm, understanding sound. "I'll tell you what's odd, sweetie. I've seen you go out with guys. And I've heard you talk about the guys you've gone out with. But I've never seen anything like this color—" she traced my cheekbone with the tip of her index finger "—when you talked about any of them." She looked thoughtful for a moment. Then: "I'm taking it as a sign."

"But a sign of *what?*" I asked, unwilling, on some level, to acknowledge—or certainly admit—that talking about Gus made my color rise. After a single date. Without sex.

But Emily turned suddenly enigmatic. She wasn't giving anything away. Maddeningly, all I could coax out of her was a quiet "We'll see."

Then, because we were on a mission, Emily got us on track. It was time to shop.

Because neither of us can afford the latest creation from Versace or even Donna Karan, we both ended up with regional originals that would be difficult to spot as totally cheap and off the rack, though both were. For me, Emily chose an unpatterned white dress made in Bali. Tight in all the right places, yet almost sweeping the floor, the dress was cut so deeply I protested.

"No, no, it's perfect for you. You have, like, no boobs so you can get away with showing all that skin without looking skanky. Me—" she indicated her full, lush figure "—I'd look like a tart. Worse, the dress would look as cheap as it is. On you, though, it's understated. Trust me, it is *the* dress for this do. For you."

For her part, Emily bought an elegant, shimmery tank that she planned to team with a very good black skirt she already owned. "That skirt cost me a mint, but I knew I'd get at least three seasons out of it. And I'm on four!" Her wardrobe rationale: good pieces (i.e., well made, expensive and recognizable labels) form the foundation of what she wears. Every season, she goes out and buys inexpensive trend items to tie the older pieces into the latest styles. And it really works for her: she always manages to look effortlessly together. Only a few of us know what it costs her (not much) and how much work she puts into it (a fair amount).

I, on the other hand, was one of those girls who spent a lot of time in high school and college at the track and in the pool. While doing that, I seemed to have missed the dress-up lessons that the other girls must have gotten. I've always had a *great* wardrobe of what my mom disdainfully calls "active wear": things made with a lot of Lycra and spandex that can take you anywhere as long as it's jogging, biking or the dry parts of a decathlon.

When I got to Merriwether Bailey, the New York City stock brokerage house where I worked, I naturally had to weave grown-up dressing into my repertoire. And I did—and I *do*—manage business casual very well. But because in New York I (a) worked such crazy hours I didn't have very much time to shop, and (b) was making so much money it was stupid (especially since I worked so much I didn't have time left over to spend it), I would force myself to book off a couple hours every few months and buy myself some sincerely good clothes for the office and any other bits that might have worn out in the meantime—bras, underwear, socks, track pants...

As a result of this forced shopping, I still have an excellent wardrobe that really isn't good for much besides a job at a New York City brokerage firm or some other place where it's beneficial to look as though you spent a bundle on whatever feminine version of a power suit you've chosen to doll yourself up in. And none of it makes much sense for the life I lead in L.A., except the rare occasion when I want to make sure someone knows they're dealing with someone who knows how to drop a couple of grand on a suit. Trust me: that doesn't come up much for me anymore.

So, not only do I not have much in the way of suitable L.A. party clothes, I don't have much in the way of anything. Emily knows this and saves my life when the need arises. Like now.

For footwear, Emily forced me into strappy sandals way strappier and higher-heeled than anything I would have chosen for myself. "It's for the *dress,* Madeline," she insisted. "The shoes finish the picture. If you insist on wearing crapola comfortable shoes, you'll end up having to spend twice or three times as much on a dress just to look as good as you do now."

"Really? That'd work? 'Cause I have those eight-hole Doc Martens…"

"Madeline, please." I knew she wasn't as exasperated as she sounded. But she wasn't putting up with any bullshit, either. "Just buy the shoes."

By the time I got home in the late afternoon, I felt fairly pleased with my purchases. It was a Hollywood party. There would be honest-to-goodness movie stars there. The kind of people who get to wear designer clothes for free, just so they can be seen in them. Clearly, no one would take me for a princess or a slumming socialite in my got-it-in-the-market-looking Bali-made dress. But I wouldn't look like a schlepp or a schmuck, either. Two states of being I seriously try to avoid.

After I got home, the phone rang just as I was carefully hanging up my dress.

"Guess who's not at your house," It was the first time

I'd heard his voice on the phone. I knew who it was, any-way, and he sounded good. Husky and smooth at the same time. A pretty neat trick.

"Gus! You sound so good," I said, before I had a chance to check myself. He didn't mind: I could tell from the satisfied-sounding chuckle that spilled out of him.

"You sound pretty good yourself. Are my guys out of there for the day yet?"

"I guess. I just got in from shopping and there was no one here. No vehicles up top, either. But I can see some of the work got done."

"I was going to try to get up there myself before they knocked off for the day, but I'm working on a job in the valley that didn't want to let go of me today."

"Is she a stockbroker?" I chirped.

"Nope. A very professional drag queen, actually. She gave me tickets for a show she's doing in Las Vegas next month." A beat. "Maybe we can go?"

I'd heard the hesitation in his voice. *We.* Both of us knew it was too soon for any kind of *we.* And yet. "Maybe," I agreed quietly.

"But listen," he resumed with more confidence. "A little closer to now—I know we just had dinner last night and I'm fully prepared that you might already have plans for tonight, but I'd love to see you again. Tonight, I mean. For dinner." Another beat. A self-deprecating laugh. "In my head just now, when I played that back, it sounded completely lame. Needy, almost. And I hope it didn't sound that way to you. I just…I just really like you, Madeline. And I find myself anxious to spend more time with you." He took a deep breath.

"It didn't…it didn't sound lame," I twirled the phone cord around my index finger. Something I hadn't done for a long time. But, when I was a teenager, the phones in our house had perpetual knots in them. "It sounded honest. I like that. And I like food, too. Dinner again would be fun."

He sounded relieved when he replied. Relieved in a totally confident way. I liked this about him, too: the way he struck me as entirely male and, at the same time, entirely able to be vulnerable. Gus seemed mature enough to show the world—or at least, me—the sides of his personality that less-secure guys try to hide. I found it incredibly sexy.

Gus gave me his address in Santa Monica and told me to meet him there for appetizers at seven o'clock, followed by dinner at his favorite neighborhood restaurant.

I got off the phone feeling desired and desirous: I felt girlish and I had trouble making the smile go away. There was this incredible feeling of *rightness* for me around Gus. Like finding a part of something I hadn't known was missing. I didn't know where this was going, but I had a pretty strong feeling that, wherever it was, Gus and I were going there together.

The address Gus gave me was on California Avenue in Santa Monica, very close to the beach and, from the vantage point of his ninth-floor outlook, it felt even closer. Gus had a spectacular view. The building had a pool, a weight room and a concierge. The apartment itself was sumptuous and, I could see at a glance, professionally decorated. The black leather sofas, the rugged and expensive art, the manly carpets on an artfully rough wood floor: all of it created an entirely different picture than the one I'd been building of Gus.

"This place is so not you," I said once he'd taken my wrap and led me into the jazz-and-candle-filled living room. I wanted to bite the words back instantly, even though I'd meant them. There was something about him that made me just spill whatever was in my head. I knew I'd have to watch that: total frankness is not always a good thing.

I was relieved when he laughed. "You're right. It's gorgeous though, isn't it?"

I nodded, still embarrassed. "Sorry. That was in the top ten of tactless things I've ever said."

He laughed some more. "No apologies necessary. It *is* total batch-guy pad, isn't it? And it isn't mine. A friend of mine got offered a year-long contract in Dubai right around the time I was moving out here. Since he owns this place, it made sense for him to just rent it to me until he gets back. And they've been renewing his contract every year ever since, so I've just stuck around. It's a good deal. And it's a two-bedroom so it works pretty well. When he has time off, he gets to stay in his own place while he's in town, meanwhile I make the mortgage payments for him."

"Sweet," I said, hoping to make amends. But it made more sense now. I wasn't quite sure what I'd been expecting of Gus's domicile, but it hadn't been the kind of babe-magnet apartment you'd expect to see in the pages of *Maxim* magazine. Frankly, I was a little relieved to hear it wasn't his.

He smiled at me. Took my hand and tugged gently. "Come see the kitchen."

I tend not to be impressed with kitchens, but the room took my breath away. It was a wonder of high-tech Tuscan design with an amazing view of the ocean.

"Wow," I breathed. And there was still more wow: Gus had made snacks. He poured us each a glass of a very robust red wine he'd had breathing in anticipation of my arrival. He'd artfully set out a selection of Mediterranean-style appetizers: ripe olives, goat cheese drizzled with olive oil, hummus, tzatziki, baba ghanoush and pita bread.

"I made it all myself," he said with some pride.

"You did not," I said, surprised.

"All except the olives and the goat cheese, of course. And the pita bread. I could have done the bread, but I didn't have time."

"Wow," I said again, dipping a bit of pita into the hummus and savoring the perfectly blended flavors. "*Wow.* This is wonderful. I don't even know how you got the time to do this."

"I cheated," he admitted, partly proud and partly sheepish. "I...I plotted a bit. I thickened the yogurt for the tzatziki when I got home last night. Likewise soaked the dry chickpeas for the hummus and roasted the eggplant for the baba ghanoush."

"Last night?" I was amazed.

"Yeah. Then, when I got home tonight, I just sort of had to throw it all together."

"Wow," I said yet again. This time I would have been hard-pressed to translate. He must have been fairly confident I'd agree to come over to go to all that trouble. Also, it meant he probably decided on this course of action pretty much right after he'd dropped me off. Just thinking about it made me a little breathless. Last—but not at all least—I had once again managed to attract a man who could cook. I savored the smoky flavor of the baba ghanoush on yet another piece of pita bread. A man who could *really* cook. "This stuff is all so great, Gus." I fluttered my eyelashes at him coquettishly. "I think I might just have to keep you."

He smiled at my antics. "You know, Madeline, that really *was* my evil plan."

"So, tell me. I didn't even know you could make hummus. I mean, that anyone could, not just you. I thought it just, you know, came from plastic containers in the gourmet section of the supermarket."

"Sure. You can make it."

"How?"

He looked at me speculatively. "You really want to know?"

I stuffed another piece of hummus-dipped pita into my face, washed it down with another mouthful of the perfectly selected wine and almost purred. "Sure," I said.

"Well—" He moved toward me. "Some day I will actually give you a cooking lesson if you're so inclined." Cupped the back of my head in his hands and looked into my eyes. "But not today." Kissed me deeply. I felt something inside me that had been closed for a long time open, turn over. He moved back from me slightly and said into my hair, "Today is not for cooking lessons."

I wanted him then. As much as I've ever wanted anyone, I wanted Gus. I could see, in my mind's eye, the two of us locked in an almost deadly embrace. I could imagine us slick with sweat, our faces contorted with pleasure, the world outside the bedroom door a noisy dream that we didn't want to rejoin.

I wanted to make all of that happen. I knew it would. I *knew* it would. I took his hand and began leading him out of the kitchen, to the area of the apartment where I thought the bedrooms would be.

Gus stopped me. So gently I almost didn't realize I had been stopped. He dropped his head, nuzzled my neck—softly—and said hoarsely, with an almost imperceptible shake of his head, "We're going for dinner. I've got reservations."

I pulled back from him slightly. Looked up into his eyes. Smiled. And said softly, with a shake of my head, "I have no reservations."

And we both laughed then, because it was funny, if not entirely original. And I liked that about him, too: that he laughed at my jokes. That I thought his jokes were funny. That we understood each other on some very basic level. And, I guess because of that, I understood when he said warmly, "I'd really like to take you to dinner, Madeline. I want…" He cleared his throat. Trying to clear it of passion, I thought. And when he spoke again, it was a whisper. "I want to wait for you."

"Wait?" I breathed the one word question into his neck.

"When it happens—and it will happen—it will be special. It will be—" he cleared his throat "—beyond belief."

Beyond belief. And I believed him.

So that was how, after another wonderful dinner, I ended up in my own little bed that night, in my own little canyon instead of someplace sumptuous and overdecorated in Santa Monica.

I would have cause to regret our self-denial. But, by then, regret would be available in economy-size.

Six

On the day of the Livingstons' party, Emily drove up to Malibu with her gear so we could get ready together. "It's not that I don't trust you to do it on your own…" she said as she breezed into my little place, the scent of lavender and bergamot trailing behind her.

"Sure. Yeah. Right. Whatever." I said, half laughing. Half because I was sure there was a part of her that was afraid that, if left to my own devices, I would, in fact, turn up in Doc Martens.

"So what were you planning for your hair?" she asked me seriously.

I looked at her. "Planning? You *plan* hair?" I grinned. Ran several fingers through my shiny and clean mop. Grinned again. "There. All done."

"C'mon, Madeline. Quit it." She was moving as she said it, pulling various implements of hair torture out of her bag. "I mean, we're past the point of joking now. Down to the wire."

The thing was—and I'm pretty sure she knew this—I wasn't joking. Not really. Had I been going to this party alone, that's exactly what my hair would have been doing: nothing. It's the only thing I'm good at getting it to do.

I let Emily fuss with it and pull at it and otherwise use various sprays and tools to force her mastery on my usually uncooperative tresses. Emily is good at it: her own hair, while quite unlike mine, also requires firm guidance and discipline in order to do anything that remotely resembles a coif. Personally, the best I can manage on my own is a kind of messy chignon: fine for running or cooking and not much else. Most of the time I let it spill over my shoulders in unruly splendor: I have good hair and am lucky that it's naturally the color it is (or it wouldn't be that color at all). But Emily didn't feel this party was the time or place for au naturel, and when she'd wrangled my hair into an updo that was neither fussy nor messy, she pushed herself back with a satisfied sigh to survey her handiwork.

"Perfect," she pronounced as she finished it with enough extra-stiffening hairspray to lower the national need for Viagra. I had to agree with her: my hair looked good. I knew that I'd never be able to accomplish anything similar on my own.

My makeup was, also, not up to snuff for Emily. "It's *evening,* Madeline. That means evening makeup."

Fool that I am, I hadn't even realized there was a difference. I have two basic modes: makeup and no makeup. You can tell them apart because one has mascara, blush, a dab of shadow and lipstick in it and the other, well…doesn't.

Emily's nighttime face for me didn't take much longer than the daytime face I seldom bother to put on, but it looked quite different. Foundation gave me a dewy glow that I had to admit was more than acceptable: it looked good. She did my eyes dark and smoky and chose a shade of lipstick from her own stock—what I had on offer just produced a sort of disparaging wave of the hand from Emily. And she *definitely* chose an evening shade: a bright brick-red that was way louder than anything I would have picked on my own.

"That's the point," Emily said emphatically when I protested. "You're supposed to wear noticeable lipstick in the evening."

Supposed to? And here I'd been going blithely through my life completely oblivious to the fact that there were rules that I'd been constantly breaking. What had I been thinking?

We decided to take Emily's SUV up to Beverly Hills. My car is just such a *car*. Emily's big, black off-road-capable vehicle is so much more L.A.

Though I'd been to Larkin House several times before, I'd not been at night and certainly not when the house and gardens were decked out in full party regalia. In the driver's seat, Emily, for whom this was a first visit, was also speechless.

The large ornamental security gates, normally closed and monitored by a hidden camera, were thrown open, the huge cursive *L* over the drive seeming to invite all comers. And I do mean "seeming." The grounds were ablaze with lights, but as you reached the house, a liveried attendant compared the names of those arriving with a list.

"Madeline Carter and guest." I leaned over Emily to reply to the attendant's polite request.

I could feel Emily holding her breath while he scanned his clipboard. When he found my name, he smiled and nodded to one of the waiting valets. We climbed out and Emily's SUV was whisked away while the two of us were ushered toward the house.

"This is *so* A-list," Emily whispered as we made our way up the marble staircase, through the foyer, to enter the throng. Even I could see the truth in what she said: the faces all around us were familiar to me from movie screens, as well as some I just knew were headed for that destination.

As always, at Hollywood gatherings, there were lots of behind-the-camera people in attendance, as well. People who, like Emily, who is a first assistant director, or Maxi and Tyler, who produce and direct feature films, are seldom recognizable to the population at large: i.e., me. But these types were overshadowed by the glamourpusses who sucked the light and energy from any room they entered.

And there, among the stars and all the behind-the-scenes people and the also-rans, I spotted Keesia. She was more exquisite than I'd ever seen her in a dark red gown that looked as if it had been made for her, which, when I thought about it, it probably had.

Keesia was more than holding her own in this crowd. She was on her own turf, mistress of Larkin House, hostess of what would be one of the hottest parties of the season and loving every second of it. There was no hostessy strain on her face at all: just—while she felt unobserved—a smug satisfaction that did nothing to detract from her glowing beauty. All her dreams had, I think, come true. If there was anything more that she could ask for, she wasn't thinking of it at that moment. She was in her element and, for just a second, I envied her that surety.

When she spotted me she beamed a huge smile in our direction and made her way across the ballroom-size foyer toward us.

"Madeline, you came!"

"How could I not? I wanted to see the place decked out for a party."

"She decks out beautifully, doesn't she?" she said fondly. Then, turning to Emily, "And who's this?"

I did the introductions, and then Keesia turned hostess and introduced us to the people nearest us. I was surprised at how pleased I was to be introduced as Keesia's "mentor in the stock market."

A lull in arrivals followed and Keesia quietly pointed out a few of the men she considered eligible and worthy of my attention. Emily listened more attentively than I did. "I've met someone," I confided to Keesia quietly.

"You have? Madeline, that's wonderful. Promise to tell me about it soonest." I nodded. "Now, go find drinks. Mingle. Tyler and Tasya are here somewhere, you know. I saw them earlier. And likely some people Emily knows, as well. And remember what I said at your house, Madeline," she said sotto voce but with a smile in her voice. "If things get boring, I'll meet you in the conservatory for a beer! You can tell me about The Guy."

I couldn't imagine things getting boring in this crowd—there were perhaps two hundred people already there and more arriving all the time. Emily and I ambled off and found drinks. Red wine for me, a vodka martini for Emily. "She's super nice. Nicer than I expected. Very, you know…" She struggled, looking for a word.

"Normal?" I supplied.

"Yeah, normal. That's it," Emily laughed. "Maybe not so much what you'd expect."

It was nine o'clock and the party was just starting to heat up. The older A-list was in place, the younger stars just beginning to make their appearances. Emily and I found an inconspicuous place to stand and watch away from the foyer, but not quite in the main drawing room. When Maxi Livingston ambled across our line of vision, Emily poked me in the ribs under cover of her evening bag.

"There he is," she hissed, though I wouldn't have needed her to tell me: his raptorlike features enfolded in cushions of fat and set off by his shiny head made him easy to spot. More distinctive than the unappetizing way he looked was the weight his appearance carried in this crowd. As he made his way across the foyer toward his wife, people alternately made way for him or tried to engage him in conversation. He wasn't having it and stayed focused on Keesia.

When he reached her, he put a possessive hand on her elbow and she focused down on him. In flats I knew she was only about five-seven. In heels she was probably five-ten or -eleven and I could see that Maxi was maybe five-six. The difference in height was exaggerated by their physiques. Keesia's slender and worked-out body accentuated her husband's dumpiness. Seeing them together this way, I wondered again why rich and older men often seem so fascinated by very young women. Keesia's extreme beauty and lush youth seemed, if anything, to make Maxi appear even less attractive, more physically diminished. Did he gaze into her face and feel youth reflected there, back to him? Looking at them together did nothing of the sort. To me the comparison just made him look older, less powerful. I wondered how Keesia could even stomach him.

Keesia leaned down and Maxi seemed to whisper something fiercely into her ear. She straightened, looked down at him as though considering his words, then leaned down to whisper something back. At his reply, she nodded to him almost imperceptibly, then swept out of the room, smiling here, nodding there, but I could see a new strain on her face.

I watched her disappear into the drawing room by another door.

"Come on, Emily," I said to my friend. "Let's see what sort of mission he sent her on."

The room Keesia blithely referred to as the drawing room was more like a ballroom and big enough for a small convention. The ceilings were easily sixteen feet high, and you could imagine the room as it might have been in a different era, where young girls with dance cards penciled partners in with machinelike precision.

There was no dancing here tonight, though. Just rafts of jovial guests, fleets of well-trained servers and carefully placed alcoves of chairs and tea tables to allow small groups to move aside and chat and probably network. And—on the far side of the room and easy to spot because of her red dress—Keesia had been cornered by a striking redhead in a black sheath dress. They seemed to be having some sort of mildly heated discussion.

"That's Bronwyn Barnes," Emily said. I looked at Emily quizzically and she continued, "You mean you don't recognize her?"

I shook my head, "Not at all."

"Well she's an actor, for one. Though not an especially good one. A lot of TV movies about a decade ago. And guest appearances on some of the not-so-great TV series." Emily scrunched her face up as though consulting a mental Rolodex. "And I think she shot a pilot once. Same period. It was something really awful that didn't get picked up. Then she married Maxi."

Emily had my full attention now. "Seriously?"

"Yeah. I think she might have been wife number three. Or four. Maybe four. What's Keesia?"

"Five," I answered.

"Right. Then Bronwyn is definitely number four. She's the one Maxi dumped to marry Keesia."

"Nice," I said dryly. "What on earth would she be doing here?"

"Well," Emily said pragmatically, "it's a company town, isn't it? And Bronwyn's in the business." Emily dropped her voice. "Though, to be honest, since the divorce, I think Bronwyn's biggest business has been cashing Maxi's checks."

I turned back to have another look, but was disappointed: both Bronwyn and Keesia had disappeared from view.

Seven

"I never thought I'd say this," Emily announced after a while. "But I'm tired of looking at big stars. I'm hungry. Think we can find some food in this dump?"

I laughed. "Hmm...I dunno. It might be possible. We can poke around and see. I've been wanting to explore more of the house, anyway." I'd been to Larkin House a number of times, but I'd only seen the foyer, the conservatory and the dark labyrinth of hallways between.

We didn't have to go far to find food. The immense drawing room spilled out onto a concrete veranda, affording a view of the pool and the gardens—both lit and almost as bright as day. The city glittered, at once inky-black and jewel-bright, beyond. On the veranda, the scent of evening on the west side of L.A.—the hint of oil and humanity, the odor of near-tropical vegetation and a trace of sea air—mingled with the smell of the roses that had been trained to clamber up the edge of the veranda near where we stood.

In all open parts of the mansion and grounds, cater-waiters wound their way between guests with trays heavy with food and drink. The canapés were ample and varied enough that you could pause to inspect what was on offer before making a commitment: chicken satay, California rolls, Swedish meatballs, delicate little taquitos, gyoza—both vegetarian and not—oysters on the half shell, various types of bruschetta, goat's cheese and caviar quiches, foie gras on toast points, shrimps and prawns in half a dozen incarnations…if it was finger food, it was here somewhere, traveling through the house on a tray.

Braydon—my ex-husband, the chef—would have turned his nose up and called the whole thing déclassé. For food to work, he would have said, all aspects have to be considered. What goes with what? What enhances what? What is the desired mood? What is the venue?

Braydon would have been right. And he would have been wrong. The food, as much as anything here, spoke volumes about the event. It wasn't about perfect execution and an enhancement of the senses, as Braydon had always insisted on. Rather, the point of it all was what would have bothered Bray most: it was about excess. The menu—and the decor and the floral arrangements and even all those wives—said, quite plainly: See how powerful I am? I don't have to make choices. Who cares what goes with what? I can have it all.

Thinking of food that went together made me think of Gus for a second, and the little feast he'd prepared before we'd gone out for dinner in Santa Monica. And thinking of him made me smile. I liked the way that felt. Two dates and no sex yet: he certainly couldn't be called my boyfriend. And yet, Gus made me feel as though there was some Other in the world for me. I knew Gus would want to hear about everything I'd seen here tonight. I took special note of the food and some of the big names I'd seen stuffing their faces with it, so I'd have extra-good details for him. And, of course, for my mom.

Aside from the moving food, there was plenty situated on tables, as well. Bowls of cracked shrimp on ice nestled in floral arrangements on candlelit tables near the pool. A chef was making crepes on the veranda, another at the edge of the drawing room drizzled truffle oil onto tiny but perfectly presented plates of seafood risotto. There was probably more—each corner turned seemed to produce additional creative ways of serving food—but after a while, Emily and I couldn't choke down anything more and figured we'd stop before we got ourselves thrown out. Not that that was likely.

Hollywood A-list party. Many of the people here probably made more in a single week than I had in a whole year as a broker, but a lot of these folks were stuffing themselves as if they were first-year university students who'd blown their food allowance on beer. The mood of the room seemed to be: if Maxi Livingston is buying, we'd better take advantage before he turns off the tap. And he will.

I had almost made the third foie gras toast point disappear, which I'd told myself was my last, when I was enveloped in a huge hug.

"Madeline Carter! What are you doing here? And looking more beautiful than ever."

It took me a minute to get my bearings, to clear the toast that had nearly choked me, right the wineglass that I had been precariously balancing between foie gras and evening bag and stand back enough to see who my cheerful assailant was.

"Clipper?" I breathed, not believing my eyes. "What are *you* doing here?"

"I might say the same to you. I'm the film person of us two, remember?"

I spread my hands in answer, I really couldn't come up with anything clever to say. "So what happened?"

"Happened?" he repeated, sounding mystified.

"To you," I supplied helpfully.

Now it was his turn to spread his hands out. He looked as though he really had no idea what I was talking about.

"The other night, Clipper. At the restaurant."

Emily looked from me to him with interest, her eyebrows raised. "The other night?"

I ignored Emily—I could fill her in later—and fixed Clipper with a hard glance.

"C'mon. What the hell do you mean 'the other night'? You disappeared. I thought you'd died in the men's room or something."

To my surprise, he laughed. Not cruel or hard, just as though he thought it was the funniest thing he'd heard all day.

"Seriously?"

"Well…" I tried to think of something scathing to say. And failed. "Well, duh! What the hell did you think I'd think?"

He had the good grace to look slightly more sober. "I guess I didn't think about it."

I shook my head, as though trying to clear it. The words that were coming out of his head didn't make much sense. "So what happened?" I insisted.

"Happened?" It was like a recording of the earlier part of our conversation.

"To you!" I was aware that my voice had gone up a couple of decibels and people nearby were craning nonchalantly to look at what the fuss was about. I really didn't care. It felt like a sort of road rage. Without the car. Sort of a notching up of the volume of my anger without much participation on my part. "You just disappeared. Now tell me how your mother got sick or your dog ate a lamp or you couldn't stand the noise I made when I sipped my wine. Or…something!"

"Oh, no. None of those things. I had a really good time."

I just squinted at him, willing him to continue. He did.

"It's just that I hate saying goodbye."

I squinted at him some more. "You hate saying goodbye," I repeated.

He nodded agreeably.

"But you *have* to say goodbye, Clipper. It's like a rule."

He shrugged. "No, not really."

"No," I said firmly. "Really. I sat there for forty-five minutes thinking you were dead in the bathroom." And sure, I'd been laughing about it by the time I got home, but I was mad again now.

If I'd hoped to injure him with my direct and scathing approach, I had another think coming. He laughed again, deep and real, reminding me of why I'd agreed to go out with him in the first place: his laughter charmed. And it was infectious. I knew I wouldn't make the same mistake again—going out with him—but I really couldn't find it in myself to hate him. Not at the moment, anyway.

"Ah, well…you seemed to be enjoying the food a lot more than you were enjoying my company." I didn't have anything to say to that. It was sort of true. "And," he went on, "like I said, I hate goodbyes."

"Okay," I said, and turned on my heel. Not caring at this point if Emily followed or not.

To my surprise, it was Clipper who followed, catching up with me on the open veranda. "Ah, Madeline," he said. "Don't be like that. We had fun, didn't we?"

"You're a crazy person, Clipper. I mean, I thought you were a crazy person, but now I know. That was…it was…well, it was *rude*."

"You think?" He was truly amused now. Far more amused with me than he'd ever been through our dinner. "Can you reach for moronic?"

"I'll go beyond," I said, but I was smiling now, too. "You're childish and ridiculous."

"Oh, ouch!" he said as if wounded, though the smile didn't leave his eyes. "And touché. But I still hate goodbyes. In any case, let's leave that for now." He was leading me back into the drawing room where we'd left Emily, who I could see was now talking to a drop-dead-gorgeous blond woman. "Introduce me to your friend and I'll introduce you to mine." The blonde. Great. The man who dumped me over ice wine was going to introduce me to his date. Could this evening get any better?

I introduced Emily and Clipper introduced us both to the woman he was with. "Nadine Pruitt," he said. She was perhaps only slightly on the wrong side of forty—though in L.A., this can be very difficult to tell. Her figure was lovely, if slightly lush by the most fashionable of standards. She had the kind of body that sent men howling, no matter their age or income bracket. Golden hair cascaded down her back; the color and length was not dissimilar to my own, but my hair does not—ever—cascade. Nadine's waved gently and fell over her shoulders smoothly in a delicate golden cloak. Shampoo-commercial hair.

Her features—like her body—seemed drawn by Vargas's hand. Even, angular, ever so slightly Nordic, her eyes were pale blue, her lips full and red. All of the disparate bits added up to beauty, and yet, there was something distinctly unbeautiful about her, something that had to have come from within, because everything the eye could see added up to stunning.

Clipper was talking, "Nadine used to live in this house." Nadine made a shushing motion with her hand. It was an obvious enough gesture that couldn't have been missed, but Clipper, being Clipper, went on anyway. "She was married to Maxi Livingston." He turned to Nadine. "How many wives ago, honey?"

Emily and I exchanged a glance. And neither of us said it—and, to be honest, we didn't have to—but we were both wondering how many of Maxi's ex-wives were actually at this party.

"Clipper, please." Like the rest of her, Nadine's voice was lush: slightly husky and very well used. "I didn't come here for any of that."

"Oh?" he said, one of his ruddy eyebrows arched in her direction. "What did you come here for, then? I thought that was exactly what you dragged me to this shindig for." His voice held no malice, but the words were enough.

"Clipper, please. Let it go," Nadine said firmly, though I heard the plea in her voice.

"You just wanted to see the old man, huh? Or was it to see the new Mrs. Livingston?"

Nadine looked as though she'd been slapped. She seemed to collapse into herself slightly, but she made no further move to shut Clipper up. I decided I wouldn't mind doing those honors myself.

"Clipper, shut the fuck up." I wasn't even that surprised by the curse that came out of my head. Clipper was, though.

"Ooh," he said, casting around for a sympathetic audience and finding Emily's eyes on me carefully and Nadine looking at me with hope. "Sounds like you mean it."

I decided not to answer, opting instead for a question, "Clipper, why do you have to be such an asshole?"

The fact is, and I could see it now, Clipper *was* an asshole, in the classic, girls-will-know-what-I'm-talking-about sense. I just hadn't seen it so clearly before. It was why he liked laughing at people. It was why he'd left me at the restaurant. It was probably even why he had hooked up with a beautiful and broken bird like Nadine.

His asshole factions were warring now. In the approximately fifteen seconds before he replied, I could see him quickly turning responses over in his head. I could practically hear the thoughts forming, the tumblers clicking. The possibilities: stoop to the level I'd dropped to when I'd made this blatant attempt at turning his attention from Nadine? March away from me, back straight, and ignore me for the rest of the evening and the rest of my life? Laugh and pretend it was all a big joke, one that wasn't on him? In true asshole fashion, he chose the easiest of the three and threw back his head and laughed, though I could see the effort it cost him.

"Madeline shoulda been a comedian—you are one funny chick."

"That's me," I said wryly, "har, har, har." But I knew I could go back to name-calling with very little provocation. Heck, kicking him in the shins with the pointy toe of one of my strappy little sandals felt like a real option just then.

"Well, fun running into you guys. Me and Nadine hafta circulate now."

"Yeah, circulate. Excellent," I said, turning my back and focusing on a nearby display of iced shrimp.

"Whoa!" Emily said as soon as the pair were out of earshot. "You actually *dated* that loser?"

"One date. *Not* dated. There's a difference." We'd moved back onto the terrace as we talked. Safe for the moment, probably, from running into Clipper again.

"Still," Emily breathed. "I can't believe you went out with him at all. Your standards must be lower than I thought."

"Standards schmandards," I said, my humor coming back now that he was gone. "It was a slow month. What can I say? We can't all have a Tristan to fall back on."

Emily nodded at this: it was true. Tristan and Emily had been something like an item since I'd introduced them a while before. A screenwriter, Tristan works about as much as Emily does—which is to say a lot—on the same kind of low-grade B movies she works on. When he isn't working, he always has his head stuffed into some type of electronics. He loves computers. Emily had been known to say he could make computers sing. None of that mattered, though. As Emily likes to point out, at least he can read and has an income. Into the bargain he's also a terribly nice guy who thinks the sun rises over Emily's head. Don't kid yourself: those are awesome qualities in a boyfriend.

"Which reminds me, Madeline, Steve still asks about you."

I looked at Emily closely over my wine. Steve was a guy I'd seen a lot of for a while. He was Tristan's roommate and the introduction I'd made had actually been sort of a double date: Tristan and Emily, Steve and me, while Steve and I were just getting to know each other.

I still cared a lot about Steve, but not enough. He was almost ten years younger than me, and in the end, I'd found that to be too big a gap to bridge. Especially when he'd started pushing for a deeper commitment. I'd known from the beginning that Steve wasn't someone I could tie myself to long term: our frames of reference were so different. And, when all was said and done, it just hadn't been what I wanted.

Emily knew all that, so her bringing Steve up now surprised me. "You know how I feel, Emily."

Emily nodded while snagging a fresh cocktail from a tray as it passed. "I do know that, Madeline. But he's so pathetic about you sometimes. And he made me promise I'd mention him."

I sighed. "Okay. You did your duty. Steve has been mentioned. It's just never going to happen, Em. You know that."

Emily nodded again. "Yes, I do. But still, Madeline." Emily shook her head in concern, and indicated the direction Clipper had disappeared. "That guy is a serious loser. Even for a slow Wednesday. You need to raise your standards. And in a world that Steve is in…"

"Can we give it up, Em? Let it go." All this discussion of men and relationships was making me think of Gus, but I opted not to go there just now. It was one thing to tell Emily about him, but if I started mentioning Gus all over the place she'd know for certain what my feelings were. And my feelings were so new I didn't really understand them myself. New and fragile, that was really the thing. I didn't want to jinx whatever it was Gus and I had growing. "You can tell Steve you did what you said you'd do. But Clipper? That was a weak moment, okay? And he tricked me."

"How'd he trick you?"

"He tricked me into thinking he wasn't an asshole. It won't happen again. Now, let it go."

But I could see it was already gone. Emily's attention was refocused on the distance, into the garden. "Is that Keesia?" she asked.

I looked. It was. The blood-red dress made it difficult to mistake her. "She's talking to someone."

The someone in question was tall—Keesia had to tilt her head up to address him—and though they were a fair distance away, my impression was of someone uncommonly attractive, even in this crowd. His hair was dark and smooth and licked at the collar of his tux jacket. Said jacket made his shoulders appear linebacker wide, and truly, that was about all I could make out from far away, other than the iconic grace of his movements.

"He is seriously hot," Emily said, with her usual subtle grace and tact. "Hot, hot, hot. Do you know who he is?"

"No idea."

"What do you think they're talking about?"

We were at a quiet end of the veranda, shielded somewhat by the profusion of roses. Neither of us felt conspicuous in staring at our hostess deep in conversation with the mystery hottie. I couldn't begin to guess at their topic, though I *could* guess that, whatever it was, they probably thought they were unobserved. The garden was lit brightly, but they were in a dark corner right at the edge: they couldn't be aware of how the ambient light had traveled to illuminate their tête-à-tête.

"Well," Emily said, "I can't decide whether it's romantic or not. I mean, look at him. You want it to be romantic, don't you?"

"He *is* yummy," I agreed.

"But their body language doesn't say that. Unless, you know, they're being careful because of all the people."

"Could be."

"Yeah. But he wouldn't inspire circumspection in me."

I looked at Emily's face, frank admiration apparent in every line. "What would, Emily? What does?"

She laughed. "Never mind! It's just fun to think about, though, isn't it? The two of them, so beautiful. And her husband…"

"Uh-oh," I said, because—as though this mention of him had caused him to pay attention—Maxi Livingston could be seen striding across the garden to where Keesia and the mystery man stood. "He doesn't look too happy, does he?"

"Gawd," Emily said. "Look at that little troll! I can't believe he's her husband. Yuck, Carter. Can you even imagine?"

"Well…" I tore my glance away from the scene that seemed likely to unfold: it was starting to feel like watching a car wreck. "Keesia and I have actually talked about it a little."

"No way!"

"Way. And she—" I lowered my voice still further, not wanting to be overheard "—she talks about it all like it's a job, you know? A career. She seems to think of this whole thing—" I indicated the house, the gardens, Maxi "—as her, you know, profession."

"Really?"

I nodded.

Emily seemed to consider. "Well, I guess I can see it. I mean, hell—it beats waiting tables, doesn't it?"

I nodded again. "For some people it would beat a lot of stuff."

We looked back to where the couple had stood: arguing or exchanging loving words, we'd never know. The mystery man had disappeared into the garden at Maxi's approach. Now Maxi and Keesia were talking. It looked slightly heated, at first. Then Maxi seemed to open his arms and Keesia melted into them. What I saw was inexplicable: a man transformed. With Keesia now, he no longer looked like a troll to me. He looked like a man in love.

"Yeah," Emily said, and it took me a moment to realize she was replying to my last comment. "But there's lots of stuff better."

When Maxi and Keesia moved back toward the house and the party, there was nothing left to look at in the garden, and with the onset of full evening adding a note of chill to the night, Emily and I headed back indoors.

A lovely woman with auburn hair and shiny, plum-colored lips pulled herself away from a little group at the door as we came inside. It seemed as though she'd been waiting for us. "Emily Wright," the woman said, only a touch of the South apparent in her voice. "It's been ages!"

Emily and the woman air-kissed in old Hollywood style. "Madeline Carter," Emily said, by way of introduction, "this is Celisa Taylor. Celisa, Madeline." I shook hands with her dutifully while she beamed at me. I knew that beam from Tyler's parties: Celisa was covering her bases in case I was someone important. That particular beam would dry right up when she realized I wasn't.

Celisa looked to be in her late twenties, so I guessed she was probably well over thirty. She was lovely in that single-faceted, predictable way that I'd quickly learned gets to be tiresome at Hollywood parties. She was somehow drop-dead gorgeous and entirely bland at the same time. Her bright plum lips added a note of interest, but in a key that was slightly off. And she looked, I thought, somehow hungry. Not for food—though she was certainly lean—but as though she feasted on something other than the calories and carbohydrates the rest of us require.

"Madeline is Keesia's mentor in the stock market," Emily said, reiterating Keesia's description of me from earlier in the evening. And I could see a certain minxishness in Emily as she said it, something I didn't understand at the time.

For her part, Celisa seemed to shrink away from me slightly, as though I might have something that was catching. And, as I'd predicted, the beam fell right off.

"So," she said to Emily, ignoring me entirely, "what are you working on these days?"

"Well, you know, this and that," Emily said airily. "I just got back from Romania, you know."

I suddenly realized this was going to be a fun conversation to watch. Whenever she'd spoken to me of her trip to Eastern Europe, Emily had been entirely—not slightly—disparaging. As though it was something to be gotten through, preferably as quickly as possible. A necessary step on a career that could only go up. Now, however, she dropped the word—Romania—as though it were the promised land.

"Something exciting?" Celisa prompted, a delicate gleam in her eye.

"Ah…well," Emily smiled, cat-with-cream-style, "you know how it is…" And Celisa nodded, even though she hadn't been told what "it" was. "I can't really talk about it."

"Really," Celisa breathed.

Emily nodded, sagely, I thought. "Yes. And you *were* in my mind. There was *one* role but really, Celisa, you would have been too young for it."

Celisa seemed to preen like a cat and deflate ever so slightly in the same moment. Their conversation faded to small talk and then Emily made few bones about washing her hands of the woman. When Emily ended the conversation, she made no pretense about a future lunch.

"All the gossip columnists called," I whispered to Emily when we were barely out of earshot, heading to the bar at the far side of the room. "They said they want their bitchiness back."

Emily shot a glance at me from under her lashes while she neatly scooped a drink from a passing tray. "Oh, really?" she said, looking pleased with herself.

"*Really.*" I replied. "I mean it. What *was* that?"

"Worlds within worlds, Madeline," Emily said cryptically.

"Hello," I said brightly, "earth to Emily." We got our drinks and retreated to an empty table nearby. "You wanna fill me in?"

"That was Celisa Taylor."

"That part I knew," I said grumpily. "You introduced me, remember?"

Emily rolled her eyes, a plea-to-be-patient look visible on her face. "You probably already gathered that she and I have worked together before. It was a few years ago. She was the female lead in *Night of Luna.*"

"I don't remember you telling me about that one."

"I never mentioned it."

"That bad, huh?" I asked.

Emily nodded. Hesitated. Then: "Maybe worse. It's better forgotten."

"Oh."

"Silly plot, bad script and terrible, *terrible* talent." Emily shrugged. "And in the end it got shelved, so, you know. But I don't think Celisa ever realized how terrible it was. And the thing is, when she was signed for the role, she was still married." Here Emily dropped her voice. "Her divorce *killed* the movie, Madeline. The studio shelved the project two weeks after the breakup. The result—another unfinished piece of crap." She sighed. "No loss, I guess. But it still hurt. With the backing we initially had, it was the kind of crap that can go places."

I didn't even try to puzzle out Emily's words this time. Upwardly mobile crap is still crap to me. I mean, in my world, if you polish a turd all you end up with is a shiny turd. Hollywood had different standards.

"But you said her divorce killed the movie. How could that be?" I grappled with the idea for a moment. "You mean she had severe emotional problems? She was broken up because of the divorce? Couldn't work right?"

Emily cast me an *oh-Madeline-you're-so-naive* look. I recognized it because she'd given it to me before. And Emily said, "No, silly. Not because of the divorce. Because of *who* she divorced."

My forehead wrinkled. "Who?"

"Who do you think?"

I spread my hands helplessly. "I have no idea."

She dropped her voice a little further. "Maxi Livingston."

"Get out," I said.

"Seriously."

"What the hell is this? Some kind of ex-wives' convention? Don't you think their being here must make Keesia crazy?"

Emily shrugged, as though she'd lost interest in the whole thing. "Whatever. I mean, you saw. Celisa isn't here as Maxi's ex. She's here as yet another reasonably untalented actor. Think about it—she was zooming *me* for work. Come on, Madeline," she laughed unselfconsciously. "You'd have to be pretty desperate to think of *me* as a contact. I *never* have anything at all to do with casting. She knows that, too. But, like I said, she's desperate." She got up, flicked an imaginary piece of lint off her fine black skirt. "Being catty makes me hungry. Let's see if there are any more of those shrimp skewers around."

By eleven o'clock the party was just getting going and I had had enough. Hollywood parties are amazing but entirely not my scene. To be honest, I'm not even sure what my scene is anymore, or if I even have one, but I knew this wasn't it.

We'd not run into Tyler and Tasya, though Keesia had said they were at the party. If at least three of Maxi Livingston's ex-wives were here—along with his current wife—and even Clipper, it seemed likely that so was half of Southern California's film industry.

I hadn't seen Keesia for a while, but that didn't really surprise me. Whatever had happened in the garden had looked as though it was intense enough to make her look for privacy.

I left Emily in the drawing room at the center of a small group that included a talk-show producer and a ballet star and headed for the conservatory. It seemed like a good chance that, if Keesia had decided to ditch for a while, that's where she would have headed. If she wasn't there, I could at least use the bathroom in the conservatory. It would be empty, and there was currently a bit of a lineup for the bathrooms in the main part of the house.

I was surprised to find the conservatory dark when I entered. I'd only ever seen the room during the day. Then all the greenery and maybe just the cheerful feeling Keesia gave the room made it a bright and happy place. Probably, I thought, the lights had been turned out to discourage guests from entering this part of the house.

"Keesia?" I called out, not expecting an answer, nor did I get one.

Well, never mind, I thought. I'd use the bathroom and then head back to the party: perhaps find Keesia there, say goodbye and then see where Emily had gotten to and try to prize her away in time to go home and get a good night's sleep.

I opened the bathroom door and saw too much red, saw those topaz eyes. The screams obliterated all thought, but I'd known at a glance that Keesia Livingston was dead.

Eight

It was a long night. Thinking back on it, it seemed to last three days. My screams were eventually answered—in a minute? an hour?—by Maxi Livingston himself. I didn't think it was odd, at the time.

"Oh, my God," I heard him say. "Oh, my Keesia. Oh, my God." I felt myself pushed away from Keesia's body—by the force of Maxi's personality or his hands, I wouldn't later be sure.

Maxi leaned over and touched his hand to Keesia's bare wrist, something I hadn't thought to do. Something I wouldn't have been able to do, even if I *had* thought of it. Even if I'd felt it was necessary. And it wasn't: the sagging of Maxi's shoulders, the breath that seemed to go out of him in a whoosh showed me that.

My screams had alerted people and pretty soon the small room seemed full, though there could only have been three or four people there. Someone dressed like a cater-waiter led me back to the conservatory. I was half lowered, half pushed into a chair. Where minutes before the room had been darkened and empty, it now seemed ablaze with light and activity. There weren't a lot of people there—my screams had only alerted those closest—but I felt as though it should still be dark here, and silent. Especially silent, now that Keesia was gone.

Maxi emerged from the bathroom minutes after me. He looked diminished, stricken. For his wife, I wondered—perhaps unkindly—or for the fact that all of this had taken place during a party he was hosting?

While I sat, shocked beyond helpfulness by what I'd seen, Maxi made a phone call, then another, then another after that. By the time he'd finished the last, responses had come to his earliest calls and a uniformed guard stood at his elbow awaiting instruction.

The party's own noise had drowned out my screams and, for the moment, the party went on: dancing, eating, laughing, networking. The thought of it made my stomach constrict.

Time passed. I couldn't say how much. I kept getting the feeling that I should be getting up. Doing something. But I couldn't quite determine what that something might be. And so I sat. I know I was conscious, but not very. I was aware of my heart, in motion, it seemed, in my chest. I was aware of the ebb and flow of people across my field of vision, but they registered to me as pieces of motion rather than individuals. I think it's likely that I was in shock, but part of being in shock is not recognizing it while you're in it.

"Ms. Carter? Can I have a word with you please?"

I forced my eyes up to the man standing in front of my chair. His suit was brown and fit him neatly, though it looked as though he'd been wearing it for at least a couple of hours too long. His eyes were sad and compassionate, like those of a basset hound with too much to do.

"I'm Detective Brown, Ms. Carter. I'm with the Beverly Hills Police Department." He flashed a badge but I barely glanced at it, I'd seen so much tonight—too much—that I really didn't care who he was. Plus, I was taking in the air of irony this cop had enveloped himself in: brown eyes, brown hair, brown suit, brown name. Did he do it on purpose? At another time, I would have laughed, maybe even come up with a sprightly comment. I was beyond that tonight. I just looked at him.

"Ms. Carter, I understand you found the body."

"Keesia," I supplied quietly.

"Right. Mrs. Livingston. You found her."

"Yes. Yes, I did."

"How long were you alone with her?"

I refocused on his face. On his eyes. What was he saying? "I wasn't alone with her, Mr. Brown."

"Detective," he corrected.

"I just found her. And then I guess…I guess I started screaming. I don't know…" I stopped myself from saying: It just happened so fast, because didn't everyone always say that? And yet it had: the moments were imprinted on my brain, would play themselves out in my head in countless ways in the future, yet my mind refused to focus on the smallest aspects when they were shepherded away from the rest of the thoughts that made up the whole experience.

He asked me more questions, took a brief statement. I don't think I was very helpful. I didn't know anything, hadn't seen anything. Just Keesia. And Keesia's blood. The sight of it, the metallic smell of it, pushed everything else out of my mind.

"I understand that this will have been a shocking experience for you, Ms. Carter." I parsed his words carefully. Was he saying I was in shock? Was that, in fact, what I was feeling? I admitted detachedly that it was possible. Brown was droning on. "When you're feeling up to it, I'd like you to come in and make a full statement." He handed me his card. "Please call me tomorrow afternoon and we'll schedule a time. Meanwhile—" he pasted on a jovial smile "—don't leave town."

I assured him that there was nowhere I needed to go. But I was thinking: What did he mean? "Don't leave town." Why would he even care?

By now Keesia's lovely oasis was crawling with civic employees: lots of uniforms and bad suits. While I'd been talking with Brown, I'd seen someone with a camera slung over one shoulder head toward Keesia and the bathroom. Minutes later I could hear the sound of a motor drive helping a camera make a visual record of the place Keesia last walked among the living.

Paramedics arrived and waited quietly on the sidelines while the police did their thing. It was apparent there was no reason for them to hurry.

Maxi paced among us like Julius Caesar: a ruined hero cut to the marrow. He was, I could see, either mortally wounded by his loss, or a hell of a good actor. Or, possibly, some of both. I wouldn't have placed a bet either way.

But, like any good ruined hero, Maxi was a man of action. He'd do anything he could to make him feel he was part of things, making stuff happen.

In a quiet moment, Maxi seemed to scan the room, as though for details not yet dealt with. Before long, his eyes stopped on me.

"Did you come with the Becketts?" he asked.

I shook my head. "No. With my friend, Emily Wright."

"O'Ryan," he barked at one of his own uniformed staff, a man with the size and countenance of an ex-linebacker, "go and find Tyler Beckett. Bring him to me." Then, as though as an afterthought, "Alone." I wondered if O'Ryan knew what Tyler looked like. There were a lot of people out there. I did not, however, wonder if he'd bring him back.

With O'Ryan gone on his errand, Maxi turned to another similarly built minion. "Halpern, please escort Ms. Carter out the side entrance." Then to me, "I'll have Tyler's car brought round, Ms. Carter. I'd like you to wait for him there."

"There's no need for an escort, Mr. Livingston. I can just wait here for Tyler...."

Maxi wasn't in the mood for opinions. "It would be best if you would allow me to do this for you. There's no need for you to be here for all of this." He indicated the uniforms. The paramedics. I had a sudden flash of them taking Keesia out of there in a body bag and I knew Maxi was right: I really *didn't* need to be there for that. He took my silence for agreement—or maybe he was just used to getting his way—because he went on, "Tyler won't be long."

Like all good mansions of its generation, Larkin House had a network of back corridors and staircases intended to help keep invisible the phalanx of servants necessary to run a house of its size. To keep us away from the partygoers, Halpern used these back passageways now. We emerged into a long, spacious corridor with blue walls. My mind registered gilt mirrors, a Chippendale demi-lune table and a massive painting I recognized instinctively as an *actual* John Singer Sergent: all stuff that would have made me gasp and examine on a normal day. Now, however, my mind was numb. I wasn't even sure I'd be able to find my way back by myself should the need arise.

Halpern led me out the side entrance where a paved walk led the way to the front of the house. I couldn't decide if Maxi was orchestrating my quiet exit for his sake or for mine, but on one level, I was grateful not to have to deal with anything more.

I was unsurprised to see Tyler's luxury SUV idling at the front of the house, nestled between a half-dozen emergency vehicles. However, I hadn't expected Tasya on the passenger side, beautiful in her party-going finery, her eyes wide with apprehension as Halpern handed me into the back seat of the SUV.

"Madeline, what's going on?" Tasya asked, her Eastern European accent more noticeable under stress. "Some men came and got us. The police questioned me and then other men brought me here, but—" her voice broke slightly "—they took Tyler away."

I've been getting Tasya's personal story from her in bits and pieces since we met. She doesn't give any of it up easily and I gather there are parts so ugly, she'd rather never look at them, let alone share them. Still, there is much more that I don't know about her. One thing I am sure of: she knows what it is to have people taken away and never returned. I suspect that she knows more than her share about loss.

I was glad to be able to reassure Tasya now. Comforting her was a welcome diversion from the horror of the evening. Of all the things I didn't know, I felt very confident that Tyler would appear probably sooner rather than later.

I told Tasya what was going on, focusing especially

on the part where her husband would be returned to her momentarily. She seemed to relax slightly, though she kept one eye trained on the front door.

"But what happened, Madeline? An accident?"

"No. Not an accident. Keesia was killed. I think…" I took a deep breath. Forced myself to go on. "I think she was stabbed. More than once."

"And you found her?" She turned her attention back to me as she spoke, her face registering concern for me.

I nodded. "How awful for you, Madeline. You two had gotten to be friends, hadn't you?" I nodded again, willing myself not to cry in the face of Tasya's sympathy.

When Tyler joined us in the car, he looked drawn and concerned. Tasya seemed to wilt slightly with relief when she saw him.

He sat behind the wheel for a few seconds without looking around. Beyond the window, I could see Halpern and O'Ryan talking to emergency personnel. Vehicles were being moved so that we might take our leave.

Tyler cleared his voice twice before he spoke. "Hell of a night," he said. He reached across the console, ran a hand gently over his wife's forearm. "Hell of night," he said again. A spot in the driveway had been cleared and O'Ryan and Halpern stood glowering at us gently. Clearly they were anxious to have their current assignment completed.

"Tyler, let's get Madeline home now, please. It'll be better for her away from here." Tyler didn't need prompting, he put the SUV in gear. When the gates to Larkin House were behind us, I felt a sudden and unexpected relief. The sooner I could put miles between myself and the horror I'd seen, the better I thought I'd feel.

Back in Malibu, Tasya and Tyler led me straight to

the guest room in their part of the house. "You're stay-ing with us tonight, sweetling," Tasya said. She brought me Russian tea, black and strong. Tyler brought me brandy. Neither liquid helped or even wanted to stay down. I kept seeing Keesia's beautiful, vacant eyes, the horrible wounds, her glorious hair fanned out and the way her skin had looked against the marble floor of the bathroom. And her dress. Her wonderful dress. Fuel for nightmares I didn't care to have.

"You want to talk about it?" Tasya said gently. I was enveloped in the luxurious bedding of the guest room wearing one of Tyler's T-shirts. Tasya perched on the edge of the bed, a steaming mug of tea in her hands. Tyler sat in a chair across the room, a glass of brandy in his. On the nightstand, my tea was cooling and my brandy scenting the air.

I shook my head no to Tasya's question, but said, "You guys are being so terrific. Thank you. I don't know what I would have done without you."

"Never mind that now, honey," Tyler said paternally. "Try the brandy again." Tasya passed it to me and I took a small sip. It burned. It didn't feel restorative, but it also didn't threaten to come back this time. I sipped again.

"Emily will worry about me," I said after a while. "We went to the party together."

"She have her cell on her?" Tyler asked.

"I'm not sure. Probably."

Tyler passed me a cordless phone and I dialed Emily's cell number from memory. After one ring, her voice mail clicked in. I almost didn't feel up to leaving a message. "Em, I'm at Tyler and Tasya's place. Sorry to bail on you, it was an emergency. Call me here when you get this," and I left the number.

Tyler and Tasya sat with me for a bit, but there really wasn't much they could do. After a while they left. Tasya returned in a few minutes with Tycho. She installed him on the bed with me, then dimmed the lights. "We're just down the hall if you need us."

This is why we have friends, I reminded myself as I uselessly tried to find my way to peaceful sleep. They'd fitted love and warmth around me when nothing—including those things—was truly going to make me feel entirely right. But it was infinitely better to be here and cared about than it would have been to be alone.

I turned the light off and snuggled into Tycho's comforting bulk, focusing on the rhythm of his breathing. I didn't sleep for a long time and, when I finally did, I didn't dream at all.

Nine

I woke to the sound of hushed voices. Morning light illuminated the unfamiliar surroundings and startled me for a moment. Then all the images and feelings came flooding back. I felt a heaviness and a sadness and the sense of responsibility that unavoidably accompanies an unexpected death.

What if I'd been a few minutes earlier, could I have saved her? What if she wasn't dead when I saw her? If I'd moved more quickly and gotten her medical help... I stopped the what ifs there. She'd been dead when I saw her, I'd known that right away. She'd maybe even been dead for a while. There was nothing I could have done. The feeling lingered, but I ignored it. I knew it was normal to feel that way, but I didn't have to like it.

Someone—probably Tasya—must have looked in on me when they got up. Tycho was gone and a robe lay on the foot of the bed, obviously for my use. I used the bathroom, washing sleep and sadness from my face. Then, wrapping Tasya's dressing gown around me, I followed voices out to the deck.

The weather jolted me. It was textbook: a perfect, cloudless, bright blue SoCal day. Fingers of mist played around the blue-green sage that hugged the hills. Later on, I knew, that mist would be burned away by the warmth of the day. And it *was* going to be a warm day, but not unbearably hot. At least not here, so close to the ocean. The sort of day meant for long walks and leisurely outdoor lunches. How could it be this beautiful? Keesia was dead. Where was the rain? A seriously overcast sky would have felt so much more appropriate.

Tasya, Tyler and Emily were out on the deck under the morning sun, steaming mugs of coffee in their hands. Tycho was a big fuzzy lump nearby. When he saw me, his tail thumped the deck in greeting, but he didn't get up.

"There she is," Tyler said with strained heartiness, getting to his feet and heading for the house. "I'll grab you a coffee."

"Did you sleep all right?" Tasya asked.

I shrugged and nodded—nothing much else was expected of me—and greeted Emily. "You got my message."

"Yeah, but I didn't think to check my voice mail until I was almost here. When I couldn't find you—and everything got so crazy at Larkin House—I couldn't think what to do. I decided to see if I could find you."

"Good instinct," Tyler said, returning from the house with my coffee.

"Things got crazy?" I asked.

Emily buried her face in her hands. "Oh, Madeline. What an awful thing. Keesia was so young."

People always say stuff like that. And they're right: seeing someone cut down in their youth is unthinkable. But, on one level, it didn't figure here. What I'd seen would have been horrible, regardless of Keesia's age.

"I found her," I said quietly.

"I know," Emily said. "These guys have been telling me. It would have been awful for you. They have no clue about who did it, either."

"How do you know?" Tyler asked.

"Stuff I overheard while I was waiting to give my statement. And *that* was a zoo, as you can imagine. All those party-happy people and suddenly the lights are on and no one is going home. I waited hours for someone to talk to me so I could go." She looked at me again. "That's why I figured something was going on with you. I was sure I'd catch up with you while everyone was waiting around to talk to the police, but no one had seen you."

"But you said you overheard stuff," Tyler prompted.

"Right," Emily said, taking a sip of her coffee, "but just snippets, you know?"

I didn't say anything, but I know Emily is very good at that. I've seen her in action. She loves watching people and she loves knowing stuff she's not intended to know.

"Like what?" Tyler asked.

"Well, odd stuff, really. Pieces of stuff. Like I heard one cop saying to another cop—sotto voce, you know— that it didn't look premeditated."

"That's odd," I said. "That's an odd thing to hear."

"I thought so," Emily said nodding. "But that's how I knew it was bad." She coughed slightly and I could see she was more upset than she was letting on: something that likely wasn't helped by the fact that she'd been up all night. "They said they figured it was too much of a mess to be premeditated," she said quietly.

I could hear Tasya gasp at this, then look at me.

"You didn't tell us that part," she said looking at me, her eyes wide and alarmed.

I flashed on the vacant eyes, the dreadful wounds, all that blood. "I didn't want to think about it too much. It was pretty horrible."

"Plus," Emily continued, "they kept questioning people all night long. I thought that, if they had someone, they would have stopped and let us go."

"Not necessarily," Tyler said. "With a crowd that big, they'd want to make sure they knew everyone that was there. I think they'd do that even if they had someone in custody. Just in case—even if they didn't suspect people, they'd want to know if there were witnesses."

"Poor Keesia," I said somewhat absently. "I still can't believe it."

The feeling of disbelief followed me around. Despite my initial misgivings, I'd discovered I liked working with Keesia, liked showing her my ropes and watching her grasp at concepts new to her and run with them. And I'd liked Keesia for herself, as well. The gallant way she'd assimilated her world and the cynical yet cheerful way she'd come to look at the reality she'd created. I felt that, somehow, my life would be a less cheerful place without Keesia in it.

Ten

In the afternoon Emily went home to sleep and I went back to my apartment. I wasn't allowed to leave until I'd assured Tyler and Tasya I was all right and that I'd call one of them if I felt the least bit like talking.

It felt funny to be fussed over that way. Funny but oddly reassuring. I'd lived in New York for ten years with my family at the other end of the country. I'd forgotten what it was like to be part of something larger than myself. It wasn't a bad feeling.

At my place, the construction in the kitchen and bathroom meant that most of the house was in disarray and filled with workers. It was Sunday, but Gus had said he felt bad about the days part of the crew had missed during the week when he'd pulled them off for another job. Though I'd told him it was okay, he'd insisted on sending a small crew on Sunday, just, he'd said, to make up some of the lost time.

Craving privacy, I took the phone into the bedroom, then pulled it with me under the duvet. I loved my bed. It was what had sold me on my tiny, perfect apartment.

The bed was built into one wall: I'd only had to supply a futon and bedding. The opposite wall was a window and, out of it, I could see down into the canyon and, beyond that, to the ocean.

You could never tire of the view: it changed every day, sometimes every hour. In the evening, just before dark, the canyon would be draped in deep purple, the ocean beyond just a hint of endless blue-green. In the early mornings, as I prepared for my trading days, there were often layers of mist moving down the canyon. It was possible to feel you were living inside a cloud.

Today was bright and the sky was blue enough to doubt. If there were clouds overhead, I couldn't see them; they were camouflaged by the pale of the sky. The canyon was shot with green and gold: the tenacious plant life that grew year-round. The ocean was an invitation: it was so clear that I could make out tiny whitecaps even at this distance.

I mused like this for half an hour, wasting time until I felt I really couldn't put off calling Detective Brown any longer. When I called him as he'd asked me to, I was relieved to get his voice mail. I left my name and number, and told him to call me back whenever he liked. Having done my civic duty, I forgot about him. If he wanted to talk to me, he knew where I was.

I was relieved when the workers knocked off at five o'clock and I could have my place back. Though it was intrusive living with construction, the results were going to be worth it. Having met Gus had been a total bonus and I usually didn't mind the construction craziness. Now, however, the crew beavering away was a constant reminder. Tyler was making good on his promise of expanding my little sky cave. I'd held up my end of the bargain, now he was holding up his. The fact that my student had died hadn't nullified our agreement. Still, I found myself wishing that construction hadn't already been started when Keesia had died. Under the circumstances, if they weren't already so close to done I would have called the whole thing off.

Despite these feelings, the renovation was going to be lovely. Tyler had gotten Gus and his crew to take every one of my suggestions and had enhanced the plans with additions of his own. Though it would still be small, the kitchen was going to be a wonder of modern technology. It made me wish I actually cooked.

"That's the beauty with this stuff," Tyler had said when I'd mentioned it. "It's not even going to look like a kitchen. The appliances are mostly hidden." There was nothing above eye level: including the refrigerator, which was being replaced by two counter-height refrigeration units with front panels that matched the new cabinetry. "Because it's such a small space. You don't need anything visually heavy in there." The cooktop was smooth glass yet, Tyler said, would be as responsive as a gas stove—not that I cared. But I remembered from my Braydon days that gas for cooking was a Good Thing. With the small space in mind, the dishwasher was tiny, but European-made: it actually could fit quite a bit and was extremely environmentally friendly.

"At the rate I use dishes," I'd told Tyler, "I'll be doing a load every two weeks whether I need to or not." I generally used a cup or two a day for the coffee I favored while trading, the occasional glass when I had wine or opted for bottled fizzy water rather than a squirt of spring water from the sport bottle I keep in the refrigerator. A bowl for cereal, a plate for a sandwich, a spoon for my coffee: I couldn't imagine I'd actually use the dishwasher for anything other than a fancy draining board or a place to hide kitchen clutter.

Understanding my lifestyle, Tyler had ordered a fair-size island to replace the small piece of counter that had previously jutted slightly into the living room. "It'll give you work space if you decide to make cookies or something," Tyler explained. As if. More important, it would give me a place to spread papers—from financial reports to newspapers—and even have a small, very informal dinner party if I chose.

In the bathroom I was getting all new cabinets and modern fixtures—a new toilet and a pedestal sink. They looked Victorian, but would blessedly work without the gurgles and chirps I'd only started to get used to. The claw-foot tub would remain, but had been refinished and repositioned in the roomier room that had emerged with the main house's storage closet removed. The additional space had provided a place for a closet that would include a stacking washer and dryer. This last was another of Tyler's suggestions and I protested less than I had for the dishwasher: it would be nice to be able to do laundry on my own schedule for the first time in my adult life.

Though construction in my apartment continued, I was slightly relieved to find Gus wasn't around. When I asked, one of his workers told me Gus was at another job site. Though part of me would have loved to see him, another was glad he wasn't there.

I was conflicted when it came to Gus. On one hand, I knew I didn't want to see him at the moment. The sad and echoey place my insides had become was not something I wanted to share with Gus at this delicate beginning stage of our relationship. But I also knew that, for the first time in a long while, I'd found someone I felt I could really care about. Someone I *could* take my troubles to if I chose. That surety made me move more cautiously than I otherwise might have done. I knew I liked him. A lot. I suspected we had more in common than either of us had even begun to understand. I felt very comfortable in his company and I looked forward to seeing him again. But I knew I was weakened at the moment, not quite myself. Gus's shoulders were so broad, his arms so welcoming, the temptation to lean on him could, potentially, be a physical thing. It might prove overwhelming. I would do best, I told myself, to avoid the potential altogether. The only thing I wondered was if I'd be able to explain any of that in a way that he would understand. I barely understood it myself.

When I called Gus at home that evening I told him about Keesia, told him I'd found her, and let him know that the best thing for me right now was to be alone to lick my wounds. He sounded as though he would have preferred to march right in and do his best shining knight, but he was grown-up enough to know that wasn't what was called for in this instance.

"But let me know if I can do anything at all, okay, Madeline? Even if you just want to take your mind off things, see a movie. Whatever."

I told him I would, and that I'd probably see him on the job site early the following week. I spent what was left of the weekend moping around my disheveled but blessedly empty apartment, screening my calls and not bothering to shower. By the time Monday rolled around, I almost felt like myself again. And I would have, too, except that Keesia's funeral service was going to be held in the afternoon.

As Tycho and I tore up the hills in the morning, I thought about whether or not I would attend. Realistically, I'd only known Keesia a short time. It was also true that, in that short time, we'd gotten to be good friends.

Running is a tonic for me. Whatever misgivings I'd had when I started got blown away by a good sweat and the familiar tingling in my limbs that let me know I'd had a good workout.

I don't know why physical excess so often seems to bring me mental peace, but it does. By the time Tycho and I walked our final cool-down half mile, I was feeling more confident, more directional, more like my usual self. I shoved aside some of the construction debris and sluiced the weekend's accumulated grunge and indecision down the drain in the shower, then hit my computer right at the 6:30 a.m. opening bell. I wanted to get some trading in before my apartment turned back into an episode of *This Old House*.

My work this morning was optimistic. I'd purchased large chunks of shares in two companies on Friday afternoon because prices overall tend to be a little softer on Fridays when a lot of players are "profit-taking": turning stocks into cash to show profit for the week, even if it's not actually the result of a profit.

I'd been watching a couple of companies for a while and had felt fairly confident that both were on the upswing. Both had released their previous quarter's earnings after close on Friday and I was sure the market would respond positively to their news.

I was right. One, a financial institution based in New York, had announced not only a healthy profit in the previous quarter, but the prospects of still more healthy happiness in the quarter to come. When the stock's price ticked upward on the first trading day after the announcement, I put in a market sell order, which meant that my three thousand shares would sell at the rate going when my order hit the exchange. My shares sold for forty-seven cents more than I'd paid for them on Friday, which doesn't sound like very much, but it translated into a profit of just over fourteen hundred bucks for sitting on them over the weekend. Still, not a lot of money, but a few trades like that every month is all I need to keep me in rent, gas and rice cakes, not to mention covering me on the months that don't go quite as well.

The other was the troubled electronics company whose seesawing I'd been watching with some apprehension over the past few weeks. Knowing that things could still go either way with them, I put in a sell order at $47.95 per share: two dollars higher than the trading price at the moment. At the same time, I put in a buy order for another five hundred shares at forty-five dollars. And, again, either way I felt covered. If the high sell order executed, I'd have made about fifteen hundred dollars. If the stock went down instead of up, I'd have another five hundred shares at an even better price than I'd paid for the original five hundred. The per-share price on my one thousand shares would then be that much lower.

If you do the math, you can see why I need to keep a fair amount of cash in my trading account at all times: Sure, I was hoping to make two or three thousand dollars on what, in the end, amounted to a few hours' work in research and actual trading time. But, to make that money, I had to pony up almost twenty-three thousand of my own hard-earned bucks. Over $40,000 in total if

I managed to buy an additional five hundred shares today. And since I maintain a fairly balanced portfolio of long-term investments along with a few intended day trades that the market forced into longer holdings, I feel it necessary to never let my available cash drop below two hundred thousand dollars. Though, to be honest, I include my long-term investment stock in that two hundred large: I can always turn blue chips into cash if I need to.

I don't often tell people that. Two hundred thousand dollars seems like a hell of a lot of equity to most people. They don't get it. People think that, with two hundred thousand cash dollars I should own my own house or at least have a better car and some decent jewelry.

The thing is, though, if I *didn't* have that money available, I wouldn't be able to trade. And if I couldn't trade, I wouldn't be able to make more money: money that I can spend. And if I couldn't do that, I'd be forced to do something else for money, like get an actual job. Since there are days when that prospect—of giving up my way of life and working for someone, probably in an office—is a fate worse than taxes, I try to make sure my available capital never dips too low.

With my day's trading packed into a few hours, I got myself ready to go to the funeral early. I'd asked Emily to accompany me for moral support and she'd agreed gladly, but I'd need to stop and pick her up.

I dressed appropriately for a funeral. In an ankle-length black skirt, black boots, a black turtleneck and black leather jacket, I felt that I looked like either a crazy blond priest or a beat poet. As I wound my way down the canyon, I tried not to think about my ultimate destination and why I was going there. I thought instead about sunshine on sand and the play of light on the water. It just seemed easier that way.

The commercial Emily was working on was being shot in Culver City so I swung by to pick her up on my way to the funeral. There are many things I don't mind doing alone; attending this funeral wasn't one of them.

Like me, Emily was decked out in black on black. We looked like rejects from an Amish farm. It's okay these days not to wear black to funerals. To just look somber and respectful. But Emily and I seemed to have tacitly decided that full mourning was in order. However, it was shaping up to be an extremely hot day. Emily, who has lived in Los Angeles quite a bit longer than I have, had taken this into consideration when she chose her ensemble. Though her getup was just as dark and somber as mine, it was a lot more sensible. Emily's dress was linen and light in feel, though dark in look. The day was a scorcher and we were heading inland, so she'd opted to dispense with hose, though with her bare feet stuffed into sober black slides and a wide-brimmed black straw hat on her head, she look respectful enough for even a Kennedy funeral.

I, on the other hand, had dressed in Malibu when the sun had yet to burn the mist off the canyon. It had been chilly in the morning and, still thinking like someone from a different climate, I'd gauged the day by looking out the window. Silly me.

Oh, I looked fine, but a wool skirt and sweater under a leather blazer and finished off with leather boots was just dumb. I realized this now, but it was too late to do anything about it. I soldiered on.

On the drive to the funeral home, we talked about Keesia and speculated gently on who might have killed her. There was the husband, of course, but with all those divorces, why kill Keesia? And, speaking of all those divorces, how about one of the wives?

"That Nadine seemed pretty flaky to me," I offered while negotiating a lane change on the Santa Monica Freeway.

"I guess I spent more time with her than you did," Emily said. "She seemed… I dunno. She seemed really nice."

"You know what they say, Emily."

"No, Madeline. What do they say?"

"About killers. How they can be anyone. You know, 'He was such a nice young man…'"

"'…Just kept to himself a lot,'" she supplied. "I know, but still. I mean, look how she was *dressed.* Who would wear Dior to kill someone?"

"A *killer,*" I said emphatically. Yet I thought about what she'd said. In a weird and completely Emily way, she'd made a good point. "Anyway, if not her, then who?"

"Well, if we're looking at it strictly from the police's point of view—" Emily looked at me carefully before she went on "—then I guess you'd be looking pretty good for it."

"Me?"

"Sure. You found her, didn't you?"

"I didn't kill her, Emily."

"Of course you didn't. And you were wearing *white* for crying out loud." I rolled my eyes and laughed despite myself. "And even if you weren't," she went on, "I know you didn't do it."

"How?"

"No motive, for one. There always has to be a motive," she said knowledgeably.

"I think you've been watching too much television again, Emily."

"Even worse—Romanian television. All those badly dubbed old movies. Ugh! But it's true. I mean, you *liked* Keesia. And she didn't have anything you wanted. Why would you have killed her?"

"All true. *And* the white dress. I guess that's why the police haven't been bothering me." I took my eyes off the road while I shot a glance at Emily. She just shrugged as if to say: You see what I mean, then. I nodded at the gesture. I did see.

We drove the last couple of miles in silence. Emily busy, I guess, with her thoughts. For my part, I focused on something Emily had said. It seemed to me to be important, though I couldn't quite figure out why. How had she put it? She'd said that Keesia didn't have anything I wanted. Was that what it was? If so, all it would take was discovering what Keesia had. And who had wanted it badly enough to kill her.

Keesia had been the wife of one of the most feared and respected men in Hollywood. She had died in a horrible and fairly public way: violently, at a party in her own home. As a result of both of these factors, even though her funeral seemed to me to be taking place an alarmingly short period of time after her death, her send-off had turned into one of the A-list events of the year, just, I thought with some irony, as her parties always had.

Though I'd prepared myself for the possibility, I was still surprised and somewhat shocked to see the open casket at the front of the room assigned to the Livingston funeral. The custom seems so unthinkably barbaric, so completely of another, more primitive time, that I'm startled whenever I encounter it. Also, considering how Keesia had looked the last time I saw her, I couldn't imagine how a casket could be open after the horror that had been visited on her.

Emily and I arrived early so, before the service began, we had time to file past the casket and pay our final respects. Keesia had been miraculously restored by some artful undertaker. She was perfect in a white linen suit, her features arranged into a picture of peaceful slumber. I could have sworn that the hint of a smile played about her lips. Any violence that had been done to her appeared to have been erased. When I looked at her, I found myself wondering if everything I'd seen that night had just been an awful dream. You could even, if you weren't careful, trick yourself into thinking that she was sleeping. That she'd sit up at any moment, run a brush through her hair, and sail out the door to go shopping on Rodeo.

I shook myself mentally. Who was I kidding? Dead was dead. Keesia's shopping days were over. And how surprising was it, anyway, that a Beverly Hills undertaker should be a genius at making even dead people look good?

Emily and I took seats at the back of the room, out of the way of the grief-stricken family. From this position we could see people coming and going. I welcomed the diversion of watching people. It was better than thinking about what it was we were actually doing there.

When Maxi entered, the eyes of the assembled mourners focused on him. I felt my breath catch when I saw the older woman on his arm. She looked so much like Keesia. Or, more accurately, as Keesia would have looked if she'd gotten the thirty or more years still coming to her. Though bent with obvious grief, the woman was beautiful. Stately, elegant and, at present, completely beyond thought. This had to be Keesia's mother.

While Maxi tucked his mother-in-law solicitously into her seat, I noticed the man who had followed Maxi closely into the room, and I gasped again. I knew Emily had noticed as well, because I felt a sharp poke in the ribs.

"Madeline," she whispered. "Do you see him?"

Of course I saw him, though I didn't say that. But how could I miss him? It was Keesia's mystery man: the Hollywood hottie from the garden. Not such a mystery, then.

I found it difficult to keep my mind on the service; my eyes kept going to the tall, attractive man next to Maxi. Who was he? I wondered. And what connection could he have to Maxi and Keesia?

The service was simple, beautiful, nondenominational—as befitted the venue—and completely lost on me. I found it difficult to buy the stuff about the gentle, generous God who had called His servant, Keesia, home to Him. I figured *that* God would have used a more graceful invitation. His servant Keesia had deserved better than to die violently in a bathroom in her own home while several hundred people partied nearby. That wasn't God's will, I thought angrily. It was some kind of sick, cosmic joke.

With that thought I gave myself up to the real purpose of funerals: I cried and released some of the anger I was feeling up to the universe. And even to God if He was listening, which, over the last week or so I'd seriously begun to doubt. Emily, always prepared, passed me a purse pack of Kleenex and I snuffled into a few of them gratefully.

After the service, Emily and I sat and watched while six pallbearers carried Keesia's casket out of the funeral home and to a waiting hearse. I thought two strapping young men with familiar coloring and sharply cut features might be Keesia's brothers, three more were men whose identity I couldn't guess. The last was the man from the garden, which confirmed what I'd thought during the service: he'd had some close tie to Keesia, or still did with her husband.

The hearse led a train of cars the few miles from the funeral home to the graveyard. Emily and I followed in my car, my headlights on appropriately. I wasn't sure I wanted to do this part, but I didn't see how I could get out of it. Again, it seems barbaric: this planting into the earth of mortal remains, which wouldn't be so bad if the way they were planted didn't preclude those remains ever actually being rejoined with the earth. If anybody ever asks, I want to be cremated. But I'm not making a big stink about it: I have a feeling I'm not going to care, either way.

Every part of a funeral is for the living, no matter how we may kid ourselves. A proper send-off: remember them well, so we can go on with our lives guilt-free and knowing we did the right thing. It all just works so much better on the East Coast, I've discovered. In the East there's at least a chance that the weather will cooperate and you'll have a somber, overcast day. With luck, even a light drizzle or a gentle rain. Weather to suit your mood.

We were inland and in the graveyard, as we prepared to pay our last respects to Keesia Livingston. It felt like it was over one hundred degrees in the shade, the sun overbearingly cheerful in a pale blue sky. I was soon regretting what I'd thought was appropriate dress. Even though I'd left my leather jacket in the car, my skirt was soon sticking to my legs like a sodden rag. My feet were screaming for air from inside my boots and I wished I'd thought to be more creative than a black sweater: I could feel rivulets of sweaty water running between my breasts. It all made me wish I was Catholic so I could have worn my perspiration like a shiny, thorny crown. Instead I was just miserable.

I tried to pay attention to the last part of the service—I really did—but I kept focusing on my own misery. And though I heard something that sounded very like "Yea, though I walk through the shadow of the Valley of Death," I couldn't make myself feel the loss and regret for Keesia that I should have in that moment. That I *wanted* to feel. I thought instead about shadows and valleys and all of that coolness.

After the service, Maxi and the woman I'd taken to be Keesia's mother stood to one side and people filed past them, paying respects. The man from the garden stood slightly behind and between them, as though providing some type of invisible support.

"My deepest condolences, Mr. Livingston," I said as we filed past, wondering while I did so if he would remember who I was. He did.

"Good of you to come, Ms. Carter. This is Claret DuBois, Keesia's mother." Then directing himself to Mrs. DuBois, he added, "Ms. Carter was a friend of Keesia's, Claret. She was teaching her about the stock market."

"I'm pleased to meet you, Ms. Carter." Claret DuBois's voice was like her daughter's had been: honey on silk. And up close she wasn't as old as I'd taken her to be. Grief and loss can do that. Probably around sixty—close to Maxi's age—and reedlike, as her daughter had been. "Keesia mentioned you to me. It's Madeline, isn't it?"

"Yes, ma'am, Madeline." I found myself close to tears again: Keesia's mother confirming the friendship I'd lost almost before I knew I had it. "This is my friend Emily Wright." Emily shook hands all around. "She was at the party with me…the night…" I shut up, before I entrenched myself too firmly. It was okay, though: both Claret and Maxi responded with sympathetic nods, like people for whom sympathy has gotten to be a second language.

I knew that our brief audience was up, that I should move on, but the man from the garden, still at Maxi's flank, hadn't said a word. His position there, and his continued silence, was a clear sign: he was no one of importance. He was an employee. A lackey. Intended to be put into position and then forgotten. I ignored the etiquette that said, given his bearing and where he'd placed himself, that he was not to be noticed. I put my hand out.

"Madeline Carter," I said, meeting his gaze. If he felt uncomfortable, he didn't show it, and his grip, when his hand met mine, was firm and cool.

"Ah, sorry, Ms. Carter," Maxi said instantly, "this is Lark St. George. My personal assistant. Lark, this is Madeline Carter and, um, Emily…"

"Wright," I supplied. "Emily Wright. Nice to have met you all. My condolences again, Mrs. DuBois, Mr. Livingston."

Emily couldn't contain herself until we got back to the car. "You did that on purpose, didn't you?" she said once we'd traversed the little hill that shielded the parking lot from the graveyard.

"What?" I asked, my mind far away.

"The guy." I must have looked at her questioningly, because she restated, "The *guy*, Madeline. His personal assistant? He looked pretty personal that night, didn't he?"

I was about to agree when I heard my name and turned to see a man half jogging toward me. He didn't look too happy, with me or with the world in general, I couldn't be sure.

"Hello, Detective Brown. This is Emily Wright," I said. Emily looked mystified but held out her hand to be shaken. "Did you get my message?" I asked. "You didn't return my call."

He ignored the gentle barb, if he noticed it at all. "I could see you looked quite uncomfortable back there, Ms. Carter."

It wasn't a question, so I didn't bother formulating an answer. "At the funeral? I didn't see you there, or I would have said hello."

"Ah… Okay. Well." He looked at Emily, then back to me. "Can I have a word with you please, Ms. Carter?" I shrugged. Why not? I gave Emily the keys to my car so she could run the air-conditioning.

"Sure," I answered. "As long as we can talk in the shade." I led him to a couple of trees that provided said shade but little relief on a day without wind.

"So… Okay, I said, you looked pretty uncomfortable back there." His voice said he was telling me something and I was missing it.

"I'm sorry, Detective Brown. I heard you the first time. I just don't get what you're driving at. It was a funeral. Of course I looked uncomfortable." Because wasn't it practically a rule to look uncomfortable at a funeral?

"No, Ms. Carter. You looked *really* uncomfortable. As though it was painful for you to be there."

"Look, if you have something to say, just say it, because I think I must be missing your point. I'm not happy about this, of course. Keesia was my friend. There are a million places I'd rather be."

Detective Brown smirked at me then. He *smirked* as though he knew something that I didn't. All *I* knew was that I was getting irritated as hell. His next words did nothing to alleviate that. "No, Madeline—" he'd dropped the *Ms.* stuff, I noticed "—I didn't say you looked unhappy. I said you looked uncomfortable. As though you could barely contain yourself. What do you suppose *that* was about?"

I looked at him, uncomprehending for a second before light dawned. "You're not serious?" A beat, then, "You're serious? Okay." Road rage was back. No car. "I'll *show* you uncomfortable." Before I'd thought things completely through, I'd grabbed his hand, pulled my sweater aside and made him feel my stomach. It was towel time in there. Really. Like a steam bath. He pulled his hand back as though I'd stung him. Or worse: like I might bite.

"Does *that* feel uncomfortable? And that's nothing…. I'm wearing ridiculous thick, black clothes. And *boots*. I'll probably be two sizes smaller by tomorrow. How's *that* for uncomfortable? Now, you wanna tell me what all this is about?"

There's something to be said for the righteousness of the innocent. I was all *over* that at the moment.

"Okay." He seemed somewhat abashed, but still like a terrier with a toy. "I'll buy that as uncomfortable. But can you tell me where you were between eleven and one today?"

"Today? Sure." I completely could not see where this might be going, but at least I could remember where I'd been. "I was at home in Malibu."

"That whole time?"

"Yes. Longer."

"And you can verify that?"

I thought about it. "I guess. I bought and sold several stocks during that time." I honestly didn't know if that would verify my location well enough for him. Truly, the trades could have been executed from anywhere, but it seemed to placate him.

"Now," I said, "are you going to tell me what this is about?"

He seemed to back off his aggressive stance a bit. I'd watched enough television to know that this might not be real, it might be a trick. But it didn't matter, because I hadn't done anything and I could prove it if I had to. That righteousness of the innocent, again.

"Someone was killed today..." he started. Hesitated. I pounced on him.

"Someone gets killed every day. Are you going to tell me who it is, or am I going to make you touch my stomach again?" It was a lame attempt at levity, but it was also effective. He backed up a couple of paces.

"Okay. I might as well tell you, because it'll sure as hell be on the news tonight." He sighed and looked as if he wasn't too happy about this last, or any of it, for that matter. He shifted his weight from one leg to the other. "Bronwyn Barnes Livingston was pushed off an overpass onto the Santa Monica Freeway at around noon today."

I flashed on the gorgeous redhead Keesia had been arguing with at the party. "Someone pointed her out to me. That night at the Livingstons'. But I didn't know her. I never even met her." I really wanted to ask what any of it had to do with me, but I had the feeling we'd get to it.

"You say you never met her?"

I nodded my head.

Detective Brown didn't look even slightly convinced. "She died on impact," he said, looking straight into my eyes. Watching, I felt. Detecting. It made me feel as though I were guilty of something, the same feeling I get every time I go through a metal detector at an airport. Like the metal detector will scan me and start screaming and suddenly Security would have me down on the ground and—inexplicably—find two handguns and a switchblade when I own no weapon more dangerous than a curling iron and I'm not even sure *that* works. It's almost like the high school dream when you can't find your locker. And you're naked. Except, with the airport-security one, you're never asleep. This was like that.

"As I said, it was off an overpass," Brown was saying. "And a truck…"

"Omigawd, I don't think I even want to know." I had another thought. "But you said she was pushed. How do you know she didn't jump?"

"No, she didn't jump. We've got a witness. Says she saw someone push her. Said it looked like a tall, blond woman."

A woman? Tall and blond? A light dawned. I could feel myself pale, my anger drain away, replaced by something fluttery in the seat of my stomach. "That's why you were asking all that stuff." It wasn't a question. "You thought it might be me."

He didn't look embarrassed or caught out. "Yeah,

well." He shrugged, pointed a lazy finger at my hair, the length of my legs. "You're a tall, blond woman."

I looked at him evenly. Calmly. "I didn't have reason to kill her. I didn't even know her. And there are a lot of tall, blond women in West L.A. We're practically a sub-species out here. You have to have a better reason than that." I thought for a second, remembering what Emily and I had talked about in the car, then added, "Anyway, I didn't have a motive to kill anyone."

"Well, you've got me there." He smiled, though it didn't touch his eyes. "For the moment. But you *are* a tall, blond woman." He slid his eyes over my stomach insinuatingly and I was instantly sorry for the road-rage-induced episode. "And you have a connection with the Livingston family."

"Not the 'Livingston family,' Detective Brown. With Keesia Livingston. Period. Look, if you're out of questions, I'd just as soon get out of this heat."

"No. No more questions. For now. But, like I said before…" He winked. I could have slapped him for it, but he *winked*. "Don't leave town."

Emily had the air-conditioning running in my car. When I slid behind the wheel it felt so deliciously cool I felt the urge to cry. Though maybe relief from the heat wasn't the only thing making tears threaten.

"Did I see that cop—uh—cop a feel?" Emily was fairly bubbling over with it.

"Don't go there," I muttered.

Emily is a goddess mood sensor. Really. She picks vibrations up off of strangers sometimes. Clearly, she can grab a vibe off a friend most of the time. She didn't fail me now.

"Whoa, Madeline. What happened? What did he say?"

I thought about manufacturing a lie: I really didn't know if I could face thinking about it anymore at that moment. But it was *Emily*. I might as well save my breath. Her antennae are as sharp as Atom Ant's.

I gave her the whole deal. At least, as much as I could remember. When I had finished, she just looked at me for a minute, digesting.

"He said Bronwyn Barnes Livingston was dead." It wasn't a question. I nodded anyway. "And you're, like, what? A suspect?" I nodded again. Then shrugged my shoulders. Was I? "I guess. Or, at least I'm a shot in the dark."

"That's too bizarre," she said thoughtfully. "Actually, the whole thing is too bizarre."

"*Way* too," I agreed.

"Something's bothering me about this, though."

"Everything is bothering me about this," I replied quickly.

"No, Madeline. I mean it." Her forehead was scrunched in a way that meant she was thinking hard, but that would not bode well for her skin when she was in her forties. "It's sort of like déjà vu," she finished lamely.

"All over again?"

She laughed dutifully at my weak joke but still looked bugged. "I dunno. If it comes to me, I'll tell you."

"Okay," I said as I pulled out of the parking lot, "I'll hold you to that," forgetting the words the moment I'd spoken them.

Eleven

A few days passed without incident. Gus was busy with my floors as well as the small things that still needed finishing and he was busy with other clients. The full crew wasn't needed at my house and Gus told me on the telephone that he'd come by later in the week to do the finishing work himself.

I heard nothing more from Detective Brown, and the place in my life where Keesia had been receded to a dull throb.

It was hot. Hotter than the season demanded, and Tycho and I got up for our run through the hills earlier in the morning than usual in order to avoid the heat of the day.

Wednesday was particularly hot. The ocean-view canyons like Los Flores tend not to get as hot as other parts of the Los Angeles area, but a complete lack of any type of air movement had us sweltering in no time. I kept trying to work—I *really* did—but I kept thinking about Tyler's pool. Electronics firm up...

and the water would feel so cool today...

…financial company down.

it would cool off my toes and my knees and my nose.

In short, I spent the day in personal and professional turmoil, and when the phone rang, I answered automatically.

"Madeline Carter," I said.

"Ms. Carter, this is Maxi Livingston." I was so surprised I didn't say anything.

"You were helping my late wife with her online trading," Maxi said without much preamble, and as though we hadn't seen each other a few days before.

"That's right," I agreed.

"We're putting her affairs in order," Maxi said, cautiously, I thought. "And the matter of the online trading account is not settled."

"Not settled," I repeated. I didn't understand what he was saying. Nor did I understand why he was saying it *to me.*

"Right. That is, her computer needs to be accessed. No one seems to be able to get past the encryption."

"Encryption?"

"Is there an echo in here?" Maxi shouted. I could visualize his jelly-doughnut face screwed into a noisy grimace.

"I can't help it if you're not making yourself clear," I shouted back. I used to yell on the telephone for a living. No one is better at it than me. And I know how to deal with it. I had to deal with *traders* on a daily basis.

I heard a rustling sigh that told me pretty clearly Maxi was trying to calm himself down. Whatever he wanted from me, he wanted it pretty badly. Maxi Livingston was a man who usually got what he wanted when he shouted. He wasn't used to having to try a different tack.

Another calming breath, then, "What part of *encryption* did you not understand?" Coming from someone else, the words would have sounded uncivil. With Maxi, I knew it was as good as I was going to get.

"That there was any. It's not usual. And I don't remember there being any on Keesia's computer."

A beat, and then, "It's possible I'm not being, as you said, perfectly clear." He definitely wanted something. "This has been a time of great grief for me—" yet grief wasn't what I thought I was hearing "—and I'm not that fluent with computers." He was being notably polite. I thought about the effort it must be costing him. Maxi Livingston wasn't known for polite. From what I'd heard, it was debatable that he was even wired for it, so I wondered why he was exerting that effort now.

"Would it be possible for you to visit Larkin House, Ms. Carter?" he continued. "Have a look at Keesia's computer and see if you can't spot whatever it is my boys might have missed?"

I considered. "If your people can't get in, I doubt I'll be able to. My expertise is in the stock market, not high tech. I'm a broker, not a computer geek."

"Still, Ms. Carter, I'd appreciate it if you'd try." There was a tightness in his voice. A control. "For Keesia's sake. And for Tyler's."

Now it was my turn to sigh. Either way—or both— it was a low blow. Maxi knew it because he didn't wait for me to fill the space after his subtle threat with words. "Let's say Larkin House at two tomorrow?" was all he said before he hung up.

The following morning it felt good to start my day in what had become, for me, the normal way. At

5:00 a.m., when I pulled on my cross trainers after I'd donned my sweats, Tycho's tail started thumping against the floor. He knew that particular sequence meant we were going for a run.

Ask three runners why they run and you'll get three different answers. From me, you'd get three different answers if you asked on three different days. And I'd mean it, too. On one day I'd tell you that running is the ultimate tool for good health. Seriously: I can't log a five-mile run without feeling like I've touched bases with every part of my body. Checked in and said: Are you awake and in good form? And, believe me, if I'm not, my body is not shy about letting me know.

On another day I'd tell you that running keeps me in touch with my environment and the universe. I'd mean that, too. But on this day I ran because I felt as though a snake was loose in my brain. There had been murders near me, I thought I might be in love, a producer wanted me to look at his late wife's computer. I just seemed to have more questions than available answers and I didn't know what to do about it. And so I ran.

I got home, made coffee, showered, had a bowl of cereal, then spent a little while on my computer and planning my day. Around eight-thirty I heard a knock on my door. I wasn't surprised when I opened it. Maybe I should have been, but I wasn't. It was Gus.

"Good morning, Ms. Carter," he smiled. "I'd like to consult with you on something."

"Please come in," I said, just as formally.

I was in his arms before the door had properly closed. "You taste so good," he said as he kissed me. "I've missed you." Then he pulled away just far enough to look into my eyes very seriously. "Do you feel this, too, Madeline?"

I nodded at him, suddenly shy. Something was growing in me. Something was growing in me so quickly I could barely contain it.

"I'm glad," he breathed to the top of my head. "It would be terrible to feel this by yourself."

Gus and a small crew were planning on putting the finishing touches on my place on this day. To celebrate the completion—and because we felt like it—the two of us made plans to have dinner. Gus had proposed an evening meal in Santa Monica again and I had a pretty good idea I wouldn't be driving home that night.

I had several hours and a lot of miles to cover before that.

Since construction had been going on for a few weeks, I'd had time to rethink my working arrangements. Some days the noise and dust didn't bother me. On others, I found it unbearable. On those days I'd taken to spending my working hours at an Internet café on the Third Street Promenade in Santa Monica.

I love the Promenade. The brainchild of some forward-thinking civic planner in the 1950s or '60s, it is perhaps three square blocks of downtown Santa Monica that are closed to traffic. I've been told that there was a time between then and now—sometime in the late 1970s and early '80s—when the Promenade would have been that civic planner's greatest embarrassment. Drug dealers and various flavors of ne'er-do-wells claimed the three blocks of turf, making it a place that most people didn't venture into, even in daylight. Now it's transformed again. Smart shops and eateries line the street, kiosks and public sculpture create a boulevard, and all sorts of people—most of them smiling because they're going somewhere fun—line the street every day.

My away-from-home workplace of choice was in the center block. Kordor was a long, narrow storefront on the Promenade. The tables were rough and homemade, amoeba-shaped tabletops with garage-sale chairs. Each table was meant to fit ten or twelve people. As a result, when you sat at a table on a busy evening, it was mostly with a bunch of people you didn't know, which was cool because everyone ignored one another, anyway.

At night there was generally live music. Not the kind that was booked in advance, but the kind that showed up. Some guy with bongos, some chick with a guitar— casual, like someone's living room. People would nurse their espressos and eat muffins and scones and carrot cake and clap and laugh and maybe sing along. Wonderful for NYC expatriates, like me. A place of belonging without involvement. My kind of place.

During the day, however, Kordor's tables were generally covered with laptops as well as coffee cups. And, judging by the non-suit types and generally artsy atmosphere, it's a good guess that more than a couple of novels and master's theses had been written there.

A half-dozen rental computers lined Kordor's back wall. None of them was less than three years out of date, and a couple had keyboards so sticky I suspected the occasional cup of coffee had been poured down there. But Kordor's Internet connection was fast and daytime business always light, and the café was open 24/7, making it the perfect location for my purpose.

I spent a few hours at Kordor, working, bolstering myself for my afternoon encounter with several well-made lattes. Then I headed up to Beverly Hills.

When I arrived at Larkin House at two o'clock, as requested, the uniformed maid who answered the door told me that Mr. Livingston sent his apologies, but he'd been detained downtown at his office and would I care to wait in the lounge? I decided that I didn't. It was really too nice a day to be stuck in the dark, dreary old house where it seemed likely that the ghost of Keesia might be around any corner. I'd never before had the chance to walk around the gardens which, from a distance, looked world-class. I told the maid that would be my preference. She sniffed her displeasure but did nothing to stop me when I headed toward the double hedge that flanked a long fountain in the style of royal gardens I'd seen in Europe.

The gardens were vast and lovely, with what seemed like acre upon acre of mature and formally arranged displays of vegetation. I tried again not to think about the cost of keeping such a huge garden viable in the heat of Southern California, though, unsurprisingly, it's kind of my business to keep my eye on everything's bottom line. And it's just the way I'm wired.

The overall effect of the garden, as viewed from the house, was one of well-tended opulence. This closer look, however, indicated that parts of the garden were in worse repair than I'd imagined when I'd seen it all from a distance. For instance, I came upon what I'd at first taken to be a grove of trees growing unusually closely together and realized, on closer inspection, that I was looking at something very like a hedge maze. However it was so overgrown that even my untrained eye could see the blur where sharp edges should be.

I walked around the man-made forest, trying to determine whether my hedge-maze assessment was correct and, if so, whether I could find any openings, when a voice surprised me.

"It's pretty amazing, isn't it?"

The speaker was a woman likely past sixty but with the air and energy of someone much younger. Her voice held traces of England, though softened by years away: she didn't sound as though she'd just gotten off the boat. She was tall and slender, the skin on her hands and face bearing testament to a lifetime spent in the sun. Her long hair was silver shot through with gold and caught up in the sort of haphazard arrangement I favor myself: quick and dirty. She looked as if she woke up and got going in too much of a hurry to worry overly much about her coif. She wore dark glasses, but her voice was kind, friendly. And there was a proprietary air about her: she looked like she belonged here.

"It *is* amazing, I agree. I was just trying to see if this was some sort of hedge maze."

"Good eye," she said approvingly. "It is. Or, rather, it was." She came toward me with an extended hand, "Myra Haskins," she said, shaking my hand, then indicating the fabulous garden all around her. "I'm a landscape designer."

"Wonderful work," I complimented her as I introduced myself.

"Well, that's the funny thing about a job like this," she laughed. "It *is* wonderful work, but it's mostly not mine.

"What do you mean?"

"Well, the gardens here, like the house, are about sixty years old. The gardens were designed by Cathryn S. Frye, one of the best-known British landscape architects of her time. Lolita Larkin was famously wealthy and she had Mrs. Frye brought in to design this little bit of earth."

"I suspected something like that," I told Myra, nodding. "It has a very British look and feel."

"It does, doesn't it?" I didn't miss the pride in her voice. "The gardens had fallen into disrepair when Mr. Livingston hired me some years ago. I've been trying to find the drawings for the original garden, though no luck yet. They probably don't exist anymore. But, for a lot of it, it's possible to see what was intended."

"And so you guess? Based on what's left?"

"Pretty much. An educated guess, but still, you're right—it's guessing. This hedge maze, for instance. It isn't really a hedge maze at all. The maze part leads to what I understand is a garden accessed through a specially made door that has a lock."

"A secret garden?" I must have sounded enchanted, because Myra laughed.

"Exactly. A secret it shall remain, as well. We're kept so busy with other parts of the garden you'd almost think we were being prevented from opening closed doors!" Her face fell then, as though she'd remembered something unpleasant. I thought I understood.

"The garden was one of Keesia's projects?"

Myra nodded. "I still can't believe it. She had so much life. Did you know her?"

"Yes," I said resolutely. "We were friends." And I regretted that the first time I'd had cause to say this aloud, she was already dead.

"Well, you'll understand, then. About her passions. She was so determined that we work together to make this place beautiful."

"But you said that Maxi hired you."

"He did," she said, nodding. "Before they were married. But it was really Keesia who got the steam going to do it up right, the way it was. Your guess is as good as mine about whether Livingston will still want the restoration work done. I'd hate to leave it, but with Keesia gone, he might go back to wanting it just to look good, not necessarily the way it was. It's just all so sad." She swept a well-muscled arm over the garden that spilled out all around us. "So young and beautiful." She shook her head sadly. For a second I thought she was talking about the garden, then realized that, of course, she meant Keesia. "And for it to be such an echo of how Lolita died. It's odd, really. Don't you think."

I looked at her blankly. "What do you mean?"

"You didn't know?"

I shook my head.

"Lolita Larkin died in the same room they found Keesia. In the conservatory."

This was news to me, though it wasn't correct. "Actually, Keesia was found in the bathroom."

Myra fluttered a hand, as though this were inconsequential. "Yes, of course. But it wasn't a bathroom when Miss Larkin owned the house. Keesia added that herself when she became mistress of Larkin House."

"Was Miss Larkin murdered?"

"No. Suicide. But I understand it was quite dreadful."

"Myra, did you know Bronwyn Barnes Livingston?"

Myra laughed, though it wasn't a happy sound. "Bronwyn! Yes, there was a whisper that they were going to charge her with the murder." This was news to me. Were all the wives suspect? "Isn't that ridiculous? Bronwyn is a mouse. A beautiful mouse, but a mouse nonetheless. I can't think of anything sillier than her killing Keesia. I can't even think of her cutting up vegetables, let alone—"

"Then you hadn't heard?" Myra looked at me, an eyebrow arched. Clearly, in her domain, she expected to be the one breaking news. "Myra, Bronwyn is dead. It looks like murder."

"When?"

"Yesterday. Not long before Keesia's funeral."

"But that's bizarre, isn't it? Can it be coincidence?"

"What do you mean?" I asked.

"Well, it's odd, is it not, that both women were married to the same man? Or had been, as the case may be. And that both died within a few days of each other."

Of course it was odd. Too odd, certainly, to be a coincidence. What else, I wondered, linked the dead women? Other than having shared different eras in a single man's life and having both been once mistress of Larkin House.

Twelve

I could have thought of a hundred places I'd rather be.

Behind the wheel of my car, speeding toward my canyon, the scent of eucalyptus and the sea growing stronger as I got closer to home.

Safe at my own little desk, the ocean whispering to me to leave my work behind and Gus in the kitchen, offering me the promise of future food.

Even back in the garden, with its beauty and its secrets. Really, anyplace but in Keesia's beautiful conservatory, where everything was just the same as it had been…yet completely altered.

There were a hundred places I'd rather be, but I reminded myself why I was here: Maxi Livingston still hadn't agreed to finance Tyler's film. Tyler had told me Maxi was "this" close. And it was probably only the tragedy that had invaded Maxi's life over the last week or so that had prevented him from deciding, one way or the other. On the phone, Maxi had made it clear that my coming would be a point in Tyler's favor. I figured that, at the rate that I was currently racking up Maxi points for Tyler, I'd end up with a new living room and bedroom soon. Maybe a better parking space, as well.

Central to the change in the conservatory today—aside from the absence of Keesia, herself—was the presence of her husband, the newly widowed Maxi who, with the exception of the night of the tragedy, I'd never seen here.

Though his appearance repelled me, Maxi's presence seemed to alter the dimensions of the room itself. When I had visited before there had been pleasant angles and a perfectly drawn balance between light and shadow. Now it felt out of harmony, out of whack.

All of this was perhaps less New Agey than it might sound—what I was experiencing wasn't an illusion. Everything in the conservatory was actually, physically different. Keesia's plants had been rounded up, retrieved from their carefully placed positions and grouped haphazardly together in one corner. Likewise, the comfy sofas with the table between where Keesia and I had shared such pleasant chats had been pushed up to the wall, a protective blanket thrown over them. The computer was still set up on the large desk, but considering the state of the rest of the room, it felt as though this might be a temporary measure: that after I left, the computer would be disassembled, Keesia's office furniture sold or put in storage, all memory of Keesia's domain obliterated from the house she'd loved. I blinked back tears. This wasn't the time or place.

"Tell me," Maxi said as he guided me toward the computer. "What were you and Keesia up to, anyway?"

Up to? I wondered. It seemed an odd way to put it. I decided to couch it all in the simplest terms. The terms I already knew that *he* knew, but perhaps was just looking for confirmation. "I was teaching her the basics of online trading. How to buy and sell, what to look for, that sort of thing."

As I'd suspected, Maxi didn't look surprised by any of this. "And how did she do?"

"What do you mean?"

"In the stock market," Maxi insisted.

"Oh, it was very early days. She'd just begun. I think she'd only bought and sold one or two things."

"Do you know what they were?" he pressed.

I shook my head. "Not at all."

"Or what types of things…?" he prompted.

"No. As I said, she'd only just begun." I thought about it for a moment. "She probably would have told me. She just…just never got the chance."

Maxi sighed as he guided me to the desk, indicating I should take a seat. "So have a poke," he instructed.

"Okay," I agreed. It was, after all, what I'd come for. I resolutely kept my eyes from the bathroom door and my mind from what I'd found there.

"But as I told you on the telephone, Mr. Livingston—"

"Maxi," he insisted, spreading his hands in a pleading gesture. "Everyone calls me Maxi."

"Maxi, of course. As I told you…Maxi…I don't really know that I'll be able to do anything."

"Sure," He seemed much more agreeable today than he had on the telephone. "That's what you said. But thanks for trying."

While we waited for the computer to boot, Maxi paced the room, as though all of this couldn't happen fast enough for him. Was he uncomfortable so close to where they'd found her? Or just anxious to get on to whatever busy thing his schedule demanded next? Either way, I wondered at the fact that Maxi was here with me himself, rather than any one of a score of underlings who might have fulfilled this mission for him.

Though he'd told me about it on the telephone, when the encryption screen came up, I was surprised. And it didn't look to me like the cheesy encryption screens one encounters in a computer store, either: where you just reboot the computer to thwart the system, or bypass it completely with a well-placed CD.

"I don't understand this," I told Maxi honestly. "I'm almost positive this wasn't on Keesia's computer the last time I was here."

"Almost?" he said.

"Well—" I thought hard "—I don't remember ever seeing her type in anything to bypass it. Though it's possible she had everything ready to go when I got here. But it just seems—" I struggled for the word "—it seems excessive. Keesia never struck me as the secretive type."

Maxi looked away quickly, out toward the pool. "Me, neither," he said after a while, without looking at me. Then he looked back and shrugged. "But there you go. So—" he waved a hand at the keyboard "—give it a whirl."

I tried a couple of obvious passwords—PASSWORD, KEESIA, MAXI, CLARET even MAD and MADELINE, but none of them yielded results.

I was disappointed but not terribly: one didn't have something like this installed on their computer without reason and, since he'd obviously not been informed, the reason was probably standing right in front of me.

"Sorry, Mr....Maxi," I corrected. "But I warned you I don't know much—anything, really—about encryption. And you said you've had people look at it?"

"Yes. The best. The best we know of. They told my personal assistant it looks like I can't even copy the contents of the hard drive without damage to whatever is on there."

"Well, like I said, I don't really know about encryption, per se. But I *do* know that someone will be able to do that for you. There are a lot of people that would find this a pretty trivial matter. I'm not one of them, but…"

Lark St. George came into the conservatory under full steam. He was nattering something about a project that he'd obviously been sent to get information about. He wore a pale suit that looked as though it might be made of silk.

He pulled himself up when he saw me. "Ms. Carter," he said, looking from me to Maxi as though surprised at my presence. I had the feeling he didn't know why I was there and that he didn't like not knowing. "I hadn't expected to see you again so soon."

"I brought her in to see if she could help with Keesia's computer," Maxi explained.

"I told you I was working on that, Maxi."

Maxi shrugged. "Madeline was working with Keesia. I thought she might have an inside track."

Lark looked at me. "Any luck?" Was I jumping at shadows again? Maybe. But I had the distinct impression that Lark had a stronger interest in my answer than what was strictly necessary.

"Not at all," I replied, oddly relieved I could answer in the negative honestly. "I told Mr.…Maxi on the telephone that I don't really know very much about that end of computers. And I'm afraid I don't have a clue about the encryption."

"I think Ms. Carter and I are done here," Maxi

said. "If you wouldn't mind, Lark—" it was phrased as a request, but I didn't think a negative answer would have been acceptable "—please see Madeline to her car."

"That won't be necessary," I protested, heading for the door, relieved. "I know my way." But there was no sense arguing: Maxi Livingston had given an order. I got the feeling that Lark would just as soon have disobeyed as wear denim.

The carpeted corridors had never felt so long to me, my car so distant. We walked in silence until Lark said unexpectedly, "You and Keesia got to be friends, didn't you? Near the end."

"We did, yes," I said, honestly. "We discovered we had more in common than I would have thought."

We were crossing the immense foyer. No one was in sight. Unexpectedly Lark stopped and faced me, an accusing light in his eyes. "What the hell is that supposed to mean?" he said.

"Mean?" I was taken aback. "What on earth do you think it means? Nothing. We were friends, that's all. We enjoyed each other's company. What did you think I meant?"

He resumed walking, the slope of his shoulders as he walked ahead telling me he'd do anything to recall his words. "Nothing," he said without looking back, trusting I was following. "It didn't mean anything. Forget I said it."

"Forget it?" I trotted to keep up. "This isn't Court TV, you know. You can't just strike a remark." He stopped so quickly I nearly careered into him.

"Where did that come from?" he snapped.

"What?"

"That Court TV crack. Why'd you go there?"

"Jeez, Lark, I dunno. You told me to forget something you said. On television that works, but not in real life."

He looked, if anything, even more mortified by my explanation. "Sorry, Madeline. I'm… I guess I'm sorry. Everything has been so crazy around here lately. I'm a little sensitive."

"You and Keesia were…involved," I ventured.

His eyes swept all around us, seeing, I guess, if the coast was clear before he answered. "She told you that?" he asked. "I guess you did get to be friends. She said she'd never tell anyone." He suddenly looked very tired. "I wish she hadn't done that."

We were at the port cochere and my car, miraculously, was already waiting for me. "Why? Why do you wish she hadn't done that?"

But Lark, having fulfilled his master's orders—and then some was already beating a hasty retreat.

I realized, as I pulled out of the impressive driveway, that this visit to Larkin House had given me way too much information. I hadn't been looking for anything, but I seemed to have stumbled over quite a bit.

I thought about Myra and the secret garden and Lark, who my shot in the dark had distressed so visibly. And, of course, I thought about Maxi, who had—mysteriously and effectively—been locked out of his wife's computer.

I found the initial issue of the computer encryption to be the most perplexing. I hadn't known Keesia well, but the things I did know about her I felt I knew thoroughly. She was smart and savvy, but she was no kind of computer whiz. I didn't think it would have occurred to her to put encryption on her computer. And, as I'd told Maxi, she hadn't struck me as the secretive type. Why would she even have cared if Maxi did poke around in her stuff? She knew he was extremely busy. What would she have thought she had that was worth going to fairly rigorous lengths to protect from prying eyes? Surely not her trading account. With a measly $25,000 in there, what would there have been for Maxi to see? Yet that was the reason Maxi had given for wanting me to come over and look at his late wife's computer: he'd wanted to settle the matter of his wife's trading account. That's what he'd told me.

Yet anyone who's spent even five seconds with an online trading account knows that the software that propels most online brokerages isn't machine dependent. That is, it can be accessed from any Internet-connected computer as long as you have the right passwords and account information.

I'd helped Keesia set up her account, so I knew this to be true in her case. For security and for other reasons to do with expediency, everything to do with the account lives on a distant server and is accessed entirely through a Web browser.

And I knew this, of course, while I poked at Keesia's computer in a desultory fashion under Maxi's eyes. I knew it and I didn't say anything and I wasn't even sure why. I rationalized around the whole issue effortlessly. After all, Maxi Livingston was a bigshot tycoon-type with flotillas of sycophants and consultants to do his bidding. If he didn't know about online trading, someone in his organization was sure to. Someone would point it out. Me? I'd been Keesia's consultant. I'd been Keesia's friend. If there'd been something on her computer she didn't want Maxi to get at, I wasn't going to be the one to lead him there. Anyway, it was entirely possible that the encryption was protecting something that had nothing to do with Keesia's stock market activity. Love notes, maybe, though I wouldn't have thought so before my run-in with Lark at Maxi's estate.

And, there again, who would I be to lead Maxi where Keesia hadn't wanted him? Even if I'd had the technology to slip past the encryption, which I didn't. It was the first time in my memory that I was actually happy not to possess information.

I pointed my car toward Malibu and home when I left Larkin House, but before very long—and even before I really knew I was doing it or why—I found myself heading to Santa Monica, back to Kordor for a second time that day.

Sometimes I'm so sneaky I surprise myself. Consciously, I didn't think about wanting to access Keesia's trading account to see what—if anything—the fuss was all about. Or the fact that the way the Internet works is mysterious enough to me that I'm never totally comfortable doing completely secret-y things from my own computer.

Even though I'd been going to Kordor a lot lately, the staff was indifferent enough that I would have bet no one remembered me from day to day. And that was a good thing because, right now, I wanted what I was about to do to be untraceable. Kordor also makes a very decent latte, so it was the only place to go for this particular piece of business.

To be totally honest, I'm not sure why I felt the need to be so cautious with Keesia's stuff. I mean, Keesia was dead. I was pretty confident it was not legally okay for me to go snooping through her account. But morally? That's a whole other deal. Morally I was sure Keesia would have wanted me to not let go too easily. Did I have a hunch something was rotten in Denmark? Maybe. More than that, I was curious. And my instincts were telling me that nothing about this whole deal was as it should be. And my instincts seldom steer me wrong.

I was lucky: when I got there, Kordor's only customers were a couple of scraggly young guys who looked hell-bent on writing the great American novel on beat-up laptops as far away from each other as the café's modest boundaries would allow. There was no one else in the place, aside from two bored-looking baristas. After I got my coffee I chose the Internet terminal farthest from these few people and logged on.

Once on the Redi-Trade.com home page, I hesitated. It was entirely possible Keesia had changed her passwords since we'd set up her account. I would have, but somehow I doubted she had.

My hesitation was filled with second thoughts and rationalizations. Did I really want to find out about Keesia's trading account? What business was this of mine, anyway? And so what if no one was ever able to access her account? It wasn't like Maxi needed the twenty-five large Keesia had been playing with—that probably wouldn't have covered the smoked salmon and shrimp bill at his party. If no one ever touched Keesia's account, it wouldn't hurt anyone.

So I hesitated. Looked at the curving red-and-yellow shapes that made up Redi-Trade's logo and log-in screen. I told myself I was still debating whether or not I should do it as I moved the mouse over the log-in box. As I typed in her user name, as I hesitated over typing in her password, did it anyway, then hit the enter key.

I was as familiar with the options on Redi-Trade as

I was with my own apartment: I spent a lot of time on this site, myself. The opening screen offered options to go to pages to check the account, change passwords and user information, see the account's trading history, get real-time quotes on individual stocks, and see the portfolio attached to the account. I clicked on the first button, then, after the page loaded, sat looking at it for a full minute while I waited for what I was seeing to sink all the way in.

What caused me confusion, initially, was simply a matter of zeros. I'd expected to see an account total of $25,000, give or take a few thousand, depending on how Keesia's earliest trades had gone. What I saw was very different. There was more than a million dollars in Keesia's trading account, not in cash on hand but in the current value of the securities she'd purchased.

Keesia had told me she was going to play with $25,000, but it was possible she'd had more money available to her and just hadn't wanted to say. This didn't seem like Keesia, though I'd only known her a short time. I realized then that it was possible I hadn't known Keesia as well as I thought I had.

More than a million dollars. The sum made no sense to me: it was quite beyond anything Keesia had even hinted at. Opening the account history page left me further in the dark. It showed that Keesia had opened her trading account with the $25,000 we'd discussed. I checked my Filofax and, sure enough, on roughly the day we'd decided she was ready to begin trading on her own, she'd bought two hundred shares of a cosmetic company at $22.47 per share. I felt a small rush of pride when I noted she'd sold the shares three days later at $23.95. Of course, that would have meant her total gross profit—before brokerage fees and taxes—on the trade was just under three hundred bucks. But it wasn't the amount that mattered so much: it would have been the first completed trade she'd managed entirely on her own. And she'd made money, not lost it. I checked the stock price now. The cosmetics company had closed the day at $21.79, the bottom of a downward trend since the little jump when Keesia had sold. Keesia's instincts about the company—whatever her instincts had been— had been right. It made me sad to think that, had she lived to see it, she would have been pleased.

I scanned down the columns of figures. Keesia had been busy before she died. She had, as she'd indicated to me, been serious about the stock market. There was a half score of other little trades. Ten thousand shares of a down-on-their-luck media company at fifteen cents per share. A hundred shares of a high-flying media company at forty-five dollars per share. Lots of trades in the first two weeks, but all little trades: a few hundred here, a few thousand there. Trades that made me think she had been testing the waters, building her confidence with amounts she felt she could afford to lose, all pretty much according to the plan we'd laid out together.

Then, after buys and sells in publishing companies, clothing manufacturers and pharmaceutical companies debuting revolutionary methods of teeth whitening— none of them amounting to more than a few thousand in total dollars and a few hundred in profit or loss— several new deposits showed up in Keesia's account totaling just under a million dollars. I blinked at the amount. It was so far beyond anything she and I had discussed. Over the three days following the logging of the last deposit, Keesia purchased a total of 450,000 shares in a company I'd never heard of—one that traded as NWZ. She'd bought them in fairly small batches in a very regular way. On the first day she'd bought about 50,000 shares for an average of seventy-five cents each, but each purchase had been a few pennies higher.

On day two, she'd bought a hundred thousand shares in total, though this time the average was higher still: $1.50 per share. On day three, she really went on a buying spree, snatching up three hundred thousand shares at prices ranging from two to three dollars.

I checked the stock. At the moment, it was trading around two-and-a-half dollars per share, though, for the half year prior to this, it hadn't traded at over a dollar. If someone had told Keesia she was getting a bargain, they'd given her a bum steer.

I sat there for a bit, letting all of this sink in. Willing the information I'd gleaned to align itself in a way that made sense. It didn't. There were things I'd learned today—too many—that were giving me a picture of Keesia I didn't want to see. A million dollars she hadn't told me about had turned up in her trading account. Where had it come from? Had she somehow taken it from her husband without his knowledge? If you added that up to the fact that—at least according to Lark St. George—Maxi's personal assistant had been her lover, a different picture of Keesia Livingston began to emerge. I wasn't quite sure if it all had meaning but, whatever else it added up to, it *did* give Maxi something I didn't have: motive to kill Keesia Livingston.

Thirteen

These were the things I pushed around inside my head as I packed up my gear and headed back to my car, barely seeing the dreadlocked barista or even the angry-looking meter maid preparing to write a ticket as I got to my car.

As I drove, I kept trying to put it all out of my mind, thinking that nothing could possibly come of any of this. Even if I had suspicions, it wasn't as if I could take anything I found in Keesia's trading account to the police. Clearly, I had been an electronic trespasser. The thought didn't make me as uncomfortable as it should have.

I could see the light on my answering machine flickering madly as soon as I opened my front door. The first message was from Gus, who apologized for not being at my place with his crew to do the finishing work, and apologized some more for having to take a rain check on the dinner we'd planned for that evening.

"I know it'll sound silly," he'd told my tape. And I listened raptly, enjoying the echoey timbre of his voice, "but a media-room job I've had a crew on this week is turning into a status-one priority, likely to turn into a first-rate catastrophe if I don't drag the whole crew down there today to do some damage control. Yes, m'dear, I can imagine your delightful smirk at the thought of a media room demanding my emergency ministrations. But, hey, this is what I do for a living, as mirthful as I know you'll find it. I'll call you later. Bye."

I liked hearing the sound of his voice so much that I would have rewound his pleasantly long message and listened to it again if there hadn't been another message waiting for me.

The second message was brief. "Madeline, it's Jilly." Her voice sounded high and excited. "Listen, sweetie, call me the instant you get this, all right? I simply must talk to you."

She'd left a cell and an office number. I checked my watch: it was 5:00 p.m. Eight o'clock New York time. No way I'd get her at her office. I tried it, anyway. She answered on the first ring. Which reminded me about something I'd already forgotten about New Yorkers: they never know when to leave the office.

"Madeline," she said when she heard my voice. "I'm so glad you called me! Marshall is beside himself about the photos you sent."

"Beside himself?" What did that mean?

"Completely. It turns out that 'hunk of rock,' as you described it, is at least nine hundred years old."

"Wow." I was surprised but not floored. I mean, who ever knows how old a rock is?

"But, more important, he seems quite certain that the piece is part of a collection the Brits have been look-ing for for more than half a century."

"That's not good, is it?"

"Well, maybe yes, maybe no. It depends on the provenance of the piece, you understand? If you have good documentation for it, can prove how much you bought it for, et cetera. You know the drill—you've bought impressionists."

I was quiet for a moment while I thought. Then, "Jilly, that's just it. It's safe to say that there is *no* provenance for this piece. As far as I know. And it was given to me as a gift."

"Well, can you ask the giver where they got it? And do they have papers for it?"

"No. Not at all. The person who gave it to me is dead. She died less than a week later."

"Oh, well. That still might be all right." I told myself Jilly wasn't being cold, just assessing things from her angle. Still, it hurt to hear Keesia dismissed so easily. "But it will make a sale more difficult. If the Brits' claim is a good one, and if they have documentation, they might be able to make a good case for it being restored to their government."

"Are you saying that my little rock is some kind of lost artifact?"

"Yes, yes, that's it precisely, Madeline." She seemed pleased that I'd easily grasped what she was saying. "But, as I said, that doesn't necessarily preclude a sale. These things can be very difficult to prove."

"But I don't want to sell it, Jilly. I'm just trying to find out what it is."

"Oh…well, then." Jilly didn't try to mask her disappointment. Sales were what she lived for, after all. "I'm sure Marshall will be happy to talk to you about it. He's sent me a bit of a valuation. I can fax it to you, if you like. I'll include his contact info, in case you want to get in touch with him directly."

The fax came buzzing through my machine about forty-five seconds after Jilly had hung up—she's nothing if not efficient—and Marshall's valuation astonished me. The rock wasn't a rock at all. It was, it said in his note, a keystone, clearly Celtic and dating from about 1100 A.D. I could barely think about years with numbers so low.

"The item in question," read his note, "seems sure to have been part of a collection from Melton Court, an estate held by the British Trust since 1955. However, the keystone—if it is indeed the same stone—had disappeared from Melton Court some years previous, along with the sister stones and the door they opened. A public sale of this object would prove difficult, considering the British government's interest in the return of stolen artifacts. However, if the item's provenance could be verified, the keystone in question could be expected to bring between four and five hundred thousand dollars at auction."

I'd done enough buying and selling at auction to know that this valuation made it official: with this note, Bartleby's had placed a half-million dollar estimate on Keesia's gift. And, since auction-house estimates tend to be conservative, it was fairly safe to say that "the keystone" was something very like priceless.

I walked over to my desk and picked the object up from where it had been keeping some very important papers from fluttering in any breeze that might find its way into my apartment. I turned the rock over in my hand, examined it closely, looking, I guess, for whatever it was I might have missed on earlier examination.

There was nothing. To me it still looked like a rock. I wondered if, though Keesia probably had no idea of its value, she'd known what it was. A key. And if she'd known what door it opened. After I'd given it some thought, I realized that was something I might already know.

After I'd spoken with Jilly and then carefully perused what she'd sent from her man Marshall, I put the fax carefully on my desk and just stood in the center of the room for a moment, willing the world to make sense.

My heart was pounding. I couldn't believe I was thinking what I was thinking, but there it was. And the more I thought about it, the more I was actually aware of the blood coursing through my body. I could feel it the way you can feel a river when you trail your hand in it. You believed in it because you could feel it and knew it was there.

I went into my devastated little kitchen and rummaged around in a box until I turned up a bottle of wine. It was domestic. Something from Napa, yet unremarkable. I rummaged around until I found my corkscrew and pulled open the bottle of wine.

All of this activity was good. Soothing. I could almost believe my blood was going to behave.

My kitchen was in disarray. I was living out of boxes. I'd done pretty well in finding the wine and the corkscrew. I wasn't going to push my luck looking for a wineglass. Instead, I found a small juice glass and filled it halfway up with the passable wine—*vin rouge ordinaire*—in rural French style.

I took a folding chair and my wine out onto my little deck and tried to focus on the gathering sunset. It was going to be spectacular. Wispy clouds were visible and the late-day sun was colorizing them: bright yellow here, pure gold there, indigo, mauve, dull green, rainbow colors touching the edge of the clouds at sunset. It was beautiful.

I left it all for a moment to go back into the house for Jilly's fax. Just directing my thoughts that way caused my heart to start pounding again. *How could you?* suggested one little voice. *How could you not?* said another. Both were right. Neither produced an entirely steady hand or quieted the fluttering of my heart.

And so it went, for a good half hour. A war on the surface, but not really a war. At some level, I'd known what I was going to do all along.

There was a time in my life when I did not act on instinct. Life teaches you better, if you let it. One too many securities unpurchased. Or too many not sold. A course not taken, a road not followed, all of these can be cause for regret.

But following the path, selling the stock—doing the thing my heart was telling me—has never given me reason to look over my shoulder with sadness. Even when things don't turn out as I'd planned—even when things don't turn out *well*—it's better, I've found, to take the advice my instincts give me. For me, life is just too short to do it any other way.

I couldn't try it during the day. I just wasn't completely sure I'd be able to find it in the dark.

I toyed briefly with the idea of taking Emily with me for moral support. Or Gus, for physical *and* moral support. In the end, though, I was glad I knew both of them were busy: Emily on set and Gus rescuing a media room. I wasn't entirely sure I wouldn't have begged one of them to accompany me had I known they were available. And on some level I had to have known that one of these two would try—and perhaps succeed—in talking some sense into me. That was something—the sense talking—I couldn't risk. My instincts were hollering that loudly.

I felt ridiculous as I dressed in dark clothing. Like I was playing dress-up. Like I was pretending to be a cat burglar. Like I aspired to be Lara Croft or Indiana Jones. It didn't matter, though. There's a reason that cat burglars have the reputation for such catholic tastes in fashion: if you don't want to be seen, wear black.

It was a warm night, so I chose black jeans, a black stretch knit top, black cross trainers and, as a final, finishing touch, a black watch cap to hide my bright hair. I hadn't worn the watch cap since I'd left New York and then it'd only seen the outside of my closet on the coldest of my winter runs. I dropped a bottle of water, a small flashlight—a gift from my brother-in-law who thought no one should be without one—and Keesia's stone into my messenger bag along with a pair of dark gloves. I tucked a couple of Tycho's dog biscuits into the bag, as well. I'd never seen guard dogs patrolling at Larkin House, nor seen any advertised, but the biscuits made me feel a little better. Just in case.

As an afterthought, I pulled off the watch cap and stuffed it into the messenger bag with everything else. No point advertising I was planning on sneaking around until I had to start sneaking.

Deciding what to wear and what to pack turned out to be the least of my worries. It was L.A., and Benedict Canyon was a long way away—hiking or running there was out of the question, as was simply driving up there and parking. There was no place near Larkin House where a car parked on the roadside wouldn't arouse suspicion. No place where that sort of vehicle wouldn't get called in by either police or a private security company. In the end I left my car in the parking lot of a convenience store on Sunset and called a cab to take me the rest of the way to Larkin House.

"Here, lady?" the cabbie asked when I indicated where he was to stop.

"Yes, please," I said as I paid him.

"But there's nothin' here."

"I feel like walking." He kept looking at me. "All right, if you must know, I'm planning on sneaking up on my husband." I let his imagination fill in why a wife might be doing that. "That's why I didn't drive myself."

I didn't know if it was important that the cabbie be satisfied with my explanation, but I was glad when he stopped asking questions. I was less glad when he was gone and I was alone on the road. In the dark. It was scary. I pulled the watchcap out of my purse, plunked it on my head and trudged along.

Clearly, if I'd really thought I was up to no good, I would have considered this plan more carefully. But what I'd thought through so rationally back in Malibu with a glass of wine at my elbow and the sunset casting fire into the sky seemed a lot less doable once I had the cab drop me at the darkest part of Benedict Canyon Drive at 2:00 a.m. I shuffled along in the dark with only the distant city lights to guide me and the crickets serenading my every step.

You think about things in the dark. Think about things in a way that you don't in broad daylight when warmth and safety are things you take for granted. First of all, dark is dark. Even with pleasant sounds and fragrant scents all around me, it was hard to avoid feeling as though I'd suddenly dropped into a David Lynch movie, and not one of the more lucid ones, either.

For maybe the second time in my life, I wondered at my Luddite thoughts about cell phones. It was, I knew, a holdover from my days in New York when I'd said—strongly and often—that I was determined to hold on to the few minutes in my life that were my own. "If God had intended us to talk on the phone while walking," I'd said often in jest, "she would have put an antenna on the top of our heads."

Now, creeping about on a dark West Coast night, I thought it might be time to rethink my position. I would have given a lot not to feel so completely alone.

Larkin House's decorative gates looked less decorative at night with no partygoers expected. The gates were closed, and while I felt fairly certain I could scramble over them, the security cameras perched on posts on either side convinced me that wouldn't be such a good idea.

But it's a big property. It's an old house. While the gates with their security cameras looked big and impressive, farther down the wall things were less tight. About one hundred yards away from the main gate, the wall was lower and there were no cameras that I could see. Fortunately, with all the running I do, I'm in pretty good shape. When I scrambled up and over and landed on the soft grass on the other side—on the *in* side—without breaking a sweat, I felt extremely pleased with myself. Once again, I'd checked in with my body and found everything to be in the right position. Life was good.

The self-congratulatory warmth lasted a total of twenty-five seconds. Before I'd even had time to plot my next move, the quiet was broken by a sweep of lights and the unmistakable sound of a slow-moving car. I ducked down behind the bulky form of a low hedge just in time to avoid being seen by the well-marked security vehicle cruising the driveway toward the road. The smell of the lavender I crushed beneath my hands and my own stale fear seemed to blend into something bittersweet while I crouched.

My heart was pounding, and I could feel a film of sweat forming on my shoulder blades and between my breasts, but I smiled to myself in the dark: this cruising car wasn't about me. It was a routine patrol, a security check. Had I hesitated a little longer before climbing the wall, they would have seen me and—certainly—asked me what I was doing. As it was I was safe. The security vehicle had left by the gates, presumably to continue their rounds, and I was inside the wall. It seemed likely it would be a while before they'd be back. The next question, of course: now what?

I hadn't anticipated just how dark the dark would be. And there was no way I could risk using the flashlight at this point. It didn't look as if anyone was around, but I wasn't tempting fate. On the other hand, it was difficult to get a fix on my location. I didn't know the gardens that well and the lights from the house weren't penetrating out to wherever I was. A good thing, from the point of detection. A bad thing from the point of finding my way around.

Though it was tempting to stay where I was, immobilized by possibilities, the fact that dawn might come while I was waiting for an idea finally got me going. In the end, I simply decided to walk straight in, away from the wall I'd climbed over, thinking that—eventually—I'd hit a landmark that would instruct me.

Unfortunately, this plan turned out to be exactly right. I didn't see the reflecting pool until I was standing in it. The good news: it was only six inches deep. The bad news? I now had two wet feet and my cross trainers squished noisily and unpleasantly while I walked.

But I'd traded wet feet for getting my bearings. I remembered that, from the reflecting pool, the hedge maze was the next large obstacle from the road. In the dark, however, I discovered that the key word here was *large*. Little wrought-iron benches, stone urns and neatly trimmed hedges might not look like much in daylight, but in the dark they were quite capable of putting me completely off course.

More than once I questioned the sanity of what I was doing. No matter how you looked at this, I was trespassing. The worst of it was, I wasn't exactly sure why. I knew I was lugging what was possibly a priceless artifact in my messenger bag, and somewhere, at the bottom of this garden, I felt sure there was the answer to what it was. My instincts told me that when I found that answer, I'd find still more. And so I pressed on, squishy feet and all.

When the dark shape of the hedge maze loomed in front of me, I felt like sagging against it in relief. Instead I skirted around the outside of it, feeling like a mole, trying to locate the entrance I felt sure must be there.

It was slow going. And, while I searched, for the first time I wondered what the years of neglect since Lolita Larkin's death might have done to what lay beyond those trees. It was possible that the entrance would be overgrown completely. If not that, I might find what I was looking for only to discover that the balance of the maze was impassable.

I'd traversed the perimeter of the hedge maze twice—and come close to giving up and letting reason win out many times more—when I found what I was looking for. The entrance was almost completely overgrown. It was a space only slightly wider than the nonspaces that surrounded it. Once through I finally allowed myself to pull the flashlight out of my bag and turn it on because, protected as I was on all sides by the dense hedges, I had no fear of the light being seen, except perhaps by a passing night bird or a plane.

And now I could see what thirty-odd years of growth can do to the best laid plans. What had at the design stage probably been wide corridors between tightly planted trees, there was now only enough room for a medium-size dog to walk comfortably. I'm bigger than a medium-size dog. But the path was discernible and I took it, forcing the brambly growth away from my face as I walked.

As I made my way—slowly and carefully—I inhaled the deep green scent of forest that the evergreen maze gave off. The incongruity of an evergreen hedge maze in Southern California came to me. While the outer trees had been dutifully watered over the years, the tightly packed trees inside the maze hadn't gotten much moisture. Most of them were alive, but the trees that had died along with those that were malnourished made my progress possible if somewhat slower than I would have liked.

I realized something else as I walked: the path I followed was just that, a path. Someone—or something—had made their way through here. Recently. And often.

Going down paths in the maze, doubling back over retraced steps then doing it all again down a different path, I lost track of time. I didn't have an awareness of that until I noticed the sky lightening above me. A glorious red, shot through with gold, almost the reverse of what I'd seen from my deck in Malibu the evening before. It was a display that would have made my heart sing if I'd been running through the canyons with Tycho. As it was, the approaching daylight filled me with equal amounts of dread and panic. What helped me get over that was the fact that, suddenly, I could see. I no longer had to creep forward carefully and feel my way, even with the flashlight. I tucked the light back into my bag and made my way forward at a reasonably normal pace and angle.

Another thing that helped me overcome my fear of being discovered in daylight in the maze was the realization that I wouldn't be. As sunshine flooded the world, I could hear the sounds of Larkin House—and the city beyond it—waking up. Before long I heard the automated sprinkler systems start up as well as the occasional laughs and shouts from the troops of gardeners that attended the estate. It all reassured me: I was no longer alone in the garden, even if no one knew I was there. The creepy nighttime things my mind had been manufacturing were no longer a possibility. How I'd get away from the Larkin estate undetected was another story, but I'd deal with it when the time came.

After many wrong turns and lots of needless doubling back, I found what I'd come for: a solid stone door. It was impossible, from where I stood, to gauge how large a garden the door protected, but since the hedge maze itself covered perhaps a quarter of an acre, it seemed likely to be quite spacious. When I tried to push through the trees nearest the gate I was stopped by a solid stone wall. I looked up, trying to determine how high the wall might be, but I found the exercise impossible. The trees were so tall and dense, they gave no clue about the walled area they protected.

The gate itself was somewhat obscured by the dense growth and the passage of time. In order to see how my "key" would fit—that is, how I was going to manage to open the door with a fistful of rock—I'd have to clear away at least some of the prickly hedge covering it. How I proposed to do that, I wasn't exactly sure. Beyond the flashlight and the key itself, I hadn't thought to bring any tools. But, at the moment, the thought of tackling that job overwhelmed me. It was now fully morning, I hadn't gotten any sleep the night before, I was hungry enough that I started being afraid that people passing the maze might hear my stomach grumble and—hardest of all to ignore—I had to go to the bathroom, a fact my body was starting to let me know was quite urgent.

I tried to ignore this last for a while but my physical self wasn't having it. I could barely focus on what to do about that, let alone complicated thoughts like opening locked garden doors. Every now and then, I've found, our bodies have a way of reminding us we're not quite as sophisticated as we think.

I solved the problem by backtracking a couple of turns of the maze, then squatting against the hedge as closely as I could. There was certainly no fear of being seen but, even if there had been, I was far enough gone that I probably wouldn't have cared and the relief I felt was worth almost any price, at least during the thirty seconds it took to achieve it.

My most immediate needs taken care of, I went back

to what I'd determined must be the gate. Looking at it from a different angle I could see that, while there was a lot of growth in the area of the door, it had been cleared at some point. I stood back to assemble what I was seeing into something that was meaningful to me. It was difficult.

I knew that I'd come to the right place for a couple of reasons. In the first place, Celtic runes like the one on the rock Keesia had given me were in evidence on various places on the door. There was a circular indentation at a height that was even with my face, around three inches deep and nine inches in diameter. Three pieces similar to the one Keesia had given me were already there. I could, I found, remove these if I wanted to. A good twist and a pull and I held one in my hand. Placing it back where I'd gotten it from was easy: like fitting a piece into a jigsaw puzzle.

I pulled the piece Keesia had given me from my messenger bag and fitted it into what I could see was its place: the runes of my stone matched those on the door and fit perfectly. And nothing happened to the door. As good as the fit was, I knew the door wouldn't open. It was easy to see what the problem was. With the addition of the one Keesia had given me, there were four pieces in place. Something was missing.

Another piece. The fifth.

I sat on my haunches opposite the stone door, the four runed pieces in place. The disappointment I felt was far deeper than I would have imagined. I hadn't known how badly I'd wanted this to work. And then all of it—the scary walk, the squishy feet, being forced to pee next to a hedge—all of it would have had meaning, somehow. All of it—except for the outdoor peeing, maybe—would have been worthwhile.

I chided myself for these thoughts, while I rubbed the dirt from my face, wished the tiredness from my bones. What, really, had I expected to find? If the door opened, then what? A garden. A lost, secret garden. Romantic enough, sure. But meaning what?

And now I had another problem. With little accomplished, I had to find my way back through the maze and away from Larkin House undetected. Dressed like a cat burglar on a clear, blue Southern Californian midmorning.

I debated for a few minutes about what to do with my stone. Should I leave it here with the other three? Should I take it? Or should I take all four? Though I found myself leaning heavily toward the latter, in the end pure practicality won out. Four stones would have added a couple of pounds to my load. Since I was walking, this didn't seem like a good option. I tucked the stone Keesia had given me back into my bag and reluctantly left the other three in place.

Getting back through the maze was no problem. I think I surprised a couple of creatures—probably rats, their scurrying gave them away—but they were as much intruders as I was. They weren't looking for a fight. Like me, they just wanted to be left alone.

I found my way out without any major missteps. At the edge of the maze, I hesitated, listening for sounds that would tell me someone was working in the vicinity. Hearing nothing, and with my watchcap safely back in my messenger bag, I sauntered into open view as nonchalantly as possible under the circumstances. Hoping that anyone who saw me would think that—black garb notwithstanding—I belonged there.

I almost made it, too. Just as I approached the portion of the estate wall I'd swung over the night before to gain access, I heard a voice call my name.

"Myra," I called back, formulating quickly. "How are you?"

When she caught up with me she was slightly out of breath. I could see she'd run from wherever she'd been when she spotted me.

"I thought it looked like you. What on earth are you doing here so early?" she asked. I watched her face closely for signs of suspicion, and was honestly surprised not to see any. I surmised that, with a staff as large as the one at Larkin House, there would be people coming and going quite regularly. Knowing that I'd worked with Keesia and that I'd been here to see Maxi the week before, she might even think I had business there. As tempting as it was to plead that was the case, I thought better of it. It was too easy a lie to get caught in.

"I was running with a friend who lives near here."

Myra looked at my clothes half critically but didn't say anything. I was wearing trainers and carrying a messenger bag. Did they balance off the black jeans, I wondered? "Near here?" was all she said.

"Yes. Loma Vista? Loma Verde? Loma something, anyway." Which seemed a safe bet. All parts of Los Angeles seem to be lousy with Lomas.

"Ah," said Myra. Which told me nothing about how she was taking all of this.

"Yes, so we were running," I had a sense of myself as a little slimy green creature, trying like hell to get up the side of a well. Making three painful steps forward, then sliding back four. I banished the image and soldiered on. "We were running and I noticed where I was and I just had to come over…over and…see how…how lovely the garden is in the morning."

To my intense relief, Myra smiled warmly. "It *is* especially lovely in the morning, isn't it?"

I nodded, wishing I'd thought to stuff my shades into my bag: they would have shielded my eyes. Not from the sun, but from detection. I don't know why I ever bother lying, I'm crappy at it. Crappy or not, Myra bit. And why not? She was hearing stuff that made her happy.

"And the rudbeckia are in bloom just now," she said. "Come, I'll show you." I stifled the groan I felt rising, pasted a smile on my face and followed her back into the garden, trying to ignore the clamoring of my stomach, the tired tightness in my eyes and the twin damp puckers my feet had become.

When I'd dutifully oohed and aahed at all of Myra's babies, she walked me to the gate and waved me on my way. The good part of all this, of course, was that she provided cover from anyone who would have been less receptive to me trespassing on Livingston property. To someone watching at this point, it would have looked as if I was Myra's garden guest.

I trotted down the road in a good imitation of a joyful jog until I was sure I was out of sight of Larkin House's driveway. I could have kept jogging but I knew I was a good five miles from my car. I was starting to feel light-headed and I would have done anything—literally—for a cab and some good old New York City street meat.

Sometimes—occasionally, but not often—I hate L.A. It's just so vast and, in some ways, can seem quite empty. Especially when you're looking for a taxi. Because taxis can't find you here the way they do in more civilized places. In New York they cruise: they are the predator, you are the prey. In L.A., it's the other way around. The big openness of the place demands different rules. You call the taxi—like, from a cell phone—and they come and pick you up. But if you're just walking there's never one around. In L.A. there are times when you could quite honestly die for want of a cab. At least, these were the things I mused on as I trekked back to my car.

I thought about that and I thought about the fact that, after twenty-four hours of being awake and some of those hours filled with adrenaline-raising stuff, I'd cease being able to think if I didn't soon get a shower, a nap and some food.

Fourteen

I couldn't wait to get home to eat, so I stopped at a fast-food place on Sunset and grabbed an avocado-and-cheese quesadilla to munch on while I drove. It wasn't street meat, but it was almost as good, especially since it was getting increasingly difficult to remember the last thing I'd eaten.

At home, Tycho greeted me like a long-lost soldier. I didn't mind his moist canine fuss. It felt good to be welcomed, good to have been missed and worried about, even if it was by a dog.

Unsurprisingly—since I'd missed nearly a whole day out of my life—the light on my answering machine was flickering maniacally. I knew I had a whole bunch of messages, I just wasn't sure I wanted to deal with any of them while I was so dirty and tired. Normally I would have ignored it and gone ahead and hit the shower, but—and I hate to admit it—the possibility of hearing Gus's smooth and confident voice proved too big a draw. I wanted something good, something happy. A message from Gus would have supplied that. But it wasn't what I got.

Instead I discovered that a mini-Armageddon had occurred in my absence. While I'd been out making like Jane Bond and trying to be invisible, I'd somehow slid right into the middle of the public eye. And, in all of that, I discovered something: when the wife of an important Hollywood producer dies under mysterious circumstances, the press is interested but not rabid. Shit happens. And, in Los Angeles, for Keesia's death to have made headlines, Maxi would have needed to be standing over her body with a smoking gun. He hadn't been, so life and the press had—more or less—moved on. It's a busy city in an ugly world.

If that same producer's *ex*-wife dies a few days later under mysterious circumstances—as happened with Bronwyn Barnes Livingston at that overpass—it's cause for a segment on *Entertainment Tonight* and maybe a mention in all of the newspapers, but it's certainly not the stuff page one is made of.

However, if the life of still *another* ex-wife is threatened and the circumstances are also at least a bit mysterious, all hell breaks loose, which was what had happened when I wasn't looking. In cases like that, the press starts sneaking the word *serial* into their copy and any angle even remotely connected with what has now become a Story is explored and discussed and dissected. These are the facts as I see them. Unfortunately, I discovered it all at quarters that were way too close.

Sometime during my overnight foray in the garden at Larkin House, my telephone had started ringing. And, basically, didn't stop again until my answer machine was filled to overflowing and clammed up. The minute I started to clear the messages—before I'd gotten beyond listening to even the briefest preamble to a message—the phone rang.

"Madeline Carter," I said crisply, still half focusing on what the voice on the answering machine had been saying.

"Hello, Ms. Carter, this is Jemma Heartweight." The voice was too crisp, too polite. Certainly not any of my stock market contacts and none of my friends. I was instantly on the alert. "I'm with the *Angeleno Citizen*," she said. "I'd like to ask you a few questions."

"Questions?" I asked warily.

"Yes, I'm doing a story on the ongoing danger to Maxi Livingston's ex-wives. Can you tell me how well you know Celisa Taylor?"

I scratched hastily through my mental Rolodex but drew something like a blank. The name twigged at me, but I wasn't sure why. I told the perky Ms. Heartweight as much.

"Ah…really," Heartweight said skeptically. "And am I also to believe that you didn't know Bronwyn Barnes or Keesia Livingston?"

"Wait, are you telling me that *another* one of Maxi Livingston's ex-wives is dead? Is that what this is about? Is Celina…"

"Celisa," Heartweight pronounced carefully. "Celisa Taylor."

"Is Celisa one of Maxi's ex-wives?"

"So you do know her?"

"No. I told you." I flashed back to the party. An auburn-haired beauty with jarring plum-colored lips. "I may have met her briefly at Larkin House on the night… on the night that Keesia Livingston…died."

"You *might* have met her?"

I ignored the question, the ramifications of having decided on a listed phone number currently too clear for me to ponder. Instead of answering, I opted for a question of my own. "What happened to Celisa?"

"Someone tried to drown her. In the pool of her house in Hancock Park. Now, if you can just answer some questions…"

"Sorry, Ms. Heartweight," I loved saying her name out loud. It was a good name. Too good. It sounded made up. "I really don't have any answers for you." And I hung up.

The phone rang almost before it had settled into the cradle and, like Pavlov's dog, I picked it right up. Another reporter. From network television, this time. I got rid of him. When the phone rang a third time, I ignored it. I brewed a pot of coffee and sat transfixed and staring at my ringing telephone and overstuffed answering machine. While the phone kept ringing, I listened to the messages that had come in before I returned home. Nestled among calls from various press agencies was one from Gus.

"Hey, baby, sorry I missed you." There was a smile in his voice. I smiled back. Amid all the calls from the rabid press and the constant ringing of the telephone, Gus's voice felt like fresh air. "And we keep missing each other. But no more missing. You'll note that some of my gear remains at your place. It's small stuff, though. I have to throw some sealant on your tiles, and that's about it. I'm going to do that tonight. Yes it's true—I'm going to make an evening house call. This media-room thing has been taking all my time and I feel bad for not finishing your place yet. Especially since the end is near. So, I'm going to swing by your place around seven, do a bit of work and then—surprise!—you're going to make me dinner. Oh, and if you have plans, cancel them—we can't go on not meeting like this." His voice took on a softer note. "I'm looking forward to seeing you. Later."

Despite the crazy night I'd had and the kooky day this was shaping up to be, I found myself grinning idiotically by the time Gus's message had finished. And he sounded so good! And, really, the prospect of an uncomplicated meal with him sounded wonderful. I was making dinner, was I? Great. I'd pick up a pizza and a bottle or two of red wine and call it done.

Thoughts of my pleasant evening were washed away when the phone started ringing again. I let the machine get it but picked up when I heard a familiar voice.

"Detective Brown," I said into the phone. "I'm here. And screening. My phone has been ringing off the hook."

"Reporters?" he said, not waiting for an answer. "It figures. This has all of the elements that the vultures love. What have you been telling them?"

"Nothing! Like I said, I've stopped answering altogether. I don't know anything, anyway."

"Here's the thing, Madeline. We now have two dead women and one attempted murder and you're connected to all of them."

"Me? How do you figure? I hardly knew Celisa Taylor and I'd never even met Bronwyn Barnes. Keesia was my friend but that doesn't mean anything. She must have had a million friends."

"Well…" He seemed to consider. "Let me put it this way. Were you at Larkin House last night?"

I thought quickly. Was there any way he could possibly know that? I didn't think so. Still, it felt wrong to lie to a police officer. "Can I take the Fifth?"

"Take it where? We're not in court. I'm just asking you a few questions, casual-like."

He had me there. "Look, Detective Brown, I don't know anything about anything, I promise. If I did, you'd be the absolute first person I'd tell."

Well, but…that wasn't *exactly* true. I thought about correcting it. There were things I knew that I felt the police should know. Things about weird stock purchases and odd keystones. But it didn't feel like the time.

"This whole thing is crazy," I said. "It's like some kind of bad dream. A nightmare. And it keeps seeping into my life and I don't know why. But I have no idea about it. You must see that."

"The only thing I see is that, wherever I look, you turn up."

"Oh, come on. Surely that's not true."

"Let's do this. Can you come in this afternoon so I can take a more detailed statement from you? Maybe you'll remember something helpful to us."

I agreed, of course. It wasn't like I had a choice. He gave me an address in Beverly Hills and directions and I told him I'd see him at five o'clock. Then I had a shower. And I tried to have a nap, but discovered I was in the middle of a conundrum: I'd been up so long and had so much stimulus I was actually too tired to sleep.

Before I left the house, I called Gus on his cell phone but got his voice mail. "Hiya, handsome," I said into the phone, trying to inject my voice with an exuberance I completely didn't feel. "It looks like both our lives are going crazy. I hope you fixed your media-room problems and now I've got problems of my own. I'm already planning an *incredibly* elaborate meal." I smiled, thinking of pizza. "If I'm a little late,

let yourself in. The food and I will arrive not long behind you."

At that moment, Gus seemed like a distant island, the
balance of the day a rough sea to be negotiated. But is-
lands are special. I had a feeling that my destination
would be worth the journey.

The Beverly Hills Police Department is located in
the city's civic center, a beautiful art deco building
that I thought looked more like an art gallery than one
of the most famous law enforcement agencies in the
country.

When I gave the desk sergeant my name, he told me
I was expected, gave me a visitor's badge, had me sign
in and had a passing officer lead me to where I'd find
Detective Brown.

I would have had trouble finding him on my own in
the labyrinth of offices and veal-fattening pens, but a
sharp female voice drew me in like a beacon. Detective
Brown was in an interview room with the door open.
The blinds on the window that separated his space from
an open office area were unshuttered, as well. The ten
or twelve officers seated at desks in the open area were
alternately trying to ignore the scene in the interview
room, or looking on mirthfully. None of them, I noted,
were getting any work done.

I saw Brown before he saw me. His attention was diverted. Though her auburn hair was swept up into an elegant chignon, and her lips weren't plum today but a
deep ginger, I didn't have any trouble recognizing Celisa
Taylor. From her words, I gathered Brown had been
having a more difficult time.

"Do you have any idea who I am?" she asked, her

tone just slightly south of insulting. Brown's face, I noted, was devoid of expression.

"Of course I do, Ms. Taylor." Brown's voice was soft. Placating. It hadn't been a tone I'd imagined him capable of. "How could I forget? I took your statement this morning, remember?"

She seemed to squint at him slightly, as though pulling his features into focus in order to remember him properly. It occurred to me that the glance was a bit myopic, as though she normally wore glasses to clearly see things a few feet beyond her nose. The sunglasses in her hand verified that for me. Probably prescription.

"Well then, if you know who I am, you'll understand why this must stop. At once!"

"What must stop, Ms. Taylor?" Brown's voice had taken on a dull quality. I think I liked him like this: a little beaten. Slightly backed up.

She pitched her voice lower and I strained to hear her clearly. "The newspapers are suggesting someone is trying to kill everyone who has ever been married to Maxi Livingston. That's unthinkable. It shouldn't…it shouldn't be allowed to happen."

"What are you suggesting, Ms. Taylor?" I didn't know him well, but I thought I detected a note of steel in Brown's voice. Wherever this was going, Brown saw it and was not amused.

"Maxi Livingston is a very powerful man. Very rich." She spoke as though to a child. "Very *connected.* Do you know what I'm saying?"

"I do. But go on." The steel was still there. I doubted that she heard it.

"It's unthinkable that we should be subjected to this."

"Subjected?"

She goggled at him as if he were a learning-deficient lapdog. "Should I draw you a picture?"

"Yes, please."

She sighed pointedly. Arched her neck aristocratically. "I was nearly *killed* today. Someone tried to drown me in my own swimming pool. If the pool man hadn't come by when he did...well I don't even like to think about it." She fanned herself with her hand dramatically, as though the mere thought of all of this might make her expire.

"I know all of this," Brown said with more patience than I would have had. "The statement, remember?"

"Well, there is no one in this town more powerful than Maxi Livingston. No one."

"All right," Brown said.

"Someone is trying to kill his wives."

"It appears that may be the case."

"And you're trying to tell me you have *no* clues. Nada. Zip. Nothing."

"Nothing that we'd share with you at the moment, that's correct."

"But how can that be?" She looked genuinely perplexed, as though the answer to this riddle hadn't occurred to her.

Brown sighed. Straightened. I thought I saw him brace his back slightly, as though a pain were growing there. When he started to speak, I could tell the patience I'd noted before was not thick. "Madam, listen closely and please try to understand. As I told you this morning, we are unsure just what it is we're dealing with. We are making every effort to find out who it was that attacked you and if it is, in fact, related to the other incidents you mentioned. You are under surveillance, as you know. We're doing our very best for you, Ms. Taylor. Just as we would," he said pointedly, "for any other citizen."

Celisa sat up straighter at this. This thought had obviously not occurred to her. "What are you saying?" I would have laughed if she didn't seem so pathetic.

"We don't solve cases based on the size of your tax bill," he said quietly, but I heard a gentle thunder and liked him better for it. "Your position in society, your income and who you are or are not married to have no relevance. We're working very hard on this case, Ms. Taylor. But no harder—and no less hard—than if you were a street person. That is the way the law works."

Celisa looked at Detective Brown agape for perhaps twenty seconds. She seemed genuinely at a loss for words. Underlings, I'm sure, weren't supposed to speak to her in this way. "Just who do you think you are? I can have you fired for this...."

Brown cut her tirade off in mid-rant. "Please Ms. Taylor, do as you see fit. I'm sure you will, no matter what I say. Now, if you don't have anything of import to tell me, I'd be pleased if you'd let me get back to work." He waved a hand toward me, partly in greeting and partly to indicate my presence to Celisa. I hadn't realized he knew I was there. "I have people waiting to see me."

Celisa Taylor passed me without a glance, leaving in her wake a thick cloud of perfume. I wrinkled my nose thoughtfully. The scent was expensive, certainly, but I couldn't place it. I was just glad I didn't have to go anywhere in a car with her. I would have had a screaming headache in ten minutes.

"What on earth was that?" I asked Brown when he'd indicated I should enter the interview room and take a seat.

"Par for the course in this office," he said dismissively. "We get at least one of those in every high-profile case. I don't really understand it. Some people get the idea that wealth and position give them some sort of exclusivity." He paused, thoughtful. "Or maybe, more like immunity. Like bad things can't happen to them because of who they are, or who they've slept with. It's sort of bizarre, because all of that exclusivity can buy the attention of a wider range of criminal types." He stopped his philosophizing abruptly, as though he'd suddenly remembered he was potentially in the presence of one of those criminal types. But he'd not stopped soon enough for me to wonder at his eloquence. Watching television just didn't prepare you for dealing with clearly educated cops.

"Sorry," he said now. "I get caught up. Thanks for coming in. Let me just buzz my partner. He'll be joining us to take your statement."

Brown and his partner, a low, squat man called Detective Usinger, sat across the table from me, a tape recorder between us. They alternated in asking me questions—by design or force of habit from having worked together for a long time, I couldn't tell, but I didn't have the sense that they were trying to railroad me or make something stick. They just seemed desperate, clutching at straws and hoping they'd missed something on earlier sweeps. If Celisa Taylor's display was any indication of the heat they were getting, I could certainly see why.

"So what you're saying—" Usinger was supporting his head with one hand. Despite the efficient air-conditioning, he was sweating freely. He had the look of a man who'd stepped up to bat one too many times over the last couple of weeks and hadn't gotten around to showering yet. I was glad not to be downwind. "What you're saying is that you'd never met Keesia Livingston until—" he checked his notes against his watch "—until less than two months ago. Is that right?"

"Right," I agreed.

"And, in that time," said Brown, "you became friends."

"That's right."

"But would you say fast friends?" It was Usinger again. I didn't see where this was going.

"Just friends. Nothing special. Friendly."

"And, in that time, you've said that you had cause to be at her home on several occasions," said Brown. "You were teaching her the stock market." He'd read this last off a file, and the way he pronounced the words—*stock market*—made it sound like a foreign language. I just nodded. They were reiterating, at this point. I figured they'd let me know when they actually expected an answer. They did.

"When spending time with Ms. Livingston—" back to Usinger "—did you ever notice her with anyone… suspicious?"

I smoothed the sleeve of my powder-blue sweater self-consciously. I ran my fingers through my hair.

"Ms. Carter…" Brown prompted.

"I know," I said, clearing my throat. "I'm sorry. I'm just…just gathering my thoughts."

"Take your time," Usinger said, but I wasn't sure he meant it.

"Here's the thing," I said finally, keeping my eyes on the wood-grain finish of the table between us as we spoke. "I have… I have discovered some things that I think you need to know."

Brown and Usinger exchanged a glance but didn't say anything.

"The thing is, I don't *really* know anything, okay? Some things just seem...well...funny." These guys were pros. I did not sense impatience. On the other hand, I knew I didn't have all day. I primed myself to just get to it, already. The thing that made me hesitate, the thing that was sticking in my craw was the fact that Keesia Livingston had been my friend. It was difficult for me to believe really bad things about her. And yet...

A deep breath, and then, "I've discovered that Keesia Livingston and Maxi's assistant may have been lovers."

"Who is that person?" Usinger said carefully while he wrote in his notebook. It seemed unlikely to me that they wouldn't know who Maxi's assistant was, which told me that they weren't giving anything away.

"Lark St. George. But there's more. Keesia Livingston had more than a million dollars in her trading account when she died. Her stock market account," I clarified.

Both Brown and Usinger looked at me carefully. I had their attention now. I'd known I would. All those zeros will do that.

"How do you know?" Brown asked blandly.

"I've had...have access to Keesia's account." I didn't elaborate. And they didn't ask. For the moment. From the guarded way they looked at me, I suspected this might be something I'd hear about later. I hurried on. "I think it may have been Maxi's money, put there without his knowledge. And, if Lark was her lover, I guess it's possible they were up to something no good together."

"That would be pure conjecture," Brown said. It wasn't a question.

"Oh, absolutely," I agreed. "But I guess I was thinking that these are easy things for you to check out. But, if it's true, it gives Maxi Livingston a motive."

"You're a detective, Ms. Carter?" Usinger said, the acid only slightly apparent in his voice.

"I am not," I replied firmly.

"I think what my partner is getting at—not so subtly," Brown said, shooting a quick glance at Usinger, "is that this is a serious matter."

"A *very* serious matter," Usinger said. Seriously.

Brown shushed him with a gesture and went on. "It's a serious matter to which our whole department is giving our complete attention. Two people are dead, Ms. Carter. One more was nearly so. And we have reason to believe you paid an uninvited visit to Larkin House last night."

"What reason?" I said as innocently as possible.

"Your car was parked at a strip mall on Sunset last night and this morning," Usinger said.

I didn't blink. "That's hardly conclusive."

"A private security company reported seeing someone who matched your description on Benedict Canyon Drive very early this morning."

"Still…"

"Still," said Brown, "when we checked with the staff at Larkin House, a gardener reported she'd chatted with you there midmorning today. She said—" and here he consulted a notebook, though I had the feeling he wouldn't have had to "—she said you claimed to be in the neighborhood and said you'd wanted to look at the garden."

"So?"

Brown shrugged. Usinger just looked mildly annoyed. "So," Brown said, somewhat languidly, "we thought you might have something to tell us."

I looked at my feet. Shook my head. "Uh-uh. And I've told you lots, anyway."

I was relieved when they let it drop. But the relief didn't last, they were just changing tack. "Now, Celisa Taylor…" Usinger let his sentence drop off ominously.

"I told you on the telephone, I was introduced to her at the party."

"Maxi and Keesia Livingston's party?"

"Right. We exchanged perhaps four words. That's all."

"And Bronwyn Barnes?"

"Even less. Someone pointed her out to me at the same party. From across the room. We were never introduced."

Their questioning continued in this vein for a while, clear attempts at finding things that weren't there. I played along. I didn't blame them for wasting my time. In their shoes, I'd likely have done the same. They had dead bodies, somehow related, and from what I could see, they had fewer clues than corpses. Perhaps, worst of all, from their perspective, this thing now had all the elements it needed to become a media circus: a powerful man, beautiful women in his periphery, Hollywood glamour and oodles of dough. It was the stuff of novels, not just headlines. Under the circumstances, I didn't blame them for pressing me—they didn't have much to go on—so anything that looked even remotely suspicious would require following up. I just didn't like knowing that, from where they were sitting, they could probably think of lots of suspicious stuff around me.

"So…" Brown prompted. "Larkin House. You were there. Why?"

I sighed and tried to think quickly, something that an

extreme lack of sleep wasn't helping. It was, perhaps, that mental fuzziness that kept me from answering honestly. I had been trespassing and snooping around in a way and in a place in which I had absolutely no business. I was completely in the wrong. And I *loathe* that feeling.

"All right," I said finally, "I was there. I told Myra, the gardener, that I was jogging with a friend in the area. I *was* jogging—that was true—but I don't have a friend there. I was hoping, I guess, to see something. Something that would help your case."

"In the garden?" Usinger snorted.

I looked embarrassed. It wasn't hard, it was how I felt. "I just had to do *something*. I've been feeling so helpless."

"Look, Madeline," Usinger said, looking pained and, to his credit, only slightly patronizing. "This case is at least as important to us as it is to you. And we're trained to deal with this kind of situation. It would be better all round if you'd leave the investigating to us, okay?"

I nodded, but Brown had his own two cents to chip in, just in case I needed my ears cleaned out, I guess.

"No, seriously," he said. "What Usinger says is right—no good can come of you poking around. If you have any serious leads, you call one of us immediately, but other than that, please leave it to us."

From the no-nonsense tone and the severity of the words, I had a hunch that if I could guess the reasons for half of their seriousness, I wouldn't even be close. One thing was sure, if either of them had any vacation time coming in the near future, they'd need to be canceling it: they weren't going anywhere. Neither, it turned out, was I. As Detective Brown saw me out, he stopped me.

"I know I keep saying this, but I do mean it. Don't leave town, okay?" His manner with me was softer than it had been before. I knew it meant I'd turned a corner somewhere in his mind. I told him as much.

"Why? I get the feeling you don't think I'm a suspect anymore."

"I don't. We really can't place you anywhere near anyone other than Keesia Livingston. But I have a hunch—call it a cop's hunch—that you know something that maybe you don't even know." He shrugged, perhaps embarrassed by his words. "I just think it would be better if you stuck around."

Before I hit the Pacific Coast Highway for Malibu, I stopped at a liquor store and picked out two very nice bottles of wine. A big, fat barolo to have with dinner and a nice sparkling Australian Shiraz for after. As an afterthought, I snagged a small bottle of Canadian ice wine. It was the easiest dessert I could think of making— opening a bottle and bringing out two more glasses— ice wine is candy to wine lovers. It would make a fantastic dessert with a bit of cheese and some fruit.

Did I think Gus and I would drink more than two bottles of wine? Not really, though I like to be prepared. And if we did, well…if I had anything to say about it, Gus wouldn't be driving anywhere later on. When I stopped to get the cheese and fruit, I grabbed a container of orange juice and a pack of bagels for breakfast. Just in case. Then I went back and grabbed a dozen eggs. It seemed likely he'd know how to scramble them to go with breakfast. I couldn't help smiling at the thought.

I picked up two pizzas at a place on PCH close to the turnoff for Los Flores Canyon. Two because I love girlie stuff on my pizza—chicken and cream sauce and curry and artichokes. And even though I'd discovered Gus was something of a foodie, I didn't know what he'd like on a pizza, so I opted to get another one covered in lots of greasy meat. And, I rationalized, you can never have too much pizza.

My drive up the canyon was—unsurprisingly—filled with pizza. The warm, cheesy smell filled my car and woke up my previously slumbering stomach. I was suddenly famished, and found that, after a few minutes, I could barely stop myself from pulling over to the side of the road and stuffing pizza into my head.

I would likely have ridden a wave of pizza lust all the way home, except that, as Los Flores Canyon Drive brought me toward the house, I happened to glance up and see a plume of smoke where my home was supposed to be. It pushed everything else from my mind.

Understand that Malibu cliff houses are not delicately made, though they can have a filigreed appearance. When you look up from the bottom of Los Flores Canyon, Tyler's house looks teeny. And you can only see small portions of the roof when you look down from the road above the house. But the house cantilevers out over the cliff over several levels.

The main level sprawls, hacienda-like, over a larger piece of land than the eye would at first believe. Below that large main level is another level and then another still. My apartment was below the deck on the main level. It quite literally hung off the deck adjacent to the kitchen and dining areas of Tyler's home.

My apartment was an afterthought, an addition, added to the six-bedroom home to provide a place for Tyler's daughter's nanny to live yet still be on the property. When Jennifer got too old to have a nanny, Tyler rented the apartment to me. I was a friend, as I've said, of his old friend and he liked having someone he knew he could trust—i.e., me—around to keep an eye on things when he was out of town. This was especially important because he has a teenage daughter. And in Malibu, just like everywhere, teenagers tend to get into trouble if they're not watched the way you'd watch a crocodile: carefully.

A good Malibu cliff house is a feat of engineering, and Tyler's is one of the good ones. But even at that, the very nature of a Malibu cliff house makes it a precarious proposition. At various times, Tyler's house has been subjected to earthquakes, storms and even fire. In some ways, it was a wonder the house was still standing at all.

Even while I began to push the pedal to the metal in my good but not especially speedy American car, two fire trucks and an ambulance raced past me, sirens screaming.

Bedlam greeted me at the house. Three fire trucks, two ambulances and other emergency-response vehicles, a police car and a couple of vehicles I suspected might belong to the press, were blocking the road. I pulled to the side as best as I could and ran for the house. At the top of the stairs that lead down, I was stopped by a police officer.

"Sorry, miss. You'll have to stay here, out of the way, for now."

He shook his head. "Sorry, miss."

"But I live here!" I almost screamed, frantic with fear.

"But what's happened?"

He started to tell me there'd been "some type of explosion" when I saw Tyler coming up the stairs, laboring under the weight of the tattered gray bundle in his arms. I fell into step beside him as he headed for his car, noting the life in Tycho's eyes as well as the pain.

"Your car is blocked," I said, indicating emergency vehicles. "You'll never get it out. Take mine." We changed direction, heading toward my car. I ran ahead, grabbing the pizza and the bag containing the wine off the back seat and throwing everything into the trunk to make room for the injured dog.

"Tyler, what happened?" I asked while he settled Tycho in the car as gently as he could.

"An explosion." His breathing was labored. Tycho weighs a lot. "In your apartment."

"Omigawd, Tyler. Is Tasya…" Though, I knew instinctively she must be okay. Tyler wouldn't have been preparing to take the dog to the vet's if his wife was injured.

"Tasya is on set today," he said. And I knew Tyler's daughter, Jennifer, was in Taos, staying with her mother.

I allowed myself a shallow breath. "Oh, Tyler. Thank God."

"I'm not so sure about Gus, though," Tyler said as he settled Tycho on the back seat with a grunt.

My heart stopped. In all the excitement, I'd forgotten that Gus had planned on working on my apartment.

"Gus," I whispered. I looked. His red van was parked down the street. "He's all right, isn't he?"

Tyler shook his head. "He must have been close to the blast. He was thrown down the cliff. The paramedics are with him right now."

I sat cross-legged on the diving board of Tyler's pool; bits of charred paper and debris floated on the pool's normally immaculate surface. Sitting there was all I could think to do: as much energy as I could muster and the closest any of the emergency teams had let me get to the "event site."

I decided I was probably in shock. At least a little. I couldn't feel anything. They'd carried Gus out on a stretcher. I'd tried to scramble into the back of the ambulance with him but had been denied by a firmly compassionate paramedic.

"It's critical, ma'am," he'd said quietly. "Let us do our stuff. You can come to the hospital later and see him."

Critical.

The word kept reverberating around in my head. I knew that, when the word was in that condition—all by itself—it had a special significance. I just couldn't bring myself to pull it into focus.

I simply didn't feel able to do anything beyond looking at the smoking, gaping hole that had been my apartment. It seemed miraculous that the house was standing at all. My apartment had been so completely obliterated—my computer, my furniture, my clothing, my *stuff*—yet the deck above it was intact and seemed to want to hold. And Tyler and Tasya's portion of the house didn't look damaged at all.

Though I'd not been allowed inside, from what I could see in the dark, my apartment looked like a moonscape. My little deck hung precariously but was otherwise in one piece. Fortunately, I'd been told that's where Tycho had been reclining when the explosion came. He'd been tossed down the cliff, as had Gus: only Tycho not only had a protective dog-hair suit, he also had been spared being pushed through a plate-glass window. Gus had not been as lucky.

The impression of moonscape was underlined by the view: incredible as always. From my position on the diving board I could see the canyon taper down to sea level. In the dark, the ocean was just a hint—more sound than sight. The sky above me was an inky star-shot canopy. If I held my head a certain way, everything looked as it always did: wonderful and promising. But move my head just a few degrees to the right and...devastation. Nothing was as it should be.

A policeman was standing beside me. I hadn't seen him approach.

"Do you have anyplace else to go?" he asked.

"This is my home," I said evenly.

"I realize that." I noticed absently that he had nice eyes, warm honey-colored eyes. And that he looked genuinely sorry that this had happened. His sympathy almost made me cry. "And I'm sorry. But we don't know what caused the explosion yet. And we don't know if the rest of the house is safe, either."

"But my stuff." It was a whisper, but he heard it. His own voice was quiet when he answered.

"There's not much left."

"Have you heard yet what happened to the man who was in there?" I thought it was too soon to know, but I had to ask.

"He's at Santa Monica General," he told me. "He's critical—" then went on quickly when he saw my distress "—but alive."

Critical.

When Officer Lopez left, he gave me his business card and told me to call if I had any concerns. I almost laughed. Concerns? I had nothing but concerns right now. Just none that he could help me with.

After a while, I lay down on the diving board. I couldn't think what else to do: couldn't summon the energy to poke around as far as the police would let me or take myself off to some other place, even if I'd been able to think of another place to go. I don't think I slept, but I drifted off, encouraged by the ghosts of clouds that scurried through that inky sky.

The sound of Tyler's voice didn't make me jump. I guess I'd been expecting it sooner or later. "Does that feel like the only safe place?"

I lifted my eyes to where he stood, Tasya at his elbow. I nodded, too filled with unclaimed emotion to do much else. "I guess." I pulled myself into a sitting position and Tasya plunked herself down next to me while Tyler sat cross-legged on the ground across from us.

"The police have said we can't stay here tonight," he said after a while.

"I know. They told me that, too."

"They say they have to figure out what happened. And figure out if the rest of the house is stable. They think it's possible that the explosion might have caused structural damage."

"Gus is in the hospital," I said dully, my eyes on the horizon. "He's…" I hesitated, cleared my throat, and, even so, when I spoke again my voice came out in a whisper. "He's critical."

"I know. Tycho is in the hospital, too. He's gonna be okay, though. They did X rays, bandaged him all up. I could have brought him home, but I thought it was better if he stayed there for a few days. They can keep an eye on him while we figure out what to do."

All three of us looked toward the house. The smoke

coming out of what used to be my apartment was tapering off and there were fewer emergency personnel running around, but it was still depressing, a clear message of destruction.

"I think I'll rent us a bungalow at the Beverly Hills Hotel," Tyler said suddenly.

"Oh, Tyler. Good idea." Tasya nodded approvingly.

"Yeah, it'll be easy for you to get to the studio," he said to his wife, "and all of us will need to do some shopping while this is being sorted out."

"You guys go ahead," I said. "I can stay with Emily or something."

"No, seriously, Madeline, you come stay with us. This has been an awful thing. I'd rather we stayed together." Then, as though it were an afterthought, he added, "You know Sal would have my ass if he thought I let you go off on your own."

I smiled then. It was a weak smile, but it felt good. "Okay. If you're sure I won't be in the way…"

"Don't be silly, Madeline," Tasya said. "Those bungalows are like little houses." She looked at Tyler. "You'll get one of the two-bedroom ones, right?"

Something warm and secret passed between them when he nodded. All he said was "9A." I looked away, embarrassed to intrude on their private exchange. Then he said more briskly, "Right, then, let's go. We'll take my car. I'll make a reservation on the way."

Normally the prospect of staying in a bungalow at the Beverly Hills Hotel would have filled me with excitement. In fact, when I first moved to L.A., I made a beeline for the hotel, holing up there for a few days while I got my bearings. And that had been in a room, of course. Not one of the bungalows, which were as steeped in history as they were expensive. Now, however, I had other things on my mind.

"You guys go ahead, I'll catch up with you later. I want to go to the hospital. See how Gus is doing."

I hate hospitals. I don't think I'm alone in that. On one level, it's very likely hospital administrators all over the world have conspired to make them unwelcoming and unappealing. Or maybe it's just what happens when you fill a big building with sick people.

It was close to ten o'clock by the time I got to Santa Monica General and found parking. Ten o'clock on what was proving to be the longest day of my life. I found the information desk easily enough, though getting actual information proved to be more difficult.

"A friend of mine was brought here tonight," I told the tired-looking woman behind the desk. "His name is Gus Barclay."

"Barclay, Barclay…" She consulted various screens and charts. "You said Gus?"

"That's right."

More checking, then, "Sorry, no Gus Barclay."

I stemmed my rising panic. Could that mean he was dead? Though I supposed even toe-tagged bodies in the morgue needed names to identify them. "But he has to be here. The police said they were bringing him here." I thought about it. "The ambulance driver as well. Please check again."

She sighed but did as I asked, lucky for me it wasn't a busy night. "Well, there's an *Augustus* Barclay in ICU. Could that be him?"

Augustus? I really *didn't* know much about him, did I? "I…I guess it is."

I must have looked saddened by the fact that I didn't know his real name, because the woman seemed suddenly to feel sorry for me. "It's okay, honey. Lots of people don't go around saying their real names. Especially with a handle like that. You go on up. It'll be okay."

It was way past visiting hours, but this hospital—like many—doesn't worry much about visiting hours in ICU. In that department, it's pretty much life and death. No one is going to hang around chatting for hours in the intensive care unit. And, in life-and-death situations, they're not going to make you wait to say your goodbyes. As long as you have the creds—and even sometimes if you don't—they let you in.

I didn't have the creds but I made them up. "You related?" the duty nurse asked me. When I hesitated, she said, "You have to be related, or I can't let you in."

"Yeah," I said, "I'm related."

She just looked at me, waiting for something more.

I looked at my feet. "I'm his wife." Then wondered where *that* came from. Somehow "sister" hadn't even occurred to me.

When she looked at me quickly I thought that maybe she didn't believe me. After I saw Gus, I realized it was more likely that she was checking my mettle. Was what I saw going to rock me? Would they need to have people standing by with a stretcher and smelling salts? I guess I passed muster, though, because she pointed out the part of the ICU Gus was being treated in, and no one followed me to his bedside.

With tubes up his nose and in his arms, his pallor visible under his tan where he wasn't covered with bandages, he looked completely un-Gus-like. Standing near his bed, seeing him with all of the essential Gusness drained out of him, I realized I'd never seen him without a smile on his face. Until now.

For the moment, there were no nurses or doctors hovering near him, but I had the feeling this was new and perhaps temporary. Various machines seemed to sprout from him, monitoring his pulse, his breathing, his brain activity.

The nurse who had directed me to him popped her head around the curtain to see how we were doing.

"Is it as bad as it looks?" My voice was small.

She met my eyes. Nodded. "I'm afraid so. The doctor is concerned that there might be internal damage. He's already been out for X rays and a CAT scan. We're waiting for the results. I'm sure the doctor will call you when we know something."

I pulled a chair over to the side of the bed and just sat there, looking at Gus, wishing him better. Wishing him safe. There was no response when I took his hand, stroked the fine, sun-darkened skin of his forearm. I could feel the life in him pulse beneath my fingers.

"I got two beautiful bottles of wine," I told him softly after the nurse had gone. "And ice wine for dessert. It'll hold, though. That stuff just gets better and better." At first I felt silly talking to someone who was completely unresponsive—as though I were acting out a role in some bad medical soap opera. After a while, though, how it looked ceased to matter. I imagined my voice, soft and strong, rising out of me and entering into him at whatever vulnerable place he currently lingered.

"I don't know what I'll do with the pizza, though. But there are a lot of pizzas in the world. We'll get another one when you feel like it. You can tell me what kind. I didn't know this time, not for sure, so I got something

I thought you might like. I got a couple, actually." Babble. All superficial. All things that wouldn't touch the essence of a person. Yet it made me feel better to talk about these mundane things. The evening we'd planned. Not surrendered, just put on hold.

I don't know how long I sat there like that, stroking his hand and forearm, silently trying to send him strength, but after a while, the beeps and buzzes and comfy caretaking noises of a hospital at night seduced me. Or maybe it was just the fact that I'd now been up for something like thirty-six hours. I only know that, before I fell asleep, my eyes were on Gus's face and my hand was touching his lightly.

"Mrs. Barclay?" I could feel myself being shaken gently, but the unfamiliar name confused me. When I opened my eyes and saw a nurse above me and the hospital around me, it all came flooding back. Too quickly. I looked over at the bed. Gus was gone. At the doorway, two men pushed a gurney with Gus on it toward the elevator. I felt something like panic grip my heart.

"It's all right, Mrs. Barclay, they're taking him down to prep him for surgery." She was speaking to me loudly, as though I might be hard of hearing, not just sleepy. I checked my watch. It was 2:00 am. "The scans came back—your husband has suffered more internal damage than the doctor initially thought. They're going to operate right away."

I must have looked terrified, because the nurse rushed on sympathetically. "I won't tell you it's going to be all right, because it's a serious matter. But Dr. Kruger is a very skilled surgeon. Why don't you go down there right now? You should be able to catch them before they begin. He can explain everything to you. Let you know what's going on."

I thanked her and hurried off the ward in the direction she'd sent me. In the elevator, I even punched in the number of the surgical floor. I pulled myself together before I got off the elevator. What was I thinking? It was one thing to pass myself off as Gus's wife in order to see him. But getting briefed by his surgeon prior to something as important as this? The doctor might even expect me to help in the decision-making process. As much as I felt that my current feelings for Gus could grow into something larger—much larger—I knew I had no place contributing to decisions that might alter the course of his life.

When the elevator doors opened, I punched in the number for the main level and kept going on down. Back at my car, I got behind the wheel and just sat for a while, contemplating my next course of action. It didn't take me long to realize, though, that I had no course. I was out of ideas, completely dry. More than anything, I wanted to redial the clock. I wanted it to be yesterday afternoon. I wanted to call Gus and say: No working tonight. I'll meet you at your house at six o'clock. I wanted to make him safe. I wanted to make all of this right.

Of course, life never works like that. Not ever. Not at all. And that thought—on top of everything else I'd been through recently—that thought undid me. I crossed my arms over the steering wheel, put my head on the soft vinyl and cried for a very long time.

Fifteen

When I first moved to L.A., the lobby of the Beverly Hills Hotel delighted me. All delicate pinks and greens and wood, like a movie set for a posh hotel in the 1950s. Just so perfect. You expect to see Doris Day and Rock Hudson sweep through arm in arm. Not to mention Marilyn and any number of beaus—the Beverly Hills Hotel was a special favorite of hers, as it was for many stars.

Today, however, it didn't delight me at all. I barely saw it. "I'm staying in a bungalow with the Tyler Beckett party," I told the concierge dully. I was relieved to see he was well trained and used to working at a venue that caters to the eccentric rich—if he noticed my bedraggled appearance, red-rimmed eyes and lack of baggage, he didn't say anything. Instead he checked his computer.

"May I have your name, please?"

"Madeline Carter," I said, hearing a mental echo say *Mrs. Barclay*.

"Very good, Miss Carter, you're expected." He produced a card key, handed it to me, then called a bellhop to guide me out to the bungalow.

Again, under different circumstances, I would have been charmed and delighted by all I saw—the Hollywood-tasteful decor, the well-tended gardens, the scent of hibiscus that seemed to overlap everything else. Now, however, I just felt sad for all of the delight I didn't feel. And there were other sources of sadness, as well, though I was trying hard not to think about those.

Despite holding a key card, I knocked softly at 9A. Tasya opened the door wrapped in a thick pink bathrobe with the hotel's logo embroidered on the left breast. She half dragged me inside.

"Madeline, where have you been? We were sick with worry."

"Sorry, Mom," I said, trying for my usual joviality.

"Don't make jokes, please. We were very concerned. Where did you go?"

I told her about Gus and the hospital. I even told her that I'd lied to be able to go see him. Tasya was sympathetic, as I'd known she'd be.

"But that is awful, Madeline. Come—" she was leading me into the bedroom "—we must tell Tyler. He can fix it," she said confidently. "He can fix anything."

Despite his wife's confidence, some things are beyond even Tyler's ability to repair. He could not, of course, fix this. He could, however, use some of his contacts to make sure he was looped in regarding Gus's condition. And while Tyler was concerned about his contractor, he must have sensed something extra from me.

"When did you and Gus get involved, anyway?" He asked it softly, in a way not intended to give offense. It didn't.

I answered him honestly. "We're not even really involved. Just, I guess, heading there."

Tyler didn't take his eyes off my face as I spoke. He watched as the color stained my cheeks then quickly receded. Then he smiled, though it was a sad smile, respective of Gus's current location. "He's a good guy, Carter," he said finally. "You could do worse."

I ducked my head. "Yeah, I know. I have before."

Tyler told me that, in the time I'd been at the hospital, he'd been in touch with the police. They'd told him that, though it was too early to be certain, it looked as though a tank of oxyacetylene that had been in my apartment for reconstruction had somehow ignited, causing the explosion.

Something about this didn't feel right to me, but I was too tired to think about it now. My eyelids felt as though they had grains of sand behind them and I could hear a rushing in my ears like wind on waves. I knew I had to sleep soon.

As lovely as my bedroom in the bungalow was, the thing I appreciated most was the quiet. No part of Beverly Hills is as peaceful as the part of Malibu where I lived, but the hotel did a good imitation. The walls were thick and sound-dampening, and the mature plants outside the bungalows were lush to good effect.

In any case, I was *that* tired. Not counting my uneasy catnap at the hospital, I'd now been awake for close to two days. As much as I had a lot on my mind, and as upset as I was about some aspects of the things that were unfolding around me, my body was clamoring for some respect.

When I lay down and closed my eyes I felt sure I was too wired—and perhaps too tired—to sleep. It seemed as though, in the next instant, I opened my eyes and sun was streaming into the room and neurotic city birds were chirping maniacally. I checked the clock on the bedside table and blinked when I realized that it was telling me it was after two o'clock. Was that even possible? I thought about it. As trashed as I'd been, it was entirely possible.

There was a bathroom adjacent to my room and I used it, stripping off clothes that had seen too much— the aftermath of an explosion, the hospital—and spent a blissful half hour under a roaring shower, availing myself of all the wonderful goodies the hotel left in the super-deluxe bungalow suites. After my shower, there were more goodies to avail myself of, including a bathrobe identical to the one Tasya had been wearing the night before. I was happy for the caress of the fat pink pile against my skin. All I had to do was get my hands on some new clothes and I'd be ready to head back to the hospital and see how Gus was doing.

I moved into the bungalow's sitting room feeling refreshed and ready to face what I knew would probably prove to be a challenging day. Clean, warm and dry, and with a good night's sleep behind me, I felt immeasurably cheered. Today, I felt, would be better. Today I'd help put the pieces back together.

Tasya and Tyler were waiting for me in the sitting room. As unlikely as this seemed, one look at their drawn faces and the tense way Tasya perched on the edge of the sofa pulled away the momentary feeling of well-being I'd had as though it had never been.

"What?" I said when I saw them. "What is it?"

Tyler came from where he'd been pacing and tried to lead me to an armchair. "Sit, Madeline." And when I hesitated, "Please, sit."

I did as he asked, noticing while he sat gingerly next to Tasya that she avoided my eyes when I tried to catch them.

"Madeline…it's Gus," Tyler started.

I shook my head. "No."

"I'm sorry. I talked to his doctor half an hour ago. Gus died this morning, postsurgery. There was some internal damage that…that couldn't be repaired."

I thought I should feel something. Some deep, draining something. But I didn't. That would come later, but for now, I just felt a kind of pathetic hollowness where feeling was supposed to be.

Perhaps to force something into the silence, Tyler kept talking, filling in blanks. "I was…I was concerned about what would happen to the…to Gus…now," Tyler struggled to say. I lifted my eyes to his for the first time. I hadn't thought that far ahead yet. That would have made it too real. "It happened on my property, while he was working for me, so I feel somewhat responsible." Tyler stopped. Checked to see how I was holding up. Looked at Tasya, who gave him a nod. He sighed and went on.

"Madeline, his family in Illinois have been notified. The hospital was able to contact them through Gus's medical insurance. I spoke with his brother half an hour ago. They're making arrangements for his…for him to be flown home. The funeral will be in Chicago."

Funeral. Gus. Together the words made no sense. Gus was energy, taut and controlled. He was strong hands on the steering wheel of his Lexus; he was laughter in a moonlit restaurant; passionate kisses and sweat in his overdecorated apartment…. Here I drew myself up. That last had been fantasy, not reality. There had been a few passionate kisses, sure. But not as passionate as I'd wanted. And all of the sweating had happened in my mind. What had he said? *I want to wait for you.* I hadn't wanted to wait, but what he'd said had made sense. At the time.

My silence must have frightened them, because I saw Tyler and Tasya exchange a look. Then, perhaps instructed by some marital telepathy I had no part in, Tasya got up and dropped to her knees in front of my chair.

"I'm so sorry, Madeline." She put her arms around me. Hugged me. I felt myself tense against her at first, then relax into the blanket of sympathy she wanted to give. Still, I felt nothing. So much of nothing I began to wonder what was wrong with me. Shouldn't I be crying? Or wailing? Or railing against an unforgiving God?

Tasya must have intuited what I was feeling, because she dropped back until she was looking into my eyes, picked up my hands in hers and said, "I understand this thing, what you're feeling now. It isn't real to you. It might not be for a while. But if it comes to you, as it can very suddenly, please come and find me. I, too, have had more than my share of such pain. When the time is right, we will mourn together."

With that she stood up, kissed the top of my head and beckoned Tyler to follow her from the room.

I wasn't focusing on them, but I heard him say, "Are you sure? Will she be all right?"

And Tasya answered, "*Da*, my love. It's best to leave her for now."

Tasya, of course, was right, as she so often is when it comes to matters of the heart. She knew I had some emotional wound-licking to do, even while I asked myself what right I had to do it. Two dates, really, was all we'd had. And a few weeks of getting to know each other while he worked on my place. Everything we'd shared—everything we'd been to each other—was really about promise, maybes, might-have-beens. And somehow that seemed to make it all worse, not better.

While I was thinking about all of that, I went back, in my mind, to the explosion. Tyler had said some of Gus's equipment had malfunctioned. Yet, at some level, that didn't feel right to me. Gus had struck me as a very conscientious workman. After all, he'd done what he did out of passion, not just to log hours or to get through yet another job. He'd done everything carefully, caringly. It was one of the things I'd loved about him. How likely did it seem that his carelessness had caused such destruction? Had, in fact, killed him in the end? Not very, I thought.

On the other hand, two of Maxi Livingston's ex-wives had died recently under circumstances that could only be described as mysterious. A third had had a serious attempt on her life. That seemed to indicate that some sort of serial killer—or even serial contract killer—was on the loose. And I'd been poking around a lot of it. The explosion had happened in the evening when I'd been away from home all day. The only person who should have been there was me. This was borne out by what I'd seen and heard about Tyler and Tasya's part of the house: the explosion had been localized. My apartment was totaled, their portion of the house was intact.

What did all of this mean? I suddenly felt as though I knew. The explosion had been intended for me: either to warn me off of poking around Maxi Livingston's business or to silence me altogether. Permanently. I had no proof, of course, but all of my instincts were telling me this was no kind of accident. Gus had been an innocent bystander. I had been the target. Of course I had. Did that mean that I was closer to knowing what was going on than I'd believed? I thought about that for a while. Thought about what I knew and didn't know. And, really, in all of this, only one thing made sense. The thing that really connected the dead women wasn't me, as Detective Brown had said. It was the fact that they'd all been married to the same man. You didn't need a finely developed instinct to tell you that all of this could be laid at the feet of one man: Maxi Livingston. What or who else, I asked myself, could it be?

Though it would have been easy for me to sit in the bungalow all day and mope and mourn and self-recriminate and fret, it seemed healthier to move. There was a wolf crouching deep inside me. I could feel the beginning of an exquisite anger taking hold. And an exquisite sadness. Feelings so intense that, if I let them, they could sweep me away.

Action didn't change these feelings, but it dulled them. Kept them at bay. And it was better to feel I was doing something. Even if, at the end of the day, I wasn't sure I'd accomplished much at all.

The only clothes I had with me were not clean. Apparently, hanging around the site of an explosion will do that. I hated the thought of putting them on, but I didn't have a choice. But it would only be for a short time. For once the gleaming towers and carefully laid-out shopping plazas at Century City did nothing to cheer me, but I managed to get what I needed very quickly. The day was warm and I couldn't think beyond it. I bought an overpriced cotton dress in a muted print and a pair of designer flip-flops, not because I desired designer flip-flops, but because they were easiest thing I could wrap my mind around.

Then on to Kordor. As I settled in at my usual terminal with a latte, I tried not to think about the fact that I no longer owned a computer. Or rather, that I owned one, but it was likely in little pieces all over Los Flores Canyon.

I checked my portfolio. I'd managed to sleep the entire trading day away, which meant I'd been three days away from the markets. That was some kind of record for me.

After logging on to my trading account, I found I could generate no enthusiasm for what was happening in the market. Though I was relieved to see I hadn't taken a bath on any of the securities I was holding, on this day I hardly would have noticed if they'd tanked. A couple of stocks had inched up higher than I would normally have allowed them to go without selling them. I put two market sell orders in for the following morning, then, wanting to turn my brain to something other than fretting, I looked closely over my account.

While scanning the dates of my most recent trades, something twigged in my brain. I could feel it, almost like something snapping into place. Without even really being aware of it, I logged out of my own account and logged right back in: this time as Keesia.

With my Filofax open in front of me, I checked the dates of Keesia's trades—the big deposit to her account had been made a week before her party, the day before Keesia came to my house and gave me her gift. A week later, Keesia had made her inexplicable purchases: ponying up nearly a million dollars for a stock whose price she'd helped inflate.

I consulted my Filofax again and compared the dates.

And I sat there for a bit, letting all of this sink in—willing the information I'd gleaned to align itself in a way that made sense. I failed. It didn't. Make sense that is. When she'd started making her big stock purchases, Keesia Livingston had been dead for two days.

Now, clearly, dead people don't make trades. That's, like, one of the basic rules. Being dead is the final trading halt: all action stops. At least until they figure out who gets all your earthly toys, which, obviously, hadn't happened yet. Especially since, as far as I knew, Keesia's next of kin—her husband—had yet to figure out how to get into his wife's trading account.

Dead women don't make trades. Though, theoretically, with an online trading account, it's possible. For a while. As I'd just demonstrated, as long as you had the user names and passwords, you could log on whenever you wanted. Today, checking Keesia's account from an Internet café, I *could* have sold some of those securities and used the cash gains to invest however I chose. Actually getting the money into my pocket would be a different matter altogether, but I could keep making trades indefinitely—at least until someone realized the account was there and made the powers that be aware of the fact that the account's owner was no longer able to use a computer due to deadness.

So what the hell was going on? The most obvious possibility was also the most unlikely: that Redi-Trade's software had somehow screwed up and was reflecting the wrong dates. But online trading, because of its intimate ties to the Internet, is heavily regulated and carefully scrutinized and self-scrutinized. That's not to say that nothing can ever go wrong—there are machines involved as well as error-making humans, so stuff can happen. But dates? That was about as likely as a bank error in your favor outside of Monopoly.

Then there was the nature of the transactions themselves. These stock purchases had a structured feel to them. To me there seemed to be a great deal of intent involved. There was some sort of meaning or pattern, though I couldn't quite see what it was. And the fact that all of these posthumous trades were of a single security seemed important.

NWZ. As on that first day, the letters didn't trigger anything for me, which, in itself, isn't that surprising. A lot of stocks are traded on the various North American exchanges. A *lot*. Quite literally thousands. It would be impossible for any one person to know all of them.

NWZ, I found, were the letters that the Northwest Zylonite Corporation traded under. This seemed to me to be a name so generic that it wasn't at all illuminative. It did make the fact that NWZ was headquartered in Olympia, Washington, not so much of a surprise. Especially since Washington is my home state and I grew up with Northwest This and Northwest That all around me.

When I dug a bit deeper, I discovered that Zylonite wasn't some sort of generic term: NWZ actually made a substance called Zylonite. They'd been making it longer than just about anyone else in the United States. Just exactly what Zylonite might be was less clear.

Interestingly, the company had been privately held until just a few months before. Interesting because companies that old—the Northwest Zylonite Corporation had been incorporated in 1880—seldom are very cheerful about laying their books and cupboards as open as they need to be to go through an initial public offering.

Frankly, you had to want it bad to take a very old company public. I'd seen a few start the incredibly harrowing and expensive process and fail.

Part of the problem is that privately held—especially family held—companies get used to doing things a certain way. *Their* way. When a company goes public, it's just that: public. In theory, every Tom, Dick and Dinah who buys a single share has as much right to information and answers as the biggest shareholder. The CEO and board are, effectively, the shareholder's employees.

In practice this is a lot of blah-blah-blah. There are too many crooked CEOs and boards who treat their shareholders like rube dupes and who manipulate facts with such alacrity they turn those facts into fictions. But it takes a company a lot of time before it can go from shiny new IPO to a culture of lies and deceit. And it's not for want of trying. Sometimes it's just that, in the beginning, everyone is watching you pretty closely.

So, on my first cursory inspection, I thought NWZ odd on a couple of counts. First of all, it was a very old company. Doing the postmodern thing and going public just struck me as off or, at least, certainly highly unusual. In the second place, they made something that sounded archaic—Zylonite—and though the investor-related bumph I could find said that they were "first in their field," and that they had "the very largest corner of the market," nowhere did it specify just what that market might be. A company Web site might have clarified all of that, but they didn't have one of those, which made me think that Zylonite was a low-enough tech thing that it didn't need to be flogged in cyberspace.

I scanned a list of the company's board members, looking for familiar names. This is a tactic that has helped me on trades in the past. I went to Harvard. After that I worked for a huge brokerage firm in New York. I've made it my business to know a *lot* of people. But I didn't know any of the people who worked in executive positions at NWZ.

The amount of information I had easy access to for a company that had so recently gone public—and one without a Web site—was limited. In an hour I'd exhausted the few ideas I had. The research, and probably the lowness of spirit I was feeling, gave me a sudden desire to talk to my old boss Sal. Though I could have gone to EDGAR—the Web-accessible Electronic Data Gathering, Analysis, and Retrieval database that is used by all public companies to send filings to the Securities and Exchange Commission—Sal seemed like a friendlier option. And Sal would have more than the regulatory stuff that EDGAR could produce—he would have the Street information that no database can give up. Sal's sources of information were much deeper than mine, plus he had been my friend and mentor for so long, sometimes his wisdom and general cheeriness were welcome for their own sake.

It was evening in New York—after seven o'clock—he'd be home by now. I checked my Filofax for his home phone number, packed up my gear and found a pay phone.

"Malibu Barbie!" he chirped when I identified myself. "How the hell are you?"

"Not Malibu right now. You haven't spoken to Tyler, I gather."

"Not for a while. Why? What's up? He finally come to his senses and throw you out?" he said jovially.

I told him about the house and the fact that we were staying at a hotel.

"Gosh, Carter, that's rough. Tyler taking it okay?"

I was both sad and glad that Sal didn't ask me if anyone was hurt. Sad because part of me just wanted to lay it all out for my old friend. Glad because the sympathy I knew he would have sent my way would have caused a meltdown. And the fact that I was standing at a pay phone on the Third Street Promenade wasn't the only reason I didn't want that right now.

"Listen, Sal, there's also a sort of professional reason I'm calling you."

"Well, this isn't office hours, but shoot."

"I'm looking at a company that trades on the Northwest Stock Exchange as NWZ."

"Never heard of it," he said unsurprisingly. "Should I have?"

"Probably not. The company is the Northwest Zylonite Corporation. And, get this, that's what they do. They make Zylonite."

"What the hell is Zylonite?"

"That's what I haven't been able to find out yet. I thought maybe you'd know."

"Yeah, right," Sal chortled. "I could guess, though. Have anything to do with Superman?"

I thought about it. "I don't get it."

"Kryptonite," he said placidly.

"I still don't get it." I've never been a big comic book fan.

"It's this material—from outer space—that is the only thing Superman is afraid of. You seriously don't know that?"

"Nope. Sorry."

"Man, Carter. You have to get out more."

I laughed. It was *so* good to hear Sal's voice. "Tell me about it. But, Sal, I don't think it's anything like that."

"No. Probably not. Still, *that* would be an interesting offering, don'tcha think, Carter? A company with a material from outer space."

"I still don't think that's it."

"Well, listen. I *could* boot up my computer and poke around for you, but I'd really rather not. It was *that* kind of day."

He didn't have to say anything more. *That* kind of day meant he'd been going since 3:30 a.m. and had likely been putting out fires most of the time.

"That's okay, Sal. I wouldn't ask you to do that, anyway."

He laughed again. "Well, we both know you would, but since you're not pushing, I gather it'll hold. Call me an hour or so after the closing bell tomorrow, all right, Carter? I'll see what I can have the boys drag up."

"The boys" were Sal's innovation and his special pets: two research geeks he'd hired at the height of the tech boom for projects just like this: getting the skinny on companies too new or elusive for there to be a lot of material lying around on the ground. They were the kind of computer whiz kids who, at the time he'd hired them, were demanding base salaries higher than the traders and brokers at the firm, despite the fact that neither was over thirty. The demand for supergeeks had softened, but Sal had kept them on at full salary. Between them, they'd developed sources and contacts so wide, they were irreplaceable. Even if, occasionally, it was best not to ask how they'd come by some of their information.

I thanked Sal and told him I'd call as asked.

Zylonite. The word was starting to take on mythic proportions for me. I was anxious to know what it was.

* * *

"So let me get this straight." It was hard for me to believe that I'd seen Detective Brown only the day before. Considering all that had happened since, it seemed like a lifetime ago. "You're suggesting that Maxi Livingston is trying to kill you?"

"Think about what I've told you. It's the only thing that makes sense." I was back at the Beverly Hills police station. This time, though, Detective Brown had dispensed with the interview room and was seeing me in his cubicle. And, mercifully, today his partner wasn't there. It was easier dealing with just one of them, and I felt as if I'd gotten to know Brown slightly. Having felt a man's hand on your stomach will do that, I guess.

"I dunno, Madeline. Maybe it makes sense to you. It doesn't make a whole lot to me."

"Well, look at it this way. Two of Maxi's ex-wives have died under odd circumstances lately." I kept my eyes on his while I spoke. "A third was physically threatened. Because of my relationship with Keesia, I'm may be a little closer inside than a lot of people. I've seen things from a different angle. I'm thinking, maybe Maxi noticed this and thought it'd be better to get me out of the way."

Detective Brown seemed to consider my words for a while, then pierced my theories neatly. "Here's the thing, Madeline. I've been a police officer for fifteen years. I've been a detective for ten of those years. After a while, you get to have a sense of things, you know? You start getting a feel for what's what."

I nodded blandly. What was what. Whatever. He continued. "And I've spent a lot of time with Maxi Livingston since his wife, Keesia, died. Maybe more than I would have liked to have spent. But I've talked and talked and talked with him and I just don't get that he did this. He may not be the most forthright guy, but killing these women? I just don't think he's good for it."

"Who else would do it?"

"Well, Madeline, that's the million-dollar question, isn't it? A lot of people would like to know the answer to that one. Yours truly included. But I'd be willing to bet money that it wasn't Maxi Livingston."

"But why?"

"Well…" Detective Brown seemed to consider his words carefully while he answered. "No motive, for starters. He was married to Keesia, of course, but he was done with the other two women. They were out of his life. No kids to haggle over. And, sure, there was alimony. But I've seen his financials, Madeline. Maxi Livingston is not hurting. So, okay, first we look for motive and we don't find any. Then what?"

I nodded expectantly.

"Well, opportunity, for one. His alibi is *not* airtight on Keesia Livingston's murder."

I stifled the "aha" I felt coming, but he saw it in my face, anyway. "But, Madeline, that's true for a lot of people. Yourself included."

"True enough, but—"

"But nothing. He's *well* covered on the other two incidents. Credible witnesses, you name it. Including, in one case, the funeral of his most recent wife. And you and I both saw him there."

I thought about mentioning that the same alibi hadn't stopped him from questioning *me* on the day of Keesia's funeral, but realized that the situation here was different. On that day, he'd had no other leads and was shooting into the dark—in this case, at me. It made sense that, in a case like that, you would beat some bushes and see what flew out. With someone like Maxi Livingston, though, you'd have to be more careful. With someone actually connected to the case you'd want to make sure you weren't closing any doors that would be better left open. Especially when the someone in question wielded as much power as Maxi Livingston.

I said none of this. What I did say: "Who says he did it with his own hands? Couldn't he have hired someone?"

Detective Brown nodded. "Sure, but we've thought that through as well. In the first place, of course, we go back to motive—still none. But, also, none of these feel like professional hits. Like you, he's the only one we've been able to connect to all three women. But he's covered, Madeline. He didn't do it. I'm about as sure of that as I'm sure I'm sitting here with you right now."

"Still…" I ventured.

"Still nothing. That's it, Madeline. Case closed. So to speak."

"No, let me finish. I was going to mention the teensy fact that someone was trying to kill me. Someone, in fact, killed someone else in my home. It's connected, you know. And will you please tell me your first name? I'm tired of calling you Detective Brown. Especially since, somewhere down the line, you decided to call me Madeline."

Detective Brown grinned. Sort of sheepish-like. "True enough, Madeline. It's Brian."

"Brian Brown?" I said before I could stop myself. "Your parents like alliteration, or what?"

Brian had the good grace to smirk, whether at me or his parents' sense of humor I couldn't be sure. "Something like that. But, anyway, you say you think someone was trying to kill you. Right now the Malibu police think it's an accident—'worker's incaution' is what they said."

I hit my fist on the desk while I pushed myself to my feet. Brian jumped but didn't say anything. "I *know* they did, Brian. But it's complete bullshit. I *know* it is."

Brian looked at me speculatively, his eyes narrowing not unattractively while he did so. "Madeline…"

"What?"

"There's something you're not telling me." It wasn't a question.

I slumped back down into the chair I'd recently vacated. Sighed deeply. "Oh, man," I moaned into my hands, "I don't even want to go there."

"I can see that."

I looked at him closely. "This is *so* not the time for humor."

"I wasn't exactly kidding."

"Okay, there *are* a couple of things I haven't told you."

"Is this the part where I'm supposed to act surprised?"

"Do you want to hear this or not?"

He just looked at me. Then: "What do you think?"

"Look, if I tell you anything, you have to promise it's, like, a secret. Between you and me."

"Madeline, you know I can't do that. I'm a cop, not a psychiatrist."

"And what the hell is that supposed to mean?"

"Nothing. Bad analogy, maybe. It's just that, well, several crimes have been committed. It's my job to figure out who did it. You know, get the bad guy. If you know something that will help me, it's your duty to tell me. I mean, legally you have to tell me. If you don't, it's called obstructing justice. Have you heard that phrase before?"

"Sure," I sniped back. "I've watched several flavors of *Law & Order*."

He grinned then, and the grin held genuine warmth. "Look, Madeline, we both want the same thing. If you're worried about betraying a confidence at this point, I say go for it. This is a really serious situation. If what you say is true, three deaths are linked to this. And the attempt on Celisa Taylor hasn't made anyone feel more comfortable. So, cut the crap already. Spill."

"Okay, I'll spill. But I'm not signing any statements or anything. I just want you to know in case it has some meaning I'm not seeing."

He kicked back in his chair a bit and laced his hands behind his head. "I see, so I can help you solve this puppy."

I sighed, ignored him and plunged in. "Well, first off, I already told you I looked at Keesia's trading account. After she died, I mean."

"Yes, you did," he said quickly. "And, as far as we've been able to determine, there is no financial aspect to any of these deaths."

"Let me finish, okay? It's just that, when I told you about it, there was something I hadn't noticed. Something pretty important. I felt like I'd missed something, so I logged back in."

"I don't know a lot about the stock market, Madeline, but I'm pretty sure you weren't supposed to be doing any of this."

"No, you're right. I'm not. But that's not the point. The point is that Keesia bought a lot of stocks. About a million dollars' worth. Two days *after* she was dead."

Brian didn't say anything for a while. And I understood why: the stock market is a field that not everyone is familiar with and, not everyone finds accessible. He was running my words through his head and seeing if he could arrange them in a way that made sense. I recognized the expression. So I let him throw it around. I knew he'd say something sooner or later. He didn't disappoint me. "Okay, I don't get it. Are you saying someone was into her trading account? Someone who wasn't supposed to be there? Besides you, I mean."

"To be very honest, Brian, I'm not sure what it means. But I'm pretty sure it means something."

"Well, that helps."

I ignored him. "I've thought about it and thought about it, and I just can't figure out a way to find out if the other two wives had trading accounts, or were involved recently in any type of odd financial activity."

"And you figured I was in a better position to find that out?"

I smiled at him. "Exactly. Like you said, *you're* the detective."

"Well, I guess you're right about that. And it's something to make note of. Follow up on. Thank you."

"You're welcome. Will you let me know if you find anything?"

"I'll think about it." And this time I could tell he wasn't kidding.

"Fair enough," I said.

"What else?"

"What makes you think there is anything else?"

He looked at me patiently. "Like you said, I'm the detective, remember?"

I smiled at that. How could you not? "Point taken. Well, Detective, the other thing is a little weirder. And this one you have to absolutely promise me you won't, you know, lay charges on me or anything. Or…or take anything from me you think I shouldn't have."

"You have a gun?"

"No! Of course not. Now promise."

He chewed this over for a bit, perhaps rolling procedure against possible information. In the end, information won, as I knew it would; as information always should. "Okay. I promise. As long as you don't have a gun and you didn't kill anyone. Now…"

"Like I said, this is kind of weird. And sort of long and drawn out. It's about why my car was up on Sunset that night."

That got his attention. I told him the whole story of Keesia's rock. How she'd given it to me, what she'd said when she'd given it to me. I told him about meeting Myra that first time in the garden and I told him about calling Jilly and what Jilly had reported. Before I told him about my moonlight foray to Larkin House, I took a deep breath before jumping right back in.

While I talked and talked Brian just sat there watching me closely, perhaps detecting whether I was lying, or what parts I was lying through. In the end, though, I think he decided to take what I'd said at face value. That motive thing again: I didn't have any.

"Going there, in the dark at night, by yourself, was potentially a very dangerous thing."

"I know that."

"If what you believe is true—that Maxi Livingston murdered these women—you were putting yourself in extreme danger."

"I guess I was."

"Why did you feel the need to risk your life?"

Now it was my turn to think. And, really, I couldn't

come up with a good answer. I suppose that, in a way, that's what I've always done in the stock market. Only now it was a little more literal. Another market left-over: my hunches. My instinct. I believe in these things implicitly. And I believed—even then—that there was *something* in that garden. I didn't say any of that. What I did say: "I'm…I'm not sure. Keesia was my friend."

"So, between what you've told me and what I've gleaned, you think you've discovered something, but you need my help with some details."

I thought about it. Was that what I was doing? "No. Maybe. Well, ask me tomorrow. I'm not sure."

"Uh-oh."

I didn't bite.

"Aren't you going to ask me why I said 'Uh-oh'?"

I shook my head.

He said, "Aha."

I looked at him. Rolled my eyes. Looked away.

He laughed. "Okay, have it your way. And I guess we'll talk again tomorrow. Meanwhile, Madeline, please don't do anything so goofy again. This is a dangerous, dangerous situation. I can't stress that enough."

"I *know*," I said.

"No, seriously, Madeline. This is an official police investigation. As a private citizen—hell, as a potential suspect—you should *not* be getting involved."

"I'm still a suspect?" I was surprised.

He looked at me, clearly exasperated. "Did you hear anything I said?"

"Of course," I said. Chagrined.

"Madeline, please. Remember what I've said, okay? And stay out of trouble."

"Of course."

"And, don't leave town."

"Jesus, Brown, will you give that a rest already? Where would I go?"

On my way to the airport, I stopped at Seventh and Fig and bought myself a new Kate Spade tote, a pair of jeans, two T-shirts, some underwear, socks, a pair of kicky little boots and a cream sweater with a deep, smooth V-neck. I made a mad dash and bought some moisturizing cream, toothpaste, a toothbrush and a tube of Mac lipstick in a shade paler than Emily would have approved.

While I shopped I tried not to think about my stuff strewn all over the side of the cliff. Would I get any of it back? Possibly. But, in the meantime, I needed something to wear. Something clean that wasn't a sundress and flip-flops.

Flying into Seattle brought a lump to my throat. So much in my life had changed since the last time I'd been home. I felt so irrevocably altered, that, on some level, I'd expected the city to be likewise changed. Unrecognizable to me. But it wasn't. There were differences, and as I drove my rental car from Sea-Tac airport to the North Seattle neighborhood I'd grown up in, I could see them—an old strip mall gone there, a new high-rise here, a new off-ramp where one had always been needed—but the pulse of the city felt unchanged. The fact that it was raining helped with this feeling.

My mother just stood and stared at me when she answered the door. Then she burst into tears.

"Oh, Madeline," she said through her tears as I hugged her, "it's so good to see you!"

"Mom…" I said into her hair, surprised that I was crying, too. Funny how sometimes you don't know you've missed something until it's in reach again. The smell of my mother's hair, the feel of her—tiny, seemingly frail, surprisingly strong—under my hands, the gleam of the banister in the hallway. The smell, the sense, the feeling of home.

"Look at us," she said. "Crying like big sillies on the front porch. The neighbors! Come on in. I'll make you some tea."

This was home, as well. In the wider world I'd taken to drinking coffee, strong espresso with foamed milk. At home—the home of my youth—it was tea, strong and black, with sugar if you wanted and milk if you insisted. Some British forebears had entrenched this tea thing in our genetic code because nothing—and I mean *nothing*—couldn't be gotten through or better understood with a cup of Mom's good tea.

Mom led me through the living room, where nothing much had changed, into the kitchen at the back of the house. I just stood there looking at it and blinking.

"I know," Mom said, seeing my expression. "It's something, isn't it?"

Unlike everything else I'd seen thus far in Seattle, time had *not* stood still in my mother's kitchen. It had been completely redone since I'd seen it last. Everything I remembered had been gutted and replaced. The new cupboards were a perfect, blinding white. The walls were ochre and deep blue. The floor was bright slabs of industrial linoleum: deep oranges, vivid blues, lemon yellows. The appliances were of a retro design but brand-new. I couldn't believe my eyes.

"So, what do you think?" she said as she filled a stainless-steel-and-black retro kettle with filtered water.

What I thought was that my mother had lost her mind. Truly. The room was like a set for a hip sitcom set in New York and peopled by twentysomethings. It was *so* not my mom. "It's very bright…very colorful."

To my surprise, my mother put back her head and laughed. I smiled, despite her obvious insanity. No one's laugh is as merry and inviting as my mother's. "Oh, Maddy. Your face! It's okay, you can tell me if you hate it. I had nothing to do with it."

"Nothing?"

"Zip. Zero. It's all Miggin's doing."

A light dawned. Meagan's latest passion was interior design. She'd recently finished an associate degree at a local college. "So what was this, her finals project? And isn't she supposed to ask her 'client' for input?"

"Oh, she did. She did! I told her I was tired of the old look. I wanted something bright and modern and—as you can see—she took me quite literally. This is bright. And modern. I went to Vegas for three days and when I got back…"

I covered my mouth with my hand, stifling what felt like a shocked giggle. "Oh, Mom. Did you tell her you hate it?"

Mom looked at me sternly, but her eyes were smiling. "What do you think?"

"But you can't just live with it if you hate it."

"Sure I can." Mom winked. "For now. And it *is* very good, don't you think?"

"Sure. It's good. In someone else's house. It's just so…" I looked around, reaching for the word. Failing. "It's just so *lurid.*"

I was relieved when my mother pulled her teapot out of the cupboard—her old brown Betty, complete with the same hideous red-and-white tea cozy it had been wearing since I was a child.

"She let you keep that?" I said, indicating the teapot.

"Even she knew better than to mess with that." Mom sighed. "Well, that's not strictly true. We had words about the teapot. And the cozy. But there's just so much you can take."

Mom's tea tasted wonderful, as did the little biscuits she produced to go with it. It all tasted perfectly like home. We sat across from each other at the kitchen island and Mom filled me in on my sisters' lives.

I talk to my mom and my sisters on the telephone regularly, but there is always minutiae that never seems appropriate for long distance. The trouble with the car, the new guy at work, the garden hose that insists on dripping no matter what. All of the things that make a life can only be shared in person, one-on-one, preferably—at least in my family—over a cup of tea.

On the second cup, Mom got to it. As I knew she'd been wanting to for a while. "So what brings you to Seattle? I'm not complaining, mind, but you've never done this before." She thought about it then reiterated. "No, never. Just cruised in unannounced. Must be something up."

This demonstrates one of the things I appreciate most about my mother—as she asked this, she looked at me alert and curious. She'd like to know everything that goes on in my life, but if I told her, "Never mind, don't worry about it," she'd put her curiosity away and simply enjoy my company. I guess that's respect, she respects me and my choices and my needs. And it's not just me, but her other offspring, as well, and everyone else's, too. And, as a result, she gets a lot of respect back. So it didn't occur to me for a moment to tell her to mind her own beeswax. In fact, I did just the opposite. Over endless cups of tea, I told her everything and—here in this ultimately safe place—finally got to the meltdown that had been building.

When I was done, she didn't say: You never told me about Gus! And she didn't say: But it could have been so dangerous alone in that garden in the dark! She just nodded and occasionally reached out to touch my hand. When I started crying in earnest, she led me to the sofa in the living room, a new box of Kleenex in her hand, and in a room untouched by my sister's newly educated aesthetic, my mother held me in her arms while I wept.

"Oh, kitten," she crooned into my hair. "What a rough time you've had lately, huh?" And there, in my childhood home, with the smells and sense of a child's version of safety all around me and in the arms of the woman who had given me life, I fell asleep.

I awoke to the sounds of soft voices, raised occasionally in quiet laughter. I was only disoriented for a moment, the room and the location were not that unfamiliar to me. I was surprised to see it was morning. I'd slept through the night on the sofa.

I looked out the window and saw the Seattle that visitors don't get to see often enough: at least, if you hear people from other places talking about Seattle's gray, moist climate.

To native Seattlites, the rain has purpose—it makes you appreciate other types of weather so much more.

Sure, it rains. Three-quarters of the year, it rains almost every day. For a while. And then the rain stops, and the sun comes out and the city is this incredible, sparklingly clean jewel. Nothing compares.

I got up and walked groggily to the kitchen to join the coffee klatch—over tea—that I knew was going on. "Madeline! You look terrible," Miranda said cheerfully as she gave me a huge hug.

"Oh, too true," Meagan chimed in, "you look like absolute shit."

"Miggin!" my mother reprimanded as she put a cup of tea in my hand.

"It's okay, Mom. It *is* true." I hadn't dared peek at myself yet, but I knew my hair was probably doing something close to standing on end, and my eyes would be puffy from all the crying I'd been doing.

Both Miranda and Meagan, on the other hand, looked wonderful. Miranda is the eldest of us three. She has a perfect life: a perfect marriage, two perfect children—a girl and a boy, of course and both blond, golden replicas of their mother—a wonderful husband who works in high tech and a gorgeous home in Redmond. She even has a golden retriever. Like me, she wears her blond hair long and, also like me, she has inherited our mother's birdlike metabolism—she can and does eat virtually anything and never gains a pound. After childbirth—twice—her friends all hated her because she went right back to wearing low-single-digit-size clothes within a month.

Meagan, on the other hand, takes after our father's side. Where Miranda and I are both blond, like our mother, and have that pale, thin-skinned girl-next-door complexion, Meagan is olive-skinned and her hair is dark. When we were children, she used to complain that she was adopted, which, of course, she was not. But it's always seemed as though her darker coloring reflected—or maybe produced—something darker on the inside. Happiness eludes Meagan and so she's constantly searching. The youngest of us three, Meagan is thirty-one, has been married twice and changed careers so often we've stopped keeping track.

On this visit, I was relieved to see she'd passed through the Goth phase she'd been in the last time I'd seen her. Her hair was its natural dark auburn instead of the matte black she'd previously worn, her makeup was less severe and the black lipstick seemed to mercifully have been relegated to a drawer somewhere.

I realized I was looking at interior-design Meagan, which was like a new version of Barbie. Her hair was cut into a short, flattering cap, her makeup was flawless and understated and she wore a tailored plum-colored suit that, at a glance, I identified as Marc Jacobs.

"You guys, on the other hand, look amazing." It was true. Plus it felt good just to look at them and have the three of us under one roof. The inseparable, invincible Carter sisters. We'd *owned* our high school. "But, Migs, I can't believe what you did to Mom's kitchen."

"Madeline!" my mother said sharply.

"What do you mean?" Meagan asked. "It's beautiful." Then to our other sister, "You think it's beautiful, don't you, Miranda?"

"Sure." Miranda shrugged, uncomfortable at being put on the spot. I knew what it looked like: I'd been on that spot. "It's just not exactly…Mom."

Meagan cast outraged eyes at our sister. "What the hell does that mean? You don't agree, do you, Mad?"

I was about to hold up my hands to deflect the wrath of Meagan, when my mother intercepted. "Girls, please! The kitchen is wonderful. Beautiful. And, as Madeline commented when she saw it last night, it's very bright. And it's functional. Now, just leave it alone, please."

Meagan sent a few rebellious looks to me and Miranda, but didn't say anything more. Mother had trained us well. Arguing with Mom when she used *that* tone wasn't something any of us thought of as a possibility. Even now.

"What brings you home, Madeline?" Miranda asked, as much to skate the conversation onto safer ground as anything. "Mom didn't tell us you were coming."

"Mom didn't know," I said, then gave them an abbreviated version of the whole story I'd told my mother the night before.

"So you're here," Miranda restated after I was done, "to check out this company? The one in Olympia?"

"Yeah. That and to see you guys," I dropped my eyes. "I felt this sudden need to have my family around me."

"You didn't tell them about Gus," my mother said softly.

"No, I didn't, did I? Look, I need a shower. Can you please tell them while I'm gone? I don't think I could handle thinking about it that much right now."

Meagan looked ready to burst with desire for information, but Mom respected what I'd asked and waited until I'd gone upstairs to shower before she gave my sisters the skinny on my life.

I hadn't been upstairs since I'd been home, but there were no surprises there. After my father died, my mom moved into the room that had been mine and Meagan's. Miranda's bedroom—as the eldest, she'd gotten her own—had been turned into a little study where my mom could go over golf course accounts or sit comfortably and read. The big front bedroom that my mother and father had shared had been turned into a beautiful, airy guest room. It didn't get a lot of use, but Mom said she was happy to have a place for her kids to stay, should the need ever arise.

My parents bought the house when us girls were small. The Victorian had needed careful handling, not only to restore it to its original splendor, but also to seamlessly add the things a modern family counted as necessities. A small fourth bedroom adjacent to my parents' room had been refitted as a walk-in closet and bathroom, creating a master suite for a couple that needed their privacy in a house full of growing girls. While I was growing up, Mom and Dad's bathroom had generally been off limits, which made using it whenever I was visiting Seattle extra special. A formerly forbidden pleasure, now available to me whenever I chose.

This is where I went now, to rejuvenate from a night spent on airplanes, crying in my mother's arms, then sleeping on a sofa. The shower was strong and good, just as I'd remembered it, just as my father had insisted it be.

Oddly, even the tap water smelled like home. Not something I would have ever been able to put my finger on when I lived here, but now that I'd been away so long, it smelled like chlorine and mountains, slightly metallic, yet wonderful to drink. I did that, too, while I was in the shower—I stood beneath the hard driving water, lifted my head and opened my mouth, gulping at what home tasted like.

In my new jeans and T-shirt, and with the sleep

washed out of my hair and off my face, I felt almost
fully human again. The crying of the night before—
wrenched hard from deep within me—had left some
marks. My eyes were less clear than usual today, but I
knew the puffiness would recede as the day progressed.

By the time I rejoined the other Carter women down-
stairs, they'd moved into the living room, the inevitable
cups of tea perched on coasters on the coffee table. As
soon as I entered the room, I could tell Mom had told
them everything: six concerned eyes moved to my face,
checking for signs of breakage, I supposed. Or the strain
that can lead to that.

Miranda spoke first, "Madeline, I'm so sorry."

Meagan started to say something as well, but I cut
her off. "Guys don't, okay? I appreciate it, really. But
if I start thinking about it now I know I'll start crying
again. I just want to enjoy your company."

Grabbing a hint, Mom asked, "So what's next,
sweetie? Much as I'd like to think you are here just to
see us, I have a hunch it's something about that kryptonite company."

Again with the kryptonite. And I hadn't even known
my mom knew who Superman was.

"It's Zylonite. And yeah, you're right. I thought I
might pay them a visit."

"Wait," Meagan said. "Zylonite?"

I perked my ears toward her. "You know what it is?"

"Yeah. Totally. We talked about it a lot in one of my
design classes. The instructor was just a total *freak* for
the stuff. It was invented in the late nineteenth century.
He collects things made with it."

"Are you serious?" I couldn't believe my luck. My
sister not only knew what it was, but it sounded as

though she had a bead on a genuine expert. "So," I re-peated. "You know what it is?"

"You're kidding, right?" She looked at me, my sis-ter and my mom with a disbelief I knew was genuine. "Madeline, you know *everything,* how can you not know this?" I just kept looking at her. Waiting. With Migs, sometimes waiting is enough. "Mad, Zylonite is just another name for celluloid."

eagan said, it most on the verge of (?)

Sixteen

Celluloid. I just looked at Meagan, allowing this to sink in. I had the feeling everything was on the verge of making sense to me. But just the verge: there was still a lot I didn't know.

"So why would you have been learning about it in a design class?"

Meagan rolled her eyes, something I was annoyed to see she still did. "Come on, a lot of cool modern American stuff is made out of celluloid."

"Like what?"

"Well, these days mostly just eyeglass frames—high-end sunglasses and designer prescription glasses. But, in the olden days, just about everything. And that's the stuff Professor Rice would just go on and on and on about."

"And on?" Miranda quipped.

"Exactly," Meagan said, ignoring everything but her words. It's amazing how sisters get really good at doing that at an early age. "Celluloid was one of the earliest plastics. Zylonite is like a trade name, but more specific than that. In their catalog descriptions, for example, department stores would say that these billiard balls were made out of Zylonite, or that comb or mantel clock, or whatever. Like a prestige thing—plastic, only better."

"Why did your design teacher go gaga over it?" I asked.

"Well, early Zylonite items are *way* collectible. The stuff was like this miracle material. Companies used it to make things that had been really expensive and difficult to manufacture before. Combs and dolls' heads and Christmas ornaments, you name it. Anything that could be molded, basically. And my prof also liked Zylonite specifically because they're based right here in Washington State and have been, like, forever." She stopped, looked at me, her eyes wide. "Oh, I *get* it, Mad. *That's* the company."

"Right."

"So what are you going to do?" Miranda was always the practical one of us three.

I sat back, laced my fingers behind my head, absently perused the collection of hand-painted English plates my mother has mounted over the mantel. Finally, I had to admit it—because nothing had come to me, "I'm not really sure yet. I thought maybe I'd just drive down there and see who I could get to talk to me."

Meagan surprised me by being completely negative. "Oh, Madeline, that is such a bad idea!"

"It is?"

"Yeah, just cruising down there without a plan. I have a better one." She looked incredibly self-satisfied.

"Well, good. I guess I could use one."

Okay, so, truth be told, Meagan's plan was silly. Not to mention convoluted. But it was also entirely doable so I went along. Meagan has been the baby in our family forever. After a while, you get used to giving in when you can.

We drove down to Olympia in Meagan's Porsche Carrera—a souvenir from her last marriage. "Hah!" she snorted when I commented on it. "This was Lloyd's car. Just let him try to pick up chicks in my minivan."

We'd stopped at Miranda's to get clothes for me for our little charade. I still wasn't so sure any of this was a great idea, but about a million years ago, we all got into the habit of indulging baby Meagan. It was proving to be a hard habit to break.

Because of the obsession of her former professor, Meagan knew that the Northwest Zylonite Corporation maintained a museum based on all of the items the company had made since the company was founded. Naturally, this was a collector's Mecca, and taking advantage of this, the museum and company did sales of some of the higher-end items.

Meagan's bright idea was that we go down there posing as an interior designer—her—and her wealthy client—me. Hence the Porsche rather than my rental. Hence also the stop at Miranda's to outfit me appropriately. Miranda, being an actual wealthy client herself, had just the getup I'd need—a powder-blue suit with a medium-length skirt and a fur-trimmed jacket. Meagan opted for the artsy contractor's special uniform, black on black on black. That is, a black knit top, well-cut black trousers, a black leather jacket and boots. I thought she looked sensational and I told her so.

On the freeway heading south I settled in and enjoyed the landscape, still as fresh and green as in my youth. Meagan, meanwhile, kept up a steady stream of conversations on her cell phone. She seemed incapable of driving without blabbing.

One of the calls was to the Northwest Zylonite Corporation. "Hello," she said when she'd gotten the department she wanted on the phone. "This is Meagan Weiss from Meagan Weiss Designs." Weiss had been Meagan's married name. I was surprised she was still using it. And it was the first time I'd heard her company name or her snooty designer phone style. "I'm in my car *this instant* with a client who's doing a house in Medina. She heard about the Zylonite escutcheons in your collection and now *will not* rest until she acquires some." She paused while, presumably, whoever was on the other line did some blabbing. "Wonderful. We'll be there in half an hour. I'll ask for you."

"What are escutcheons?" I asked when she'd disconnected.

Meagan took her eyes off the road long enough to pantomime openmouthed shock. "I can't even believe this— *two* things in one day Little Miss Know-it-all doesn't know and I do."

"Yes, it's true, sister darling," I said, picking up a banter that had been discarded for most of the last dozen or so years, but still came to me as effortlessly as silk on skin. "It is indeed a day of miracles when such a thing should happen. Seriously. Escutcheon. What is it?"

"It's the little plastic thingy that goes around a light switch."

"I always thought that was called the Little Plastic Thingy That Goes Around a Light Switch."

"And it's other stuff, too, stuff like that. Things that go around things. But we'll look at the light thingies because it makes sense, from a decorating perspective."

"Does it?" I had my doubts. "Who would drive all this way—Seattle to Olympia—for the right…whatcha-macallit? Escutch—"

"Escutcheon. And you'd be surprised, Mad. This design stuff is a kick-ass interesting world in the circles I'm traveling. Thanks to Lloyd, my new clients are the wives of his old pals."

"Cool."

"Yeah. Very," she snorted. "He may as well have been useful for *something*. And since they're all friends, their purpose in redoing a house can just be to get one over on *their* pals. And if that means collector escutcheons— or antique bed skirts or postmodern art or whatever it is that week—off we go, on the big search. They don't always come with me, mind. Sometimes I just step and fetch and bring samples to Her Ladyship. But sometimes they come along for the ride. Makes 'em feel involved."

"When did you get to be such a cynic, Meagan?"

She looked at me. Smirked. "It runs in the family, doesn't it?" She had me there.

I felt simultaneously faintly ridiculous, and as though we were on the greatest adventure ever when we stormed the gates, which, in this case, turned out to be the building's original late 1880s structure, enhanced and enlarged over the years.

Meagan pulled her Porsche into a spot marked Reserved even though there was guest parking farther up the lot. She marched us in the front door, despite the one at the side clearly marked Zylonite Museum and told— not asked—the receptionist that hers was the Porsche and that it was parked in a reserved spot.

"I trust you'll ensure it's not towed," Meagan said. The woman opened her mouth as though to protest, then shut it again quickly as she bought what Meagan was selling—that anyone this imperious was not to be messed with. I tried to remember the technique, though I doubted I'd be able to pull it off as well as my sister did. She was, after all, the youngest child. She came by her imperiousness honestly.

When the receptionist didn't argue, Meagan favored her with a thin smile, reached into her bag, pulled out a business card and handed it to her, saying, "Please tell Jerome Moretti that we're here."

Then she marched us both over to a waiting area and indicated that I should sit. She didn't sit—just paced impatiently as though if Jerome didn't show up pronto, her head would explode.

"You're making me nervous," I whispered to her.

"That's the idea," she whispered back.

"Why do you want to make me nervous?"

She favored me with a withering look. "Not you—" a thumb over her shoulder at the receptionist "—her."

"Oh," I mouthed at her silently.

Jerome Moretti didn't look like a Jerome Moretti at all. He was painfully tall and thin, with a complexion like clotted cream and wispy mouse-colored hair.

"Ms. Weiss." He recognized Meagan as the designer by her uniform, no doubt. "So good of you to come. And Mrs. Carter," he gushed when Meagan introduced me, the Mrs. being Meagan's additional creative flourish, "we're always pleased when a designer brings us one of her clients. Extending the world of Zylonite, if you will."

He talked as he ushered us toward the museum entrance. "Ms. Weiss told me you were especially interested in escutcheons, but she didn't specify. Were you looking for picture frames or door plates or wall plates, or…?"

"The light things," I said with as much confidence as I could muster, describing a light-switch-size rectangle in the air in front of me with my index finger. I shot a glance at Meagan, who gave me an almost imperceptible nod of approval. I've had clients. I know the drill. Clients aren't expected to know a whole lot. That's why they hire pros. I didn't know a whole lot and so was playing my part perfectly.

The museum was housed in a single large room that had so much character I was sure it was probably a place where preunion employees who worked incredibly long hours for crap wages under horrible conditions had once "crafted" the "historic items" that Jerome Moretti now showed us. Huge barred windows on either side of the long, high room cast spiderwebs of bright light onto the polished concrete floors.

A myriad of Zylonite items were displayed in glass-fronted cabinets and on long mahogany tables. The mind boggled just looking at all the stuff: combs and brushes and cigarette cases and lamps and ornamental objects that looked intricately carved out of precious materials but were actually molded out of plastic. Er... Zylonite.

Moretti let us peruse at will while keeping up a running monologue on the wonders of the material his company manufactured. It was interesting to me, but after a few minutes I'd stopped listening. In fact I think that, for just a few seconds, I stopped breathing. Because there, halfway down the room and commanding the largest piece of wall between windows, was a huge gilt-framed portrait of Lolita Larkin.

Seventeen

Seeing her there, as I'd seen her looking in films from the heyday of her career, was like seeing a ghost. The artist had captured her at the height of her beauty and her screen powers, titian hair flowing over bare shoulders, head cocked coquettishly to one side, lips barely parted, inviting gently.

"Ah," Moretti said, breaking into my startled observation. "I see you've discovered the portrait of our patroness. Do you recognize her?"

Meagan looked baffled, but I nodded. "Yes."

"She was quite the beauty, wasn't she?" Moretti said.

"Who is it?" Meagan asked.

"Lolita Larkin," I said. "The actress. But how is she—what did you say?—your patroness?"

"Really, she was much more. She bought the company, you see, in the middle part of the twentieth century."

"She did?" I felt as if I should have known this.

Moretti led me past rows of Zylonite combs and Christmas ornaments and jumping dogs and totems to the far corner of the museum. "If you're a fan of Lolita

Larkin's," he said as we walked, "then you simply must see this." He stopped in front of a wall covered in photos of Lolita Larkin. Lolita dancing, Lolita at the beach, Lolita on the sets of various films, Lolita at home, the gardens of Larkin House visible behind her.

Other people were visible in some of the photos. In the publicity stills and the on-set photos, for instance, and I could identify the faces of various leading men of her day. But one face cropped up again and again—a male face—and I couldn't place it.

"Who's this?" I asked, pointing.

Moretti looked closely but shook his head. "Sorry. I couldn't say." Then he went on to point out the faces he did know in other photographs.

"Why is this here?" I asked, indicating the photographic shrine.

"Lolita bequeathed it to us—to the company—upon her death. She wanted these things displayed in a place where her public would have easy access to them." He smiled warmly. These were likely questions he fielded on a regular basis. "Her public is smaller these days," he said without embarrassment. "A lot of people don't even remember her work. But you'd be surprised at the number who do."

"So, you were telling us," I prompted, "before. That she purchased the company around the middle of the last century...."

"Yes. She was an extremely astute businesswoman. And ours was not the only celluloid company she purchased. She bought several others, throughout the United States, and united them under the Northwest Zylonite banner."

"Celluloid?"

"That's right. By the time she was done, Miss Larkin effectively controlled the North American celluloid market. A shrewd move, you'd agree, for someone whose career was tied to the production of film."

Shrewd? Sure. Though in some ways that didn't begin to cover it. Why hadn't I thought of it before? Celluloid was what early film was made of. Still, this felt like another piece of the puzzle: not the whole answer. There was a lot I didn't know.

"When did she sell the company?" I asked.

"Oh, she didn't. When she died, it passed to her son, George. And when *he* died last year, the board of directors elected to take the company public."

"George had no heirs?"

"Well—" the formerly forthright Moretti seemed suddenly evasive "—there was no one to take over the company. Now, Ms. Weiss indicated you had an interest in escutcheons?" Since I'd already confirmed that this was the case, his question seemed an obvious ploy to steer the conversation back to the present day. Whether this was because he didn't want to talk about it, or because he had more important things to do than blather away to us, I couldn't say. But, after a few more moments of looking up at the photographs of Lolita Larkin, I followed Moretti and my sister to another area of the large room to look at what was on offer.

Though Victorian design isn't one of my things, the majority of the plastic-that-goes-around-the-light-thingies that the Zylonite company had made had been influenced by that period, as well as a few items that were obviously more arts and crafts and art deco. Later design periods were not largely represented. It was easy to see why this was so; celluloid—or rather Zylonite—

could be easily molded to look as though it were any number of more rare and expensive materials. It would, I imagined, have been revolutionary at the time these objects were first made.

I honed in on half a dozen escutcheons that represented the Victorian era. Four were original late 1880s Zylonite Corporation creations. These had been crafted to look like carved ivory, as though brought back from India by some seafaring uncle. The other two were also Victorian, but Moretti explained that these had been made recently—reproductions of original Zylonite company designs, though, of course, made of Zylonite right at the factory. These two looked so much like carved jade it was astonishing, at least to me, who is no kind of expert on jade.

Since my parents had restored their Victorian house and—aside from my mother's newly *très moderne* kitchen—every room gave a nod to the period in which the house had been built, I thought these six escutcheons would make a cool gift for my mom. I knew I'd probably have to get back to L.A. before I had a chance to do any shopping, so this might be my only opportunity to find a fun present.

"I can't decide for my own house today, Mr. Moretti," I explained. "And I will, of course, need Ms. Weiss's input. However, I'll take these six, for my mother's home."

To my surprise, Meagan interjected. "Oh, Mrs. Carter. I don't think that would be a very good idea."

"No, really," I said carefully and slowly, so Meagan would understand my reasoning. "I was thinking I haven't bought my mother anything nice for a while and this seems a good chance."

Meagan shook her head. "As it happens, Mrs. Carter,

I've seen your mother's house. I don't think these would compliment her decor."

Meagan really was the limit, I thought. Now that she was a designer, no one else could have any taste or offer a design opinion. Well, I'd show her: I happened to really think these *escutcheons* would not only look great in Mom's house, I knew she'd love them.

I ignored Meagan and pushed my selections toward Jerome Moretti. "Wrap these up for me, please."

"Wonderful choice, Mrs. Carter. I'm sure your mother will be very pleased." And off he trotted to do my bidding and prepare an invoice.

"What's wrong with you?" Meagan hissed when Moretti was out of earshot.

"With me? What's with you? Do you seriously think I can't even pick light plates now that you're a designer?"

Meagan just looked at me, eyes wide for a moment. "You think *that's* it? Oh, Maddy." She shook her head as though very sad for me, then flashed me an evil grin. "Fine. Get your *light plates*. You'll see why I was trying to stop you."

Somewhat miffed at her, in the way one only can be with a sibling, I busied myself looking at more Zylonite historic wares. There really was a lot of it: electric "candles," light stands, children's toys, the list went on and on. Some of it was quite beautiful, but I found a lot of it to be tacky beyond compare: garishly hand-colored objects that were obviously inexpertly painted. Not my idea of museum pieces.

While I waited, I wandered back to the wall of photographs and saw a postcard rack I hadn't noticed before. The images were mainly of what I gathered were star pieces of the collection, as well as a few that had fetched high prices at auction. Near the bottom, though, I found a few dusty postcards with images of Lolita Larkin, some of them the same images that were reproduced on the wall. I picked up one featuring her and the mystery man and turned it over: "Lolita Larkin and friend, at home in Beverly Hills© Northwest Zylonite Museum, Olympia, Washington." Not nearly enough information.

I was still holding the card when Jerome Moretti came bustling toward me, Meagan trailing at an interested distance. "Here you are, Mrs. Carter," he said, passing me a carefully wrapped package and an invoice.

I handed the card to Moretti. "I'll take this, as well."

He tucked it in with my other purchases. "Consider it a gift from the museum. And how will you be paying today?"

Without glancing at the invoice, I started opening my bag, "Is cash all right?" I jested, not looking up. I'd gotten a few hundred dollars at an ATM at the airport in L.A. while waiting for the plane.

"Cash?" Moretti said. At his tone I stopped. Looked at the invoice. And tried to keep the shock from my face. I kept my tone neutral when I said, "Eighteen hundred and seventy-six dollars."

"And twenty-nine cents," Moretti finished. "I had to add tax, of course. And that gives us these funny uneven numbers." He smiled, perhaps to cover his embarrassment. It must have been clear to him I hadn't expected the amount.

"Do you take credit cards?" I asked weakly.

"Oh, your *face*, Maddy. I wish I had a camera," she laughed as she drove North on I-5, back toward Seattle. She laughed hard. "It was priceless."

"Well, shit, Miggs, almost two grand for half a dozen wall plates."

"Escutcheons," she corrected. "And that should have been your clue. Don't you know people charge more when they use those fancy names?"

"What*ever*. They're light plates."

"Come on, get real. You used to collect art, right? We were in a museum. Can you not *buy* a clue?"

She had a point. "But light plates, Miggs," I said weakly. "I mean…how much could they be?"

This brought a new bout of laughter from my sister, always sensitive to my feelings. "Well, the two later ones—the jadeish ones—won't have been much. Check your invoice."

I did. They were $79.95 each. Which I figured was pretty hefty. I said so to Meagan.

"Well, sure, if you'd gotten something like it at some hardware store they would have been, like, four bucks. 'Cause what are they? Fancy plastic, right? But these were *designer* wall plates—escutcheons—made from original early twentieth-century designs in the actual Zylonite factory."

"Who cares?"

"Well, my dear Maddy, you'd better hope our mother does, or you'll have some very fancy light plates when you get back home."

I sighed. "Okay. And those were the cheap ones. Where do they get off charging several hundred dollars for each of the other ones?"

"If you'd been paying attention you'd have heard Jerome say that the company collects original Zylonite both for the museum and for resale to collectors. You happened to choose collector pieces."

"Great," I mumbled. "So now Mom has an escutcheon collection."

Meagan's laugh was slightly more sympathetic now. She's never offended by a joke on other people, but she isn't mean. "She'll love them, Madeline. And they'll go with most of her house, you were right about that. And this Zylonite stuff actually has some pretty passionate collectors. Those plates will probably appreciate in value." She hesitated. "Is it okay? The money, I mean."

I thought about it. I'd been living pretty cheaply the last few months, if for no other reason than—like during much of my adult life—I simply didn't have a lot to spend on. "Actually, it's all right. It won't put me over budget."

"Really?" Meagan took her eyes off the road to read my face for a second. "Cool. Does that mean you can afford to hire a decorator? I'd love to redo your place when they fix it."

I settled back into my seat with a sigh. I didn't even want to think about what my place looked like at the moment. "Just drive," I muttered.

The good news: Mom loved her gift. "Why, they're exquisite, Madeline. Just beautiful. Your father would have loved them, too." They'd redone most of the house together and both had an equal say about all matters relating to the restoration.

Mom wanted them up right away, and zipped down to the basement to get a screwdriver. I found myself less than enthusiastic to see the light plates installed.

"Mom," I said to her in the living room, "are you sure you want that one in here where everyone will be touching it all the time?" It was the most filigreed—and expensive—of the historic ones. This one alone had set me back more than five hundred dollars. She insisted, and it looked great in place, even if I carefully avoided touching it when I came into the room.

While she busied herself with the installation, I went up to the guest room to change back into my jeans, hang up Miranda's suit for later return and make some phone calls.

The Beverly Hills Hotel advised me that "Mr. Beckett and family have checked out," which meant that the police must have told them they could go home.

I called and got Tasya. "Madeline, it's good to hear your voice," she enthused, and I realized that, as odd as it seemed when I was staying with my family, it was good to hear hers as well. I supposed that meant that home really did have a new location now. "So much has been happening since yesterday, you would not believe. One thing you know already—the engineers pronounced the house structurally okay, so we came home this morning."

"That's wonderful, Tasya."

"Yes. It is." She sounded somewhat sad. "Now the bad news. Your place is no more. The apartment? Gone."

I sat down on the bed, the receiver in my hand, hard to my ear. "So it was worse than we thought?"

"Much, much worse. Tyler is hiring people to come and collect what things of yours he can. Right now the things are all over the canyon. I'm sorry."

"Me, too."

"You will, of course, stay in the guest room while we figure everything out." I started to protest weakly, but Tasya cut me off. "Tyler and I have talked about it. He's going to have what stuff that is good is found put in there." I could visualize her pulling off her signature shrug. "So, it is done."

"Thank you."

"No, Madeline. You are family." And she said this last so naturally, so easily, I knew it to be true.

"Well, thank you for that, as well."

"Now, more bad news…" More? How could there even be more? "The police say the explosion was not an accident after all. They had, what do you call them? Special police…"

"Forensic investigators?" I offered.

"*Da*. That's it. Forensic guys. They found, they called it, a timing device."

"In my apartment?"

"That is right. And that is why we are so worried, Tyler and me. We are worried that you are not here because a timing device means someone was trying to kill you. Otherwise, why your apartment?"

Why indeed?

"How is Tycho?" I asked, really wanting to know and also wanting to change the subject. Not wanting to think about the fact that someone wanted me dead badly enough to risk killing innocent people and a dog.

I could hear her smile at the question. "Tycho is home again. He is horse healthy. He will be happy to see you. When are you coming home?"

"I'm not sure. Later today or tomorrow, I guess. Thanks so much for the update, Tasya."

"Oh, wait, someone has been trying and trying to talk to you. Detective Brown. He's called many times. I'll give you the number."

"Never mind," I said, stopping her. "I have it already."

Brian Brown was less happy to hear from me than Tasya had been.

"Where the hell are you?" he boomed when I identified myself.

"I don't really want to say," I hedged.

"Well, you *better* say. All hell is breaking loose around here." He lowered his voice and I could almost hear him struggle with himself for control. "There've been some interesting developments, Madeline. And we think you may be in danger."

"I know. I just spoke with Tasya Saranova. She told me they found a timing device in my apartment."

"Yes. And the house is under surveillance. But it's not just that."

"What then?"

He hesitated, sounded like he might be getting to ready to tell me, then changed his mind. "Look, I'd rather not say until I have you in my office. Just be careful. And get here as soon as you can, okay?"

I quelled the fear I'd felt rising since I'd spoken with Tasya. Fear had no place here in my mother's house. "When are you on duty?"

"Never mind that. You have my cell number. Call me the minute you get back so we can get together. There are things we need to talk about."

It was already afternoon and Miranda had planned a family dinner in my honor at her house. I hadn't seen my niece and nephew in a while and I was pleased at the opportunity to catch up with them and see how they'd grown.

"Too bad you didn't know about dinner when we were at the Zylonite factory," Meagan said to me quietly. "You could have spent another couple grand on historic toys."

I punched her lightly in the arm and her protests emerged around a mouthful of giggles that ended up with both of us in a wrestling tickling match on the living room floor at my mother's. Some things you're never too old to do with your siblings. Cheerfully beating them up, I've found, is one of them.

Before we left for Miranda's I called Sal, as I'd told him I would the day before. "I don't know what it is with you and these shaky securities, Carter," he said when I got him. "You had a look at the financials?"

"What I could get my hands on. There really wasn't much."

"Good reason, too. They're in such deep financial doo-doo, they're sinking in it."

Doo-doo. Sal's raspy voice made the gentle curse all the more incongruous. "The picture I got wasn't exactly rosy," I said, "but doo-doo was not my read."

"Yeah, looks like a lot of sleight of hand to me. The boys got to the bottom of it, though." He sounded especially self-satisfied at this.

"Tell me."

"Well, the company was always privately held. *Family* held, to make matters worse. So, of course, we don't get any of those financials. When the family patriarch died a year or so ago the shit hit. They'd been doing the spiral for a long time, probably. You know what I'm saying?"

I did. I think that anytime that happens to a company they feel like they're unique: that it's never happened before. The market has changed and they have not. They spend just as much money as they've always spent, but they're making a whole lot less. Maybe they even spend more money to make less money, because they're scurrying around trying to drum up business that just isn't there.

Having seen the Northwest Zylonite Corporation up close and personal, I could imagine how this could be the case. Who really needed Zylonite escutcheons anymore—besides me, of course? And the eyeglasses thing couldn't be that lucrative—not enough to become the mainline when it used to be the sideline, and there are offshore companies with cheap materials and new polymers lining up to steal the teeny customer base you have left. And the mainline? The mainline was dead. Most production companies didn't even *use* film stock anymore: a lot of stuff was now filmed direct to tape or even digital.

"So the IPO was, what? A last-ditch attempt?"

"Pretty much. They needed a cash infusion. So... who you gonna call?"

"Exactly. Did it work?"

"Somewhat. Can you guess what happened?"

"Lukewarm IPO followed by an all-out tank?"

"Ten points, Ms. Carter! Exactamundo."

An exactamundo practically on top of doo-doo? Sal must have had a good day.

"Chapter 11 is looming?" I asked.

"Well, it was. Then, a few weeks ago, another cash infusion from an unexpected source. Every available share was bought up over the course of a few days."

"Buoyed the stock, huh?"

"Yeah. And since a huge chunk of family-held shares had just become available, more were on the market than would usually have been the case."

"Family held?"

"Yeah. George Larkin."

"But he's dead." More dead people playing the stock market? The morgue would be getting a little crowded.

"Nah…his kid. George Larkin Jr."

I'd been standing in the guest room, next to the bed. I sat down now. Heavily.

"Sal, are you sure that's who it is?"

"Of course I'm sure, Carter," he boomed. "I wouldn't say it if I wasn't sure."

I let it go for the moment. But the coincidences were piling up hot and heavy. Lark, Larkin, not to mention that gorgeous profile. Why hadn't I seen it before? "That seems like incredible timing, doesn't it?"

"Yeah, lucky. Normally, a large inside-held chunk like that would have caused the stock price to plummet."

"But an available buyer had the opposite effect." I didn't bother trying to keep the excitement out of my voice. "Pretty good timing, huh? With someone buying, it made the price rise."

"Exactamundo again, Carter. Exactamundo precisely."

My impromptu trip to Seattle couldn't have worked out better if I'd planned it. Though I didn't doubt I would have found the connection between Lolita Larkin and the Northwest Zylonite Corporation without leaving Los Angeles, there had been something about being in Washington and discovering it for myself that had really rocked it home. In one way, seeing that huge portrait of Lolita Larkin had alone been worth the trip.

More important at this point, though, it had done my heart good to spend time with my family. The personal losses I'd experienced had drained me more than I'd realized. The single sleep spent in my childhood nest had steadied me somewhat. Grounded me. And though part of me felt like holing up in my mother's guest room indefinitely, I knew I had to head back to L.A.

After a family dinner at Miranda's so warm it made me miss everyone before I'd even left, I said goodbye to my sisters, brother-in-law and my niece and nephew and went back to my mom's house.

In the morning I bade my mom a tearful farewell and headed off to the airport in my rental feeling as though I'd accomplished everything I'd come to Seattle for. And more. I got into LAX just after noon.

And then all hell broke loose.

Eighteen

Disorientation was all I felt when I came to on the rough concrete floor of the parking structure at LAX, sirens screaming in my ear and my left cheek feeling as though someone had tried to exfoliate it with a belt sander. When I touched that cheek gingerly, the tips of my fingers came away lightly dotted with blood.

I picked myself up carefully, fully expecting at least one limb to protest, but I was relieved to find I was more battered than broken. I put weight on each leg, stretched my arms and extended my neck, trying to get a feel for the extent of the damage. Nothing, other than my cheek, seemed hurt. That was something.

While I did this self-examination I tried to shake off the disorientation, tried to put together whatever path had led me here. It didn't all come right away.

I could remember making two attempts just to locate my car. All of the parking structures at LAX seem identical to me and I always forget to take note of the letter-number designation that would ease the process. I got back to where I thought my car should be, only to find a late-seventies Monte Carlo sitting where I was *sure* I'd left my Impala. I just stood and stared at this intrusive car for a moment, trying to think what might have happened.

In the second parking structure I tried, I was relieved to find my car just where I'd left it. I fumbled in my bag for my keys and, without taking them out, pushed the remote door lock—or in this case unlock—while I walked. The car beeped at me agreeably three times: I'd hit the wrong button and opened the trunk. I do this a lot. There are four buttons on my remote keyless-entry fob: one unlocks the doors, one opens the trunk, one starts the car and—inexplicably—one beeps the horn. I quite often don't look at the buttons when I hit them and depress the wrong key. The general rule, however, is that I *never* accidentally hit the horn button unless it's really going to embarrass me. Murphy's Law?

I'd been traveling light on this Seattle trip and I'd just planned on popping what little I had on the back seat but, what the hell, the trunk was open and the Hummer parked on the driver's side of my car was taking more than its share of space. Since a pillar was neatly blocking my passenger side, I was going to have to squeeze in as it was. The trunk was unlocked, anyway, so I pulled it open to put my stuff in.

I was immediately sorry I'd even started the exercise, though I imagined things would smell bad even in the car's main cabin. The pizza was, of course, still there, and a couple of days in the trunk of a hot car hadn't done much for its disposition. It didn't smell bad, exactly. It just didn't smell good. The pizza, however, wasn't the worst of it. In the heat, the sparkling Shiraz had exploded and my trunk looked as if someone had died in there—it looked like a bloodbath—and smelled like the inside of a wino's head. And while the bagels had probably fared all right—I wouldn't have wanted to eat them, but they didn't stink—the eggs and the orange juice were adding their own pong to the odorific melody my trunk had become. It was truly awful.

My first instinct was to be cowardly and just run: take my stuff, hail a cab and call some cleanup service to get my car, sterilize it and deliver it to me all nice and shiny and new. Since this really *did* seem cowardly—not to mention impractical—I bit the bullet. I opened the passenger side door, walking sideways to avoid the pillar, put my stuff on the seat, reached in and got the towel that I always kept on the back seat to tidy up after Tycho has been keeping me company on a road trip.

With my limited materials, it took me a long time to clean up. The messenger bag with Keesia's rock and the other supplies from my nighttime foray was the least affected by the mess. Since I wasn't going to be throwing that away, I mopped it up first with the still-clean towel and slung the bag over my shoulder with my Kate Spade tote just to get it out of the way.

The chunks of glass from the wine bottle were mercifully large. I plopped the pieces into one of the pizza boxes, then mopped up all of the wine I could with the towel. While I worked I tried not to think about the potential symbolism of that ruined last supper. The one Gus and I hadn't gotten to have. Broken glass, spilled wine, putrid pizza. And breakfast: stale bagels, rotten eggs, spoiled juice. Too many thoughts like those, I knew, would have me crying into my trunk.

The cleanup was an imperfect job. Without actual soap and water, it had to be. When I was satisfied that the worst of it was dealt with and that it was as good as it was going to get under the circumstances, I scrunched the pizza boxes up as well as I could, with the broken glass safely on the inside, popped the orange juice container and the egg carton on the pizza and, as an afterthought I plopped the towel on top of the whole mess, then made my way across the parking structure to where I could see a garbage can. I beeped the door locked before I left the car. I'd only be gone for a minute, but this was, after all, L.A.

With the mess properly disposed of, I made my way back to the car, rubbing my pizza-and-wine-stained hands on my jeans when no one was looking. Is that not, after all, the purpose of jeans?

Halfway back to the car, I fumbled again in my purse, thinking to use the remote entry to unlock the door. A small click from the car confused me—the wrong sound, not unlocking. I'd hit the remote start button, instead.

Just as that thought registered, the world ended. At least, that's what it felt like. My next coherent thought came some time later, though it took me a while to even figure out how much later it was.

Two police cars, a fire truck, a fleet of airport security vehicles and an ambulance burst into the vicinity just as I was picking myself off the pavement. "What happened?" someone shouted, and I found there was no answer I could formulate. Not only did I not know what had happened, I seemed momentarily completely without words.

The action centered on my car, not me. Or, rather, what was left of my car. There was a trunk. There was an engine compartment. But what was left in the middle was a smoking mess. While I watched, dazed, from the sidelines, a brace of fire guys hauling a hose between them doused my car, stopping the smoke and dampening the flames.

All of the activity—not to mention the small amount of blood I'd lost—kept me from thinking about what all of this actually meant. For a while. When it did sink in, I felt my knees go weak. Literally.

Since I was the only obvious physical casualty, the paramedics hustled me into the back of the ambulance. It happened quickly and I was dazed, but I was aware of having my bones checked for breaks—there weren't any—and the contusion on my head quickly bandaged. I remember, also, a lot of "Does it hurt here?" and "How about there?" It didn't, and when it was clear that my only injury was on the surface and had been dealt with, they nodded at a policeman whose presence I hadn't noted before and said, "Okay. We're done with her."

"Come with me, ma'am." Ma'am! I looked at him. When did they start recruiting twelve-year-olds? And, of course, he wasn't twelve, but he really *did* look barely old enough to shave, let alone drive a real police car and carry a gun. He noticed that I was still a bit shaky on my feet and led me toward a marked car. "You can sit in the back of my cruiser for a minute." He opened the door and let me sit on the seat sideways, my feet still touching the pavement.

"You want to tell me what happened?"

I looked at him, wide-eyed, trying to formulate an answer. What *had* just happened? "My car exploded."

He smiled, not unkindly. "We've pretty much got that part figured out. Any idea why?"

I shook my head in the negative, reflectively. Then nodded slowly. Then shook it again. "Not exactly." I cleared my throat. The old vocal thing wasn't working quite perfectly yet. "But it's not isolated." I thought for a moment, then added, "Detective Brian Brown at the Beverly Hills Police Department has been working on… on…the case."

Was that what all of this was? Keesia's death? Gus's? And now my car. Did all of that add up to a case?

"I have Detective Brown's number here," I said, then did a mental inventory, and realized I was right: my new Kate Spade tote, my messenger bag and my handbag were all attached to me via various shoulder straps. There was a lot of thanks that needed to be expressed to a single bottle of sparkling wine.

"I don't need the number—" he smiled again "—our lines here are pretty direct." He indicated the computer and two-way equipment in the front seat. "If you'll just give me your name, I'll see if he's on duty."

After I'd given him my particulars, the young cop trotted off to join the other officers. From my vantage point in the back of the police cruiser, I felt the ease to really take in the scene for the first time. It was a mess. I could tell that my car was going to be a total write-off. From the looks of things, the Hummer that had hemmed me in—and probably saved my life by blocking me from the worst of the blast—hadn't fared much better. LAX is one of the busiest international airports in the country, and it was the middle of the day so, even though most people had places to go and people to see, a small crowd was beginning to collect: the inevitable rubberneckers wondering what was happening and it looked as if the press was arriving now, as well. They wouldn't know anything yet but give them fifteen minutes and they'd know more than I did.

I gathered, from the looks of the powwow happening near my car, and from the snippets of conversation I could overhear, that some kind of power struggle was going on. Which, when you thought about it, only made sense. Exploding cars in airports—even airport parking lots—make a lot of people nervous. What jurisdiction would this fall under, I wondered? City police or airport security? In either case, I could see that no one was taking it lightly. This thought was confirmed when I spotted a couple of guys with "SWAT" confidently displayed on the backs of their flak jackets securing the site perimeter and keeping press and onlookers back from the blast area. I wouldn't have been surprised if I'd discovered they were shutting the airport down while they figured out what was going on.

I could see my young officer enter the powwow and partake on some junior level for a while. Then he went off to another cruiser, presumably to contact Brian in private. When he came back to the car, he was still jovial, but with an edge. "Well, Ms. Carter, looks like you get the limo treatment today."

"Pardon?"

"Detective Brown has asked me to bring you directly to him. If you wouldn't mind swinging your legs in and…"

"Am I under arrest?" I asked, though I didn't think to argue.

He laughed. "Not even close. We don't generally arrest the victim when a car explodes."

So now, on top of everything, I was a victim. I sighed, pulled my legs in as requested and settled in.

Brian must have been watching for me because, by the time I trudged in dragging my various bags, he was waiting there himself to escort me to his part of the building.

"Wow," I quipped. "I feel privileged. First I rate a ride and now you meet me in person."

He looked as though he might say something to squash my quip, then seemed to change his mind. He smiled instead and shot back, "You should. I generally only escort hardened criminals this way."

Instead of sitting me at his cubicle, he led me to an interview room and shut the door. Once there, he didn't bother with pleasantries. He launched right in.

"You want to tell me what the hell you were doing at the airport?"

"Umm…" I stammered.

"Because I have this sneaking suspicion that you weren't meeting someone."

"Or seeing someone off?"

"Madeline." No inflection. No question. Just my name. But he didn't have to say more. Under the circumstances, it spoke volumes.

"I was in Seattle," I said quietly.

"I thought I told you not to leave town." His tone was level.

I shrugged. He was right, he had. And I hadn't even considered telling him when I left. "I just had to go."

"Why?" He was looking at me expectantly. He wanted an answer.

"I'm from Seattle. Did you know that?"

"No, actually. I didn't. I had the idea you were from New York."

"Not originally."

"So you, what?" he said sarcastically. "Got a sudden urge to see your family?"

"To be honest, that was part of it," I said with dignity. "A lot has happened to me over the last few weeks."

He looked contrite. "Actually, aside from some dirt and that scrape—" he indicated my cheek "—you look better than you did the last time I saw you."

"Thank you. I feel better, too. There was also a Washington State connection with that stock stuff I was telling you about."

He *had* looked contrite. Now he looked annoyed again. "I figured it had to be more than family. I told you before, Madeline. This is an official police investigation. You're not helping."

"Do you want to hear this or not?" I said. He nodded curtly. Since I knew that was as much encouragement as I was going to get, I told him what I knew.

"The company I told you about—the one Keesia bought shares in? It turns out Lolita Larkin bought it in the 1940s."

"So?" Brian looked unimpressed. When I thought about it, he didn't have any reason to be otherwise.

"Well, I'm not sure yet. But don't you think that's a hell of a coincidence?"

"Maybe. Maybe not. It's the one thing you find in this business—there really is such a thing, Madeline. The damnedest things happen in real life. It's not like in detective books or the movies where everything ultimately fits together. Real life is messy." He paused. Thoughtfully, or reluctantly. I didn't know him well enough to tell which it was. "Speaking of which," he said finally, "have you looked at a newspaper yet today?"

"I read the *Seattle Post-Intelligencer* on the plane."

"I meant local. No? Well…" I noticed that his face now wore what I had come to recognize as its most serious expression. "Another one of Maxi's ex-wives is dead."

"No," I mouthed. Brian nodded. "Who?"

"Margaret Harding Livingston. Did you know her?"

I shook my head. "Not even the name." And if she'd been at the party, I hadn't met her there.

"And since you were in Seattle—and I suppose you have people who can verify you were in Seattle?" I nodded. "Well, I guess that rules you right out."

"I knew that."

"How?" he asked.

I lifted my hands, palms up. "I knew I didn't do it. How did she die?"

"Horribly, I'm afraid. A barn worker found her body in Griffith Park yesterday morning. At the back of a stall. With a horse in it."

I was dumbfounded. "She was killed by a horse?"

"No, no. She was shot. Someone stuffed her body into the stall. The horse was cowering in the corner, as far from her body as it could get."

"That's horrible, Brian. Are you even allowed to tell me any of that?"

He passed me a copy of the day's paper. The headline was blaring, the story longer than the little information anyone would have available warranted. "Of course I can tell you. Everyone in the world seems to know more than I do." He took a deep breath, sat down in the chair facing me. "Madeline, I like you. At some level I even understand why you keep poking your nose in every place, even though I think it's a really bad idea. But I wouldn't tell you stuff I wasn't 'allowed' to tell, all right? If I'm telling you, you can rest assured it's either common knowledge or a detail so small I could tell the guy who brings the mail."

"Thanks," I sniffed.

"Don't mention it," he said, ignoring my tone.

"Okay," I said, "I've got something else. That company I told you about? The one based in Washington State? I found out a large chunk of family-held shares came on the market a few weeks ago. I'm guessing these are the same shares that Keesia's account bought, which drove the market price up."

Brian looked interested, but he also looked confused. "You know this financial stuff, Madeline. I really don't. Please explain why that would be significant."

I took a deep breath, thought back a few steps and struggled to keep my explanations at entry level. "The SEC—that's the body that governs stock exchanges in the U.S.—they keep track of shareholders important to the company. It needs to be public knowledge if, for instance, the CEO starts dumping all his stock. I mean, it might indicate an expensive mistress or the purchase of a new yacht. But most of the time stuff like that means the ship is sinking and the rats are trying to swim. Does that make sense?"

Brian grinned. "Perfectly, actually."

"So, okay, it's not just CEOs that you track, right? But other people important to the health of the stock. This particular company was family held until fairly recently. So when a large chunk of stock still owned by the family goes up for sale, this also needs to be known. So in *this* case, I was told that the stock was owned by—wait for it—George Larkin Jr."

I looked at Brian expectantly, waiting for a light to dawn. I didn't have long to wait, but I watched it arrive in waves over Brian's face. I knew the feeling.

"You said Lolita Larkin bought the company decades ago?"

"Right."

"And George Larkin Jr. is what? Her son?"

"Grandson."

He paused awhile longer, then spread his hands helplessly. "I feel like there's a piece I'm not getting."

"That's how I felt at first. But think about it—George Larkin? Lark St. George? I know how you feel about coincidence, but is it even possible in this large a quantity?"

"Okay, clearly I'm going to need to have another talk with Lark St. George. But that doesn't change where I want you on all of this."

I just looked at him.

"Someone does seem to be trying to kill you."

"You think?" It wasn't really the place for sarcasm. It just slipped out.

Brain sighed, looking suddenly tired. "Please, Madeline. It's not a joking matter."

"I know that," I said more seriously. "But I don't know what else to do. If I stopped to think it all through carefully, I'd be too afraid to move."

"In your case, that might not be a bad thing," Brian said wryly.

"Thanks."

"Don't mention it. In any case, we have to consider where we go from here very carefully."

"Where would we go?" I honestly couldn't see where this was leading.

"Someone wants you dead, Madeline. Or at least out of commission. Presumably, that same someone will be paying attention to see if their evil plan played out."

"Their evil plan?" I said.

"Sorry. Whatever you have must be catching. It was a weak attempt at humor," he sighed. "Obviously, I'm going to watch you as closely as possible."

I didn't know what that meant. When I thought about it further, I realized I didn't really want to know. "Okay," I said slowly.

"And—right this instant—you are going to promise me that you're going to stay out of anything that even remotely resembles trouble from here on in."

"For the rest of my life?" I said, deadpan.

"For the rest of your life." Brian nodded. "If that's what it takes. But I'm betting it won't take that long. Whoever is doing this is getting pretty bold, Madeline. If it *is* all the same person."

"It is," I said sagely.

"Well then, you've got nothing to worry about. Anyone pulling the shit this person is pulling is going to get caught." He reached for the intercom button on the phone. "I'm going to have someone drive you home," he said.

"You are not," I said, even while Brian called for an officer to come to the interview room.

"Oh, but I am. I have determined that having you loose on the streets is a really bad idea."

"So you're going to—what?—lock me into my house?" I could feel the righteous indignation building. "A neat trick, Brian. Especially since I don't even actually have a house anymore."

"No one is locking you anywhere, Madeline. Like anyone even could." Then, over my head, "Hey, Andrews. This is Madeline Carter. Like I told you earlier, you'll be driving Madeline home to Malibu, then sitting across the road from her house and following her if she goes anywhere." I knew that Brown had said this more for my benefit than for the man who had been directed to be my watchdog.

Officer Andrews looked a pleasant enough sort, pale of hair and skin. I forgot his features the second I looked away from him. "Oh, my *God,* Brian. Are you even listening to yourself? You're having me *followed?* Am I a child who needs watching? Do you seriously think I'll get into trouble without a babysitter?"

Brian looked at me without speaking for a moment. I'd ranted and now wanted an immediate response. "Well?" I prompted. "Were you even listening to me?"

"I was listening, yes. I was just waiting to see if you'd run out of steam. I thought I'd let it blow itself out."

"Is that supposed to make me feel better?"

"Madeline, it's not my job to make you feel better. It's my job to try to keep you from getting yourself killed. Though it may have slipped your mind, it has *not* slipped mine. There have been two attempts on your life in less than a week. Now, please, I have work to do. Just let John here drive you home and then, if at all possible, sit tight for the next few days. Please? It would make things so much easier for me."

He said it like he meant it. In a different state of mind, it might have hurt my feelings.

John Andrews proved a tractable sort, after some persuasion. I told him that, rather than driving me home, he should take me to a car-rental place and then follow me. He didn't cave right away but, fortunately, he soon had the sense to see the course of my logic. After all, as I pointed out to him, it wasn't like I was under arrest or anything. Ultimately, he had to comply.

Once I'd secured the small, nondescript rental car in a nothing shade of brown, I felt a lot better with Andrews behind me than I had with him beside me. This way I could pretend he wasn't there and know that I was safer than I'd be without him.

I was surprised to find a small but dedicated-looking group of reporters camped at the top of the stairs that led down the cliff to Tyler's house. Tyler doesn't have a security fence or cameras or any of the type of stuff that famous people can add to their lives to keep undesirables out. What he does have is a house that's quite far off the beaten trail. And the fact that it's down a cliff accessed only by stairs generally discourages unwanted visitors. Plus, that part of Malibu is not on an easy arc from any of the newsrooms: half an hour from Santa Monica if traffic is light. Longer if they were coming from farther east, which they generally were. The fact that they were here now brought home to me just how big this story had become.

"Ms. Carter," an eager-faced reporter shouted as I left my rental and headed toward the house, "is it true you survived an explosion at LAX this afternoon?"

How had they known that? I left my messenger bag in the trunk, but grabbed my purse and my Kate Spade tote and headed toward the house, reporters all around me but not blocking my path. "No comment," I said as I walked, not really knowing where the words came from besides a lifetime of watching television. And I really didn't have any comment to make. What was there to say? My conjectures were best left inside my head— or Brian's—and I didn't really know anything for sure.

Another reporter: "Ms. Carter, what is your relationship with Maxi Livingston?" This time I didn't even waste breath on another *no comment*. Just kept moving. I heard someone shout, "Dave, are you getting a close-up of her face?" I looked around, saw someone reangling their camera and blocked it as best as I could with my tote.

At the top of the stairs I was relieved to encounter a human wall in the form of a couple of exceptionally burly guys.

"Ms. Carter," one of them said while presenting a shieldlike back to the little throng, "this way, please."

"Thank you," I breathed as I passed the person I recognized as hired muscle.

"No problem, Ms. Carter," he said politely. "You go on down to the house. We've got the entrance covered."

And having the entrance covered meant the whole house was covered because, short of arriving in a helicopter or scaling a cliff, it was the only way in.

Once I got to the house, Tycho greeted me like a war survivor, which, in a way, we had both become. Though he was singed, I was relieved to see not only was he not permanently damaged, but even with bandages on several parts of his body, he gamboled around like a puppy when he saw me. It dawned on me that he might have been worried about me if, in fact, dogs are capable of worry.

One corner of the deck was taken up with fragments of my former life. Though whoever Tyler had hired to retrieve my stuff out of the canyon was stacking things against one of the deck rails quite neatly, there was no way they could do anything to prevent it looking as though—as Tycho had so eloquently expressed—a war had gone on. It was so depressing to see my laser printer with one side bashed in, my hairbrush slightly singed, a pile of clothes that looked largely undamaged but hurt, nonetheless, a chipped coffee cup, a tube of mascara… all the pieces of my life, disconnected by a moment. I turned my back on the distressing pile and knocked on Tyler and Tasya's kitchen door.

Tasya, though not quite as demonstrative as Tycho, was glad to see me. She hugged me, offered me some of her mind-numbing black tea and told me Emily had called several times and that she'd sounded worried out of her mind. I opted to use the guest bedroom where I'd be staying to return her calls.

"Hey, chickie!" she said a little too cheerily when she heard my voice. "You shouldn't put your bag in front of your face. The camera adds ten pounds, you know. With a bag on your head, it adds twenty."

I groaned. "You've seen it already? I was just out there, like, two seconds ago."

"Your timing was awful, then. I saw it on a news-break. Your good luck to come home when they needed something for the top of the hour." I could almost hear the smirk.

"What is it? A slow news day?"

"I don't think so," Emily said thoughtfully. "The opposite, in fact. You're in the middle of the biggest news story in L.A. For the moment. Get used to it."

"Did you hear what happened?"

"Are you kidding? Have you been listening to me at all? How could I not hear? It's taken on this whole thing, you know?"

I did. Only too well. It seemed that, at some point during the last two weeks, I'd gone to sleep and woken up in the middle of a nightmare. I shook myself out of my reverie. Emily was talking. "The other reason I've been trying to get hold of you so frantically..."

"What was the first again?" I interrupted.

"Worry."

"Right. Sorry. Go ahead. You've been frantically trying to get hold of me because..."

"Because I figured it out!" She sounded triumphant.

"Figured what out?"

"The connection. Remember I told you? After the funeral when we heard about Bronwyn Barnes and the overpass. I told you that there was something bothering me about it."

"Well, people were dead, for one."

"Yes, of course," she said impatiently. "But beyond that. I had the feeling I should know something—that I should *see* something—that I was missing. Then, when I heard about Maggie Harding's death—about how she died—it dawned on me. The connection."

"There's a connection?" If Emily was making sense, I wasn't getting it.

"Well…oh, Madeline, this is *so* far-fetched. I just had to tell you. Because who else would believe me?"

"Believe you about *what?*" Emily was doing it again. For all her cheerful grace, her casual elegance, her way with people, there are times when Emily can be as frenetic as a hamster in a wheel.

She took a deep breath, centering herself. When she spoke again, her composure was markedly higher. "Okay, be patient with me, because this is sort of complicated."

"Shoot." I had no computer. I had no television. I no longer even had my own phone or food. For the moment, I had no life. What did I have besides time?

"Well, like I said, when I heard about Maggie Harding—about how she died—something about it struck me as familiar. Well, not familiar, but like…like it meant something, you know? Something I wasn't getting. I didn't tell you, but I had that feeling when I heard about Celisa Taylor, too. But with Maggie Harding's death, it was a little more obvious."

I squelched the desire to say *What was?* And settled for a gentle, encouraging, "Uh-huh…"

"See, the horse, that made it distinctive. The shooting and then the horse stall thing. That's how Lolita Larkin's character died in *Quartet.*"

I found I was suddenly paying closer attention.

"You're kidding me, right?" I said.

Emily's voice was warm when she answered me: I could tell she was glad she'd met with instant acceptance and not the scoffing she'd perhaps feared.

"No joke, at all. Her character was shot and then her body was left in a public stable. But that's not all."

It wasn't? What more could there be?

When Emily spoke again, it was with markedly more confidence. She knew she had her audience. "So, after that twigged, I went to Cinema d'Argent—you know the vintage video store on La Cienega?—and rented all of Lolita Larkin's movies. Well, the six before and the one after *Quartet,* anyway. And I found a pattern, Madeline."

"Are you serious?"

"Yes. See, *Quartet* was the second-from-last movie Lolita made. The third from last was a bit of a stinker called *Extraordinary Promise.* In *that* one she kills herself in a swimming pool."

I could barely breathe. "That's what happened to Celisa Taylor. Maxi's wife number four. Someone tried to drown her in her pool. She was lucky—the pool guy came and scared her attacker off, but no one got a look at him."

"Right. Then Bronwyn Barnes. Wife three. Lolita's fourth-from-last movie was called *Claw of Raven.* In it she walks off an overpass and ends her life. Very tragic. And that was the one that twigged me because it was one of the terrible movies I watched in Bucharest just a couple of weeks before Keesia's funeral."

"Only Bronwyn didn't walk."

"I'm guessing not."

I thought for a moment. "So what was the last movie Lolita ever made? 'Cause I'm betting you know."

"You'd bet right—it was the biggest stinker of all her stinky movies. And it sank without a trace. It was called *The Secret of the Garden*."

"Omigawd," I breathed.

"Truly," Emily agreed. "And she plays a woman who becomes obsessed with her garden and gradually spends more and more of her time interacting with plants than people."

"What was it? Made in the seventies or something?"

"You'd think so, wouldn't you? I looked it up on IMDB." From hanging around with Emily, I knew she was talking about the Internet Movie Database. "And the critics of the time—the ones that bothered to see it— called it a metaphor for the decadence of the jazz age."

"Sounds bizarre."

"It totally is. But I think we'd better make sure Nadine stays out of gardens, don't you?"

"Absolutely. And we're missing another one— Keesia herself. Does that one fit that pattern?"

"Well, yes and no. See, I wondered about that myself for a while. Why break the pattern? But it doesn't. Not really. Because Keesia died in exactly the same place Lolita herself died. Though in Lolita's case, it was suicide."

"Right, Lolita hung herself. But they both died in the same room," I said absently. Remembering something someone had told me. "Well, sort of the same room."

"They did?" Emily sounded pleased. "Well, that's it, then, isn't it?"

"But, Emily, what do you suppose this all means? It's a pattern, right? But I don't get it. Why would anyone want to duplicate what Lolita Larkin did in movies all those years ago? It just doesn't make any sense."

"I know," Emily agreed. "It doesn't make sense to me, either. But it's real, Madeline. I'd stake my life on it."

"Please, sweetie, don't even say that. It just isn't funny right now."

Emily's theory seemed like a breakthrough to me. Though there were certainly details missing, it was too big a coincidence not to be shared.

When I got him on the telephone, Brian didn't say much when I explained what Emily had told me. I had expected his usual doubting Thomas reaction. This time, however, he just seemed to get quieter and quieter while I spoke.

"So," I said when I'd finished.

"So?" he asked.

"What do you think?"

"Madeline, I can't really tell you what I think right now. I thank you for bringing this to my attention and I won't forget it. But I'm in the middle of something. I'm sure you'll hear about it later. Have a nice evening."

I sat looking at the phone for a minute after he'd hung up. I was surprised to find I'd been counting on his usual skeptical, sarcastic attitude. Without it, I didn't know quite what to do.

Without any real mission or plan, I did what I usu-ally do when I'm stressed or distracted: I worked. Tyler and Tasya had gone out, and even though they'd told me to make myself at home, I didn't feel completely comfortable booting their computer without specific permission. There's something so personal about that.

Lacking both a computer and the desire to drive down to Kordor where computers could be found, finding something to do to take my mind off real life was a little more difficult than usual, but not impossible. Before long I found myself going through the pile of debris on the deck—the detritus of my former life—as well as the neat pile of largely undamaged-looking items that had been put in the guest room. I was trying to scavenge enough unscathed clothes for a load of laundry.

I was pleased to find a couple of pairs of jeans, some sweatpants, underwear, socks and T-shirts that didn't look too bad. And with these particular items of clothing, that was good enough—it was stuff I generally wore around the house, anyway. At least it would mean I didn't have to start from zero *and* I'd have clean clothes for the morning.

While my laundry washed and then dried, I read the financial section of the newspaper. Once my clean clothes were folded and stacked on top of the dresser, I felt a little more in control of my life.

Look, jeans: I dominate you.

I laughed at myself, but felt more relaxed, anyway. I made myself a sandwich and helped myself to a glass of a nice pinot blanc I found open in the refrigerator. Then I called my mom to let her know I'd gotten back to L.A. in one piece, relieved when I got her voice mail because that meant she couldn't grill me about my omissions.

Then I stripped off my clothes and rolled myself up in the Egyptian cotton sheets in Tyler and Tasya's guest room. With the lights off and my eyes closed, the chirping of the crickets seemed to spread and deepen into a velvety after-dark serenade. I don't remember falling asleep, but I know crickets took me there.

Nineteen

I woke up at 4:30 a.m. without an alarm and figured, what the hell? Since I was already up, I'd try to do something that felt like my normal life. I put on my sweats, borrowed the pair of cross trainers that Tasya had thoughtfully left for me and opened the sliding doors that led from the kitchen to the deck.

Tycho, alert for just those types of sounds, joined me as I put my hand on the door, his tail wagging hopefully.

"You're such an opportunist," I scolded at a whisper.

He just opened his mouth slightly so I could see his front teeth. It's what, in canine lingo, seems to pass as a smile.

When we got up to street level, I was pleased to find the narrow road almost empty. Even news vultures, it seems, have to sleep some time.

The single occupied car had the definite look of a police vehicle, though I could tell it wasn't Andrews. I decided to ignore the car. If it was a police officer sent to surveil me, I'd just go about my business and let him do his job. Tycho and I set off on our run and if the cop followed us, I wasn't aware of it.

We pounded down the road to the abandoned orange grove that looks out over Coal Canyon. Though I don't generally rest during my runs, I felt the urge to sit and contemplate in this quiet place, which I did on the foundation of a house that had slid into the canyon years before. Tycho didn't sit, but contented himself sniffing around the orange grove for rock lizards and visiting cats and news of dogs that might have passed this way earlier.

Coal Canyon, like Los Flores, faces the ocean. It drops quickly from where I was sitting, then rambles— foothill-like—toward sea level. It is a peaceful view and I drank it in, enjoying watching the full light of day flow into the world.

After I'd sat peacefully for half an hour or so, Tycho and I walked home. I couldn't get my head around running on that particular morning. I mean, why run? It wasn't like I was in a hurry to get anywhere.

Back at the house, I showered in the bathroom attached to the guest room, then changed into my newly cleaned salvaged clothes. I found myself embarrassingly pleased at the feel of my powder-soft blue jeans. It was a small thing, definitely. But it was nice to be able to wear something comfortingly familiar. Something that was mine and had been for a while.

At eight-thirty, and with all quiet from the master suite, I left Tyler and Tasya a note telling them I'd be gone for the day, gave Tycho a dog cookie and petted him goodbye, then climbed up to my rental. The police vehicle I'd noticed earlier was gone, and John Andrews was back in position. Good, I thought, better a rested surveillance officer than a tired one.

As I got into my car, I waved good morning to him, then watched in amusement as he followed, trying to keep up with me on twisty canyon roads he wasn't familiar with.

In Santa Monica I felt lucky when I found an open parking meter with thirty-seven minutes left on it on Arizona Avenue just up from the Third Street Promenade. The money left on the meter wasn't as big a boon as finding the meter itself. There are times when I have to cruise the vicinity for half an hour before I land a parking spot.

I waved at John, who had double-parked next to my car and was looking confused. He rolled his window down when I walked toward him.

"I'm heading to Kordor, the coffee place on the Promenade?" I said. "I'll be on the computers. It's a big enough place that it won't bug me if you hang there. Find a place to park and you'll find me there." He looked doubtful. "Come on," I said. "It'll be more comfy than your stinky old car. You might even be able to get a doughnut to go with your coffee."

In Kordor, I got my latte, secured what was becoming my favorite of the crappy computers—for position only. In reality, it was no less crappy than any of the other computers—and sat down. I logged onto my Redi-Trade account, opened my bag and discovered that though I'd remembered my Filofax, I'd forgotten my trading journal. It was so unlike me—this forgetting of something which (a) is essential to my trading, and (b) is a thing I never forget, that I found myself suppressing the urge to cry. It was, I reasoned, symptomatic: both the forgetting and the urge. I was living out of various bags and life as I knew it had simply ceased to exist. And what did that mean? Gus. Keesia. My own life in danger and a police shadow my constant companion.

I forced myself to stop thinking about it. To think instead about the thing I know best, but even that couldn't fully divert me today. I was alarmed to find I couldn't lose myself in the rising and falling of the stocks on my watch list, the way I usually could. I refreshed the screen every so often and noted a rise here or a fall there but found that, even on securities I was holding where a few points either way might make a financial difference to me personally, I just couldn't make myself care.

I took a stab at reading news releases, but the words swam together. None of it would penetrate to the place in my brain that assigned meaning. I kept forcing the issue: kept making my mind focus even when it wanted to wander. And after a while, I didn't have to force it anymore. The world of the stock market grabbed me and entranced me as it always has. As it, hopefully, always will. The poetry of numbers, the music of a market that rises and falls like an unpredictable sea, this offered me the promise of peace in a world that had recently gone mad.

All of the domestic markets were up just then. I nodded sagely. Of course they were—I'd just read that a "stronger than anticipated jobs report eased concerns over slower economic and corporate profit growth." In my world, when the morning papers blared reports like that, the market responded with enthusiasm. And then another item—there were fears that the interest rates were going to go up. That would mean an instant correction to the market. See: it all made sense. Sometimes there would be permutations. Say jobs and interest rates were up, along with the price of crude oil, and all of those announcements came at the same time. The market would correct. That was a given. But which way? Fortunes were made and lost with how brokers decided to answer that question with regards to the portfolios in their charge.

The point, really, was that the world gave you clues and your financial survival depended on how well you responded. But you had to be paying attention to see the clues in the first place.

So time passed. I'm not sure how much. I was pleasantly lost in the world that had absorbed me for so many years.

I'd seen John Andrews come into Kordor not long after I did, grab himself a coffee and a newspaper and take up a watchful place between me and the door. I glanced over at him now and saw him on his cell phone, getting to his feet while he talked and walking toward me. To my surprise, he handed me the phone. "It's for you," he said. "Detective Brown."

"Hi, Brian," I said brightly, the flow of the market still quickening my pulse. "How's your day?"

"Hey, Madeline. Listen, can you get here as quickly as possible? I don't have time to explain, but I'd like you here on a consulting basis."

I was mystified but knew better than to ask. All, I knew, would come clear in due course.

"Where's here?" I asked.

"Beverly Hills. The department. Have Andrews drive you. I need you here five minutes ago."

"Sure, I'll come. But I'm driving myself. I'll follow Andrews in as quickly as he can make it."

Brian sighed but didn't argue. "Okay, fine. Just make it quick, all right? Let me talk to Andrews again."

I gave John his phone back, then logged off the terminal and started packing up my gear. By the time John had put his phone away, I was ready to roll.

"He gave you instructions?" I asked.

John smiled. "Yup. This time, you're following me."

You can play at being a sophisticate all you want. You can ride a lightning-fast elevator up a tower to work every day wearing a designer suit and expensive high heels. You can arrive in a town car instead of a cab. Spend two hundred bucks a month on your hair, four on your nails. Eat at the best restaurants, vacation at the coolest spots. *Anything.* I dare you. But none of that will prepare you for the cool you will feel when invited inside a Beverly Hills police murder investigation.

Brian was waiting for us outside the building when we arrived. He dismissed John politely, then sat me on a bench while he filled me in on what had been going on.

After I gave him the Lark-Larkin connection, Brian had been able to use it to pin some pieces he already had into place. Under the circumstances, Lark hiding his identity from the police and his employer provided enough probable cause to get a search warrant. The case was high profile and they got the warrant quickly. They descended on Lark's office and his home simultaneously. Though electronic investigators were still working with his computer, they hadn't found anything very interesting at the office. But with the search on his home they had struck gold.

Lark had a house on a quiet street in a newly revitalized part of Studio City. There were pictures of Lolita Larkin everywhere. "You couldn't go anywhere in the whole house," Brian told me, "without Lolita's eyes following you." He suppressed a shudder. "It was creepy."

Most interesting—and most damning—was what Brian described as Lark's war room. Among other things, there were posters from Lolita's last five movies: the same ones Emily had rented just a few days before. In each case but two, Lolita's face in the poster had been carefully taped over with a photograph of the woman who had died.

There were so many questions. So many things to ask. The biggest one, of course, was "Why?"

"That's a little bit of where you come in. The minute we had him in custody, he broke down and started confessing. When he started talking about maneuvering the company around—"

"The Northwest Zylonite Corporation," I supplied.

"When he started talking about that, Usinger and I started getting a headache. I mean, none of it made much sense to us and it concerned us that we couldn't really even separate the truth from the lies. We had a quick confab," Brian continued, "and agreed to get you in here as quickly as possible so you could take notes or whatever and draw us a picture."

"Where is Lark now?" I asked.

"I really wanted you here for this. We've been with him almost all night. When he kept going back to the financial stuff, we decided to give him a bit of a break until you got here."

"And yourselves, I hope," I said, noticing the lines around his mouth, the bleary condition of his eyes and the slept-in look of his suit. The same brown suit, I noted, he'd been wearing on the night I met him. Unless he had a closet full of frumpy brown suits.

"We got some coffee—" he grinned self-consciously "—and a doughnut."

Inside, I was issued a visitor's badge and taken to a small room adjacent to an interview room, empty but for several chairs and a long table with a tape recorder and microphone on it. Not the same interview room that Usinger and Brian had spoken to me in before, but another, deeper in the building.

The room I was in had a bench positioned to face a piece of glass almost as wide as the room itself. On the other side of the glass I knew this wall would look like a mirror. It was like peering into a fishbowl. You could see the fish, but they couldn't see you.

The small room smelled slightly of sweat and stale Cheetos. After a while I stopped noticing it. The only other occupant was an assistant district attorney, a young man who was introduced to me as Weldon Delacruz. He had fine dark hair, compassionate brown eyes and the air of someone who had a plane to catch.

Before very long, the fishbowl filled up. Usinger entered, followed by Lark St. George, followed by Brian. All three men looked serious, but Lark looked transformed. Diminished.

They started by going over material they'd obviously previously covered. It fascinated and repelled me at the same time. Like watching television—vividly colored, life-size television—but with the odd addition of knowing it was not only live, but real.

Lark started speaking the moment Brian told him he should. He spoke in a monotone, his voice droning along so lullingly, had I not been so fascinated by his words, I would have fallen asleep. And sometimes, as he spoke, I felt as if I should turn away. Or at least close my eyes. What does madness look like? I can tell you because, to me, it has a face. It looks like Lark St. George.

So, in that dreadful monotone, he recounted killing Keesia with a letter opener taken from her desk. It had not been premeditated but an act of passion. He had been in love with her, he said, but she hadn't loved him back. Not enough, anyway. Enough to play with him: enough to make plans with him. But the night of the party she'd told him it was over, that she loved her husband and planned on staying with him. And he, Lark, had snapped. He'd followed her and in a quiet moment he'd slain her.

I jumped when Weldon Delacruz poked me gently in the shoulder.

"Here," he said quietly, holding out a box of Kleenex. I hadn't even realized I was crying.

He confessed to Bronwyn Barnes's murder, as well. And Maggie Harding's. And the attempt on Celisa Taylor's life. He spoke of all of it in the same quiet voice. As though these were things that had occurred to someone else, somewhere else. And he spoke not as though he were sealing his fate, but as though he were confessing to a priest.

"Why did you do it, Lark?" Usinger asked after a lengthy silence.

"He killed my grandmother." And here his voice rose, growing louder. I saw Usinger and Brian exchange a fast glance. Obviously, this was something new to them. "He killed her while I watched! He didn't know I was there. I wasn't supposed to be there. I was in the conservatory reading a comic book. It was after my bedtime." His voice sounded younger now, as though it belonged to a child. "I couldn't say anything, or I'd get in trouble. I couldn't turn on the *light*. But I saw him. I saw him hit her. And then I saw him—" his hands described a rope around a neck "—I saw him hang her from the rafter. I saw her *swing*. He has to pay. He *has* to pay, don't you see?" He broke then. He covered his face with his hands and cried like a child. Deep, soul-wrenching sobs. The type of sobs that made you think that, if they'd ever had an outlet, things might have turned out differently.

After a few minutes of this—and with no ebb in sight—Weldon Delacruz pulled out a cell phone and tapped in a series of numbers. A vibrating pager on Brian, I decided, because just a few seconds after Delacruz had tucked his own phone away, Brian got up quietly and left the interview room, joining us next door.

"I need you to get her out of here," Delacruz said not unkindly, but leaving no doubt that the *her* in question was me.

Brian raised his eyebrows at the other man but didn't say anything, and Delacruz went on. "This isn't what you brought her here for. And I think it's inappropriate for her to be here for this."

Brian didn't disagree, but said, "This isn't what any of us expected, Wel."

"I know. I *know*. And all of us have been working way too hard on this. We've all lost a lot of sleep and maybe some objectivity. I don't think I would normally have okayed you having her here in the first place. What I should have told you—what I'm telling you now—is get a transcript. She can look at the salient parts and give you what she gets, okay?"

Brian nodded and indicated I should follow him from the room. As I left, I looked over my shoulder through the glass. Lark had his head thrown back, though he was still sobbing. And I knew he couldn't see me, but when his eyes passed over me, I shuddered.

* * *

Feeling as if I'd been run over with a steamroller, I dragged my sorry ass back up to Malibu. While I drove I didn't bother looking in the rearview for my tail. Brian wouldn't still be having me followed. It was over—I couldn't believe it was over—Lark had confessed. *Was* confessing. He was in jail.

I dreaded explaining all that I'd been through to Tyler and Tasya when I got to the house. In the end I didn't have to. A note on the kitchen counter had been left for me, I guessed, after I'd gone in the morning. Tyler and Tasya had gone to Aspen for a few days. Tycho was kenneled at the vet's. I should, the note said, make myself completely at home. And use of the computer was specifically mentioned: I was to make myself at work, as well.

"Eat the soup, please" was written at the bottom of the note in Tasya's careful hand. I smiled. Tasya's usual response to a crisis was making amazing soup. And here she was, not even knowing my current crisis, supplying what I needed.

I reheated her good vegetable soup in the microwave, poured it into a bowl, then sat on a stool at the kitchen island savoring it slowly while I pondered the amazing expanse of velvet blue over the Pacific at night. I didn't think about the last few days. About watching a man pour out his soul until it ran over his feet like so much used motor oil. I didn't think of Keesia. I didn't think of Gus. I wished my mind into a perfect blank and pondered the stars and the moon and the light on the water while I ate Tasya's wonderful, restorative soup. And then I went to bed and slept as though I might never wake up. It was over. Dear God, it was over and I'd helped make it so.

Twenty

In the morning I rambled around Tasya and Tyler's house somewhat aimlessly for a while. Don't get me wrong. I was glad not to have to think about who had killed Keesia and Gus, and who was maybe trying to kill me anymore. I *liked* that it was over. But the fact that I no longer had all of that to think about made me realize that I had no life. I mean, I had no house, I had no car. I had no clothes to speak of. I had no computer. I had nothing. No, less than nothing. There was still that mountain of crap reclaimed in my name now living in a heap on Tyler's deck and in his guest room. And while I could have driven down the coast to Kordor and worked for a bit, that wasn't what I felt like doing. I felt like spending time absolutely alone and licking my wounds. And I felt like picking up the pieces—literally—and seeing where that left me.

Something was bothering me. A nagging something that said that, though the recent nightmare was over, there was something that we'd missed.

I knew that, by now, Brian had likely gotten to the

bottom of everything. He probably knew everything there was to know and would share everything with me in good time. Right now, however, Lark's words kept coming back to me.

He killed her while I watched! he'd said. *He didn't know I was there. I wasn't supposed to be there.*

Who had been killed? And where was Lark not supposed to be? If Brian had the answers, I hoped he'd hurry up and tell me. With considerable effort, I put it out of my mind and focused on the task at hand. Not as compelling as the stock market, maybe. But it had to be done.

Of my stuff, there was amazingly little that was reclaimable. Too much just needed to be discarded. As the day progressed, I worked off several future dinners by carting load after load of *stuff* up the stairs to the trash bins. *My* stuff. Essentially all my earthly goods.

I recognized pieces of my stereo and bits of my small CD collection. I found a corner of my desk. An intact pillow. I actually salvaged a few files. When I managed to save a small album of family photos I cried a little bit.

I found my phone and my answering machine, but neither looked as if they should stay in my life: the plastic of both had been affected by the heat from the explosion. I found a piece of my Chagall poster. It wasn't worth much, so it wasn't as though the loss was a financial hit. And I hadn't had it for long, so how sentimental could my attachment to it be? Nonetheless, finding it and discarding it brought another round of mistiness.

I decided I was well and truly losing it, but I gave myself permission for that. I'd been through a lot, I told myself. A minor meltdown now struck me as a sign of being human.

After about my fifteenth trip up to the trash bins, I

decided I'd produced enough sweat for one day. There
were bathing suits of every size in the pool house. I
found one that fit without too much trouble, then spent
the next half hour doing laps. When I realized that I was
probably working up a sweat in the water during a swim
that had been intended to provide relief from the sweat
I'd worked up making all those trips up the stairs, I had
to laugh at myself. The difference between *strong work
ethic* and *workaholic* is subtle, but it's there. If what you
do to relax from work is work—even of an entirely different type—you should be getting a pretty strong clue.

After my swim I hit the showers yet again, then sat
cross-legged on the middle of my bed trying to think of
what to do next. In my adult life I've seldom had leisure and I don't know what to do with it when I get it.
And this wasn't the sort of leisurely leisure one gets on
vacation. There was a dull sadness underlying everything I did, an awareness that my life had been altered
by forces outside of my control. And there was nothing
much for me to do.

There was a film magazine on the nightstand. I flipped
the pages looking for something that would pique my interest. Failing, I plopped it back where I'd found it.

I pulled my Filofax out of my bag and looked through
it idly, looking for something, I suppose, that would divert me. I found it when the postcard I'd purchased at
the Zylonite museum fell out.

I looked again at Lolita, her skin seal smooth, her expression as pleased as a cat's. I looked into the face of
the young man who stood behind her. The same young
man, I was sure, I'd seen in other pictures at the museum. I flipped the card over, read again the back. Then
looked at the faces once more.

"Who are you?" I asked the young man aloud. He didn't answer.

And I realized I had my diversion.

I felt only slightly self-conscious sitting in Tyler's office chair, at his desk, and booting his computer. I found I liked sitting in his office, which looked as if it had been done but not overdone. The walls were the color of chocolate, the furniture Danish modern. Light streamed in from windows on three sides, illuminating the awards in a case I could see if I sat at the desk and looked over my left shoulder: an Oscar, four Golden Globes and a bunch I didn't recognize but promised myself I'd look at later.

I wanted to Google something. "Lolita Larkin," I typed. The responses from the search engine came back quickly: thousands of them. Thousands upon thousands of them. Each match on the name was represented on-screen by a line of text, with ten such lines on each page.

The bulk of the many Web pages devoted to Lolita Larkin weren't worth the thirty seconds I spent on them. Many pages were obviously just there to sell something: a Lolita Larkin biography or poster or videotapes of some of her movies. On pages like that, the sales offers would be deep and the content light or nonexistent. It didn't matter, Google had told me there were sixty thousand references to my search topic: I could pick and choose.

It was a little overwhelming. Tribute pages and filmographies and photo galleries and more. It was in one of these last—a photo gallery devoted to Lolita Larkin—that I found images that included the young man in the postcard. As on that postcard, he was never identified as anything other than Lolita's "friend" or "companion." I kept surfing and finally, on a site devoted to films of the golden era, I found a scan of a newspaper article from a party thrown to celebrate the Oscars. The photos that had accompanied the piece were grainy in the low-res on-screen image, but in one of them, Lolita's mystery man was both identifiable and identified: "Miss Lolita Larkin was accompanied to the gala evening by sportsman Jaimie Welles of Hancock Park."

There was no chance that, after more than thirty years, I'd be able to find that person. And, honestly, I wasn't even sure why I'd want to. At the same time, I knew that I *did* want to. That instinct again? I knew that if Jaimie Welles was still out there, I wanted to talk to him.

I used a Web-based phone directory service and tried the most obvious thing—typed in his first and last name and the city—Hancock Park—thinking I'd get no response. And, of course, there was no Jaimie Welles listed there. However, there was a J. Welles on North June Avenue. And the number was listed.

I called Brian at the office and was told he wasn't due in until the following morning. I asked for Kerry Usinger and was told the same thing. Sleeping, I thought. Finally. I opted not to try Brian's cell. If he *was* sleeping, I'd best leave him to it. I'd seen him the day before and noticed that he hadn't had enough sleep lately.

I got off the phone and thought things through. Even if I *did* get Brian, why did I think he'd want to try to find some old guy Lolita had once known? Brian had enough on his plate. When I thought it through carefully, there was no reason for me to talk to Jaimie Welles, either. Yet I wanted to.

Better to put things to rest—just call the number and be told that it wasn't the same Jaimie Welles because what were the chances it could be after all these years?

Pretty much zero, I told myself as I dialed the number.

Someone answered on the second ring. A scratchy-sounding "Hello," as though the voice wasn't used that often.

"Jaimie Welles, please," I said before I lost my nerve.

A dry laugh. "Jaimie," he said, sounding amused. "It's been years since anyone called me that. I don't know how many. But that's me—though these days most people call me James."

I'd decided to approach Jaimie Welles with complete candor. "Mr. Welles, I understand you were a friend of Lolita Larkin."

A hesitation, I thought. A moment of collection. And then, "Funny thing about Lolita, I don't hear her name for years—*decades*—and suddenly she's in the news every day again." He chuckled. An old man's sound. "She'd be pleased, I think."

"So you knew her?"

"Who wants to know?"

"Sorry for not introducing myself," I said hastily. "My name is Madeline Carter. I was a friend of Keesia Livingston's. I've seen you in many photos with Lolita so I figured you were close. I just wanted to ask you a few questions."

That hesitation again and, in the pause, I started wondering just what the hell I thought I was trying to prove with this call. What I felt I'd accomplish. I fully expected Welles to tell me to take a flying leap, so when he said, "When can you come by?" it took me by surprise.

"I thought we could just chat on the phone."

"Phone's impersonal, isn't it?" I detected a British accent, overlaid with years of living away. "I'm over in Hancock Park. Where are you?"

"Malibu," I said without thinking.

"Fine then. No reason for you not to come by, is there? I'll put the coffee on. See you in forty-five minutes." He gave me his address and, before I even really thought about what I was doing, I'd agreed to drive out and see him.

While I drove, I tried hard not to think about Brian's face—about what he'd think about all this. And it wasn't hard to imagine. But I knew there was nothing to be afraid of. I'd heard something in the old man's voice, something that dampened my fears. It was loneliness.

Hancock Park is a very odd neighborhood. In the time that Lolita Larkin was the queen of Hollywood, Hancock Park was one of *the* places to live. Stars lived there. Society folks. Captains of industry. You name it. Then, being so close to downtown, it slid to a sort of no-man's land of living. Imagine: palatial homes built between the 1920s and 1940s, by the 1980s they were white elephants. By then, no one wanted to live that close to downtown Los Angeles, especially in a huge, old-fashioned, falling-down house. With taxes and maintenance high and the economy bad, a lot of people walked away from high interest rates and ownership, letting the bank take their houses back. Before very long, squatters moved into some of the boarded-up houses. It was that kind of economy.

In the late 1990s things changed. People were tired of commuting and the old, out-of-fashion white elephants were now *très* cool. The multistyled mansions—Italianate, arts and crafts, neoclassic—were just the ticket for newly affluent young couples who didn't feel like spending an hour in the car to get to work.

Because Jaimie Welles's phone number hadn't changed since Lolita had been alive, I deduced he'd probably been there a *long* time. Buying during the first cool wave, shaking his head in wonder and staying indoors at night when the neighborhood must have—quite literally—felt as though it had been sent to hell. Parking in front of his ancient Tudor-style house, you couldn't even see what might have been. The streets were tidy and welcoming, and I figured he might have been floored to discover his museum from another era was now worth in excess of two mil.

He greeted me at the door, quickly after my knock, as though he'd been waiting. He looked every inch the well-preserved septuagenarian, and his eyes held a youthful light. A wide smile creased his face when he saw me, and he held out a weathered hand. "Madeline Carter, I presume," he said quite formally, though still with that smile. "Please come in."

The wide foyer was all honeyed wood and gleaming plaster moldings. I imagined things in here probably didn't look much different than they had forty years earlier, save the smell of a house that has been well loved for a long time. Jaimie led me to a small, homey sitting room and said, "Make yourself comfortable, Miss Carter."

"Madeline, please."

He smiled again. "Madeline, then. I'll just go and fetch our coffee, shall I?"

During his brief absence, I surveyed the room. It

seemed likely to me that whoever had initially decorated Larkin House had done some work here, as well: the same tastes seemed to prevail. Muted but apparent colors, good antiques—or excellent reproductions—representing a wide swath of styles. All punctuated by good—though not remarkable—art. The personal touches in Jaimie's house, however, set it apart. One wall was given over to photographs. Mostly, I noted, black-and-white glossies and none more recent than a couple of decades ago. I recognized Jaimie in almost all of them. Though he was a lot older now, the warm smile was the same.

Here he was taut and tanned at a beach. There he was with a marlin in the back of a boat. Here he was dancing at some soiree, his partner glowing in an iridescent gown. I looked closely at her face and, sure enough, Lolita Larkin, smiling prettily—graciously, like the empress she'd been—for the unseen camera.

Coffee was served from a silver service into delicate hand-painted cups with matching saucers. He'd also brought out suspicious-looking little cakes and some fairly benign-appearing cookies. Not wanting to be impolite, I settled on one of the latter.

"Now," he said with coffee installed in both our cups and the cookies and cakes properly offered, "you said you were a friend of Keesia Livingston's?"

"I was. Yes," I said, trying to swallow the bite of gingersnap that was threatening not to go down.

He shook his head sadly. "Dreadful, dreadful business that. And by all accounts a lovely girl."

"You didn't know her?"

"No, never had that pleasure," he chortled, as though at a private joke. "I wasn't precisely welcome at Larkin House with Maxi in residence, as I'm sure you know."

I looked at him blankly for a moment. "No, I'm sorry. I don't know at all."

He looked at me, as though assessing, but I had no doubt he'd tell me. From what I'd seen of him, I knew the assumption I'd made on the telephone was right: he was an old man, likely alone in the world, and most of his friends were either dead or close to it. He was lonely. And I'm a tall blonde. Old guys like to talk to me. It's not always been an attribute I've been happy with, but it didn't seem to be doing me any harm now. Especially since, aside from appalling taste in confections, he seemed like a genuinely nice old guy.

"Well, that Maxi," he laughed. "He was such a parasite, wasn't he? And not at all Lolita's type, if you ask me. Which, by the way, no one ever did. But her…er… companions—quite frankly—generally fit my description more than Maxi's."

I must have looked at him askance, because he said, "Oh, don't look so surprised, Miss Carter."

"Madeline," I said again.

He nodded. "Madeline. Lovely name, by the way. Madeline. But no one these days should be shocked. None of it was shocking, not by today's standards." He shrugged. Sighed, as though with resignation, but I could see he was enjoying himself. All these great stories, no one to tell. It was more than a little sad.

"Lolita was very rich," he went on, "wasn't she? All those films. And, when she was done buying up all those celluloid companies, she was very powerful. That was the idea, you see.

"Age—for women, anyway—was everything in Hollywood in those days. She could see the parts getting thinner, the scripts coming less frequently. These days an actress would start a production company, wouldn't she? Start making her own movies. In those days, that wasn't an option. Lolita was a child of the studio system. It's not something she felt she could fight from the inside. But she got the idea that, if she could buy every celluloid company in the country, she'd control the market on the stuff and then the studios would *have* to offer her roles if they wanted anything to shoot their movies on."

I sat silent for a moment. Maybe even openmouthed. The audacity of that! More: the insanity. That's what I said to Jaimie: "But that's crazy."

Jaimie nodded. "Certainly. In fact, I pointed that out to her," he sniffed. "She didn't listen."

Jaimie had confirmed something I'd suspected: that's why Lolita had developed her interest in Zylonite. It had nothing to do with business in general and everything to do with her business, in particular.

"Were you an actor?" I asked.

Jaimie surprised me by laughing. "Well, you could say that, couldn't you? But no, not in the way you would think of an actor. That is, I was never in any films. Never on the stage. I acted my way through life, didn't I?" he said with a flourish of his hand. "But no. I was never an actor."

"You described Maxi as Lolita's 'companion.' And, the way you said it, I thought you might have been her companion as well," I smiled at him and my interest was genuine. "I want to hear about that."

Jaimie laughed and refilled my coffee. "Well, I was getting back there, not to worry. As I said, she was rich and, after a fashion, powerful. She didn't need men the way a lot of women in those days needed them—to make mortgage payments and drive the car, maybe settle a kid on them, you know. She had all of that as covered as it needed to be. She needed men the way you yourself might need a fur wrap, you understand? She needed men draped on her arm, more fashion than function." Then a little more quietly, into his coffee, he said, "She needed men draped on her bed." He sighed, shook his head as though clearing it of old business, then forged ahead. "You look at me now and, I guess, you see someone in their dotage." He ran his hand self-consciously through hair that was yellow-white though still surprisingly thick. "But, I don't mind telling you, for a while I *was* Lolita's 'companion.' And it wasn't anything to complain about, either, let me tell you." He stopped abruptly and I was afraid he wouldn't go on.

"So what happened?" I prompted gently.

"Can't you guess?" he said.

I shook my head. Smiled. "Not even a little."

He smiled back, though his offering was somewhat rueful. "Maxi Livingston. That's what happened."

"Maxi," I said. "I don't get it."

Jaimie chuckled. "Maxi was Lolita's flavor of the month that summer. Her last flavor, as it turned out."

"Wait," I said, somewhat startled now. Jaimie had said it before, but the word in this context with relation to Maxi hadn't fully sunk in. "Are you telling me that Maxi was Lolita's…companion." I thought of Maxi as a Lothario. The jelly doughnut without the soft center. The thought wouldn't gel.

Jaimie helped himself to another cookie. "Bingo."

"Why doesn't anyone know that?"

Jaimie shrugged. "People know. *I* knew, didn't I?" He nodded, half to himself. "Other people knew. Anyway, I don't think it was something Maxi wanted advertised. Not with the way things turned out." I just looked at him and he took my prompt. "Well, Lolita ended up dead, didn't she? And I always had my doubts about Maxi."

"Doubts," I said, still prompting.

"Sure. It was all a little too neatly wrapped up, wasn't it? And I'd been spending a lot of time with Lolita not long before. She was *not* suicidal. Honestly? I'd have been more prepared to believe she killed someone else than believe she killed herself."

I digested this, or tried to. Jaimie wasn't what Brian would have called an impartial witness. He'd had stuff at stake. "Did you tell the police?"

"I did," he sniffed again. "No one was listening to me, though, were they? And Maxi? He had things all organized, didn't he? Oh, yes," he said, answering his own question. "He did! Somehow—and I've never understood how—he got himself made Lolita's executor. Imagine! And what do you think happened then? Maxi parlayed what he managed to gain out of that into a pretty important career, didn't he? And where did that leave me?" He spread his arms to encompass the living room and, I imagined, the whole house. "Well, it got me these digs. She was generous that way. It got me dinner invitations, for a while. But the serious dosh—" he rubbed the fingers of his left hand together in a universally understood gesture "—Maxi got the bulk of that, by hook or by crook." He sighed again, deep in thought. "One thing I never understood, though, maybe you can tell me."

"What's that?"

"What happened to the child?"

"What child?" I asked. But I thought I might already know.

"Lolita's grandson was staying with her that year. Would've been there at the time. Had to have been—she wouldn't let him out of her sight. She'd had a terrible falling-out with her son over his running of one of her companies. I got the feeling she took the child from him almost as some kind of ransom. Or punishment."

"How old was he?"

"The child? Oh, not very. Maybe this high." He indicated a spot perhaps three feet off the ground. "Maybe five or six years old. Too little to notice very much." He paused again, thinking. "She treated him the way she would have treated a poodle—doted on one moment, ignored the next. What was his name? Jerome, maybe. Jack? Something like that."

"George?" I heard myself offer softly.

Jaimie brightened, "That's it, precisely. Well done. George. George Larkin. I remember that part because it always seemed odd to me that she'd settled her own name on her brood. Don't know who her son's father was. Probably one of us." He indicated himself and I knew he'd cut a broad swath: Lolita Larkin's boy-toy club. By the sound of things, it hadn't been very exclusive.

Jaimie Welles had given me a lot to mull over and I did that as I drove. Maxi as an ornament? It was difficult to imagine. And what of the child? Lark's words in the interview room came back to me again. *He killed her while I watched.* Is that what Lark was saying? That Maxi had killed his grandmother? That Maxi had killed Lolita Larkin?

I got off the freeway to find a pay phone to call Brian.

Unsurprisingly, I knew the number by heart now. He wasn't on duty. Probably still off sleeping somewhere. I got back in my car and headed to the only place I could think of to work off the excess energy I was feeling: Kordor, where I knew I'd find a good latte and a crappy computer. Even though I was full of the charming Jaimie Welles's really awful coffee, I felt as though I really needed a hit of good caffeine.

It was midafternoon and Kordor was mostly without patrons. The guy making espresso today had neatly cut hair—almost a buzz cut—not dreadlocks. I tried to determine if it was the same guy who usually made it. I couldn't tell right away and decided it didn't matter. One surly server was as good as the next, no matter the haircut. I thanked him when I picked up my latte. He grunted and moved away.

Being on a computer again reminded me that, right now, I effectively didn't have one. The pile of junk I'd gone through earlier in the day on the deck in Malibu was a pretty good indication that the prognosis on my old machine was bad.

I was toying with the idea of getting a laptop to replace my old desktop computer. Wireless technology was so good now, there were many places in West L.A.—maybe even in Malibu—where I could make an Internet connection without being physically tethered to anything. I visualized myself on the beach, the sun kissing my body, the waves crashing and surfers glinting past while I executed my trades. It was a gorgeous image until I thought about sand in the keyboard. Well, clearly there were some bugs I'd have to work out but—overall—the idea was pretty good. And it *did* mean that it wouldn't matter where I was or where I woke up, I'd be able to do what I did: anywhere.

Meanwhile I sighed, and logged onto the old lemon at Kordor. I shook my head too often as I caught up with what had been going on in the market while I'd been variously mourning and gallivanting. What had started as a good month for me was turning into a nightmare and all, I realized, because I hadn't been paying attention. And though I'd tried to pay attention the day before, Brian's summons to Beverly Hills had diverted me before I really got going.

I was holding stocks I would have sold days ago under normal circumstances. As it was, a hiccup in the market had me several thousand dollars down. I didn't freak: it wasn't a freaking matter. It was the kind of hiccup that was possible to recover from tomorrow or, failing that, next week. Still, it made me realize how vulnerable I was and how careless I'd recently been—careless and preoccupied. And being careless just wasn't a good idea with my bread and butter.

While I worked with my own stock stuff—making another effort at reading the news releases I hadn't gotten to the day before and checking changes in the market that are essential to my financial well-being—something nagged at the back of my brain. I kept thinking about what Jaimie had told me. Lark had said he'd seen someone kill Lolita. In less shrill tones, Jaimie had accused Maxi of the same thing. I thought back to my first visit to Larkin House after Keesia died, the day I'd spoken with the gardener. Had she told me that Maxi encouraged the people who worked for him to stay away from the hedge maze? Everything for me kept coming back to that secret garden. Lolita's lost garden. And even though I chided myself for it, every bit of my instinct was telling me that an answer would be found there.

I gathered up my stuff and went out to the pay phone on the promenade. While I did so I thought again that it really might be time to cave on getting a cell.

Brian still wasn't answering. I called Larkin House and asked for Maxi.

"Sorry, Mr. Livingston is not here right now. You can try him at his office downtown."

"When do you expect him?" I asked.

"I believe he has a function this evening," I was told. "I would imagine he won't be back until quite late tonight."

I found a bench nearby and sat in the afternoon sunshine while I pondered what to do next. Pondered, really, if there was anything I *should* do. I wasn't convinced that there was.

This time I did not think about coincidence, I thought about the way life sometimes just fits together. Or maybe it doesn't, but we make it fit together. In either case, I knew that Brian, if he heard them, would laugh these thoughts right out of Dodge.

With Lark out of commission, and Maxi out for the evening, I reasoned that it was as good a time as any—and a better time than most—to pay another visit to Larkin House. In daylight, this time.

Brian had warned me to be careful and I intended to be. Safely knowing I'd get his voice mail, I called him once again and left a detailed message of what I was up to. I knew he'd be mad when he got it, but it made me feel better, anyway. Made me feel less on the brink of solitary insanity: at least someone would know where I was. After a while. Just in case.

I didn't feel afraid until I was walking through the garden at Larkin House. The gates were closed, but I parked my rental on the side of the road—doubling back to get my messenger bag after taking only a few steps—and scrabbled over the fence as casually as I could, taking equally casual strides through the garden—toward my destination.

It was near the end of the workday—the shadows were lengthening—but it still seemed inordinately quiet. None of the gardeners seemed to be around and it felt—somewhat dramatically—as though the place were holding its breath.

I wasn't afraid of detection. A lot of people work in the house and gardens at Larkin House. I reasoned that, as long as Maxi wasn't around, one person walking confidently through the gardens wouldn't attract attention. Apparently I was right, because no one raised a warning shout and I reached my destination without incident.

Even in my gloomy, determined mood, the garden was breathtakingly lovely. Even more so, perhaps, because of the stillness.

Gardens, at their very best, are meant to be places of respite. Magical creations of light and growth where we mortals can turn to escape the pressures of a sometimes confusing world. There's no room for anger in a garden. It is, by nature, a place of peace. And I couldn't help myself—I caught some of that peace now as I walked past the reflecting pools and blooming roses and budding rudbeckias and azaleas. All that growth and all those sweet scents made me hopeful, somehow. They made me believe in possibilities.

As I made my way through the garden, I kept my eyes open for a ladder or some other device that would help me get over the wall. One way or another, I thought, I was getting into that lost garden today.

I had no less trouble getting through the hedge maze

than I had on my first visit. The maze was deep and old and complete: I made as many wrong turns as right ones.

Once I heard a sound behind me. I stood very still and listened but I heard nothing more. A *rat,* I told myself, *it was only a rat.* But if it *was* a rat, it had sounded like a very big one. I stood perfectly still for a while longer and heard nothing more. Finally chiding myself for jumping at shadows, I moved on.

When I found the door, I had to look at it for a moment to process what I was seeing. And, when I did, my heart began to pound. I wouldn't need a ladder after all. In the place at the center of the huge stone door where there had previously been three stones, there were now four. And with the four in place, their symbolism began to make sense. Though the runes were crude and ancient, I thought I could determine that each stone represented an element: water, earth, fire, air. The fifth stone, the heart stone, was a combination of each of these. It was all that was missing. And it was in my bag.

Though part of my mind clamored to know how the missing stone had mysteriously appeared, I ignored it. The fact was, I could barely contain my excitement.

My stone, once inserted into the spot created for it, moved home with strong surety. I was almost certain I could feel some type of vacuum force pull it into place, though I knew this couldn't be the case.

With all five keys in position, like the pieces of some rough-and-ancient stone pie, the circular arrangement could be rotated. I did that carefully. Though I couldn't imagine where the sound was coming from, I heard a quiet clicking, as though some ancient tumblers were falling into place.

Though I didn't know precisely what to expect when

the door opened, I'd built a picture in my mind: a golden, secret place, perhaps with beautiful flowers growing—in abundance, of course, because the garden had been neglected for a long time—plus an almost overpowering profusion of green. There would be a secret, sure. But a wonderful secret. Something that would cast a radiant light over the darkness of the last few weeks. Something that would make a difference.

All of these visions of flowers and green and light left me unprepared for the reality of what I found. My attempt to push the door inward didn't bring much movement, so I pushed harder. I strained and strained with everything I had, the only thing keeping me from giving up altogether were the tiny increments of space that appeared as the door opened. I'd be close to giving up and the door would give a fraction of an inch. Lots more pushing and I'd be about to give up...and the door would give up another fraction. Finally, the disuse that had held the door shut gave very suddenly and the foot thick door swung open...on nothing.

At least, it felt like nothing. Darkness gaped beyond the open doorway. For just a moment it felt as though, were you to enter, you'd fall forever into a limitless pit.

The endless void was, of course, an illusion. What was beyond the door wasn't a garden at all. If I had thought my eyes were deceiving me, I'd have known my nose wasn't: an un-smell came out of the darkness to greet me. It didn't smell bad or good, but more like nothing than anything I'd ever experienced.

After a while my eyes had adjusted enough to the dim light that fell through the doorway to see that it was not, after all, limitless space. No more, at least, than it was a garden. It was a room perhaps eight feet long by eight feet wide and not much taller than I was: completely windowless and without furnishings of any kind. Not a garden, then, I could see at a glance. Not a garden at all, but a crypt.

And then I saw her. I stifled the groan of fear that came from some nameless place. I entered the crypt slowly, moving toward the shape of a woman huddled in the corner.

I fumbled in my bag for the flashlight I'd brought the last time I'd been here, relieved when my fingers touched the cold, European-crafted metal. When I fixed the beam on the female shape, however, I was almost sorry I'd brought the light with me this time. I was aware of making small, hurt noises low in my throat when I saw the mummified corpse. What I saw was beyond nightmare: it was the nightmare that, when you wake from it, you command yourself instantly to forget.

It was Lolita Larkin. Without question. Though her features had drawn into themselves after more than thirty airless years, the glorious auburn cascade of her hair was unmistakable, as was the jade-and-diamond brooch on the lapel of the dressing gown she wore. What was more horrific than finding the great actress here, when she'd apparently been interred at the Forever Hollywood Cemetery so long ago, was what was obvious the moment you saw her. This was not the carefully arranged slumber manufactured by a skillful mortician. Her hands were arranged into claws, the nails broken and dirty. When I inspected it with the flashlight, the stone back of the door showed minute marks, as though someone had tried to dig their way out.

I could see that, when Lolita Larkin had been entombed, she'd been alive.

* * *

I moved closer to Lolita's corpse. As close as I dared. But I wanted to see if it could possibly be true. I couldn't bring myself to touch her, but when I brought the light to her hand, I could see the stone-colored dirt clearly.

I could see the edge of a piece of paper poking out of Lolita's dressing gown. I wanted to—*had to*—see what it said. But to disturb a body dead so long? Or would it be a disturbance? Just a note.

In order to stretch my right arm out far enough to grab the note without touching the corpse, I'd have to use my other arm to hold my weight away from the wall. Which didn't leave a hand free for holding the flashlight.

I could put the flashlight on the floor, but even propped against my bag, I couldn't get the beam going in just the right way to illuminate what I was doing.

Leaving the crypt, I jammed the butt of the flashlight into the dense greenery of the maze, directly across from the crypt's entrance, shining the light directly on the area where I needed illumination.

Satisfied that I could now accomplish my self-appointed mission, I went back in, my hands free.

Back inside, I tried to control my revulsion as I worked my way carefully toward Lolita's pocket, paying extra special attention to *not* touching her in any way.

I was so intent on my quest—the piece of paper that might be a note—that I didn't notice that the light had weakened slightly. My hand closed tightly over the paper in the same moment that the door closed, very quickly. As I heard the soft clicking of the ancient tumblers, I sprang to my feet, the paper in my hand. Too late. I was plunged very suddenly into a dark so complete I couldn't see my hand in front of my face.

Twenty-One

When I was a kid, my parents liked us girls to watch as much educational television as possible. It was as though they felt that, if they filled our brains with good stuff, it would somehow counteract all the televised goop we consumed on our own time. The way I think of bran sopping up cholesterol.

One day, we saw what must have been a brilliantly executed program on the ancient Egyptians. I say it must have been brilliant because, after I watched it, I didn't sleep properly for about a week. I kept having visions—I won't call them dreams, because I wasn't asleep—of having my brains scooped out my nose and then being locked in a Very Dark Place for about a million years.

These ancient dudes had prepped for a siege—they'd taken sheaves of wheat and cosmetics and boats and servants and (most significant of all to me because I was six) they'd even taken their cats. I mean, you don't take your cat anywhere with you unless you're planning on coming back. But they hadn't come back. They'd just stayed there, in the dark until, thousands of years later, this crew of guys with television cameras had come rooting around. I found it all pretty graphic. My parents had been more careful about what they forced me to watch after that: violent cartoons never cost me any sleep.

This was like all of my worst fears—my waking nightmares—come to life. No one was trying to scoop my brains out my nose, but the way things were going, I started to feel like if I gave it long enough, it would happen. If I lived that long.

I discovered that you think about a lot of things when you're locked in a tomb with a mummified corpse. First of all, your life does *not* flash in front of your eyes. You're too busy worrying about your air supply to waste energy on such nonsense. Your thoughts are really quite primal. You maybe think about screaming, but you have such a feeling of confidence that you won't be heard that you make a conscious decision not to bother. It's the last conscious decision you'll be aware of for a while.

All of this is easier to think about in the third person because when I contemplate it too closely, it comes back quick and hard. And—quite suddenly—I'm six again.

When the door closed it was almost as though, suddenly, I was some single-celled preanimal—an amoeba or a very simple jellyfish—floating without anchor in a vast, black space. Everything that had been important to me an hour before was suddenly meaningless. It hurts me to recall it, but I remember that, at one point, Gus's face floated in front of mine and I pushed it away, trying to focus on what was important to me and discarding him as not belonging in that category.

So, what was important? Well, for starters, air was a primary concern. I didn't actually know that the crypt was airtight, but I had a pretty strong clue. Airtight is, after all, in the very nature of *crypt*. For a split second I tried to do some math: a space approximately eight by eight by six filled with air: how long did I have? But there were too many variables: the door hadn't been open that long, would the room have filled with air? I was sharing space with a dead person…how would that affect the outcome? Even if I'd known how long someone of my size and weight could last in a room this size full of air I wouldn't have been able to do the calculations, even without my variables. I tried to stop thinking about it, but it was pretty basic. The air you breathe, and all that. The mere thought of it all made me feel like hyperventilating and I knew that would be a bad idea.

The silence was deafening. That sounds like a cliché, but it's truly how it was. I could hear—literally—my heart pound, hear the rushing of my blood through my veins, the sound my hair made when I ran my fingers through it nervously. When I extended my foot experimentally and slightly in the direction I *thought* the door was in, I recoiled sharply at the crack of sound that seemed to come when my foot connected with the silk of Lolita's robe.

Breathe, I told myself. *Just breathe. But not too much.*
How much is too much?
Never mind. Just breathe.

I wanted to sink to the floor in a big, sorry heap and just think, but the possibility of my hand or some other part of me connecting with any part of Lolita's mummified corpse kept me frozen in place at first. I mean, you could think, well, she's right over there. But, with the complete absence of light I was experiencing, I barely knew which way was up or down, let alone the position of the door and me and Lolita.

Aside from breathing and position, another thought that was important and basic was one of escape. Lolita had, obviously, died trying. And she hadn't even made a dent in the stone. I couldn't get anywhere without tools or some kind of light. Clearly, a jackhammer would be a Good Thing. But I didn't have one of those.

Even though my bag weighed less without the stone or flashlight inside, I still had the bag itself with me, its heft was reassuring over my shoulder. I thought again of dropping to the ground while I groped the contents in the dark, but the memory specter of Lolita held me in position. I opened the bag where I stood. Realized the paper I'd taken from Lolita was still clenched in my now-sweaty palm. Let it drop into the bag. Felt inside. Did a quick inventory.

Four dog biscuits. Good to know, but without something more, I doubted I'd last long enough to get hungry enough to eat Tycho's PuppiGrowls.

My ATM and Visa cards. So useless to me now I felt like laughing. But I didn't.

A hairbrush. Which just made me think of Lolita's flame-colored locks. Which brought a shudder. I dropped the brush back inside the bag.

My keys. That wouldn't work on this door, even if you could unlock it from the inside, which I doubted you could do, anyway.

A bottle of Evian. So simple and reassuring. I unscrewed the top, took a sip and felt slightly better for the life-giving water that trickled down my throat. The bottle was almost full. I'd certainly be out of air before I ran out of water. I tipped the bottle back and took a good gulp, even letting a little trickle down my chin. It felt like defeat and triumph all in one mouthful. I put the top back on and replaced the bottle in the bag. I sighed and, for the first time in my life, I wished I was a smoker. Then I'd at least have some matches. Then some high school science class came back to me and I remembered that a burning flame would use still more air. So much for that thought. Though the light would have been welcome in any case.

I stood like that for a long time: too scared to move. How long is a long time? I really have no idea. I can recall one very serious cramp in my left leg. I rubbed it anxiously and carefully, concerned beyond circumstance.

At one point I tried a scream. Just a single, piercing scream that held part of the shape of "Help me!" It was a mistake that I didn't repeat. The sharp sound in the small, empty, airtight place produced, not an echo but more of a reverberation; the sound of my scream rolled off the walls toward me for a long time, first in reality and then, I think, in my mind. And, above it all, I had the very strong feeling that not even the teeniest bit of that sound would break the stone barrier that held me.

It was difficult to gauge the passing of time, but serious time must have passed, because—and it came upon me quite suddenly—the needs of my body outweighed my need to stay out of physical touch with Lolita. I had maintained my standing position for what must have been hours—two? four? six?—and, quite simply, I couldn't stand any longer.

Initially, I dropped straight down to the floor, just bending my knees and then crouching sideways, feeling quite confident I hadn't moved more than a few inches off my mark.

The stone floor was surprisingly cold and unsurprisingly uncomfortable. Before another hour had passed, my tailbone began to complain, the way it does when you're sitting through a particularly bad, particularly long movie. I stretched out my leg to ease a cramp and hit…softness. Fabric. Lolita. I could feel the encounter in the core of my being, my vivid imagination creating an indentation on her body that hadn't been there before. I recoiled with a small scream and sat panting, my legs tucked under me, for another very long time.

It was the panting that pulled me back. The sound of it rolling gently back to me off the stone walls. The sound a dog might make. Or a demon. But the thing it really reminded me of was that air was at a premium and panting would use it more quickly than normal breathing would.

Yet what would that matter, I asked myself? Lolita Larkin had died here more than thirty years ago. And, until today, no one had found her. It didn't seem likely or even possible that I was destined for a more gentle fate.

I was suddenly aware of the beginning of a headache and I was sweating, though there had been no change in temperature. These, I knew, were not good things.

That's when it really came home to me: if I was going to get out of here, I was going to have to do it on my own power. Yes, Lolita had tried to find a way—digging her way out—and had failed. But what were my options? Should I just lie down here in the dark and die?

I felt my way to the wall in what I was now certain was the opposite direction from Lolita's corpse. The wall was cold, the stone slightly gritty, roughly textured under my blind hands. I couldn't feel anything that would provide purchase—nothing that felt like a handle. Not even a door. I moved slowly and cautiously along the wall, the memory of Lolita's corpse never far from my mind, my hands instructing me about what my eyes couldn't see. When I felt the edge of the doorway, relief gave way very quickly to despair. I discovered, as Lolita had before me, that whatever the purpose of this room had been, it had not been meant to provide an exit for the living. I pushed against the door, felt as much give as from a mountain. I pushed harder and was rewarded when my headache intensified and I felt a wave of nausea.

Which was when I remembered that the door had swung inward.

I was never aware of a change in the quality of the air. I didn't notice, for example, if it became thinner and less wholesome. I just suddenly felt very tired and my pulse was racing. My headache was worse now, too. Much worse. The only plus about it was the fact that I couldn't focus on anything else.

I sank back to the ground, relieved when I didn't hear the rustle of silk as a result. I knew I was going to die here. I didn't even think it would take very long. To my surprise, I found I was ready. I didn't invite it, but if that was the hand fate spit out, I'd be damned if I'd go kicking and screaming the way Lolita Larkin had. What was the point? The end result would be the same. I thought about my family. They'd worry when I turned up missing, but they were strong and they had one another. They'd be okay. In the end.

I closed my eyes and the dark went away. I focused on breathing as normally as possible and tried not to think about the ache in my brain.

I saw me and Meagan tearing down the I-5 in her Porsche as we raced towards Olympia. I saw me and Gus in his Lexus, the sky above us diamonds set against velvet. I saw my daddy, tossing me into the air like a little sack of flour. The smile on his face confident and sweet. The laughter in my heart so intense that moisture ran down my cheeks. And then I didn't see anything. Only now it was okay.

Twenty-Two

The first thing I became aware of was the scent of jasmine blossoms, a warm and delicate smell that always moves me. I was perhaps less surprised to find that heaven was jasmine-scented than I was to discover that there was a heaven at all. I've never bothered with religion very much, nor has it bothered much with me. Religion is not very useful to a stockbroker, to tell the truth. The brokers I've known who were devout all seemed to worship for the wrong reasons.

If I expected to see cherubs when I opened my eyes, I was in for a surprise. Basset hound eyes stared intently into mine. "Brown," I croaked, surprised when my voice came out less strong than expected. "What are you doing in heaven?"

He smiled then and the relieved expression transformed him so utterly that all signs of the basset hound disappeared for the moment. "Jesus, Madeline, you had us worried."

Us? I swiveled my head around, lifting it only slightly, surprised when a wave of nausea followed the movement.

Usinger was nearby, smoking a cigarette. He probably had matches. I didn't know why matches felt so important, but they did.

"So I take it I'm not dead," I said to Brian, indicating Usinger with my head. "Because I'm sure smoking is pretty much verboten is heaven." To my surprise, this teeny speech tired me out and I collapsed back with a grunt.

"No. Not dead. Not this time." He held his fingers above my head, within sight. Two fingers, two inches apart. "About this close, though. And I'm pretty relieved to hear you sounding like yourself. The paramedics are taking their time about getting here and, you know, a deal like this—no air—you could have ended up with a head full of cheese."

"Really?" I said.

"Not really cheese. Just—you know—some cheese-like substance. But I can see you're pretty much your usual ornery self."

"Ornery?" I'd never been described as ornery before. At least, not to my face.

"Well, maybe not ornery. But adamant, for sure."

I could see we were in the garden—away from the hedge maze, but not very far. "How'd you find me?" I asked. My head was still blazing, my stomach gave the occasional heave, and my voice wasn't coming as easily as usual, but otherwise I felt all right.

"How do you think? You left pretty clear instructions on my voice mail."

I shrugged. Nodded. What could I say? He was right.

I tried a weak smile. "I may be crazy," I said. "But I'm not stupid."

"Madeline, there had been two apparent attempts on

your life. Plus you keep insisting on doing crazy-ass stuff like this. Anyway, thankfully you left that message for me, so I at least had a hint. I tried to get in touch with you. When I couldn't find you, we came out here. We found the rental registered to you out on the road, but no one on the property had seen you. So we tracked the gardener down at home and she told us where to find the hedge maze, which is what you said you were looking for."

I was up on one elbow, looking at Brian in pleased wonder. "You mean to say, you *detected.* How cool is that?"

Brian shrugged and looked away for a moment. He looked pleased and embarrassed all at once. I liked him for it. "Guess you could say so. Anyway, we opened the door and there you were."

"You opened the door."

He nodded.

"It wasn't locked?"

"No. We had to turn the stone things. They kinda clicked and 'open sesame.' *That's* the lucky part, Madeline. I bet you wouldn't have lasted another half hour."

I settled back on the grass with a shudder, too weak to do anything else. It was all a little too much to think about. Brian was saying that I'd come amazingly close to ending up with a fate like Lolita Larkin's. Which reminded me.

"Did you see the body in there?"

He nodded. "Though not really a body, exactly. More like a mummy." I could see him repress a shudder of his own. "I've called the coroner's office. They're on their way to pick it up."

"*Her* up," I corrected. "It's Lolita Larkin."

"That's impossible, Madeline. You know as well as

I do that Lolita Larkin is buried at the Forever Hollywood Cemetery."

I shrugged. "Well," I told him, "someone is buried
there, but it's not Lolita Larkin. I'd stake my life on it."

The three of us waited in the driveway in front of
Larkin House for the various emergency vehicles. The
coroner did eventually come. And a forensics team. And
the paramedics. The paramedics were for me, Lolita
Larkin left with the coroner: she'd been beyond helping for a long time.

While the paramedics gave me a once-over—checking for cheese, I guess—I mused on the fact that after
managing to get through the first thirty-five years of my
life without seeing the inside of an emergency medical
vehicle, I'd somehow done just that. Not once, but three
times in under a week.

"We have to stop meeting like this," I said to the
young paramedic I'd never seen before.

"Huh?" he said, looking up from taking my blood
pressure.

I shook my head. "Never mind." Humor, I decided,
was ill placed when you were in the middle of being
checked for brain damage.

"Now what?" I said to Brian when I rejoined him and
Usinger outside the paramedic van.

"For you, a good sleep, I'd imagine. For us? We're
going to talk to Maxi. See if he knows why there's a
dead body on his property."

"Brian, that door didn't close on its own. When I
called, Maxi was at his office and was expected to be
out all evening. I think you should find out where he
was—exactly—yesterday late afternoon and early eve-

ning. Because I'd be willing to bet it turns out he wasn't where he was supposed to be."

Brian looked as if he might argue with me. Probably as much out of habit as anything else. But Usinger answered first. "Yes, ma'am," he said as though addressing a senior officer. Though I doubted such an address would contain as much irony. "Anything else you'd like us to do?"

I knew he was kidding, but I pressed on, anyway. "Well, yes. I found something else out. Before all this crazy hedge stuff happened."

I saw Brian and Usinger exchange a glance, then Brian sighed and said, "Shoot."

I told him about Jaimie Welles and his insupportable accusations. On its own it would have been meaningless. Combined with what Lark had said, it merited a closer look.

"You'll give me the guy's number if I call you at home tomorrow?" Brian asked.

"Sure," I said.

"OK. Good. Now, Madeline, please stop it. I won't pretend there haven't been moments when you were helpful." I snorted but he ignored me and went on. "But now, please. I'm going to get Andrews to drive you home."

"I can drive!"

Brian ran his hands through his hair and just looked at me. I could suddenly see how tired he was. "Please, Madeline, just this once, don't argue with me, okay? Andrews has instructions to drive you home, secure your house, then watch the premises. Just do it, all right?"

I nodded quietly, and when Andrews pulled up in his unmarked car, I hopped right in.

Though I thought I'd make some attempts at scintillating conversation while we drove, the soft motion of the car punctuated by the chirps and squawks from the police radio had me out before we'd gone a couple of miles. Apparently, the sleep of the asphyxiated is not a restful one. Every so often a particularly loud squawk would wake me and I'd make an attempt to keep my eyes open, but I'd drift off again almost instantly.

I was surprised when a gentle shake of my shoulder announced our arrival at Tyler's house. "We're here," Andrews said, in case I'd misunderstood the gesture.

When the reporters had decamped, Tyler had let the security guys go, so Andrews and I entered a dark and quiet house. I watched with interest as he went carefully from room to room with his gun at the ready, looking for all the world like a hero on a television show. I told him as much and he grinned sheepishly. "Some of those shows aren't half bad, you know," he told me.

When he'd checked every room and pronounced it clear, he said, "I'll be up watching from the car. If you need anything…" He circled the cell phone number on his card before he handed it to me.

After he'd gone, I sat quietly in the living room for a while, letting waves of exhaustion and hunger vie for my next move. What with being locked in a very dark place for a very long time I, once again, hadn't eaten in nearly twenty-four hours. And I was so tired, I could barely keep my eyes open. Finally, I decided to do things neatly, and in order. I checked the contents of Tasya and Tyler's fridge, thinking longingly of Tasya's soup. But it was gone. Instead I found a piece of bread, threw it in the toaster, slathered it with peanut butter and consumed it while I walked to my bedroom. Before I got there I was half undressed. And probably in less than three minutes I was under the covers and on my way to sleep.

I didn't turn off the light that night.

Twenty-Three

A telephone was ringing somewhere. And ringing. It jolted me back from whatever soft and safe place I'd been. Though it had woken me, I wasn't even tempted to answer. It wasn't my phone, after all. I stretched languidly, pleased to discover that, after a good night's sleep, I felt mostly human again. And I needed more food. I'd noticed some eggs in the refrigerator the night before. I decided I might get really ambitious and scramble some. And I knew Tasya always kept a few truffles in the freezer. I'd get supercreative and shave truffle over my scrambled eggs. I knew she wouldn't mind. And scrambled eggs with truffles: *that* was what the doctor ordered.

A pounding at the front door interrupted my eggy fantasy. I thought about ignoring that, too, then decided I had to draw a line somewhere. I put on the robe Tasya had left for me, smoothed my hair with my hands as well as I could and opened the door to discover Andrews there, looking worried. His relief at seeing me was almost comical.

"Where's the fire?" I asked, knowing it was the wrong expression for the situation, yet not quite awake enough to stretch for another.

"Brown just called me in a panic," he said. "He tried to call you, couldn't get through and thought…" He let his voice trail off.

"And thought I'd gotten away from you?"

"Or worse."

"Well, I'm here. Now what?"

"You'd better call him."

"He's not *my* boss," I said. Andrews looked pained. "Just kidding. I'll call him. But I can't call him pre-caffeine. I don't talk to anyone precaffeine. I'm only making an exception for you because…well, because you're here. You call him and tell him I'm okay and that I'll call him when I'm coherent. I'm just about to put coffee on. You want some?"

Andrews shrugged somewhat helplessly, I thought.

I led the way to the kitchen and started fussing with the unfamiliar machine. "It'll be okay. I can't imagine it matters very much if you watch me from up there or in here."

While the coffee dripped to readiness, I had a quick shower, brushed my teeth and put on some actual clothes. Sharing morning coffee with a cop in my bath-robed state did not seem at all appropriate. Especially since I almost always get the nastiest case of bedhead imaginable and I never feel really human until I brush my teeth.

It was a sunny morning—no big surprise—and I led John out onto the deck, each of us with a coffee mug in our hands. I'd also brought out the cordless phone. A few mouthfuls into my coffee, I felt capable of normal, grown-up conversation. When I picked up the phone, John leaned forward and asked if I needed the number.

"Actually," I said as I dialed, "I know it by heart. How sad is that? I have less than a dozen phone numbers memorized, and Detective Brown's cell number is one of them."

Brian sounded distracted when I got him. "I had a busy night," he said.

"So tell me." Somewhere along the line—and I'd have been hard-pressed to say exactly when or where— a little friendship had blossomed between the two of us. There was no romantic layer to our connection, but we'd discovered that our constant sparring masked a deeper feeling. Maybe it was just that we both enjoyed a sparring partner who could punch back.

"I will," he said, "but I can't. Not right now."

"Did you charge him with murder?"

"Who?"

"Maxi."

"I did not. While having a body on your property is not smiled upon in my circles, it's also far from conclusive evidence. Especially since it happened so long ago."

Which reminded me, "What about the body that's supposed to be Lolita Larkin? The one that got buried? Are you digging it up?"

"Well, we're working on getting an exhumation order, but that's not such a simple thing. We're trying to fast-track it. I'm hoping that can happen this afternoon. By tomorrow at the latest."

"Tomorrow! Maxi could be in some extradition-free country by then. It has to be sooner."

I could almost hear Brian smile. "And what would that look like? If he did run and we caught him doing it. He'd be better off saying he's guilty now. No, he'll stick around. If he did do it—"

"He did!"

"If he did do it, he'll ride it out. I mean, wouldn't you? After all these years whatever forensic evidence the team managed to pull out of there is likely to be pretty thin. He'd be better off sticking around. Listen, none of this is what I called you about. I wanted to know you were okay…"

"Thanks."

"And I wanted to see if you'd come down here this afternoon and look over these transcripts. See if we can resolve the financial portion of our program."

"Sure. I could come sooner, if you'd like."

"Later would be better. I'm pretty wrapped up in stuff here right now, what with potential exhumations and everything."

"Ugh."

"So get John to drive you down here around four, okay?"

Though John said he wasn't hungry, I made enough of the truffled scrambled eggs for both of us. They weren't what Braydon would have created with the material, but they were more than all right.

My body continued to be in heavy recovery mode and, after breakfast, I had another little nap. I was vaguely aware of John doing surveillance-type things while I slept. Pacing here, checking there. It was oddly reassuring, like having a big German Shepherd on duty.

I woke in the early afternoon and had a swim. John declined my offer of finding him trunks and kept a careful watch on the whole swimming proceedings, looking decidedly uncomfortable the whole time I was out of doors.

After my swim, I made us peanut butter toast for lunch and then had another shower. A longer one this time. And by the time I was dry and dressed, it was time to leave for Beverly Hills and check out whatever interesting stuff Brian felt like showing me.

Twenty-Four

Brian was all atwitter with the fact that the body which had been exhumed from the cemetery that morning did not look to be Lolita Larkin.

"I could have told you that," I said uncharitably.

"You *did* tell me that, Madeline. As odd as this may seem to you, we need a little bit more to go on."

We were in a café close to the department. When I'd arrived at his office, Brian had told me he was ready for a break. But not the kind of break where you don't think about the matters at hand. He'd brought a file folder with him that I gathered contained the transcripts of Lark's confession. I also gleaned, though I couldn't be sure, that Brian was more comfortable talking to me about the case—cases now—away from the office. I'd been involved in so many aspects that I knew more than an ordinary civilian. I'd become a useful sounding board, the type who might actually have information to contribute. My blundering around meant I knew more than I should.

"What about the body from Larkin House?"

"Inconclusive. We can tell what she died of, but not who she is. Not yet, anyway. We will, though. We're rushing the DNA testing on both bodies and on Lark."

Lark. Right. I'd forgotten that the Beverly Hills Police Department had a sample of Lolita's DNA in custody.

Brian told me they *could* tell, however, that there had been trauma to the head not long before death, but that she'd died of asphyxiation. Just, I thought, like I almost had.

"Honestly, though, Madeline, the more I learn, the less I feel I know. That's where you come in." He shoved the folder across the table at me. "The parts you need to look at are highlighted."

As I scanned through the portions of Lark's confession relating to the manipulation of Keesia's account, I grew increasingly more excited.

"I was right!" I said at length. "He was manipulating the account to make the stock price go up."

"I don't get it," Brian said. "How could that benefit him? It wasn't even his money. It was Keesia's." He thought for a second and went on, "Well, Maxi's money, I guess, after Keesia's death."

"See, from Lark's perspective, though, that's the beauty. He was using Maxi's money to right an old wrong," I saw this suddenly with intense clarity. "From what Lark said here, he felt Maxi had stolen from him—from his family. All he had left of Lolita's huge holdings was an increasingly devalued chunk of stock. Maxi had, one way or another, gotten everything that he felt should be his—except the Northwest Zylonite Corporation."

"Maxi probably hadn't even wanted that," Brian put in.

"Exactly. So Lark grows up in Olympia with his father. He comes back to Los Angeles as an adult and no one recognizes him. He maneuvers himself into a position of trust with Maxi. From there he had access to the ex-wives and the accounts Maxi used to pay them out of."

"You're conjecturing," Brian observed.

I looked at him. Smiled. "Of course. But I'll bet it's stuff you can check on. That's why you wanted me to see this stuff, right?"

"Right. Okay. But I still don't see how Lark ever thought that spending Maxi's money was going to help him."

"Well, it helped him two ways. On the one hand, he was essentially throwing Maxi's money away. By buying chunks of NWZ at regular intervals through Keesia's account at ever higher prices, he was driving the price up. And they were unrealistic prices: sure to go down when the stock corrected itself. But the securities Keesia's account was buying were stocks that Lark—actually George Larkin Jr.—owned in his own name. Now do you see?"

Brian scrunched up his face in a way that told me he was trying hard to understand. "Um, maybe almost," he ventured.

"Okay, put it this way. Let's say that Lark owned a million shares in a company that were worth fifty cents apiece. That's half a million dollars, right? Not very much."

"Okay."

"Now, let's say those million shares are worth five bucks apiece a week later."

I saw the light dawn on Brian's face. "That five hundred thousand dollars is worth five million dollars practically overnight."

"Now you've got it," I said. "And the shares are sold all nice and legal. Lark St. George—who doesn't actually exist, anyway—disappears and George Larkin Jr. takes his cash and buys an island or something."

"Meanwhile," Brian said brightly, "Maxi Livingston is out that five million. Right?"

"Or however much Lark managed to unload before you nabbed him."

"Wow. So the plan was to make a lot of money and damage Maxi in the process?"

"That'd be my guess. Only he couldn't have known I'd uncover Lolita Larkin's body—"

"If it *is* Lolita's body…"

"It is. So what do you think, Brian? You've heard everything there is to hear. Why kill the wives if you're making the money? Didn't that just draw attention to himself?"

Brian thought things over. We weren't all the way there yet. "I think the money plan had been in place for a while. Get himself in a position of trust, then do the stock thing." He indicated the papers I'd been reading. "The idea for killing the wives came later, I think. Much later. We knew before he told us that Keesia Livingston's death wasn't premeditated. The other women, though? They were. And we know that, as Maxi's assistant, he had access to all those women and could set up meetings with them and get into their homes without anyone thinking twice about it."

"So maybe his relationship with Keesia triggered something. Or killing her suddenly triggered something deeper."

"Madeline, if you'd seen what I did at Lark's place you wouldn't say that. There was nothing sudden about it. I'd say he'd been planning it for a while. It's possible his relationship with Keesia even delayed things. Or maybe he was waiting to see how it played out with her: how useful she'd be to his ultimate plan. He says that he'd hoped that Maxi would be implicated in the deaths of his ex-wives. That Maxi would be made to suffer for killing Lolita Larkin by the deaths of the women he'd been married to."

"That's crazy, isn't it?" I asked.

"Sure," Brian said. "But how sane can a murderer be? You cross a line when you take another human's life, I think. It's the one thing all human societies agree on as a really bad—a really unacceptable—thing. I mean, who does that?" he asked with the air of someone who'd given these matters a lot of thought. "Who kills another human? And what does it say about that person's mind?"

I wanted to bring things out of the philosophical and back to the matters at hand. "When Lark was confessing the other night, he said Maxi killed Lolita. He said he saw it. What did he think he saw?"

Lark had told Brian and Usinger that, on the night he said he saw Maxi kill Lolita, he'd been hiding in the conservatory, reading a comic book with the aid of a pocket light. He'd heard voices and doused the light, fearing he'd get into trouble for being up after his bedtime. He admitted that what he'd seen had been unclear, the room was deeply shrouded in shadow. But he'd had no doubt that Maxi had killed his grandmother. Lark grew to adulthood with the vision of his grandmother dying at Maxi's hands etched on his little psyche. He'd spent his adolescence formulating revenge and his entire adulthood bringing it to fruition.

Usinger joined us just as we were packing up. "The DNA tests came back," he said in his quiet way. He cocked his thumb at me. "She was right."

"It was Lolita on the Livingston estate?" Brian asked. Usinger just nodded.

Brian and I sat back down. Usinger joined us.

"Who was in the box at the cemetery?" Brian asked.

"Don't know yet." Usinger grinned darkly. "She wasn't carryin' any ID. We'll have to work on it."

"One thing I'm afraid of," I said quietly. Brian and Usinger both just looked at me. "Who blew up my place? Who tried to kill me at the airport?" I paused. Thought about things. "Who closed the door on me in the garden? Someone has been trying to kill me. It couldn't have been Lark. You already had him in custody."

Brian and Usinger exchanged another glance. Brian raised his eyebrows, as though asking a question of his partner. Usinger just shrugged. He didn't say: "Your call." But I could hear it.

I agreed with Brian's call "We took your advice and questioned Maxi about his whereabouts the night you got locked in that tomb. Like you said, he'd been at the office and then he *was* at a function that night, but there's like an hour in there where we're not totally happy with his explanation. And it happens to have been right around the time that door shut on you."

I looked from Brian to Usinger, who just nodded his head and then shrugged and Brian went on. "He got really defensive when we talked to him, started spouting off about charging you with trespassing."

"He *what?*"

Usinger took over, waving a dismissive hand. "Never mind that, we talked him out of it. But that's what got both of us to thinking, he was just a little too noisy about everything, you know? Like, look at how innocent *I* am."

"So we did a little digging," Brian said. "He had access to explosives through one of the films he's been working on, we checked that out."

"But he doesn't strike either one of us as a do-it-yourself kind of guy," Usinger offered, as though his words were partly to confirm his thoughts. "But we have no leads on who, if anyone, he hired. And, without a little more to go on, he's basically untouchable right now."

"What do you mean, 'untouchable'?" I asked.

That exchanged glance again. "Look, Madeline," Brian said finally. "We've probably already told you more than we should have. You have to promise—*promise*—you won't go gallivanting off taking things into your own hands again."

"Why would I promise that?" I said minxishly.

Brian's eyes flashed a warning, but I think he knew I was kidding. "Because," he said slowly, carefully, as though wanting to be certain I caught the import of his words, "I won't tell you anything more until you do."

"Sure, whatever. I promise. What would I do, anyway?"

Usinger just laughed, but Brian said, "We're not even going to go there."

"So *tell* me already."

"Well," Brian said, "we just don't have enough to actually charge him with anything. Not even enough to get a warrant to search for things that might implicate him."

I looked from one to the other of the two men. "So that means, what? He just gets off?"

"Well, first of all, we don't know there's anything to be gotten off from, if you follow," Brian said.

"So you're just going to, what? Let it go?"

"We never just let anything go, Madeline." I didn't realize before he said this that Usinger had never used my given name before. "But we have to back-burner it for now. We'd need a whole lot more than what we have right now to convict Maxi Livingston of a murder more than thirty years old."

"Maybe you'll get it," I said.

"Maybe," Brian agreed, but he didn't look very hopeful.

"What about me?" I asked. "He tried to kill me. Twice. *Three* times." I looked into each of their faces and didn't like what I saw. "What about Gus?"

Brian shook his head. "It's all circumstantial, Madeline. We don't have anything that links him to those things."

Nor would we. When I thought about it, I realized that, unlike Lark, Maxi would have covered his tracks and he probably wouldn't have left great gobs of incriminating evidence lying around his house either, in the way that Lark had. Which reminded me...

"The computer!"

"What computer?" both men asked almost simultaneously.

"Keesia's. Right after she was killed, Maxi had me come out to the house to look over Keesia's computer. He said someone had encrypted it and he couldn't get past the encryption. He wanted to see if I could do it."

"Could you?"

I shook my head. "Lark came in and interrupted us before I got a chance to try very much." I paused, remembering. "Maxi said he wanted to get into the computer to check on Keesia's stock dealings. Now I'm not so sure."

"But if Maxi was so concerned about what was on the computer and he couldn't get past the encryption, why not just wipe the hard drive?" He was right: why not indeed?

"Maybe he just didn't think of it," Brian offered. "I mean, I wouldn't."

"You're a bit of a Luddite, Brown," Usinger jested.

"No, Brian's right," I said. "When you work with computers a lot, you get to thinking that everyone knows as much as you do. But, think about it. How old is Maxi? Sixty-five? Lots of people that age know about computers, but Maxi doesn't have to know about that, he's got people to do it for him."

"True enough," Brian said. He glanced at his watch, "I spoke with Maxi earlier. He said he'd be at his office downtown until late today. He should be there for another couple of hours."

"So what do we do?" I asked.

"*We* do nothing. You go home, or do whatever it is you do when you're not trying to crack murder cases, Miss Marple." His smile took the bite out of his words. "Usinger and I will figure where to go from here."

Over my protests, Brian informed me that, under the circumstances, he was going to keep me under surveillance, at least until they got a better handle on what was going on and could be certain I was no longer in danger.

Brian had initially wanted Andrews to drive me straight home. I told him to quit being a dork. I needed my rental car back and couldn't he get Andrews to drive me back to the Livingston Estate where I'd left it parked on the road? "Unless it got towed," I said mournfully.

"It didn't get towed," Brian said, then when I looked at him quizzically, he said mysteriously, "Vee haff vays off takeink care of deez tings."

"Can you fix a parking ticket I got last month?"

"Nope. Not *those* kinds of things."

When Andrews dropped me at my car, I headed not toward West L.A. and the direction we had come from, but north, toward the San Fernando Valley. I checked my rearview, Andrews was following me at an easy distance. We'd been doing this for a few days now and had fallen into kind of a rhythm. He followed at a discreet distance and I slowed down politely when I was in danger of losing him. He had no reason to think that today would be any different.

So when I accelerated into the turn leading to Clear View Drive, Andrews had no reason to think I was up to anything. With several cars and a turn between us, I knew he didn't see me deke onto Philbert Drive, which was fortunate, because it's not a very long street and there's nowhere to hide.

I drove slowly to the end of the street, trying to admire the palatial homes, but not paying much attention to anything but the beating of my heart. With the twists and bends Benedict Canyon Road took between here and the Valley, John wouldn't realize he'd lost me until he got clear to Mullholland. And maybe not even then.

"Sorry, John," I said aloud while I sat at the end of Philbert for a few minutes to make sure he was out of sight. I didn't like the idea of his getting into trouble for losing me—and I knew he would—but I knew what I had to do. What had Brian said? They'd need a lot more than they had to get anything on Maxi Livingston. I had a pretty good idea I knew how to get it.

Twenty-Five

At the gates to Larkin House I drove right up and buzzed to be let in.

"Madeline Carter," I said into the intercom. "Maxi asked that I pop by and get Keesia's computer."

"He didn't tell me about it," the attendant said, though he didn't sound suspicious.

I shrugged, knowing he could see me on the monitor. "Someone from his office called my office. That's all I know."

"You're the person who was working with Mrs. Livingston, aren't you? The stock lady."

"That's right," I said.

"All right, then," he said. And the gates swung open.

I went through the same thing at the front door: a cursory question and then in I went. I had expected that. In my experience, if you look like you belong somewhere, you can do almost anything you want.

The conservatory looked much as it had the last time I'd seen it, though all of the plants were now gone and the computer had been dismantled, the monitor was no longer in place, but the CPU was where I'd last seen it. Excellent, I thought, so much the better—less time to spend disconnecting things.

A surge protector lay nearby. With cords coming out of it and going nowhere, it looked just like a dead octopus. I selected the cord that looked most likely to belong to the computer, wrapped it up and stuck it in my bag, then hefted the CPU and left the same way I'd come in: by the front door. I smiled at the maid who held the door for me.

"Thank you," I said as calmly as I could.

At the car, one of the gardeners jumped out of a rosebush with a smile in order to help me manage opening car doors and stowing the computer all at once.

As I headed back to the beach I touched my hand to my heart. It was pounding. In one ill-considered act, I'd gone from trespasser to thief. Yet, somehow, that wasn't the part that worried me.

When I got home, I was relieved to see that Tyler and Tasya hadn't returned. If I was going to be messing with stolen property, it seemed better to be doing it with no one looking.

The phone started ringing forty-five seconds after I got into the house. I ignored it. Chances are, it wasn't for me. But there was also a chance it was a fire-breathing police detective and I didn't want to take it.

I put the CPU in the middle of the living room floor and paced around, looking at it from various angles. All right: I had it. Now what was I going to do with it? I'd not been understating my talents when I'd told Maxi I didn't know how to bypass the encryption. But I also knew I couldn't leave it at Larkin House, subject to getting its brain wiped at the whim of the lord of the manor. And it didn't sound as if Brian thought he'd be able to get his hands on it. What else, really, could I have done?

I dragged the computer into Tyler's office, plugged it in and used Tyler's monitor to be this computer's window on the world. The encryption screen came up, just as it had before. I didn't know if I should be glad or relieved. Well, mostly I was relieved—it meant the hard drive hadn't been wiped—but that wasn't getting me any closer to what I needed to see.

Finally I had a thought: Emily. I was way overdue to call her, anyway, and I knew she had access to someone who could help me. Someone who could be trusted not to blab.

Her boyfriend, Tristan, is a screenwriter, but he's also a geek, which I say with the largest possible amount of affection. He's sweet and brilliant and good-looking and he can make any computer do anything. And he does it for love, not money. As soon as I thought of Tris, I got on the blower.

"Emily," I said when she answered, "I need Tristan."

"Honey! I'm not done with him yet. Anyway, try 'Hello, Emily. It is lovely to hear your voice. I know I have been remiss in not calling you sooner. I apologize and will buy you lunch and perhaps a new pair of shoes at the earliest opportunity.'"

I sighed. She was right. Except about the shoes. I told her so. "I *am* sorry, Em. You would not believe the crazy stuff that's been happening. And I will buy you that lunch—and maybe even the shoes—but I need to borrow Tristan for an hour. Maybe two."

"Hmm," Emily said, "I'm usually done with him after forty-five minutes." Then more seriously, "What's up?"

"It's just too long and involved, but I'll tell you everything—*everything*—when I can. Meanwhile…"

"Yeah, yeah, I know, 'Where's Tris?' Right here, actually. I'll get him."

I told Tristan I had a computer that I'd come by under questionable means that was encrypted and did he have the time to look at it for me? I thought it was a challenge he wouldn't be able to pass up and I was right. Ten minutes after calling Emily, I was back in my rental with the computer wrapped in a blanket in the trunk, heading down the coast to Huntingdon Beach.

As I drove, my fingers white on the wheel, I thought about what kind of jail term I might get for breaking into a famous person's house and stealing his computer. I thought, also, about messing with evidence and screwing up a crime scene or whatever else the hell I'd done. And then I thought about Gus. And I thought again about Keesia. And I stiffened my lip. And I drove.

"I knew Tristan was good," I said, "but I didn't know he was *that* good." I had been at Emily's place for less than half an hour. Long enough only for Em to get some good snacks on the table, a glass of wine into both of our hands and for me to tell her only the very surface of what I knew. I love Emily and trust her implicitly, but I also knew I'd been entrusted with some things that I really shouldn't blab about. Not yet. Under the circumstances, I knew Emily would forgive me when she found out.

Tristan had been waiting for me when I arrived. I imagined him cracking his knuckles and doing warm-up exercises while he waited: he's that kind of maestro on a keyboard. And, truly, it seemed as though

Emily and I had barely settled in when we heard him call "Ta-da!" from Em's office.

When I'd first heard about the encryption on Keesia's computer, I'd suspected poetry from a lover. That's not what it was. What I found was Keesia's journal, as well as some fairly damning e-mail from Lark. Damning to Maxi, that is, which is why Lark hadn't just erased the computer's hard drive. Reading the material over, I realized, too, that it was likely Keesia who had, in fact, added the encryption screen to her computer. Or had it added. Though Lark had probably not tried as hard to have it broken as he'd let on. He wouldn't have known exactly what was there, but he would have had a clue.

Keesia's journal. I'd forgotten, in the weeks since her death, how hopeful she'd been. And, while she was alive, I'd never gotten the chance to discover how talented. She should have been a writer, I reflected. Some of her words just made me cry. And, in the end, all of it painted a picture that would be damning to her husband. The things she'd discovered about him—both the conclusions she'd drawn and the evidence she'd found in the time she'd been his wife.

Lark had been wrong—Keesia hadn't broken things off with him because she was in love with her husband. As I'd guessed, whatever she'd had with Lark had been meaningless to her, a flirtation, something to pass the time. She'd broken things off with Lark because he was putting her in a vulnerable place with her husband and she was afraid for her life. She'd discovered where the bodies were buried, so to speak. Ledgers and notes she'd found, things she'd overheard from the staff.

There had been, for example, the matter of the gardener who had gone missing around the time of Lolita's death. Whispers that Lolita had been gone weeks before her official death occurred. Questions about Lolita's closed-casket funeral and bribes that had been paid around that. And a sheaf of old papers Keesia had found hidden in a hollow window seat in one of the twenty-six bedrooms at Larkin House that proved—to Keesia if no one else—that Maxi had forged Lolita's signature on the legal documents that gave him control over much of her estate. Forged it, perhaps, after she was dead.

Keesia had put together a frightening picture of her husband. He had, she conjectured, killed Lolita—perhaps in a fit of passion—then somehow covered his tracks, kept her death a secret until he had found a replacement for her—someone who could be killed in a manner that looked like suicide, then buried in her place.

Now I conjectured that Maxi had been afraid I knew too much. Had perhaps even thought I knew more than I was letting on. Discovering that I'd been poking around the gardens of Larkin House at night—as he would have learned from the police the day after they found my car at the strip mall—he must have feared that his ancient secret was close to being discovered. Had he, perhaps, placed the fourth stone there himself? Hoping that it would open the door so he could finally remove the body and dispose of it someplace it would never be found. Someplace far from Larkin House.

The night I'd gotten shut in the crypt, had Maxi been the source of the sounds I'd attributed to rats? If that *were* the case, I hadn't realized how close I was with my guess. Had he followed me through the maze, closing the door on me when he got the opportunity and thinking that, one way or another, closing me up in there would solve his final problem?

Thinking about this reminded me of something so vast I couldn't believe I'd forgotten it. My messenger bag had come to Emily's with me with the computer's power cord inside. I reached under the desk and pulled the bag out now, digging around until I found what I was looking for, trapped at the bottom, in the seam. The old paper was soft, but not yellowed, it had been away from light and air for many decades. There were two pages of lined paper, together folded in half, then folded again. When I carefully opened them, I could see they were covered in spidery handwriting. Lolita's, I guessed. Though that was something that could be easily checked.

It appeared to be notes—either rough notes to herself or her lawyer—on changes to her will. The instructions were specific and detailed. She'd obviously been rethinking things she'd previously ordered and had done so adamantly. She wanted all mentions of Maxi Livingston's name taken from her will and, without question, she wanted everything to go to her grandson, George Larkin Jr.

Had Maxi discovered what Lolita was plotting and decided to end her life before she was able to enact her plans? As I read the notes, it seemed obvious to me that, even with her own words in my hands, no one would ever know for sure. More, my fishing these things from Lolita's pocket might have seriously damaged any chance of her words being useful to Brian and Usinger's investigation. I tried not to dwell on that, tried not to beat myself up. After all, had I *not* been poking around blindly, as it were, Lolita's body might never have been found in the first place. At least, not while Maxi Livingston was alive.

I went back to Keesia's journal. Before she died Keesia had held pieces she didn't know what to do with. In her journal, she pondered the questions. Should she tell someone? That would, she'd thought, be the right thing to do. Should she try to use what she knew as leverage to start a new life? I wondered what she would have decided, if she'd had time. I hoped she would have done the right thing, but sometimes you don't recognize the right thing until you're standing in it. And sometimes it gets to be too late.

I must have spent two hours in Emily's home office, poring over Keesia's journals and Lolita's careful notes. In that time, Emily and Tristan went back out to the living room, probably to eat the snacks and drink some of Em's good wine. But I didn't really know: I was lost in a world of intrigue and deception. I was lost in Keesia's thoughts.

After a while I called Brian. He'd be mad as hell. He'd tell me I'd broken my promise, and I wondered if I should let him know I'd had my fingers crossed behind my back the whole time or if that would just make things worse. In any case, I'd weather his anger—there were things he needed to know. Would any of this be enough to lead to Maxi's arrest? Somehow I doubted it. It was, as I'm sure Brian would point out, circumstantial. A lot of it was pure conjecture, yet I didn't doubt a word. And I hoped that some of what I'd found would put Maxi away. When I thought about it, though, I knew that—ultimately—it didn't matter. There are different layers of hell.

I still think about Gus sometimes. And thoughts of Gus are troublesome for me. His death froze him at a beautiful moment in our fledgling relationship. I mean, I've been in relationships before. Left to time, the rosy glow dissipates, either turns into something deeper or something loathsome, and you base your life decisions on which one surfaces.

If we'd gotten the chance to spend more time together, what would have happened? That's what I think about now. Would we have fallen in love? Pledged to each other? Or would we, after a couple of weeks or months, have decided we were ill suited and gone our separate ways? I'll never know and not knowing eats at me. It's sweet somehow, but mostly bitter.

In my mind's eye, Gus is caught forever in that rosy glow. To me, Gus will be forever young, forever golden, forever something to be anticipated, cherished, savored. And if there are soul mates, was he mine? How will I know?

How will I know?

I am homeless. I am car-less. I am not friendless, but when I'm in a very dark mood—as I have been lately on occasion—it can seem that way.

I recently bought a laptop computer—all soft angles and a pearlescent white finish—to replace the computer-shaped shards that ended up on Tyler and Tasya's deck. I can work now. The rest will take care of itself. In time. And hopefully by then I'll have sorted through the debris of my life.

Tyler offered to rebuild the guesthouse. I told him not to do it on my account. My heart just isn't there now. I don't know where it is, and the options I have won't sit still in my head long enough to be properly explored. I could buy a little house somewhere. I could rent an apartment. I even invested a couple of minutes in thinking about moving back to New York, my tail between my legs. But New York represents its own kind of pain for me. Old pain. And it's forced me to realize something, realize it better late than never: pain isn't about place. Not ever. It's something you carry around inside yourself. At least, it is until you're ready to let it go. I'm not there yet.

But I will be. That's just the way life works.

New York Times bestselling author

ROSEMARY ROGERS

When the beautiful and daring Sapphire Fabergine discovers that her real father is an earl in England, she sails to London to confront the aristocratic family who had disowned her—only to find that her father is dead and that his title has passed to Blake Thixton, an attractive yet loathsome distant American cousin.

Blake is determined to discredit Sapphire's claims of legitimacy, but she will not compromise her quest for honor so easily— not even for the man she has come to desire.

"The Queen of historical romance."
—*New York Times Book Review*

Available the first week of December 2005 wherever paperbacks are sold!